Shades of White

Shades of White

KI-ELA

Translated by Kate Northrop

Previously published as *Schattierungen von Weiss* by the author via the Kindle Direct Publishing Platform in Germany in 2013. Translated from German by Kate Northrop. First published in English by AmazonCrossing in 2015.

Published by AmazonCrossing, Seattle

www.apub.com

Amazon, the Amazon logo, and AmazonCrossing are trademarks of Amazon.com, Inc., or its affiliates.

ISBN-13: 9781477829783
ISBN-10: 1477829784

Cover design by Kerrie Robertson

Library of Congress Control Number: 2014921174

Printed in the United States of America

1

Hamburg, Germany

The majestic strains of "A Whiter Shade of Pale" floated through the sparsely furnished room. Mia closed her eyes and let the music carry her far away.

"Hey, Mia, are you listening to your song again?" Lydia set down the tray of medications on the little table by Mia's bed. "How many times have you heard it today?"

Mia didn't bother to answer. Instead, she stayed on the window seat and gazed out into the park. How many times had she heard it? How *could* she answer that? She didn't even know. And it really didn't matter. Mia listened because, for her, this was simply the most terrible song in the world. And the most beautiful.

It wasn't her problem if the others couldn't understand that. It didn't matter to her what Lydia, Robert, or Sven (or whatever their names were) thought. Mia had her own reality, and all that mattered to her was what she could see with her own eyes. She drew a happy face with her finger on the fogged-up glass and smiled.

Berlin, Germany

Levin launched a textbook into the air. He just couldn't cram anything else into his head. He'd read that last section at least twenty times, but he couldn't remember any of it. Not one word.

He brushed his hair out of his eyes. Studying had been going on this way for at least three weeks. It had never been hard for him, but right now he just couldn't handle it. He'd had an idea going through his head for about a week, and the more difficult studying became, the more he liked his idea.

He jumped up from his chair and grabbed his jacket. He had to talk to his parents. There was no way he could execute his plan without their help. It would take all of his powers of persuasion, he was sure, because his father would certainly not be thrilled by the idea. But he'd almost always been able to get his mother to let him have his way.

Levin hopped onto his bicycle and rode to his parents' villa in a posh residential area at the edge of Berlin. The fresh air blowing in his face helped reactivate his mind.

"Levin, darling, I'm so glad you came by," his mother said. She smiled and mussed his hair. "It's time for another haircut."

"Hi, Mom." Levin gave her a kiss on the cheek. "I like my hair the way it is," he said with a wink.

"I don't know," Sonja Webber said, looking at him skeptically. "But, if you say so. Your father is in his office—I'll get him."

Levin nervously waited in the living room. Of course his father was working again. He worked every day. With ambition and diligence, he'd created a well-functioning law firm and an excellent reputation. He expected the same excellence from his son: discipline, diligence, and outstanding grades.

Up until now, Levin had always been able to fulfill his father's expectations. He was a model student who'd graduated from college with straight As. From there he'd gone on to complete his civil service and start law school. He had enjoyed it and even found it easy, but now he'd lost steam and needed a break.

James Webber stepped out of his office, nodded at his son, and patted him on the shoulder. "So, Levin, what brings you home? How's school going?" He sat down in a large wing chair by the fireplace and lit his pipe.

"That's actually what I wanted to talk to you about," Levin said, hesitating. He'd hoped to make a bit of small talk first, but apparently his father wasn't in the mood for that. He'd have to be direct.

"What's the problem? Can I help?" Levin's father asked, raising his eyebrows.

"I feel totally burned out," Levin said. He leaned back into the sofa and gave his mother a pleading glance. She looked at him with sympathy—everything was going as planned.

"That happens sometimes. Maybe you shouldn't be involved in so many sports," his father suggested.

"Sports help clear my head. That's not it. I just need a break."

"A break? In the middle of the semester? How do you imagine that's going to work?" He looked doubtful.

"You have your semester break soon, anyway," his mother added.

"Yeah, but during that break I'm supposed to work at the firm," Levin complained. "I haven't had one free moment since I graduated. I just want some time to myself. I need a vacation, and I don't think that's too much to ask."

"You can go on vacation when you've got your degree. I never took vacations, and I always had a job during breaks. Pull yourself together, Levin." His father shook his head.

"I haven't been able to," Levin insisted. "I've got some kind of mental block and haven't been able to concentrate for three weeks already."

"*A block*? That's ridiculous! Get rid of it, and study harder!" His father stood up. "You'd better get used to working."

His mother got up, too, and walked over to his father. "But, James, the boy is right. He did civil service right after college and then helped at your law firm—and since he started law school, he's spent every free moment there. We really shouldn't deny him a break. The Canzen boy had a vacation before he even started graduate school."

"Typical, letting him talk you into it," he snapped.

"Levin has excellent grades. We have no reason to complain." Sonja smiled at Levin. "I think we should let him take a vacation."

"*Take a vacation*," James parroted. "Where? The Bahamas? Hawaii? Maldives? Seychelles? And who's going to pay for it?"

"You still have the old camper. Couldn't I just borrow it and take off for a little while?" Levin asked.

"That old thing?" his mother cried. "It's not fit to drive anymore!"

"Of course it is." James Webber looked at Levin. "I fixed it up with Peter and Werner years ago so we could sleep and cook in it." Now he laughed. "We had some great trips in that thing. Of course we'd have to give it an overhaul and have everything checked by a mechanic."

"I'd take care of all of that. Please, Dad, will you let me borrow it?" Levin said, feeling hopeful. He'd obviously caught his father off guard and touched a nostalgic, vulnerable spot.

"We can get it ready together." His father grinned. "But it's like a stubborn old mule. You'll need patience and intuition to drive it."

"I'll make the effort," Levin assured him.

Then his father said the magic words: "OK, Levin, you can borrow the camper."

"I'm still not sure that's a good idea," his mother said. "Driving around in such an old wreck, you never know what could happen. It might not even survive the first hundred miles."

"It's safe, my dear, don't worry." James pulled a photo album off the shelf and brought it over to Levin. He flipped through the first few pages and pointed at what looked like a rusted heap of scrap metal. Levin's mother sighed and left the room. She realized she had lost the fight.

"That's what it looked like before we started." His father's eyes shone as he looked at the photo. "And then we set to work."

Levin looked through the whole album with his father. It was strange for Levin to see his father this way. He'd rarely experienced him as emotional or enthusiastic. James Webber was more the practical type.

After they'd had dinner, his father said, "Come by tomorrow after church, and we'll take a closer look at the old darling."

"Sure," Levin said, happy. "And thanks, Dad."

"Well, if this helps you clear your head, it's OK with me."

2

"Good morning, Mia. Did you sleep well?" Lydia said, suddenly standing in the room. Mia hadn't heard her come in. She didn't answer and continued looking out the window.

"We're about to go into town. Did you remember?" Lydia asked.

Mia nodded. Of course she'd remembered. How could she forget? Taking a trip into the city was always one of the highlights of the week. She was allowed to go alone, but because she wanted to see everything and was overwhelmed by all the new stimuli, going alone caused problems. When she was with the others, there was no danger that she'd be late.

"Then please be downstairs in half an hour. On time, OK?"

"Sure," Mia said. "I'll be on time."

"I know you will. I wasn't trying to insinuate anything, Mia." Lydia smiled and moved closer. She always seemed to be smiling. Mia often wondered how Lydia did that. Always smiling, always friendly. That must take a lot of energy. But maybe she had to. Maybe it was part of her job to always be friendly to someone like Mia. She was probably that way with the others, too. Mia considered asking a few of them but then rejected the idea. She wasn't interested in talking with them, because they were just so . . . strange.

Mia arrived on time to the foyer. A few others who were allowed to come that day were already there. Lydia was, too.

"Mia, there you are! You look pretty."

"Thank you," Mia said. She looked exactly as she had half an hour ago, except she'd bound her blond curls into a braid. But hey, if Lydia liked her hair that way, she didn't mind.

They left on time. Mia hung back a bit. She didn't want anyone to see that she was part of the group. Lydia left her to herself but occasionally turned around to see if she was still there. Probably because she was afraid Mia would disappear. Mia knew the walk by heart. It took them into the center of town, where all the shops and department stores were.

"Shall we buy you something new to wear?" Lydia suddenly appeared next to Mia.

Mia hadn't registered that she was there, because she had been too distracted looking at the window displays. "No, I don't want anything," she said.

"But, Mia, you only wear white clothes. We could get something pretty and colorful."

"I don't like other colors, I like white. White is a beautiful color."

"Yes, that's true. I just thought maybe you'd like something different for a change," Lydia said, determined.

"No, I wouldn't. I like my white clothes," Mia said. She could be stubborn, too. They had this discussion every time they went into the city. And every time it was the same result: Mia stuck to her point or bought another white piece of clothing.

"With the money your grandma gives you every month, you really could buy something new for yourself."

"I don't want anything," Mia said, shaking her head. Then she suddenly stopped, distracted by a travel agent's window display. Mia hadn't seen any of these pictures before. Every week the agent advertised a different country, and now there were pictures of Morocco behind the glass. She was fascinated and completely captivated by the images. Morocco, that was in Africa. How beautiful it looked. There were huge sand dunes and mountains, palm trees and beaches. She saw colorful markets with exotic spices that she could almost smell—and camels. Mia smiled. She liked camels. They were so miraculous, so completely different from other animals. Camels were special.

Mia pressed her nose to the glass, trying to remember every detail.

"Mia, shall we move on?" Lydia asked.

"No, I want to look at these photos."

"You've been doing that for a while now. Do you like Morocco? Shall we go to a bookstore and look for books about Morocco?"

"Yes, let's do that!" Mia said.

The selection at the bookstore seemed endless, and at first she couldn't decide on anything. After much deliberation, she finally chose three picture books about Morocco. She could hardly wait to take them back to her room to examine them in detail.

The friendly shop assistant even gave her a poster of camels on sand dunes, and Mia shrieked with delight and threw her arms around the man. He was extremely surprised, and then they shared a laugh. It was a strange scene, both of them just standing there, looking at each other and laughing.

"Do you like Morocco, too?" Mia asked.

"I don't know—I've never been there. Have you?"

"No. But I'm definitely going there someday." She realized Lydia was looking at her with amazement.

Mia spread out the picture books on her bed and became completely absorbed in the photos. She read the captions carefully and soon knew which images were from which parts of the country.

"Hey, Mia, aren't you tired yet? It's two thirty in the morning." Lydia peered over her shoulder. "How do you like your books?"

"I love them," Mia said. "What a spectacular country."

"Yes, it certainly is. Maybe someday you'll go there. You've got tons of time—you're only twenty-two."

"Maybe, we'll see." Mia closed the books and put them carefully onto the shelf. "I'm going to bed now."

"That's a good idea. Sweet dreams!"

"Yes, you, too." Mia crawled into bed but didn't go right to sleep. She'd only said that to get rid of Lydia. Instead, she began to form a plan. Tomorrow she would speak to the director at the home and ask him to let her leave.

3

"So, Mia, what brings you here?" Director Schneider studied her over his wire-framed glasses. Today he was wearing a white coat, which he rarely had on when Mia came across him in the hallways. Mia was sure he knew exactly why she was in his office. After all, it wasn't as though she visited him every day. She glanced at Lydia, who gave her an encouraging smile.

"I thought Lydia might have already told you," Mia said.

"You're right, Mia. I do know why you're here, but I want to hear it from you."

"I'd like to leave."

"So you want to leave us," Director Schneider said, leafing through a file. Mia could see that the documents were about her.

"According to the court order from last May, you don't need to be here anymore. You remained with us voluntarily. May I ask why you've suddenly changed your mind?" He looked at her curiously. Mia knew this look, and sometimes she had the feeling he could see right through her.

"I just want to go. It's time."

"That's your right. But it says here you may only go if you meet certain conditions. You know that, Mia, don't you?"

"Yes, I know. I have to do outpatient therapy."

"Or live in a supervised housing facility with a resident therapist on staff, because your grandmother isn't prepared to take you in. I would advise you not to live alone at first, at least not until you've gotten used to life outside. What do you think?" The intensity of his gaze began to make her feel uncomfortable.

"I don't want to live in supervised housing. If that's my option, I might as well stay here," she argued. She had carefully considered everything, and it was important to let her wishes be known.

"It's your decision. If that's your choice, then I'd like to assign a social worker to you. Just in the beginning," Director Schneider said.

"I appreciate your advice, but I feel fine, and from now on I want to take care of myself. I chose to stay here longer than I needed to. Now it's time for me to go."

"Mia, it's very different out there. Take some time to make your decision," Lydia said. "You've never lived alone, and it will be a very big change."

"I'm aware of that. I know how to shop, do laundry, and cook. I learned all that here. And I'll continue with my therapy. That's what's required of me. I'll do everything I need to, but I want to live alone."

"All right, we won't try to stop you. How long have you been with us?" Director Schneider flipped through the pages in the file again.

"Eight years," Lydia answered for her. "We're going to miss you, Mia."

"Eight years, two months, and fifteen days," Mia replied, ignoring Lydia.

Director Schneider smiled. "That's a long time for a young woman. Promise me that you'll play by the rules out there. It's important to stick to the rules—you know that, don't you?"

"Yes, of course."

"I spoke to your grandmother. She paid for your voluntarily lengthened stay with us, and now she's required to finance the cost of a furnished apartment. I'll start looking for one right away. Is that all right with you, Mia?" he said.

"Yes, that's fine. Thanks for your help."

"After that, I'll find you a therapist, and you'll be able to make contact with her yourself. Do you understand? Same with the social worker."

"Yes," Mia said. "How long until I can leave?"

"That depends on how soon I can find an apartment."

"I'd like to leave today or tomorrow."

Director Schneider laughed. "You've been here so long, a few days more won't make a difference now, will they? I understand your need for freedom, though, so I'll do my best to hurry."

Mia nodded. What else could she do?

"Good, then I'll prepare all the papers." Director Schneider offered her his hand. "I wish you all the best. You're young—do something worthwhile with your life. Anything is possible."

"Thank you," Mia said, making an effort to sound polite. Then she left his office quickly. She wanted to pack as fast as possible. Maybe the apartment would come through soon.

She didn't own very much. A few outfits, school materials that she didn't need anymore, her beloved books, and a laptop that she'd bought with the money from her grandmother.

Mia's grandmother hated her, and she could understand why. That made her even more grateful for the financial support she offered.

Mia didn't depend on the money, but that might change someday. Maybe she'd just change everything. The idea made her giddy with anticipation.

"Take good care of yourself, darling. And stay in touch!" Sonja Webber said, close to tears. She kept hugging Levin.

"Mom, don't worry. I'm old enough to do this," Levin said, laughing.

"I know that. But so much could happen. Drive very carefully, do you hear?"

"Yes, Mom."

"And be careful with strangers."

"Mom, that's enough." He kissed her on the forehead one last time.

"Take it easy with your money, and watch your budget. We put money in your account, but I don't plan to give you more." James Webber gave his son a stern look.

"I know, and thanks for everything. I really appreciate it." Levin gestured at the old camper that he and his father had just overhauled. It had been polished to a perfect shine.

"I certainly hope so. Levin, I want you to enjoy your break. But when you return, I'm counting on you applying yourself to your schoolwork with unwavering concentration. Don't enjoy this bohemian lifestyle so much that you never come back."

"Don't worry, Dad. I already told you I've arranged to make up the work I'll miss next semester. There's nothing to worry about. I'm going to hit the road now." Levin was annoyed by his father's lecture. He'd endured it more than once in the last few days.

He hugged his mother again, punched his father on the shoulder, and slid in behind the wheel of the vintage camper that would be his home for the next few weeks.

As he turned the key and heard the motor roar to life, an enormous wave of happiness washed over him. He had no plans. He just wanted to get away and let the road take him wherever it would lead.

Finally—no fixed schedule to keep, no responsibilities, and no excuses. He was going to enjoy every moment of this trip!

Mia stepped out of the therapist's office and took a deep breath. Her session had been OK, and Mrs. Mueller was nice enough, but Mia didn't ever want to see her again—let alone come back to her office. Her next appointment was in a week and a half. By then, Mia would be gone.

She smiled to herself and set off for her apartment. She had already packed everything in an extralarge backpack. Unfortunately, her full collection of beautiful picture books about Morocco wouldn't fit. So she'd decided with a heavy heart to leave all but one of them behind.

She emptied out the fridge, stuffed the food into her backpack, and checked one last time to make sure she'd closed all the windows. She had stripped the bed that morning. Mia hadn't slept very well. It was the first night that she'd been there, and she wasn't yet used to being alone, but that would change with time, she was sure.

She took one last look around the apartment. Though she'd decorated it and made it more comfortable, Mia had known all along that she wouldn't be staying long.

Mia went outside. It was a beautiful summer day. The sun shone down, its warming rays spreading over the earth. The sky was completely cloudless, and Mia took that as an omen. A good omen for her new life. She laughed with delight, barely noticing the people turning to stare, and then she started on her journey.

4

Levin rolled down the window. The airflow created a hellish amount of noise in the old camper, but he couldn't stand being closed in the vehicle without fresh air or even air-conditioning.

He chugged along in the slow lane, going just fast enough so all the trucks wouldn't pass him. He wasn't in a hurry. He didn't even know where he was going. He'd decided to be utterly spontaneous. When he saw road signs, he chose whichever direction interested him at the moment. It was glorious to be so free.

Levin took an exit for a rest area. He was hungry for something sweet, and he wouldn't mind using the bathroom, either.

The place was packed, and he could tell that people were heading off on vacation. As Levin found a parking place and climbed out, he noticed the curious glances of other travelers. The old camper attracted the attention of vintage-car enthusiasts. Several people had already approached him to talk about it. If his father had been there, he'd have been bursting with pride.

As Levin made his way to the restroom, he noticed a girl sitting on a bench digging through her backpack. She was dressed completely in white and was humming to herself. He passed by without paying her any further attention.

He bought some chocolate from a vending machine and noticed on his way out that the girl was still sitting on the bench. She had a very pale face and dark circles under her eyes, but she had strikingly beautiful blond hair. The white outfit made him wonder if she worked in a hospital. As he passed, he saw that she was holding a handwritten cardboard sign that read "Morocco."

She didn't notice him, as she was completely absorbed in reading some kind of coffee-table book. Levin shook his head. He wanted to leave, but his curiosity got the best of him. Did she really want to go to Morocco by hitchhiking? From their location in Germany now, it was almost two thousand miles!

He decided to speak to her and cleared his throat. She still didn't look up, even though he was now standing right in front of her, blocking the sun. She surely noticed that.

"Excuse me," he said. "Can I ask you something?"

She raised her head and looked him in the eyes. Her eyes were very dark, a stark contrast to her pale skin. She reminded him of a ghost.

"You're already doing that." She smiled at him. She had a pretty smile. It gave her face a particular charm that made her look less ghostly.

"Huh?" Levin had been thrown off. He didn't understand her answer.

"Well, you don't need to ask if you can ask me something, when you're already doing it." She giggled softly, like a little girl.

"Oh, of course." Levin had to laugh, too. "You're right about that."

"What would you have asked if I'd answered with yes?" She put aside her book and looked at him curiously.

"Um . . ." Levin scratched his head. He was still slightly dazed, but he pulled himself together. "I wanted to ask if you're really trying to get to Morocco," he said.

"Oh, yes!" Her eyes shore. "I want to go to Morocco. Are you headed there?" She jumped up, excited.

"Um, no. Actually, that is, I can't really say," Levin answered. "But if you want to go to Morocco, why don't you fly? Hitchhiking will take forever."

"Fly? That would be way too expensive." Mia shook her head as her hope of finding a ride faded. She was disappointed, because the young man seemed nice. He had longish dark hair and beautiful blue eyes. Eyes that somehow encouraged trust and didn't look at her as judgmentally as others had when she'd asked about rides. So far, she hadn't met very many nice people—except for one family who'd taken pity on her and brought her to this rest area. And here she'd sat since yesterday, looking for someone traveling to Morocco, or at least in that direction.

"It wouldn't be so expensive if you go with one of those budget airlines. They can be quite affordable," Levin said.

"Budget airlines? What are those?"

Levin was speechless. Was it possible she didn't know about budget airlines? She was strange, very strange. Or was she yanking his chain? "Yes, budget airlines," he said. "You've never heard of them? They're airlines that sell cheap tickets. You should ask at a travel agency or go online. That's the fastest way to get to Morocco, and it's definitely safer."

"Hmm." Mia was at a loss. Should she take his advice? Her budget wasn't exactly huge. Her grandmother added a little bit to her account each month, and she still wasn't sure how far it would get her. She had learned how to budget, but not for unusual situations. She did know one thing, though: Flying would never be cheaper than hitchhiking. Not even with these strange budget airlines.

"Thanks for your advice," she said. "But maybe I'll get lucky and someone will be able to give me a ride."

Levin shook his head. "It's up to you. In any case, good luck!" He nodded and went over to the newsstand, where he ate one of his chocolate bars.

He watched her for a while. She was back to sitting on the bench and looking at her book, the cardboard sign next to her. She seemed completely unworried—almost enviably so. He wondered if she was scared at all. Hitchhiking wasn't exactly safe for a young woman alone, and she seemed a bit naive. Or maybe she just wasn't very bright?

Levin crumpled his chocolate wrapper and turned toward the restroom to throw it away.

"Hey, honey, you really wanna travel that far?" A burly man was standing in front of Mia, grinning.

"That's the plan. Are you going to Morocco?" she asked.

"It depends." The man's eyes wandered over her body, and she slid around on the bench nervously. She thought he was a bit strange, but if he was going in the direction of Morocco, she couldn't be too choosy.

"What does it depend on?" she asked.

"On the compensation, honey. One hand washes the other, understand?"

"No." She furrowed her brow. "I don't know what you mean. Can you explain?"

"You're a dumb, little blond thing, aren't you?" The man broke out laughing. "I'll be nice and let you ride with me for a while—and then you'll pay me back for it. I've got a comfortable bed in my truck. All clear?"

"What exactly do you expect from me? What should I do? I can't give you any money."

Levin couldn't believe his ears—this just couldn't be happening. The young woman really must be unusually naive. Did she truly not understand what this slimy, unkempt, beer-bellied pig wanted from her?

"I don't want money from you, sweetheart. You just need to get a bit friendly with me," Levin heard him say.

"Friendly? I am that, certainly."

Levin saw her reach for her backpack. It was definitely none of his business to worry about what the guy was planning. After all, he'd made his intentions perfectly clear, and it didn't seem to bother the girl. But could Levin just allow this to happen? She seemed so innocent. What if she really didn't understand what the man wanted from her? Would he take it anyway?

Levin repressed a groan as she stowed the book in her backpack and gave the man a friendly smile. The man waved her toward his truck.

"Hey, there you are," Levin called. Then he quickly approached and put his arm around her. "I've been searching everywhere for you!"

"You were looking for me?" She looked at him with surprise.

"You wanted to come with me, don't you remember?" Levin put on his most charming smile.

"Get outta here—this one's mine," the man growled.

"You're going to Morocco?" She gazed at Levin expectantly with her dark eyes, and he knew he wasn't going to get out of this so easily.

"Yeah, of course." He laughed and turned to the trucker. "Sometimes she's a bit scatterbrained."

"You could say that," the man said. "What now, honey? You gonna ride with him or me? I can surely take better care of you!"

"Take care of me?" Mia crossed her arms. The man was odd, and she didn't understand him. But she didn't have to, because the nice young man was here again, and he really did plan to drive to Morocco. Today was her lucky day!

"Thanks for your offer, but I'm going with him," Mia said to the truck driver.

He swore under his breath and stomped off.

"OK, I'm Levin. And you are?" Levin didn't know if this would be the biggest mistake of his life, but now that he'd gone this far, he'd have to carry on with it.

"I'm Mia." She held out her hand. "Thanks for giving me a ride!"

"All right, Mia, come with me." Levin took her hand. It was delicate, almost fragile. Like the rest of her, somehow.

5

She seemed totally trusting, and as she followed him without hesitation to his camper, Levin began to have doubts. How could this work? Did she really believe that he was going to drive her to Morocco? Would she want to sleep in the camper? He couldn't exactly send her out alone into the night. Levin cursed himself as a phenomenal idiot. Something like this could only happen to him. For once in his life, he was footloose and fancy-free, and now he'd voluntarily acquired a ball and chain. He congratulated himself on his stupidity.

Mia's voice roused him from his stupor. "What a wonderful car!" She was aglow as she took in the sight of the vintage camper.

"Yes, it belongs to my father. It's an old treasure," Levin said. The more closely he observed her, the more childlike she seemed.

"And he lets you drive it? That's really nice." Mia smiled.

"Yes, it's very kind of him. My father really loves this old thing. He and two of his friends fixed it up. There's enough space for sleeping and cooking. Would you like to see inside?" he asked superfluously; sooner or later she'd be getting in anyway.

"Sure, I'd love to!" she said, seeming very happy about his suggestion.

Levin opened the door and gave a chivalrous bow. "Madame, after you," he said.

Mia glanced at him in surprise, but then she giggled and climbed in. Levin's gaze wandered over her backside. Mia was very slender—almost too thin—but she still had some nice curves. At least now he had something to look at.

"Wow, it's great in here," she said. "And it's really big!"

"Well, yeah, for two or three it's big enough." She was so sweet in her excitement. She seemed completely without suspicion. He'd never met anyone like her before. Maybe that was because he'd always tried to find the kink in people's behavior. He was just like his father that way. Maybe it was a lawyer's disease, or maybe it was just a prerequisite for the job.

Mia looked around curiously. She'd never seen a vehicle like this before. She'd seen campers, but she could tell that this was something special. It had personality. She looked at Levin more closely, too. He was a good-looking guy, and she liked his blue eyes and slightly long hair. She wanted to run a hand through it. He ran his own hand through it just at the moment she was thinking about it, and she laughed.

"What?" Levin asked, puzzled. "Are you laughing at me?"

"No," Mia answered quickly. "I'd never do that! I just had a funny thought."

"Like your idea to hitchhike to Morocco?" He grinned at her.

"Why is that funny?"

"I already told you. Flying would be much more practical."

"But I don't have much money," Mia explained. "I'm on a tight budget."

"Mia, it's none of my business, but aren't you scared?"

"Scared of what?" Now she seemed more insecure.

"Of guys like that trucker, for instance. Wasn't it clear what he wanted?" Levin looked at her sharply. She couldn't be that stupid.

"Um, no," Mia said. "I guess I did think he was pretty strange, but I didn't know what he was trying to say. I was just happy he wanted to give me a ride, though." Suddenly unsure, she felt her face burning. Had she behaved carelessly? She bit her lower lip.

"Mia," Levin said, pushing his hair off his face again, "that guy offered to take you with him in exchange for . . . I mean, he wanted sex. Wasn't that clear to you?"

Mia's eyes grew wide; then she covered her mouth with her hand. "Oh, God! Do you really think so? Could that really be true?" She sank onto the bench, shaking her head in disbelief. Was that really what the trucker had been planning? And what about Levin? Did he want the same thing?

Mia looked up at Levin fearfully and asked, "How should I have known that?"

Levin sighed, and then sat down across from her. "Haven't you ever heard that hitchhiking can be dangerous for girls? Some men only take girls with them to get sex. And for some girls, it all ends very badly." Seeing how upset she was, he spoke gently. He felt sorry for her. She looked completely shell-shocked. Her carefree exterior had been blown away, but he couldn't leave her in ignorance.

"And what about you? Do you want sex from me?" Mia didn't dare look at him. She was afraid of the answer.

"No, I don't." He took her hand. He realized again how fragile she was. Her hands were so cold in comparison to his. "I prefer to only have sex with women who want it. Voluntarily, not as compensation. You don't have to be afraid of me, Mia." He gently raised her chin with his free hand to make her look at him. "Understood?"

Mia swallowed and stammered, "Y–yes."

"Shall we go?"

She nodded, her mind in chaos. Was she really so stupid? Mia had never been intimate with a man, nor had she ever kissed anyone. She'd had offers from a caregiver who'd wanted to "initiate her in the ways of love," but she had been shocked, and had turned him down. She'd come across a few pornographic websites but had immediately clicked away, disgusted. Otherwise, she only knew about sex from television—and she didn't know much. But one thing was clear to her: love and deep feelings had to be involved, because otherwise it would be impossible to let another person come so close.

Levin climbed into the driver's seat. A moment later, Mia followed and sat next to him. She seemed to have gotten herself under control again.

"Ready?" He winked at her.

"Yes."

Neither of them spoke for a while, but then the silence became uncomfortable for Levin. Now that he had a passenger, he at least wanted to know something about her. So far this girl was still a puzzle to him.

"Why did you choose Morocco?"

Startled, Mia turned to look at him. "You're not going there, are you?" she said.

"To be honest, I haven't really thought about where I'm headed. I just took off, and it didn't matter to me where I was going. So why shouldn't I drive toward Morocco? Let's see what happens," he said.

"But you still haven't answered me."

"I've seen pictures of Morocco, and I have books about it. It must be beautiful there." It didn't escape Levin that Mia's eyes were shining with excitement.

"So you've never been there?"

"No. What about you?"

"No. It's so far away," Levin said. "Which countries have you been to?"

Mia lowered her gaze. "I've never been out of Germany," she admitted.

"Where are you from?"

"Hamburg. You?"

"Berlin," Levin said. "So you haven't gotten very far yet."

"No, I only got one ride with a family who brought me this far. But I have time." Mia shrugged.

"Then you've never been to Paris, either," Levin said, glancing up at the highway signs.

"No, never."

"How do you feel about taking a little detour?" Levin grinned at her. "If you want to go to Morocco, we have to go through France, anyway."

"Do you feel like it?" Mia wasn't sure what he wanted and didn't want to presume too much. She couldn't figure him out. Was he actually this nice, or did he have ulterior motives? Ever since he'd explained the trucker's intentions, she'd become more suspicious.

"Of course I'd like to. Paris is cool. So, shall we?"

Mia watched him for a moment, then cleared her throat. "Yes, I'd like that," she said, nodding.

She looked out the window. It was starting to get dark. Neither of them had spoken for a while. She tried to recall what she knew about Paris. It was the capital of France; that was clear. She remembered pictures. The Eiffel Tower, the Arc de Triomphe, the Louvre. She'd seen all those in books. And now she was going there. On her way to Morocco.

Suddenly a song playing on the radio caught Mia's attention. She listened carefully. It was about leaving your old life behind you. Mia smiled as it came to an end.

"Do you like that song?" Levin glanced over at her.

"Yes," Mia said, happily nodding. "Yes, I do."

"Could it be that it applies to both of us?"

Mia's eyes shone. "That may be true."

6

"OK, now we're about thirty miles from Paris. Shall we spend the night here and drive into the city for breakfast tomorrow?" Levin said. He took the exit for the next rest area. He was a bit nervous, because he couldn't predict what would happen. He'd offer her the most comfortable bed and convert the sitting area for himself, but it was a strange thought, to share the camper with a girl he didn't really know.

"Sounds good." Mia looked over at him, suddenly anxious again. "And . . . how should we work this? Shall I look for a hotel?" She swallowed and twisted her fingers. What did he expect from her?

"Would you normally get a room? How did you do it last night?" Levin's nervousness was also growing.

"I slept on a bench in the rest area," she admitted.

"You did *what*?" he cried. "Are you nuts?"

Mia shrank back, squeezing herself into the farthest corner of her seat. "Why are you shouting?" she asked, panicked.

Levin immediately adjusted his tone as she cowered next to him, shaking like a terrified rabbit. He was sorry he'd yelled, but it had burst out because he was so shocked by what she'd told him.

"Sorry, Mia. I didn't mean to raise my voice, but—wow—why do you take such risks? You could have been robbed or much worse." He swallowed hard.

"But nothing happened," she said.

"No, thank goodness. Jeez, Mia." He kept shaking his head.

"Do you think I'm stupid?"

"Is that so important?"

"I don't want you to think I'm stupid. You might think I'm crazy, and that's totally fine. Lots of people think that. But I'm not stupid, OK?"

Levin looked over at her. He was angry with himself when he realized she had tears in her eyes.

"Hey, Mia." He reached over and tentatively stroked her cheek. She had very soft, fine skin. "You're not stupid. That's not what I was trying to say. But you seem to trust people too easily. Please promise me that you'll never sleep out in a public place again."

"OK," Mia said, smiling with relief. He didn't think she was stupid, and that was good.

"If you don't mind, we can both sleep here in the camper. I'll crash here in the front, and you can have the bed in back," he suggested. He wondered if she would take him up on the idea.

"Did you sleep in front before?"

"No, I slept in the back, but I don't mind giving you the bed."

"But I don't want that. I don't want you to have to change your ways for me. It's important to stick to what you normally do."

"None of this is normal for me—I haven't even been doing it that long. And if I say it's OK for me, I mean it," he said.

"I'll sleep here in the front," Mia said. "I'm so grateful that you're taking me with you, and I couldn't possibly ask you to make any more compromises for me."

"Who says I'm making compromises?"

"You must be."

"No, I'm not. At the moment, I'm not, anyway." He touched the tip of her nose. "So, how are we going to do this?"

"I sleep in the front," she said with authority, looking him straight in the eyes, "or I sleep outside."

"OK, you stubborn creature, you win!"

Levin went into the shop and bought some shower tokens. He'd already showered that morning, but the situation had changed, and he didn't want to risk it. He considered taking a couple shower tokens to Mia, but then he wasn't sure what to do. He didn't want her to misunderstand and be insulted.

He sighed. His vacation had become much more complicated, but so far he didn't regret taking Mia with him. She was so completely different from any of the girls he'd ever been with. His past girlfriends had been modern and self-assured, and Mia was . . . what was Mia, anyway? Different. Mia was very different. Levin left it at that, for now.

He knocked and waited until she asked him to come in. Levin saw that she'd emptied her backpack. The only clothes he could see were white. This girl was really a surprise package.

"I think I know what your favorite color is," he said.

Mia blushed. "Um, yes, I like white. Do you?"

"Sure, white's OK. But so are red, blue, yellow, and green. And black."

"I like white." As she took out a fresh T-shirt and shorts, he caught a glimpse of her underwear. It wasn't anything racy, but it was enough to get his imagination going. Levin swallowed hard.

"Do you think there are showers in there?" she asked.

"Yeah, there are." He suppressed a sigh of relief. The problem had resolved itself nicely. "I still have two shower tokens left. You can have them if you want." Levin allowed himself this little white lie.

Mia's eyes widened. "Really? That's great, thanks!"

Levin hadn't expected so much enthusiasm, but of course he was glad that it had worked out so well. "Do you need towels?" He opened a cupboard. His mother must have packed at least ten for him without his knowledge. He'd only discovered them that morning.

"I have one, but it's still damp. It would be nice if you could lend me one. I'll wash it right away and—"

"No problem. Take as many as you want."

Mia shyly chose two towels, then asked where the showers were.

It took her a while to understand how the tokens worked, but soon she was enjoying the warm water flowing over her skin. She'd remembered to pack a razor and took all the time she needed. She felt incredibly good as she made her way back to the big vehicle. Things had turned out so well! She had a nice companion, and she hoped very much that she wouldn't get on his nerves or be a burden to him.

Mia couldn't tell whether he was only being polite or wanted to get rid of her as soon as possible. But maybe he liked her. She liked *him* a lot, anyway. He was kind and good-looking. He had an open smile, and his eyes fascinated her. Mia got butterflies in her stomach when he looked at her or winked. It was a strange feeling but also nice.

"Hey, there you are," Levin said, grinning at her as she got back into the camper. She smiled back shyly. Her hair was wet, and she wore a close-fitting white top and shorts. He snuck a peek at her long legs. *Extremely pretty*, he thought.

"Are you hungry?" Levin said, wanting to distract himself. "I can't cook very well, but my skills should suffice for spaghetti with tomato sauce."

"I can help—I had cooking classes," Mia offered.

"That would be great. You'd be doing us both a favor."

Mia stood next to him by the stove, and he breathed in her scent. She smelled so good.

"Do you have any herbs?"

"Yes, um, sure." Levin turned his head, embarrassed, and then opened a compartment over the stove. "Ha! Here." He was relieved. "I even have red wine. Would you like a glass with dinner?"

Mia hesitated. She considered that she sometimes needed sleeping pills. Could she take the risk? She'd never had any type of alcohol before. But why shouldn't she try some wine just this once?

Levin wondered about her reluctance. "Of course I have water here. Or juice, or whatever," he added.

"I've never had wine before," she finally said. "I'd like to try it, though."

"Would you rather have a beer?"

"I don't know. I've never tried any of that . . . alcohol in general, I mean." Mia lowered her eyes.

"That's no problem," Levin said, trying to hide his surprise. "Just take anything you want, OK? And if you don't like the wine, leave it."

"OK." Mia was grateful. "You're nice, Levin."

"So are you, Mia." He winked at her, and the butterflies in her stomach started fluttering again.

Levin left her to work at the stove and went to set the table. It was very warm in the camper, and he regretted that they hadn't left the highway. Sitting outside in the noisy rest area wasn't exactly pleasant.

Mia concentrated on her task. She had learned to cook, but those were only classes, and she'd never cooked for anyone in particular before. She wanted him to enjoy it. She tried to hide her agitation as she set the bowl of spaghetti on the table. "I hope you like it."

"Of course." Levin raised his wineglass to her. "What shall we drink to? A wonderful journey?"

Her eyes lit up. "Yes, to a wonderful journey!"

She sipped at the wine. It tasted good and left a warm feeling in her stomach.

"So, do you like it?" Levin was observing her closely. She'd tasted it so carefully.

"Yes, it's delicious." She nodded.

"So is the dinner. Thanks for cooking."

"No, I have to thank you," she whispered, emotion catching in her throat.

She was careful not to drip any of the tomato sauce on herself—that would be too embarrassing. But spaghetti with tomato sauce could be tricky, especially when dressed in white.

Mia kept sipping her wine. Soon she felt her cheeks begin to glow. Could that be from the summer heat? Was it really the wine? Or maybe Levin's presence had something to do with it?

Levin kept sneaking glances at Mia. He didn't want to stare at her so obviously, but she intrigued him. Everything about her was special, and he couldn't get rid of the feeling that she had an interesting story to tell. The wine seemed to be affecting her, and her cheeks had taken on a soft pink glow that gave her face a healthier look. Her paleness had been almost scary.

Mia was relieved when she finished the meal without any accidents. She glanced up into Levin's eyes. He looked away quickly. That made Mia uncomfortable. Had he been staring at her or something?

"Did I make a mess of myself with the sauce?" She wiped the corners of her mouth with her napkin.

"Oh, no, not at all," he replied quickly. "The wine is giving your face a dose of color, and I was just noticing that." Now he felt shy himself, which surprised him.

"Oh. I'm not used to alcohol, I should probably stop." She pushed her glass away.

"Why? I think it does you good. You were so pale."

"Well, I haven't been in the sun for a while," she said. She couldn't very well tell him the truth. Actually, she'd hardly left her room at all lately. She hadn't wanted to walk in the clinic's park. The others were there, and they always acted strange.

"Will you tell me a little bit about yourself?" Levin asked.

"There's nothing interesting to tell," she said hastily. She hadn't considered the possibility that he might ask her personal questions, and there was no way she could tell him about herself. She started to have misgivings. No one wanted to have anything to do with someone like her. She could never tell him the truth.

"I don't believe it. What do you do? Did you go to college, or are you still studying?"

"I earned a high school equivalency," Mia said. "And afterward . . . well . . . I didn't do anything else. I don't really know what I want to do." She looked at him, hoping he'd be satisfied with her answer.

"Sure, it can be difficult to figure out," Levin said.

"And what about you?" Mia asked.

"I study law, but I'm taking a break right now. My head was completely blocked, and my father was nice enough to lend me this old piece of junk."

"Then . . . someday you'll be a lawyer? Or a judge?" Mia looked at him in awe. He must be very clever.

"I'm going to work in my father's firm. That's the plan, anyway," he explained.

"That's great that you have a clear goal." Mia's esteem for him continued to grow.

"And you? Do you have any goals?" Levin studied her closely. He didn't want to push her. He got the impression that she didn't like to talk about herself very much, but he was curious. He decided he'd stop asking questions as soon as she looked hesitant.

"Morocco. I want to go to Morocco." Mia quickly looked away. "I can't tell you more at the moment."

"Well, that's a clear goal, too, isn't it?" Levin said. He smiled, and she stopped holding her breath.

"Yes," she said, "it is."

7

"I'll do that." Mia jumped up as soon as she saw Levin starting to clear the table.

"We can do it together so it goes faster," Levin said.

"But I want to pay you back a little since you're giving me a ride." She looked at him with her deep, dark eyes, and Levin's resolve began to melt.

"Mia, you don't have to do that."

"But I want to, please."

Levin gave in. She might be shy and unusual, but her charm was indisputable. In any case, she could easily wrap him around her finger. Levin decided he'd better pay attention. This little lady, as unassuming as she might seem, might be a lot smarter than he realized.

Levin went to sit outside. It was still summery and warm. Several truckers were sitting in front of their vehicles. They were chatting despite all the background noise from the highway. He tried to follow their conversation, but his French wasn't good enough.

Mia cleaned up everything carefully and wiped off the table. She saw that Levin was sitting outside and climbed out of the camper, worried that she might be disturbing him. "Can I sit with you for a moment? It's so hot in there."

"Of course. Would you like some more wine?" Levin was happy that she'd followed him.

"I probably shouldn't. I still feel it." She laughed, slightly embarrassed.

"Just take anything you want. You know where the fridge is. Oh, yeah, and in the back left corner—behind the little door—is a toilet and sink. So there's no need to walk over to the facilities, unless you want a shower."

Mia got a glass of water while Levin brought out a chair for her. He stole a glance at her as she walked down the steps. Her legs had a lovely shape. In general, she had a great figure, even though it wouldn't hurt her to gain a few pounds here and there.

Mia untied her hair and ran her fingers through the blond curls. It was already dry, and it was no wonder, in this heat. Levin saw that a few travelers had noticed her. Her slender body and long blond hair were a feast for the eyes. He felt a touch of glee that *he* had the pretty blonde by his side, and the neighbors were out of luck.

"Is there anything in particular you want to see in Paris tomorrow?" he asked.

"No, not really."

"Do you want to know something about the city?"

"That would be great!" Mia sat on the chair with her legs pulled up, and she listened attentively. She absorbed everything. Levin could describe things well, and he told a few funny stories. She laughed heartily more than once. Levin was happy that Mia listened to him, because she truly listened. There was no feigned interest. She hung on every word, and the short questions she asked made it clear that she cared.

He lost himself a few times in her dark eyes. They were mysterious and expressive. Now they glittered with pleasure, but he'd also seen fear and sadness in them.

Levin was certain that she was genuine. She didn't play any games, and even if she hadn't told him much about herself, and maybe never would, she was the kind of person he felt he could trust, even after such a short time.

Mia slowly started to feel tired. She stretched and tried to suppress a yawn.

"Are you sleepy?" Levin asked.

Mia looked like she'd been caught red-handed. "Yes, last night on the bench wasn't particularly, um, restful. Do you mind if I go in now?"

"No, of course not." Levin stood up. "I'll help you make up the bed."

"Thanks." Mia stood next to him, looking self-conscious. "Can I wash in there?" She pointed to the door in the corner.

"Of course. I'll stay outside for a while. Good night, Mia." Levin playfully tugged at one of her blond curls.

"Good night to you, too. And thanks for—"

She didn't get any further. Levin put a finger to her lips. "Stop thanking me. I didn't plan to make this trip with company, but I'm really glad you're here, OK?"

Mia's eyes glowed. He was really nice. "OK," she said.

"Levin! How nice that you called!" His mother's voice vibrated loudly through Levin's cell phone. "Where are you now? What's all that noise? Did you stop by the highway?" The questions rattled like hailstones.

"No, Mom," he said, "everything's OK. I'm just outside of Paris. Tomorrow I'm going in to see the city."

He avoided using the word *we*, because if he told his mother about the unusual hitchhiker he'd picked up, she'd probably send a Special Forces team to his rescue.

"That's nice, dear," his mother said. He heard his father's voice in the background. "Your father wants to know if everything's all right with the camper."

"Yes, it's fine." Levin grinned to himself. "It's running perfectly, and you couldn't even tell how old it is."

"I'll let him know. Take good care of yourself, dear."

"I will, Mom. I promise."

Levin called his best friend, Kai, who'd just about burst with envy over Levin's trip. Kai was right in the middle of his dissertation, so he hadn't been able to come along.

But Levin was happy with the way it had worked out. He also decided not to worry too much about what would happen with Mia or wonder when they would go their separate ways. Right now everything was fine.

He sat outside awhile longer. Suddenly he heard a soft whimpering. He looked around, perplexed. The other travelers were already in their bunks. Levin walked around the vehicle, trying to locate the sound. Then he realized it was coming from inside the camper.

He entered. "Mia, are you all right?" he called into the darkness. All he heard was the quiet crying. He approached her bed. The moonlight was shining through the window, and he could see that the sheets were all tangled. She lay on her back without a cover—not so surprising in the heat—and she was drenched with sweat.

Levin was at a loss. What should he do? Wake her up and risk frightening her, or leave her to her nightmare? He decided on the former. The way she sounded, it wasn't a pleasant dream. He touched her shoulder.

"Mia, hey, wake up." He shook her gently. She didn't stir at first, seeming to be completely caught up in the nightmare. Levin placed a hand on her cheek and called her name a bit louder.

Mia heard a voice and felt someone touching her. Her eyes flew open. All she saw was a silhouette. Her heart began to race. She sprang up, and her head crashed into someone else's with a crunch.

"Ow!" Levin shouted.

Mia caught her breath and slowly began to recognize outlines. Then she remembered.

Levin, Morocco.

"Jeez, Mia," Levin said. He really hadn't expected her to jump up like that.

"Levin?" she said in a squeaky voice.

"Yes, of course! Who else did you expect?" he said, rubbing his aching forehead.

Mia swallowed hard as Levin turned on a low light. She watched him take two towels, hold them under cold water, and then press one against his head. He handed her the other towel.

"Here," he said, "we don't want to go into Paris tomorrow with huge purple bumps on our heads."

Mia held the towel to her head. "What happened?" she asked.

Levin sighed. "You were having a bad dream and crying, don't you remember? I wanted to see if you were OK, and I tried to wake you up. You sat up really fast and crashed into me. I won't wake you again, at least not from so close. Next time I'll throw something at you."

"Oh!" Mia looked guilty and lowered her gaze. It was all very uncomfortable, and she really didn't want to disturb Levin. "Did I wake you up?"

"No, you didn't. I was still sitting outside when I heard you crying." His voice was gentler now. "What were you dreaming? Were demons after you or something?"

"I can't remember anymore," she said, but that wasn't the whole truth. Now something occurred to her. Of course, she hadn't taken her sleeping pills, and perhaps that was the reason for the nightmare. True, she hadn't dreamed so intensely in a long time, but maybe the dreams were a reaction to the excitement of the last few days. One thing was certain: she would have to start taking the pills again. She didn't want to bother Levin, not at any cost.

"I'm really sorry. Please excuse me, I hope your head is feeling better."

"It's already fine. We both have pretty hard heads, don't we?" Levin gave her a lopsided grin.

Mia breathed a sigh of relief. He didn't seem angry. "Looks like it."

She hurried into the little lavatory and took a sleeping pill. As she came out, she saw that Levin was pulling off his T-shirt. He stood there wearing nothing but his shorts. It looked like he was getting ready for bed. Her face turned a brilliant shade of red. What should she do now? She quickly averted her gaze and went to her bed.

"Everything OK?" he asked.

"Yes, everything's fine, thanks," Mia said. She had turned her back to him and was staring at the wall. He had noticed her shyness and her appraising look. But he wouldn't have thought he needed to cover up in front of her. They were sharing such a small space; she'd have to get used to it. And she must have seen a half-naked man before.

What's more, she didn't have very much on herself. Since she had turned her very attractive backside toward him, he could get a better look at it. She wore a close-fitting spaghetti-strapped top and panties. Her bottom had an extremely nice shape, and he'd already had plenty of opportunities to admire her legs. And as she had jumped up from her bad dream, he would have had to be blind not to notice that she was well-endowed on top.

Levin swallowed. Mia's beautiful body was starting to have an effect on him. The pressure in his boxers made that totally clear. He turned off the light and escaped into his bed, determined to try to sleep.

8

When he awoke, the sun was shining through the little window over his bed. Levin rubbed his eyes and stretched.

With a jolt he remembered that he wasn't alone anymore. He sat up and looked over at Mia. She was still asleep, lying on her stomach. His glance fell on her bottom. There were worse things in the world than waking up to that kind of view. He stood up quietly, got fresh clothes and some money, and made his way to the showers.

When he returned, Mia was still asleep. Her blond curls were tousled over her face, and her top had ridden up so her stomach was showing. She slept peacefully and breathed evenly. Levin considered letting her sleep, but he'd brought two cups of hot coffee—and after all, they had wanted to have breakfast in Paris. He was getting hungry, and it was time to go.

"Mia," he said softly. She made an involuntary grunt. "Hey, Paris is waiting for us," he said a bit louder.

Mia registered a gentle voice and slowly raised her eyelids and pushed the hair out of her face. The first thing she saw was a pair of brilliant blue eyes. Levin. She sat up and smiled shyly. "Good morning," she said in a sleepy voice.

"Good morning. Would you like some coffee?" He held the cup out to her.

"Thank you, how nice!" She appreciated his friendly gesture.

"I hope it's OK if we leave soon. I'm hungry, and we'd planned to have breakfast in Paris." Levin sat down on the edge of her bed.

"Yes, of course," Mia said. Then her conscience got to her. "Maybe I should buy an alarm clock."

"Why? We have plenty of time."

Looking at him, the butterflies in her stomach were back. Then she noticed that Levin had already showered and dressed. "What time is it?"

"Almost nine. Don't you have a watch?"

"No."

"But you have a cell phone, don't you?"

"I don't have one of those, either," she said, feeling self-conscious. Now he'd surely think she was completely behind the times. And he would be right.

"Really? How can you live without a cell phone?"

"Up until now it's been entirely possible," she said with a giggle. The amazement on his face was simply sweet.

"And your family and friends? Can you always find a phone to reach them? What about emergencies?"

She lowered her eyes quickly. Friends? Where would she have found any? She didn't want contact with any of the others in the clinic. Levin was the first person she'd met in a very long time who might actually fit that description.

"Oh, it always works out somehow," she said, evading his question. "Do I have time for a quick shower?"

"We have all the time in the world—did you forget already?" he joked.

Mia showered quickly so she wouldn't keep Levin waiting any longer than necessary. He looked up in surprise as she suddenly appeared next to him. She really had made it back in record time. He hadn't expected it after his experiences with ex-girlfriends.

She'd braided her hair. It was still wet, and a few beads of water ran down her neck. Levin forced himself not to watch their progress so closely.

"Wow, you're ready."

"I didn't want to make you wait. You're hungry. And anyway, I already shaved yesterday, so I didn't need—" She broke off her sentence, feeling herself blush. She really hadn't needed to tell him *that*. She risked looking in his eyes, which widened with surprise, then crinkled with amusement.

"Well, then," Levin said. He looked down quickly. "We can go, now," he said quickly and escaped back into the camper. Mia followed him. She still seemed embarrassed by her comment. She put away her things, hung up her towel to dry, and then climbed onto the passenger seat next to him.

"Ready for Paris?" he asked.

"Yes," she said. Being next to him was comforting.

Even though Levin tried, he couldn't manage to completely forget what she'd said. His imagination got the better of him, and he was grateful that the Paris traffic required all of his attention.

The other drivers paid deference to the big, old camper, and Levin adapted to the French driving style fairly quickly. He remembered a nice, quiet area with lots of cafés from his last visit to Paris, so he headed in that direction first. His stomach was beginning to growl.

Mia was speechless. The experience overwhelmed her. What a quirky, loud, and extremely beautiful city. She was impressed by how Levin maneuvered the camper through the chaos. She would never be able to do that; she'd even have difficulties as a pedestrian there.

Levin was lucky that he found a large enough parking space not too far from where he wanted to go. He looked over at Mia. "Are you as hungry as I am?"

She hesitated. Was she hungry? She didn't even know right now, as she was so amazed by the city around her. She was actually in Paris. Until a couple of days ago, she hadn't even imagined being there. "Yes," she said.

They found a cozy-looking café and took a table in the sun. Mia looked around, admiring the facades of the antique houses, dreaming about what might be going on inside them. The waiter spoke, and she snapped back to reality.

Levin ordered in French, which impressed Mia, and she scratched the remnants of her school French together to order a croissant and a café au lait.

"Hey, you have a good accent," Levin complimented her.

"Thank you. I didn't expect them to understand me," she said.

Levin ordered a gigantic breakfast, and Mia was amazed at how much he could eat. She looked on with wide eyes as he finished his meal.

"Phew, that was necessary," he said after downing the last of his coffee. Then he looked over at Mia's plate. "And what about you? Only a croissant and coffee. Is that enough?"

"It's enough for me. I never eat much for breakfast."

"That's clear. You're quite slim."

"Considering how much you eat, you are, too."

Levin laughed. "Are you being fresh, Mia?"

"No, of course not," she said, turning serious again. "Sorry, I didn't mean to offend you."

"Hey, no problem!" He was puzzled by her reaction. "I know how you meant it—I was kidding."

Mia breathed a sigh of relief. She found it difficult to judge how others perceived her words. And she definitely didn't want to hurt Levin's feelings.

"Are you ready for some sightseeing?" he asked.

"Yes, I'd love it," she said.

Levin looked into her eyes, enthralled by their expressiveness.

After breakfast, Levin squeezed the camper back into the Paris traffic. "Shall we find a quieter place to camp this evening?"

"Yes, please." Mia's mouth fell open as they drove past the Eiffel Tower. "I didn't realize it was so huge," she said. "I mean, it looks smaller in pictures, and . . . wow."

"We'll go take a closer look. I'm just looking for a parking place near the center of town. From there we can take the Metro. We don't want anyone to bump into us and make a dent." He patted the dashboard.

Luckily, they quickly found a parking lot and were able to set off on foot.

"Shall we go to the Eiffel Tower first?" Levin asked.

"Yes." She looked happy. Levin was tempted to take her hand, but then he thought better of it.

When they were finally standing in front of the tower, Levin took a few pictures with his cell phone. He asked Mia to pose for him. "Do you have a camera?"

"No, unfortunately not." Actually, she didn't need one, because she'd never forget these images.

"Look," Levin said, stepping closer. He showed her the pictures he'd taken. "A beautiful subject."

"Yes, the Eiffel Tower is really beautiful and so impressive," she agreed.

Levin touched the tip of her nose with his finger. "Mia, I didn't mean that dumb steel thing. I meant the pretty girl in front of it."

Mia looked at him shyly and tried to read in his gorgeous blue eyes whether he was making fun of her.

"Me? I'm not pretty," she said softly.

"Oh, yes, you are. And you know it, too." He took her hand. "Shall we go up to the platform? From there you'll get a terrific view of the city."

Mia just nodded. She was speechless, but not because of the view of Paris waiting for her—it was because Levin was holding her hand. It was a lovely feeling. He had wonderfully warm hands, and it felt good to walk with him this way. She felt protected. She kept stealing glances at him. It was both calming and exciting to be so close to him.

As they reached the visitors' platform, she was completely overwhelmed. She covered her mouth with her hands. Paris lay at her feet, and the view was simply breathtaking. She couldn't get enough of it. Levin explained the sights to her, and she soaked up the information like a sponge. She lost all sense of time. She was so amazed that she could barely speak. She walked around the platform slowly, absorbing the beauty of the entire city.

Levin hadn't been looking at Paris for a while now; all he could see was Mia. She seemed like a small child in front of a lighted tree on Christmas Eve. She was so astonished by everything.

They had been up there quite a while, and Levin was starting to feel impatient. There was still so much he wanted to show her.

"Mia?" he said in a gentle tone.

She turned to face him. Suddenly there were tears in her eyes. On impulse, he put his arms around her and held her tightly.

"Thank you," she whispered in his ear.

At first he was surprised by her strong reaction, but then he began to enjoy the embrace. He breathed in her intoxicating scent.

"My pleasure," he whispered, burying his face in her hair. Mia closed her eyes, and Paris faded into the background. She wondered if it was improper to hug him, but she decided not to worry about it. She carefully untangled herself from him. She could tell that her cheeks were red.

"Shall we—" Levin stopped to clear his throat. "Shall we move on? There's still a lot to see."

"Yes, let's," Mia said. "It's all so beautiful."

Levin laid a hand on her cheek and looked into her eyes. "That's true."

9

As they left the Eiffel Tower, Levin held Mia's hand again as though it was the most normal thing in the world. He wondered if she would mind, but she didn't pull back. He'd never thought something like that was possible: walking through Paris, holding hands with a girl he'd only known for a day.

But it felt right, and he couldn't think of any other way to describe it. Mia was practically a stranger. He knew nothing about her, yet she'd put some kind of a spell on him that he couldn't resist—and didn't want to. He wondered what would happen between them. Would it become a friendship, or something more? But they had time, and it was nice just to let things happen.

Sightseeing with Mia was different than with other people. Not only did she admire the famous buildings, she noticed every bed of flowers, every fountain, and every pigeon. However, they still managed to see a lot. But Levin noticed when she began to walk more slowly.

"Are you tired?"

"Yes," she admitted. Mia had never walked so much. Her protesting feet were refusing to go much farther.

"There are a few nice restaurants nearby, and over there is the Metro station. We can ride back from there later. How does that sound?"

"Good," Mia said, relieved. The idea of the chance to sit down with something to eat was very attractive.

This time even Mia had a large appetite. The sightseeing took more energy than she expected.

"Just outside the city, there's a campground where we can take showers and stay the night," Levin said once they were back in the camper. "And tomorrow we can see more of Paris."

"Sounds perfect."

"Do you like the city?"

"Totally!" Mia said. "I had no idea it would be so beautiful."

As Mia enjoyed the warm water in the shower, she went over the day in her head. It wasn't just Paris that she'd enjoyed so much; it was the way Levin acted with her. She already felt so close to him. She never would have believed that such a thing could be possible after such a short time.

His smile, the way he looked at her—all that gave her butterflies and set off a delightful tingling on her skin. He seemed to like her, too, at least a little. Otherwise he wouldn't have held her hand, would he?

Mia had seen romances on television, but she had no real experience with guys. Still, she could sense something coming from Levin's side. Then she had a sad thought. How could all this work? How long would they even be together? When would they have to go their separate ways? Mia didn't want to think about it. They'd only just met. They'd had today, and they'd definitely have tomorrow. But after that, who knew?

She walked slowly back to the camper. She was tired, and her feet hurt. Levin was waiting outside for her. He'd gone to the showers first and now had set a table and two chairs by the door, along with a baguette and a bottle of red wine. He smiled as she approached. "Hey, how are you feeling?"

"Good but tired," she admitted. "I can't even feel my feet anymore."

"You're not particularly fit, are you?" he said with a wink.

"No, you're right." She sank down onto the free chair with a sigh. "I was never all that athletic." Mia pulled her legs up onto the chair. Levin reached over and pulled her feet into his lap.

She was surprised when he began to massage them. At first she wanted to protest that he didn't have to, but she enjoyed it too much. "That helps," she said.

"I know. I want you to be fit again tomorrow," he teased.

Mia looked him in the eyes. "Do you want to see more of Paris? I mean, you know it all already."

Levin was about to say that he wanted to see everything with her, but then he stopped himself. With Mia, he saw things from a new point of view. She saw everything with different eyes, making things new to him, too.

"It's always nice to see Paris again. Otherwise I wouldn't have made the suggestion to come here."

Mia was relieved. She didn't want him to change his plans for her. After all, she was *his* guest.

Levin was diligent with the massage, and Mia relaxed so much that she almost fell asleep in the chair. Soon she said she had to go to bed, but not before she'd helped Levin carry everything back into the camper.

Slightly embarrassed, she stood in front of him in her tank top and panties. "Thanks for the wonderful day. That was the best time I've ever had," she said.

"What? Really?" Levin was surprised. "Then I'm even happier about it, Mia. I really enjoyed being with you." He hesitated briefly—should he risk it?

Levin followed his intuition and took her in his arms. To his relief, she immediately returned his embrace.

"Sleep well, sweet Mia," he whispered against her neck, and then planted a kiss on her cheek. Mia was taken by surprise, but it was nice. She could really feel the spot on her cheek he'd kissed.

"Good night, Levin." She screwed up her courage, stood on her toes, and gave him a quick kiss. Then the courage left her, and she hurried into bed.

Levin must have stared at the ceiling for at least an hour. He was dog tired, but this strange girl lying less than two yards away from him was stealing his sleep.

Mia tried to sleep, too, but it wasn't so easy. She couldn't get the scene with Levin out of her head. Those two little kisses probably didn't mean anything, but she couldn't stop thinking about them. Although it had been her choice to go quickly to her bed, she wouldn't have minded embracing him longer and kissing him more. But where would it have gone from there? She didn't know anything about that stuff. And what did he think about it? Had he wanted to make love to her?

Mia's face grew hot at the thought. Of course she knew, theoretically, how it worked—and she had also discovered some Internet sites about it—but what she'd seen online had turned her off more than on.

But why was she racking her brain over it? Maybe it wouldn't have even gone that far. Maybe he just liked her. Mia sighed. It wouldn't help to think about it anymore. Being with him was so nice. Maybe she should just wait and see how everything developed. Her life had changed much faster in the last few days than she would have believed possible. And who knew what was waiting for her?

This time, Mia woke before Levin. She'd been awakened by the sun. It looked like it was going to be another beautiful day, and she hurried over to the washhouse to freshen up. On the way back, she bought a baguette and some cheese.

When she returned to the camper, Levin was still asleep. She tiptoed over to him. The temptation to gaze at him was simply too strong. He slept on his back, one arm hanging off the bed. He wore leather bracelets, one of which was worn out. His stomach muscles were toned. He obviously worked out regularly. In the clinic, Mia had never felt the urge to do serious exercise, partly because it would have meant spending more time with the others.

His skin was so smooth. Mia wondered if he shaved himself all over. He looked like he did, anyway. She stepped closer. His face was completely relaxed in sleep. She was enchanted by his gentle expression. He was a very handsome guy, and she was tempted to run her hands through his thick, dark hair. He'd surely had many girlfriends do that. She wondered if she should risk it.

She bent over him and moved her hand toward his head very slowly. With her fingertips, she lightly stroked his hair.

Levin felt something, a gentle touch like a breath of air. He cautiously opened one eye. He knew those beautiful legs well by now. He quickly closed the eye again, fiercely hoping she hadn't noticed. He concentrated on trying to look like he was asleep. He was dying to find out what she intended to do.

She ran her hand through his hair very gently, but to Levin it felt like lightning shooting through his entire body. It was so delicious that his skin prickled.

Mia pulled back her hand. She didn't want to risk waking him this way. She decided to make coffee. Maybe the scent would rouse him.

"Don't stop," Levin murmured. Then he opened his eyes. Mia jumped back in surprise, blushing. How embarrassing! He'd noticed. What must he think of her now?

"You're awake," she said.

"Yes." Levin stretched out a hand to her. "Come here."

She hesitated. Then she let him pull her down onto the edge of the bed.

"Thank you for waking me so nicely," he said, smiling at her. He sat up and pushed a blond curl off her face. "Did you sleep well?"

At least he didn't seem angry. "Yes, I did. I was going to make coffee, and I got fresh bread." Her heart hammered away wildly.

Levin gave her a kiss on the cheek. "That sounds great."

After breakfast, they drove into the city again. They hadn't seen anywhere near everything the day before. Even at a quick pace, it would take weeks to see Paris properly.

Levin wondered how Mia would act toward him today. They'd gotten closer yesterday and that morning, but basically it was all harmless. He wasn't certain he wanted more. Sure, he found her attractive, but she seemed so naive and inexperienced. He wasn't the kind of guy who would pretend he wanted something he didn't just to get a woman into bed.

Once they'd found a parking spot in the city, he took her hand again. She smiled, and they set off.

That afternoon they discovered a flea market. Mia asked Levin if he'd like to look at it with her. Of course he couldn't talk her out of it. Whenever she looked at him with pleading eyes, he melted like ice in the sun.

"Look, here are some leather bracelets like the ones you wear," Mia said, pulling him over to a leather-goods stand.

"Mine *are* pretty ratty," Levin said.

Mia looked everything over carefully and then chose a pair. "May I give them to you?" she asked, blushing.

"Give them to me? You don't have to—I can buy them," Levin said.

"But I'd like to. Then you'll have something to remind you of me," she insisted.

"Mia, if I know anything for sure, it's that I will definitely never forget you." Levin laughed and looked into her eyes.

Both his look and his words confused her. How did he mean that? Was it because she was so strange? Or did he think she was stupid after all?

She bit her lower lip, then looked at the bracelets again. "Please, Levin," she said.

"OK, I surrender. But only if I'm allowed to give you something, too."

"I couldn't possibly accept," Mia protested. "You've already done so much."

"Good, then let's forget the bracelets," he said, waving his hand at the display. "I don't want anything, either."

"But, Levin, it would mean so much to me."

"Me, too." He was trying hard to remain serious, but it wasn't easy—now she looked distraught. He resisted the urge to just take her in his arms and let her do anything her unusual mind came up with.

"Listen, we can make a deal: Neither of us spends more than five euros on the other. We're at a flea market, so that should be possible. I think that's fair."

Mia was surprised, but she agreed. That sounded good. "OK." She bought the bracelets and fastened them on his wrist. "I hope you like them." Now she was unsure again. Had she coerced him into accepting something he didn't like?

"I like them a lot." Levin stroked her cheek. *Just like you*, he added in his mind. She seemed very happy, and Levin got a warm feeling when he saw her smile.

"OK, now it's my turn," he said, winking. Taking her hand, he led her through the market. As they approached a stand with colorful scarves, Levin got an idea. Mia always wore white. That must get boring for her after a while. He headed directly to the stand, fished out a red scarf, and draped it around her neck. Shocked, Mia pulled it off and put it back in the pile. She was breathing fast, and for a moment she felt like she was seeing everything through a red veil. She had to stop herself from shaking.

"Hey, what's wrong?" Levin was surprised by her strong reaction.

"I, well, red," she said, stopping to gulp. "I just don't like red." What would Levin think of her?

"OK, Mia, sorry." He was perplexed. "I just wanted to show you how good you look in other colors."

She was overcome by a wave of conscience. He must think she was completely gaga—and, basically, she was.

"That's very sweet of you," she whispered, reaching for his hand. "Please forgive me."

"Nothing to forgive," he said. A strange feeling crept in. Was she part of some kind of sect, or something? But then she wouldn't have been traveling on her own. He needed a few answers, and now. "Why do you always wear white? Is there a specific reason?"

"I just like it."

He shook his head. "No one wears one color exclusively, not even their favorite."

"Well, I do. White is beautiful, it's so pure and—"

"Innocent," he said.

Mia's head shot up. Had he seen through her somehow? Or did he actually know something about her? She was scared, but she didn't want to let on. He must never discover the truth.

"But you're right. Maybe I should wear something else for a change," she said. It took great effort, but she reached for a beige-colored scarf. "What do you think of this one?"

"Beige is just a shade of white," Levin said, slowly getting himself back under control. Her reaction to the scarf still irritated him, but maybe he shouldn't take it so personally. Maybe he'd just taken her by surprise. Anyway, now she seemed open to his suggestion.

"You have such beautiful brown eyes. How about this?" He held up a scarf with earth tones. "Or this, royal blue."

Mia reached for the blue. "This one is really pretty," she said.

"Will you wear it if I give it to you?"

"Of course," she said. "It's a gift from you, and I'll always cherish it."

Levin found her so sweet that he wanted to put his arms around her. "OK, then," he said, handing it over.

"Thank you," Mia said, tying the scarf around her hair like a headband, taming her blond curls. "It's too warm to wear it around my neck right now."

Levin couldn't resist anymore. He pulled her close and buried his face in her hair. "It looks good on you."

"It's beautiful." Mia put her arms around his neck and closed her eyes. What had she done to deserve being with such a wonderful person?

Levin enjoyed this tender moment. Then he noticed the scarf vendor winking at him. Leven smiled and released Mia. He haggled with the vendor and paid for the scarf. "Shall we move on?"

"Yes," she said.

Hand in hand, they continued on to a stand where a child was selling toys. Mia saw a stuffed camel she liked and cried out, "Look!" She squeezed Levin's hand.

"What?" He followed her gaze.

"That camel. Isn't it the sweetest thing?" Mia had that amazing light in her eyes again that Levin couldn't resist. He checked it out. It was a camel, but so what?

"How much would you like for it?" Mia asked the boy.

"Two euros," he said eagerly.

She dug through her bag for her wallet, but Levin grabbed her hand.

"I'll get this one," he said.

"But you just bought me a scarf," she protested.

"I talked him down to three euros, remember?" He gave the child a five-euro note and told him to keep the change. The boy looked as happy as Mia had when she first discovered the camel.

Levin handed the camel to her. "Here you go, my dear."

"Thank you!" She was touched. She wanted to kiss him, and why shouldn't she? She stood on her tiptoes and kissed him lightly on the cheek.

"OK, what else can I get for you?" Levin asked. "If you always thank me like that, I'm going to enjoy this very much."

Mia felt herself turning red. "Levin, you don't know how much it means to me to be here with you," she said. "I'm so happy. You're a wonderful guy."

"Hmm, I could say the same thing about you. Well, not the guy part, just the wonderful part." He took her hand again. "And now this wonderful guy is hungry."

"There's a grocery store over there," Mia said. "Shall we shop and cook something when we get back?"

"Sounds good to me."

10

"That smells delicious." Levin peeked over Mia's shoulder as she fried steaks. He didn't mean the food as much as the girl standing in front of him. He wouldn't mind knowing what perfume she used—it had the desired effect on him.

"That was an excellent grocery store," Mia said happily. "It wasn't at all expensive, and the quality of the meat is super."

Levin stood directly behind her. It made her a bit nervous to have him watching her, but it was different from the kind of nervousness she'd felt in the past—say, when a teacher was watching her. Levin's presence made her feel that delightful tingling.

Levin resisted the temptation to put his arms around Mia's waist. He didn't want to frighten her. Instead, he went off to set the table outside the camper.

The weather forecast for the next few days promised blue skies. If it went on like this, it would be a beautiful summer, but Levin knew that his feelings about the summer didn't have that much to do with the weather.

"That tasted great," Levin said, complimenting Mia's cooking.

"Thank you. It wasn't difficult. It helped that the ingredients were so fresh." She pushed an escaped curl behind her ear.

"What shall we do tomorrow? Paris again? After that, we could move on. France is a beautiful country, and we can spend some time in other areas, too," he suggested.

"I'll go wherever you want," Mia said.

"I'd like to hear your opinion. If we go down to southern France, we could take off to the Mediterranean coast toward Tarifa. Then we could take the ferry from there to Morocco."

Mia looked at him in disbelief, and then smiled radiantly. "You really want to go to Morocco?"

"Why not? I didn't know where I wanted to go anyway, and if you're so into the idea, there must be something to it."

Mia quickly cleared the plates from the table and dashed with them into the camper. Then she returned with the big book she'd been studying so intensely the day they met.

"May I show you what I know about Morocco?" Her cheeks were pink with excitement.

Levin could have devoured her on the spot. He had to exercise a lot of self-control not to take her in his arms and kiss her. He really had to pull himself together. It couldn't go on like this. With Mia, he had to be very careful.

"Of course I'd like you to show me."

She opened the book and was immediately caught up again in the exquisite images. Mia knew every picture—and where it had been taken—by heart.

Seeing a photo of a camel, Levin said, "Aha! So that's why you wanted that little camel from the flea market."

"Yes, but I've always liked camels. They're so . . . special." Mia briefly met his gaze.

"Just like you," he said seriously, as though he was simply stating a fact.

"Everyone is special," Mia said, embarrassed. She quickly turned the page.

"But some are especially special. And you are definitely one of them," he said.

"No, you only think so." Mia knew she was blushing again and turned back to the pictures.

Levin's impulse to kiss her was stronger than ever, but he forced himself to look at the photos.

Mia had herself under control again. The book fascinated her, and she continued with her explanations. When they reached the last page, she looked up at Levin. "I hope I haven't been boring you," she said. For her standards, she had been talking a lot.

"Not at all. You've convinced me that we must go to Morocco."

Mia's heart leapt for joy. She threw her arms around Levin's neck. "Thank you, thank you, thank you," she whispered in his ear.

"My pleasure." He kissed her bare shoulder, allowing his lips to linger. He breathed in her scent, then slid his mouth toward her neck.

Mia closed her eyes. She was tingling inside, and her skin had goose bumps. What was happening? It was like she was paralyzed, but it was a lovely feeling. She waited breathlessly for what would come next, enjoying the intensity of every one of his little kisses on her skin.

The shrill sound of Levin's cell phone shattered the tender moment. Mia startled and pulled back. Levin wanted to throw his phone into the bushes.

"Excuse me," he said, picking up the phone.

Mia stood up and put the book in her backpack. She didn't want to listen in on his call, and she needed a moment to get herself back together. Her skin was still burning in all the places he'd kissed her. She ran a hand over her shoulder. She felt completely intoxicated. She had never experienced anything so beautiful.

She wondered how to interpret it and was hit by another wave of insecurity. She thought about what Levin had said about the trucker who'd offered her a ride. Was she being stupid or naive to allow this kind of intimacy? Or was she reading too much into it?

She was already twenty-two. Other women her age had had serious relationships for years, and some even had husbands. But she wasn't like other women. For the first time it was clear how much she'd missed, how much she simply didn't know—and she felt it was all her fault.

"Mom, how nice," Levin answered flatly. He tried not to sound annoyed. His mother always managed to call at inappropriate moments. But maybe it was better this way, because he needed to get himself under control. Mia's effect on him had caused him to be careless. It might be better if that didn't happen again. He shouldn't get her hopes up when he didn't know what he actually wanted from her.

"Levin, are you still there?" his mother asked.

"Uh, yeah, sure," he said, forcing himself to give her his full attention.

"How are you? Are you still in Paris?"

"Yes. Well, I'm at a campground outside the city. It's cheaper than staying in town," he explained.

"Do you know where you want to go next?"

"Probably southern France, down the Mediterranean coast, and then we'll see," he said.

"How nice. Well, we hope you have a lot of fun, dear."

"Thanks, Mom, and say hello to Dad for me. Tell him the camper is working perfectly."

His mother laughed. "Thanks, that will make him feel much better."

Mia sat on a bench in the camper. Thoughts whirled around in her head. She was confused and didn't know how she should act toward Levin anymore. On the other hand, not that much had happened. They'd flirted a little, and there wasn't any more to it. Other women her age would probably laugh at her for worrying so much.

She heard him call for her and went hesitantly back outside. "I didn't want to eavesdrop," she said.

"That was just my mom. Come back out—it's boring to sit here alone." He gave her a dazzling smile she couldn't resist. "My mother is really overprotective," he said, rolling his eyes. "What about your parents? Don't they worry about you traveling alone?"

Mia's breath caught in her throat. There they were again, those questions she wanted to avoid. "No," she said, shaking her head.

"But there must be someone who's worried. You didn't grow up in a cocoon, did you?" This actually didn't seem so far-fetched to him, considering how naive she sometimes was.

"Um, my parents . . . well . . . they're dead," she answered honestly. Even if she couldn't tell him everything, he had the right to know part of the truth.

"Oh, my God, Mia, I'm sorry." Levin reached for her hand and stroked it gently. "Did it happen very long ago?"

"It's been eight years."

"An accident?"

"Something like that," she said. She couldn't look into his eyes.

"What happened to you after that? Where did you grow up? With relatives?" He was stricken and felt ashamed of his remark about the cocoon.

"In an institution. I don't really want to talk about it—please don't be angry." She looked at him pleadingly.

"I'm not angry, of course not." Levin kissed the tips of her fingers. "If I pried too deeply, I'm sorry, Mia. It's OK, if you don't want to talk about it."

"Thank you for understanding. And for everything." She gave him a long look.

"I haven't done anything that great," he said.

"Yes, you have. More than you know." She got up her courage and leaned over to kiss him on the cheek. "You're an absolute godsend for me, and I can't imagine what I've done to deserve you."

"Stop, Mia, you're making me blush." He could tell she meant it—the look in her eyes made it clear. The sadness in them didn't escape him, either.

"I don't even know how old you are," Levin said as they sat together later that evening. They'd set up lanterns. Crickets were chirping in the distance, and fireflies glittered everywhere. It was a beautiful summer night.

"Hmm, I don't know how old you are, either," she said.

"I'm twenty-three," Levin said.

"That's nice." She didn't say any more, just stared dreamily into the starry sky.

"You can be mean, did you know that?"

Mia started to giggle. "That's not true."

"Sure, it's true," he said. He leaned over and gave her a playful poke in the side.

"Hey, stop it!" she said between giggles.

"Why, are you ticklish?" Levin flashed a wicked grin, which Mia noticed even in the dim light.

"No, not at all," she lied.

"Why don't I believe you?" Levin got up from his chair and went around the table to stand in front of her.

"I don't know," she said, trying to look innocent. His hands instantly flew to her waist, and Mia squeaked.

"No, please don't," she said, giggling.

"Sh, not so loud! We're not alone here, you know," Levin said.

"Then let me go," she said.

"I have a much better idea." Levin pulled her up off the chair and hoisted her over his shoulder. She shrieked so loudly that she needed to cover her mouth.

Levin carried her into the camper, quickly shut the door behind him, and threw her on his bed. "Now you're gonna get it, Mia."

"No, please!" she said, giggling underneath him, but it was too late. He clearly did not feel merciful. He tickled her so much that she could barely breathe through all the laughter.

He loved seeing her so boisterous, tears rolling down her face with the release. Then she whimpered for mercy, and he softened—stopping the tickle attack but still holding her down.

"How old are you?" he whispered in her ear, his fingers slowly stroking her sensitive sides.

"Twenty-two," she panted, finally catching her breath.

Levin sat up again, releasing her from his weight. He noticed that her top had ridden up, exposing her soft skin. He caressed her stomach.

Mia breathed deeply again. Something had suddenly changed. She looked into his eyes. His expression confused her. He looked different than usual. His gentle caress on her bare skin gave her goose bumps. He was so tender, so gentle, and still she felt every nuance of his touch.

"Mia." Levin's voice was rough as he gazed at her. Her mouth was slightly open, the blond curls tangled. She was breathing heavily, and her chest rose and fell under him, but then he came to his senses. Where this could lead was instantly clear. Something else was clear, too, and it was extremely uncomfortable. He quickly crawled off of her and sat on the edge of the bed. Levin hoped she hadn't noticed the obvious bulge in his shorts.

Mia was confused. What was wrong? Why had Levin pulled away from her so suddenly? She sat up and hugged her knees, regarding him anxiously. He didn't look at her; he just stared at the floor.

"Levin?"

"I have to bring the things in," he said. He stood up quickly and went outside.

Levin gulped the fresh air. *What the hell was that, you idiot? Pull yourself together!* God, he'd nearly done it. He'd almost taken Mia like the last Neanderthal. But she was an incredibly sweet thing, and the warm summer night and revealing clothes hadn't made the situation easier for him. After all, he was only a man, and it had been quite a while since he'd slept with a woman.

But not like that, he swore to himself. He was afraid to hurt her, and he couldn't judge how she would react, if it really happened. Was she very conservative? Would she believe they were a serious couple after that? No, he really didn't want it to go that far. He didn't want to hurt her or use her in any way.

Mia bit her lower lip. What had just happened? Had she done something stupid? She must have, because the mood had been so fun and relaxed, and now it was suddenly over. She wondered if she should ask him about it, but she didn't have the courage. She stood up and tidied Levin's bed. Maybe it would be better if they just went to sleep and hoped that everything would be back to normal in the morning.

She hurried into the little bathroom and brushed her teeth. Then she put on the top she'd been using to sleep in and took off her shorts.

She went hesitantly to the outer door. Levin was sitting outside, looking pensive.

"Levin?" Her voice was a squeak again. She knotted her fingers anxiously. Why was he acting so strange all of a sudden? If only she knew what she'd done wrong.

"Hmm?" He felt so incredibly stupid that he couldn't look at her.

"I'm going to bed now." She felt guilty, and if she didn't know what she'd done wrong, then she was afraid she might do it again.

"OK, good night, Mia." He glanced over at her. She stood in the doorway and had an unhappy expression on her face. "Hey, what's wrong?" he asked.

"I–I," she stuttered, and then shook her head. "No, it's fine." She made a terrible attempt at a smile and went back inside.

Levin's conscience gave him a powerful shake. Did she not know what was wrong, or had she actually noticed how much it had affected him? Levin pushed back his hair. Maybe he should talk to her. And what would he say? *Sorry, Mia, I was totally turned on by you.* And what if that just scared her again? The rest of the trip could get awkward if he admitted to something like that. But it would get awkward if he didn't say something, too.

Levin sighed as he brought everything in and closed the door for the night. He saw that Mia was lying in her bed with her back to him. His eyes roved over her curves again and hesitated on her panties for a moment. Her firm bottom was truly a feast for the eyes.

But then he reprimanded himself. He went to her and sat down. She noticed him and turned onto her back.

"Mia, is everything really OK?" he asked.

"Yes, of course." He seemed to act the same as ever, and she relaxed.

"Sleep well, sweet thing." He caressed her face. Mia sat up and pulled him close and kissed him on the temple.

"You sleep well, too," she whispered. She slid back, gazing at him while she stroked his cheek. Levin caught her hand, but he couldn't release himself from her eyes so easily.

Levin! he warned himself again. What had he just been telling himself? He couldn't remember anymore. He bent over Mia carefully and kissed her on the lips. "See you in the morning."

"Yes," she whispered. A kiss! Levin had kissed her! Mia lay on her bed with a pounding heart. How wonderful it was. But it always was when Levin came close to her, touched her, or anything else.

She turned onto her other side. Through the darkness she could only see his silhouette. In this heat, he slept without a blanket, and all he had on was a pair of boxers.

Mia wanted to lie next to him, feel his skin against hers, caress him, kiss him. A sweet stirring meandered through her lower body, and she sighed.

Levin stared at the ceiling and ordered himself to come down from his passion-induced delirium. Maybe he should go take a cold shower or stick ice cubes in his shorts. Too bad there was no freezer compartment in the camper's little fridge.

He heard Mia sigh, a sweet little sound. His thoughts wandered from the images in his head down to his lower regions. Levin turned onto his stomach. How he would love to go over to Mia now, take her in his arms, caress her soft body, inhale her scent, kiss her—and much more.

He sprang up, grabbed a towel, and headed for the showers.

11

The cold water helped him calm down a bit. He'd never known himself to get so keyed up. Maybe it had to do with the heat and the fact that Mia always wore so little to bed. If only he knew how she felt about the whole thing. He definitely had the impression that she had no idea what kind of effect she had on him. Somehow, that fit.

When Levin returned to the camper, Mia was lying in bed. He stood by her for a moment, watching. He could tell by her steady breathing that she was asleep. He was almost annoyed that this sweet little thing was driving him so crazy while sleeping so peacefully.

"Do you have any idea what you do to me?" he whispered, gently pushing a blond curl off her face. "Sweet dreams, angel."

The smell of fresh coffee reached his nose, and he slowly opened his eyes. Mia was standing in the little kitchen area, busily putting together their breakfast. He watched her for a while and had to grin. She was trying to be so quiet. As she put down a cup too loudly, she startled and looked in his direction.

"Oh, I woke you. I'm sorry," Mia said.

"No problem." Levin grabbed his cell phone and checked the time. "It's time to get up, anyway. Have you been awake long?" He pulled himself out of the bed and went over to her.

"Awhile. I already showered and prepared everything." She waved a hand at the breakfast table.

"Super," he said, smiling.

She looked so pleased and happy that he banned all his negative thoughts from the night before to the furthest corner of his mind. He had briefly wondered if it wouldn't be better for them to part ways, but now he felt ashamed of the thought. Sending Mia off alone would simply be irresponsible, and besides, he didn't want to deprive himself of her sweet company.

"Do you have a swimsuit with you?" Levin asked Mia as they strolled hand in hand through the streets of Paris.

"No."

"And how do you picture our trip down the Mediterranean coast? Do you plan to skinny-dip?" he teased.

She stopped, shocked. "What? *No!* How could you think I would do such a thing?"

Levin laughed. "It wouldn't be *so* unusual in France."

"No, I will most certainly not swim naked." Mia glared at him.

"OK, then we need to go shopping—unless you don't want to go swimming."

Mia hesitated. "I can't swim very well," she admitted. She wasn't even sure when she'd last done it; probably when she had been at school.

"I don't want to race with you, just a little splashing around. That should be enough, shouldn't it?"

"OK, for that it should work," she said.

"Fine. Look, there are a few department stores over there. Shall we?"

By reflex she reached for a white bikini, but then she changed her mind. Maybe it really was time for something different. If she wanted to be free, she had to try to break her old habits. She was determined and chose both turquoise and violet bikinis.

Levin had noticed her internal fight. He was surprised and pleased to see her choices.

"I'll try them on," Mia said.

"OK, I'll wait."

Actually, he'd always hated shopping with girlfriends. How many hours had he stood in front of changing rooms with the other poor idiots accompanying their better halves? It was different with Mia. Shopping with her was interesting.

Mia examined herself critically in the mirror. The bikinis were pretty and fit well, but weren't they too provocative? But then the girl in her decided that she wanted Levin to find her attractive, after all, and maybe he'd like the way she looked in the suits.

She peeked anxiously through the curtain and checked to see if they were alone. She didn't want to show him in front of other men.

"Could you have a look?" she asked, pushing aside the curtain.

Levin had to swallow hard—she looked absolutely gorgeous. "Wow," he finally managed to get out. "You look . . . fantastic. I mean, that bikini looks great on you."

"Do you think so?" Her eyes glowed again. "Then I'll take it."

"Do that," Levin said. After she disappeared behind the curtain, he allowed himself to take a deep breath. She had beautiful breasts, and he'd already seen her bottom. Levin was sure men would be drooling. He'd have to watch out that none of them tried to pick her up.

Mia was satisfied. She was glad Levin liked how she looked. Elatedly, she walked toward the checkout counter, and on the way she noticed some jeans and a rose-colored T-shirt. She felt motivated by Levin's previous reaction and asked for his opinion again. "Do you think I'd look good in those, too?" she said, biting her lower lip.

Levin followed her gaze. "Definitely. Do you want to look around some more?" he heard himself ask. He never would have said such a thing with any other girl.

"If you don't mind."

"Go ahead," he encouraged her.

Mia had made an excellent haul. She now owned two bikinis, two pairs of jeans (long and short), three T-shirts, and a summer dress. Not one of these new things was white. But then she had to stop, because her budget was limited. The shopping wasn't particularly expensive, but it was enough for the time being.

For their last evening in Paris, Levin and Mia decided to splurge on dinner at a nice restaurant. Mia put on her new dress for the occasion and even some makeup. She wore makeup very rarely and didn't have a lot of practice with it, but with the help of a magazine she'd bought, she was able to do a reasonable job with it.

Levin tried not to stare at her the *entire* time, but how could he not, when she looked so damn pretty?

He invited her to a bar after dinner to hear a band. Mia was enjoying the music, and Levin got up his courage. "Will you dance with me?"

"I can't dance."

"I can't, either, but with such a slow song we'll manage." He held out his hand. Mia didn't really want to. She was afraid of making a fool of herself, but she didn't want to offend Levin, either, so she agreed.

She glanced at the other couples on the dance floor leaning closely together, swaying to the music. It didn't look that difficult. She was nervous about coming that close to Levin again, but he pulled her in so quickly she didn't have a chance to worry about it. Mia smiled, then shyly put her arms around his back. Levin buried his face in her hair. Her perfume filled all his senses, and having her body so close made him feel intoxicated.

"Mia, you're so beautiful."

Her heart leapt at his words. She didn't know if he really meant it, but it was so nice of him to say it.

"You're so sweet," she said.

Levin raised his head and looked into her eyes. "I am so, so glad that I met you." His voice was full of emotion.

"It's so wonderful to be with you."

"Mia?"

"Yes?" She looked at him with wide eyes.

"I really want to kiss you." Levin's blood pounded in his ears. He was suddenly extremely nervous—he didn't want to frighten her. Maybe he was making a huge mistake and the beautiful evening would end in disaster, but the temptation of the moment was too much.

Mia was so excited that she couldn't utter a sound. She simply nodded. Levin smiled and lowered his mouth to hers. Her lips trembled as he met them. She closed her eyes, not even noticing the music anymore. She didn't care that they weren't alone, either. This gentle kiss captivated all her senses.

Levin didn't hurry. One kiss became many tiny ones. He felt her acquiescence and became more courageous. He increased the pressure on her lips and gingerly pushed his tongue between them.

Mia caught her breath. Did he want to French kiss her? That is, *really* kiss her? She had never kissed anyone. But the tingling she felt all over her body whenever he was near was simply too enjoyable, and it encouraged her to surrender.

She opened her mouth a bit, feeling how Levin's tongue slowly caressed hers. She felt electrified, and it was an amazingly beautiful sensation. She instinctively followed his lead. It felt so right, and her doubts began to melt away.

Levin held her more tightly. Her hands ran through his hair, and he began to feel a fluttering in his stomach. What was this girl doing to him? How did she manage to make him so crazy for her?

Levin wanted to keep kissing her, but on the edge of his awareness it registered that the music was getting faster now. He raised his head regretfully. Mia was just as out of breath as he was. Her face glowed pink.

Levin rested his forehead on hers. "That was so beautiful," he whispered.

"Yes," she said, and she let him lead her back to their table.

12

Mia tried not to look at Levin with such adoration, but it was difficult for her. The kiss had thrown her completely off balance—in a delightful way. He put an arm around her shoulders and kept giving her little kisses on the cheek and temple. He'd have loved to disappear with her immediately, but it was clear to him that he had to get control of himself again.

They stayed in the bar awhile longer before Levin suggested that they go. His pulse had returned to normal, and they were back to innocent conversation. But if he were honest with himself, things had completely changed between them.

Mia wondered how this could continue. For her, it was great to share such tenderness with Levin, but what if he wanted more? She'd have to admit that she was inexperienced. How would he react? Would it scare him away? She sighed, and her nervousness grew with every step closer to the camper.

"Do you want to go to sleep right away?" Levin asked when they arrived.

"I don't know. If we're trying to get to southern France tomorrow, then it wouldn't be such a bad idea," she answered, nervously twisting her fingers together.

"You're right, it's going to be a long trip. But we'll hardly be able to do it in one day, anyway." Levin smiled. She looked embarrassed, and he understood why she might be nervous. He pulled her into his arms. "Are you scared of me, Mia?"

She pulled back from him a bit. "No, of course not," she said quickly, and looked briefly into his eyes.

"Mia, I'm not going to jump on you, even if I'd actually love to devour you," he said, his voice rough with emotion again.

A smile crossed her face, and then she giggled softly. "I'm sure I don't taste very—"

"I'm sure the opposite is true," he said. But it was better not to go any further in that direction. He didn't want to scare her any more than she already was. "Would you like to use the bathroom first?"

"No, you go ahead."

While Levin brushed his teeth, Mia slipped out of her dress. The strangest thoughts were running through her head. On one hand, she found Levin so attractive and longed for his touch. On the other, she was so terribly afraid of making a fool of herself. What did normal girls do in this kind of situation?

As he came out of the bathroom, Levin saw that Mia had taken off her dress and was wearing her little top and panties again. She slipped past him with her towel.

He wondered how it would go that evening. If she really wanted to sleep, then of course he'd let her, but he also didn't have anything against continuing to kiss her. He wanted her so badly that it was almost painful, and yet she was so unreachable.

Mia smiled as she opened the bathroom door. She walked toward her bed and looked over at him.

"Wouldn't you like to come over here for a little while?" Levin said. "You can trust me. Nothing will happen that you don't want to happen."

She breathed a sigh of relief. She gratefully took him up on his offer and reached for his hand. He slid a bit closer to the wall and pulled her onto the bed. She settled into his arms.

"Everything OK, sweet thing?" His voice betrayed his level of emotion.

"Yes, very OK," she said. The look in her eyes made his heart beat faster.

"I want you to be able to relax completely when you're with me. There's nothing you need to be scared of, all right?"

"OK," she said. Then she worked up the courage to give him a light kiss on the lips.

Levin was relieved that she'd made the first move. He remained passive to see what she would do next.

At first, Mia wanted just one kiss, but kissing Levin was simply too nice, and her memories of their dance together were still fresh. Her whole body tingled just from thinking about it. This made her feel more daring, and she started using her tongue.

Levin smiled against her lips. She was so sweet in her shyness. He didn't mind her demands at all. He tried to hold himself back, knowing that with Mia, only very small steps were possible. Even though his desire grew stronger by the second, he had to keep it under control.

He put his hands gently on her stomach, and she felt his touch intensely through the thin material of her top. A shock of heat like she'd never known raced through her body.

With her innocent kisses, Mia ignited Levin's passion, from his toes to the roots of his hair. He caressed her, his hands wandering lower. As he reached the edge of her top, he let his fingers slip teasingly under the cloth. She sighed as she felt his hand on her bare skin. A sweet ache spread through her, seeming to center in her lap.

Levin felt encouraged to continue. Caressing her delicate skin made him shiver. He could hardly wait to discover the rest of her.

Mia writhed under his touch. Feelings she had never known before spread out and took over her consciousness.

His fingertips brushed the soft swelling at the top of her breasts. Levin held his breath for a moment, hoping she wouldn't stop him. He continued his exploration slowly, finally reaching the fullness of her breasts, carefully cupping them with his hands. Her nipples hardened at his touch. He was relieved; she obviously liked what he was doing. He pulled back from the kiss and pushed up the thin material of her top. He wanted to see her, at last.

Mia held her breath as Levin gazed at her breasts.

"You're so beautiful, Mia," he whispered. He then kissed her nipples very lightly. She arched her back, her hands searching for something to hold. Her fingers twisted in the sheet. Levin let his tongue continue discovering the tempting display. Mia's sighs fired his passion for her even more.

He used his hands again, caressing and teasing her hard nipples before beginning to suck on them, spoiling her in every possible way.

"Can I undress you?" he asked breathlessly.

Mia nodded, wide-eyed. She sat up to help him remove her top. He started kissing her again, but this time he was more demanding. He heard blood rushing in his ears and felt it collecting lower in his body. He was hard as a rock already, and he'd have to be extra careful now.

Levin caressed her tense belly, making tiny circles on her skin and slowly gliding downward. He stopped at the top of her panties.

Mia twitched. What he was doing was so wonderful, but now her fear started rising again. His fingers stroked her as lightly as air through her lacy panties, gently brushing her mound.

"Levin, please," she gasped against his mouth. He broke off the kiss and looked at her.

"What's wrong, should I stop? Don't you like it?" he asked. He saw the uncertainty in her eyes.

"I–I mean—"

"It's OK if you don't want to," he said, trying to comfort her.

"That's not it. I–I haven't ever, well, you know." Mia felt herself turning red, and she covered her eyes with her hand. This was all so embarrassing.

Levin was perplexed. He knew she was trying to tell him that she was a virgin. But she had the body of a goddess. It was almost impossible for him to believe that no guy had ever shown serious interest in her. Or had she been raised so conservatively? No sex before marriage, or something like that? *Please, not that*, was the thought that shot through his mind.

"You're still a virgin. Is that it?"

Mia nodded. She peeked at his face through her fingers.

"OK." Levin took a deep breath. He really hadn't expected this. He'd understood that she was shy, but this bowled him over. "Should we stop? I mean, I don't know how you feel about sex or anything." He leaned on his elbows, his hands resting gently on her chest.

"I've never had a boyfriend," she admitted. Now it was out. She looked at him fearfully. What would he think of her?

"Never?" Levin raised his eyebrows. "Really, never?"

"Really." Mia looked into his eyes, trying to read his thoughts while also noticing all too clearly what his fingers were doing. He was still playing gently with her nipples.

Levin was astounded. Lying with him was an innocent virgin. And now? What should he do? He had no problem with deflowering her. After all, he'd already done that twice, and to the best of his knowledge he'd been able to do it with relatively little pain and plenty of enjoyment for the girls in question. But Mia was another case entirely. If she wanted him, he wanted to do it perfectly. She was something special, and the fact that she'd saved herself was a valuable gift.

"I can hardly believe it. You're so beautiful. Mia, like I said—I won't do anything you don't want me to do. I want you to enjoy it with me."

"I am enjoying this," she said. "You're wonderful, Levin."

"Can I touch you some more?" He bent down again and kissed her tenderly, and to his relief she responded.

"Yes," she whispered.

"Then close your eyes." Levin kissed her more passionately. He caressed her again, drawing out one sigh after another. He wanted to explore further, and her body almost made him crazy. How could a girl be so incredibly sensual?

He slowly caressed her through her panties and carefully slid his hand between her legs. He could feel her moistness, and he was relieved.

Mia felt the wetness between her legs and realized that Levin must feel it, too. She was self-conscious about it, but it didn't seem to bother him. She instinctively spread her thighs. His kisses and caresses sent increasingly hot pulses through her body. She didn't want him to stop. What he was doing was so amazing.

Levin's hand slipped into her panties. He felt the heat that was emanating from her in waves. Her skin was smooth and soft. She felt so good to him. His fingers reached her most sensitive spot and stroked over it gently; then they slid lower, reveling in her wetness.

Mia arched her back, pushing against his seeking fingers. Levin didn't stop kissing her. He gently parted her petals with his finger, gliding deep inside.

Wow, Levin thought. *She's so tight*. He stopped himself from imagining what entering her would feel like, otherwise he'd come on the spot. Instead, he concentrated purely on her pleasure. With one quick movement, he pulled off her panties. Then he rained kisses down her velvety skin and pushed her thighs farther apart.

Mia looked up, astounded. He wouldn't?

But he did. He kissed her mound, caressing it with his tongue. He entered her again with one, then two fingers. He sucked and nibbled on her, circling her delicate pearl with his tongue, making her moan.

A gigantic wave rolled over Mia and carried her away. She smoldered and glowed, and Levin kept making the fire burn ever hotter inside her. Mia screamed. Her fingers twisted in his hair, and she shuddered like an earthquake under his touch.

Levin raised his head. Mia's eyes were closed, and her breath came fast and heavy. He carefully slid up next to her until they were face-to-face. She opened her eyes. They were heavy lidded with passion, and the adoring expression in them hit him full power. He touched his nose to hers, and whispered featherlight kisses onto her lips. "So, sweet thing?"

Mia just looked at him for a while. What he had done was incomparable. She had never known that anything so beautiful existed.

"Levin," she said with difficulty. She was still overwhelmed by the gift of pleasure he'd given her. "What . . . I mean, what about you?"

"What about me? I have a terrific girl in my arms, and I'm doing fine," he said, grinning.

"You know exactly what I'm talking about." She knew she was blushing again. This was a subject she didn't know very much about. *Another subject*, she corrected herself. "You must be . . ."

Levin decided to be merciful. He could see that she was embarrassed. "Mia," he said, "giving you pleasure was great, and I liked it a lot. Everything is good." He kissed her, and she cuddled closer to him. She came up against him with her leg, and the warm hardness she encountered let her know how aroused he still was.

"I want you to have pleasure, too," she whispered. "But I have no experience, so maybe you can help me. I mean, maybe you can—"

Levin stopped her with a passionate kiss. He moaned as he rubbed against her. He guided her hand to his shorts, looking into her eyes all the while. He resolved to stop if he noticed her getting uncomfortable.

"Stroke me," he whispered. Mia's hand slid carefully over his boxers. She tried to grasp his manhood through the fabric, but it didn't work so well. She took a deep breath, sat up, and tugged the boxers off. She gazed in wonder at this naked boy in front of her. She carefully placed her hand around his jutting member. It was very hard, but at the same time the skin felt soft as satin.

Levin closed his eyes for a moment, trying to keep himself under control. This was one moment that he definitely wanted to make last. He took Mia's hand, gently moving it up and down. She then continued to massage him on her own. Levin moaned. This girl brought him to the edge of insanity. Her movements were so innocent and unpracticed, and that's exactly what was turning him on so much.

Mia grew bolder, and he seemed to enjoy what she was doing. She remembered the porn clips she'd run across on the Internet. Tenderly, she bent down and kissed the sensitive tip of his shaft. Levin's eyes went wide, and he almost lost it. He watched as she touched him slowly with her tongue, licked him, and took him into her mouth. Now he knew he couldn't hold back.

"Come here to me, now," he said, his voice cracking with passion. Mia looked puzzled. "Am I doing something wrong?"

"No, you're doing it too well. I don't want to come in your mouth." He reached for her arm and pulled her up next to him and encouraged her with his hand to continue stroking him. He kissed her passionately, his member rubbing against her stomach. He felt the powerful pressure rising within him, and finally the tension released from him in hot pulses.

Mia felt the warm fluid run over her hands and stomach. Levin opened his eyes and looked into hers.

"Oh, man, Mia," he said euphorically, "you make me crazy." She breathed a sigh of relief. She couldn't have made too much of a fool of herself. Levin rolled onto her, covering her body with his, kissing her. He simply couldn't get enough of this girl.

After what felt like an eternity, they broke their kiss, and he pulled her into his arms. He didn't know when he'd felt this satisfied, and they hadn't even slept together. He couldn't even begin to imagine how it would feel to be inside her. He'd probably come as soon as he entered, but he wouldn't find out tonight. He wanted it more than anything, but for now, things were nice the way they were.

"Will you stay here?" he whispered to her.

"Are you sure I won't disturb you?"

"No, certainly not. I want to feel your skin against mine. I want to fall asleep with you."

Mia's eyes glowed with happiness. She gave him a little kiss and said, "I'd love to."

Levin buried his face in her hair and breathed in her scent. Now that he knew exactly how she smelled and tasted, he *really* couldn't get enough of her. He rested a hand on her bottom and stroked her for a while, and then his eyes shut.

Mia could tell that he'd fallen asleep. She considered getting up to take her sleeping pill, but she was so deliciously tired, and the way she and Levin were lying together was just too nice. She decided to risk it.

When Levin awoke, he felt something warm and soft against his body. Opening his eyes, he saw a tousled blond head on his shoulder. The memories of the night before came flooding back, and his body reminded him of an important question: Did he even have condoms with him? Then he remembered that he'd packed a few before he'd left. It was always best to be prepared.

He carefully pulled away from her and crawled out of bed. He happily picked up her top and panties from the floor and laid them on the edge of the bed. Then he allowed himself plenty of time to gaze at her sleeping form.

He still thought she was too thin, but she was perfectly proportioned. Nature had been generous with her. He hesitated— she was all natural, wasn't she? He suddenly remembered a one-night stand. That girl definitely had silicone enhancements, which felt very different. No, Mia was 100 percent real; he was positive.

She stirred, and it looked like she was waking up. Levin crouched by the bed and rested his chin in his hands as he watched her. She opened her eyes and looked into his.

"Good morning, gorgeous," he said with a smile. "Did you sleep well?"

"Yes!" She looked at him with delight. Not only because she'd truly slept like a stone, but also because she hadn't had any bad dreams, either.

"I'll go grab a shower and get us something for breakfast." Levin gave her a tender kiss. "It was wonderful last night."

"For me, too." Mia gazed at him. A warm feeling flooded her body. *Love?* Yes, she was in love; she was sure of it. Even though she'd never felt that way before, she had no doubts.

She watched him collect a few things and slip into his denim shorts. She admired his beautiful body. What about him? How did he feel about her? Was she just a distraction for him? A nice way to spend some time?

Mia had to assume it was that way, because they had no chance for a future together. She hadn't thought about what would happen when the trip was over. He'd have to go back sometime, and the same was true for her. They lived in different cities, and Mia had no place in his plans. She would only make it harder for him if he wanted to be a lawyer, and her past would stand in the way of his career. It was a dreadful truth, but Mia had to come to terms with it, and she would. That people didn't want to be associated with her after finding out what she'd done was nothing new to her.

But she decided not to think about that right now. She was still with Levin, and their trip wasn't over yet.

Admit it, you've got it bad. Levin couldn't think of anything but Mia and their evening together. Of course, he'd had more spectacular experiences in bed. The petting with Mia had been completely harmless, but *she* wasn't. She'd gotten so deeply under his skin that she'd reached the core of his being.

Mia had touched something in him the first time he had seen her. He had only known her for a few days, but these days had been the most intense of his life. And what did he know about her? Basically nothing, but that wasn't important. When she looked at him, when she spoke, she allowed him to see the world through her eyes, and that was an amazing feeling.

He couldn't predict the future, and at the moment he didn't want to. They were living day to day, and that was exactly what he wanted right now. Mia, this summer, the freedom to drive anywhere he wanted—life was just about perfect.

13

"We're almost to Clermont-Ferrand. I thought we could stay the night there," Levin explained.

He had to speak loudly, because the open windows made it noisy in the camper. But they wouldn't survive the heat with them closed.

"Fine with me," Mia said. He reached out a hand to caress her cheek. He gave her little kisses whenever he could, but not while he was driving. He could hardly wait to take her in his arms and kiss her properly again.

They arrived in the city at twilight. After they'd found a spot for the night, they explored the narrow streets and found a charming restaurant for dinner. Outside of Paris, the prices were much more affordable and wouldn't put so much stress on their budget.

Levin could have looked at Mia for hours. She wore her new clothes—nothing white—and a little makeup. He thought she didn't really need it, but it looked good on her. Plus, she wasn't ghostly pale anymore, having gotten some healthy color in her face. He allowed himself to believe that she was truly blossoming in his presence. She laughed a lot when she talked and gestured with her hands. Her obvious joy for life captured Levin and carried him along, and her way of seeing new things fascinated him again and again.

They made their way through town. It was very pretty, and it felt good to stretch their legs after the long drive, but he'd be happy to get Mia alone again. He'd have to keep his lust from getting the upper hand, but for now, what they had was enough.

"Are you tired?" Mia asked as they returned to the camper.

"A little, but not too much," he said, winking at her.

She blushed. She knew what he had in mind, and she had been longing for his touch all evening. When she thought of the night before, sheer joy shot through her body, and she wanted a lot more.

"Will you sleep with me again?" Levin asked as they got ready for bed.

"I'd love to." She slipped into his bunk, wearing her usual top and panties. Levin slid in after her, still in his boxers. Mia thought about how nice it would be to lie naked next to him, but she didn't dare take off her clothes.

"Hey, sweet thing," he said. For a long moment, they only looked at each other. Then Levin ran his hand over her hair. "Tomorrow we'll be by the sea," he whispered.

"I can hardly wait." A stray curl fell over one of her eyes. Levin realized again that she'd never been out of Hamburg, and even if there was plenty of water there, a Mediterranean beach was really something different.

"Do you like the water?" he asked.

"Yes, very much."

"Oops, that was a stupid question. You're from Hamburg!" he said.

"Yes, but I've never been to the sea," she confessed.

"Never? How come?"

"My parents . . . they were usually too busy to take me anywhere."
Here came the difficult questions again. Why had she told him that?
She'd have to be more careful.

"That's too bad," he said. Somehow he found that hard to imagine.
It was neither expensive nor time-consuming to take a child to the
seaside from Hamburg. But he also knew not to push her—otherwise
she might close up again.

He thought about all the vacations he'd had with his parents.
They had flown somewhere every year. Only now did he realize what a
luxury that had been.

"Come here." Levin pulled her close. She looked insecure, and
he was sorry. He began kissing her, and to his relief she responded
immediately.

It wasn't long before he was completely hard. Mia knew it, too; he
could tell. Levin devoted himself to exploring her body and indulging
her with little kisses. But this time she was more courageous and
returned his caresses.

As he entered her with his finger, Mia became hungry for more.
She wanted to feel all of him inside her but was afraid to say so. She
knew now that he was the man she was destined to be with, and she
longed to take that final step. Maybe not today, but definitely soon.

"Oh, it's so beautiful." Mia stood entranced, gazing at the blue
Mediterranean. It looked clear and inviting.

They kicked off their shoes and walked barefoot down the beach,
the warm sand between their toes. As they neared the water, the ground
became softer, and they sank in as the first wave washed around their
bare legs. The seawater was warm, and Mia reveled in the feeling of it
lapping against her skin.

Levin got the impression that Mia had forgotten he was there. She seemed to have entered an entirely different world.

They'd found a lovely campground on the beach at the edge of a cute village. Levin had decided to drive a little every day and visit places along the coast to look for nice spots to stay the night. Soon they'd reach Spain. Levin definitely wanted to show Mia Barcelona, but they weren't in any hurry—there were no deadlines. And if they especially liked it somewhere, they could linger for a few days if they wanted.

"Are you coming?" he heard Mia call. "It's nice and warm!" She looked so happy. The wind played with her blond curls, and she kept pushing them away from her face. His gaze ran down her slender figure and stopped on her beautiful legs. A warm feeling flooded through him.

"Levin!" she called again.

He walked over the sand to meet her. Without a word, he gave her a passionate kiss. Mia was surprised, but she enjoyed it.

"Shall we go swimming?" he whispered onto her lips.

"Yes."

She was a little afraid. It had been so long since she'd been in the water. But it wasn't possible to forget how to swim, was it?

As Mia pulled off her T-shirt, Levin was aware that she'd attracted the interest of several men. He threw a few glares at them. He wanted to make it clear that she was with him.

She looked incredibly sexy in her bikini. Levin couldn't get enough of looking at her. She seemed nervous as she walked into the water. That meant the games had to wait.

After a few moments, she trusted herself enough to swim a few strokes, and she realized joyfully that she hadn't forgotten how. She laughed with relief, and soon she and Levin were playing in the waves.

Mia delighted in the warm sun drying her skin. Levin lay especially close to her on the towel.

"It's so beautiful here," she said contentedly.

"Yes, it is." He gave her a kiss on the nose.

They looked up at the sound of children's voices. A family with two little girls had set up on the sand a few yards away. Mia smiled over at them. The smaller girl had blond curls and looked a lot like Mia had as a child. The mother took care of them lovingly, and the father helped them build a sand castle. Mia got a lump in her throat. She hadn't thought about her mother in a long time, and it still hurt so much whenever the memories returned. How often had she asked herself why everything had turned out the way it had? But then she pushed aside the dark thoughts. It was the way it was, and no one could change that.

Levin followed Mia's gaze. She'd been observing the little family for quite a while. Now he realized there were tears in her eyes.

"What's wrong?" he asked.

It took Mia a moment to realize he was there. "It's nothing," she said, shaking her head.

"Are you thinking about your parents?" he said gently. He didn't want to push, but he really did want to know more about her.

"I was thinking about my mother. She was always so loving with me," she said.

"You miss your parents." Levin stroked her cheek. "Of course you do."

"I miss *her*," Mia said. "She was a wonderful person."

Levin furrowed his brow. Mia only spoke of her mother. What about her father? When she closed her eyes and rolled onto her stomach again, he decided to stop asking questions.

They stayed on the beach for a few more hours and then discovered a grocery store and bought some food. Because the weather was so beautiful, they decided to cook dinner on the grill. Afterward, Mia wanted to go back into the water. Levin didn't mind. Sunset on the beach was something special, after all.

They sat in the sand, still warm from the sun, gazing out to sea. Levin pulled Mia between his knees and put his arms around her waist. Mia watched the natural spectacle with wide eyes. The warm light of the evening sun gave her face a special glow. Levin kissed her so hard he was afraid he'd make her sink into the sand and disappear.

As the sun slid below the horizon with spectacular flashes of green among the reds, golds, and violets, Mia sighed happily. "That was so beautiful."

"Mia?"

"Yes?" She turned toward Levin and was totally captured by his gaze.

"I've fallen completely in love with you," he admitted. Now it was he who seemed shy. His heart hammered in his chest. He hadn't planned to say it yet, but it came out anyway. There was nothing he could do to hold it back.

Tears came to Mia's eyes, and she felt shaky. It was the most wonderful thing anyone had ever said to her, and at the same time the most terrible. But this moment was too perfect to destroy with dark thoughts. So Mia did the only thing that felt right to her: she told him the simple truth.

"I love you, too, Levin. You can't imagine how much." She smiled shyly, her heart beating wildly. And his brilliant smile made her the happiest person in the entire world.

14

They found a nice bar at the edge of a harbor. Levin didn't let go of Mia's hand, not even for a second. He was so relieved that she shared his feelings. He'd never been so nervous in his life as when he'd declared his love for her. It was all so crazy when he thought about how briefly they had known each other. But their time together was even more intense because of it.

Since Mia had come into his life, everything felt different. Who was to say how long it should take for people to know they're in love? For some it takes years, and others know immediately.

Mia suddenly stiffened, and Levin gave her a worried glance. "Is something wrong?"

Mia couldn't believe her ears as she heard the first few measures. There it was again, the song by Procol Harum that had been her haunting companion for the last eight years. What was it doing here? It didn't belong—and it felt like it had come from a different lifetime. She felt dislocated from reality.

"Mia?"

She heard Levin's voice and looked at him, confused. She got up quickly. "I–I have to go to the bathroom," she said before hastily walking away.

Levin watched her in surprise. What had just happened? He didn't want to follow her, and maybe he was just imagining her confusion.

Mia closed the stall door and leaned against it, but she could still hear the music. The memories came back with a grinding force, and she willed them to go away. They'd chased her long enough. But it didn't help, of course, so Mia closed her eyes and hummed along until the song was over.

She took a while to calm down. When she went back out to Levin, he looked at her with concern and pulled her onto his lap.

"What's wrong, Mia?"

"Nothing. Sorry, it's just that song. It reminded me of something."

Levin had only barely registered the music. It was such a dinosaur of a song with strange lyrics that had probably been the result of an LSD experiment. But he didn't know anything more about it. He asked, "Did it remind you of something good or bad?"

"Both," Mia said, shaking her head. "But those memories don't belong here. Sorry, sometimes I'm kind of strange."

"If you hadn't told me, I never would have noticed," Levin teased.

"Really?" She looked at him skeptically and noticed his grin. She sniffed, offended. "You're making fun of me," she said.

Levin quickly kissed her. "Yeah, I am, but I wasn't trying to be mean." To his surprise, Mia responded to his kiss, and it started to turn into a serious make-out session. "Mia," he said. She was having an effect on him, especially because she was still on his lap. "We should probably stop. We're not alone."

Mia pulled back. He was right. She stood up and went back to her chair and glanced around. A couple at the next table was smiling at them, but no one else seemed to have noticed.

She took his hand and said, "Shall we leave?"

Something in her eyes had changed, and it made Levin's blood run hotter. "Sure," he said.

Mia was still stirred up. Maybe it was because of the song, but she felt stronger than usual, and Levin's presence gave her a feeling of security. He'd said he loved her, and she believed him.

After they entered the camper, she pressed herself against him, flashing a smile that took his breath away. She threw her arms around his neck and kissed him passionately. He was caught by surprise, but he was more than happy to comply. Mia ran her fingers through his hair, her body melting into his.

Levin's kisses grew hungrier. He'd wanted to hold back with her, but he couldn't. He had been longing to touch her all evening. Now it was difficult to go slowly, especially when she leaned into him that way.

He found it easy to fire her passion even higher. His hands wandered over her back and slipped under her shirt.

At that moment, she knew it was going to happen tonight. She wouldn't be content with less any longer. "Make love to me," she whispered against his mouth.

Levin hesitated. Had she really said that, or had he dreamed it? "Are you sure?" he asked breathlessly. His entire body burned, and he wanted nothing more than to connect with her completely.

"Yes," she said. "I want it, and I'm sure."

Levin kissed her and slowly guided her to his bed, only taking his hands off her to pull her shirt over her head. His eyes wandered over her breasts as they rose and fell. He showered tiny kisses down her neck and skillfully released the clasp of her bra. His mouth slid lower until he finally reached the pink nipples straining toward him so sensuously. He nibbled on them, but now he wanted more.

He went down on his knees in front of her, opening the button of her shorts and pulling them down. She quickly freed herself from them, watching him all the while. Levin's hand found her rounded buttocks, and his mouth pressed against her panties. He could already feel her wetness, and her tempting scent nearly drove him mad.

With a quick motion he removed the last bit of material between them and pushed Mia onto the bed. He kissed the insides of her thighs. She now lay completely open in front of him. He took a moment to enjoy the view.

She gleamed with moisture, and he gently ran a finger over her cleft. When he felt how ready she was for him, he could hardly hold back. He quickly pulled off his own shirt and jeans. Mia's eyes were closed, her hands gripped the sheets, and her breathing came fast. He opened a drawer next to the bed and pulled out a condom. He tore the plastic wrapper with his teeth and rolled the condom on. He bent over her again, kissing her tenderly. "Are you sure?" he asked.

"Yes," Mia said. Her eyes opened, and their deep-brown shade seemed a little darker. Levin took plenty of time for her pleasure, indulging every inch of her soft skin. As he arrived at her most sensitive spot, his tongue playfully circled the shining pearl. Mia moaned loudly.

Levin slid one finger into her, then carefully added a second to help prepare her. Her narrowness was incredibly exciting for him, but he knew that it wouldn't be painless for her. He plunged into her again and again, kissing and nibbling all the while.

Mia felt the tension building, felt his fingers and his tongue between her legs. A huge wave bowled her over, carried her away, and made her quake under his hands.

Levin waited until she'd calmed and poised himself carefully over her. The tension in his body made him feel like he was attached to high-voltage wires. Pleasuring her had made him painfully hard, but only she was important.

Mia put her arms around his neck and began kissing him again. Her wanting had not been satisfied. She needed him inside of her, so she opened her legs wider, feeling his hardness pulsing against her waiting flower.

"I want you," he whispered, "but it might hurt a little."

"It doesn't matter—come to me," she begged. Levin kissed her with even more desire, more possession. He wanted her, too, so much.

He slid into her moist heat with the tip of his manhood, pushing through just a bit. He gasped for air. The feeling of her narrowness almost made him come, but he wanted her to experience another explosion of pleasure while he was inside of her, and he was determined to keep control of himself.

"Does it hurt a lot?" he asked, worried.

Mia shook her head. Instinctively she wrapped her legs around his hips, and he slid more deeply inside her. She held her breath for a moment.

Levin breathed hard. He had filled her completely. Then he began to move very slowly in her. Mia moaned and closed her eyes. It was extraordinary to have him inside her so deeply. She felt every one of his movements in every nerve of her body. Every single one of her senses was focused on him.

He increased the tempo and kissed her harder. Then he couldn't hold himself back anymore—he needed to have her completely. Mia dug her fingers into his back, and another wave hit her, but this time it was much stronger. His thrusts became harder, but that was good. He filled her with his body and his love, and she felt it with every fiber of her being.

"Let yourself fall, my angel," he whispered as he sensed her release and gave himself up to his own. They both cried out. Levin gave a few final, strong thrusts as his seed pulsed out of him. He trembled, and for a moment it felt like he was floating outside of his body.

He let himself sink onto Mia, exhausted. The only sound was their breathing. After what felt like forever, he came to his senses. He kissed her shoulder tenderly as he pushed himself up to release her from his weight. "Everything OK?"

"Oh, yes," Mia said. "I love you so much, Levin." Her eyes glittered with tears. Levin kissed them away.

"Don't cry."

"But I'm so happy," she said, sighing.

"Me, too." He carefully pulled out of her and took her in his arms. "My aunt always says that nothing happens without a reason. Now I know what she means. You and I are meant for each other, Mia."

She could only look at him. Tears flooded her eyes again. She knew he was right. And she also knew it would soon come to an end.

The next day they didn't go anywhere. It wasn't possible. Levin couldn't keep his hands off Mia. He simply had to make love to her all the time, and it wasn't any different for her. She became more daring, and Levin gently showed her more variations of sex. She had an incredible erotic charisma even while seeming very innocent.

Toward the evening, like it or not, Levin had to leave the old camper. His condom supply was running out. On the way to the village, he could only think of the last night and day. It was astounding—there was no one like Mia.

He loved her with everything he had. Sex with her was purely amazing and touched him in his deepest core. He never would have believed he could feel that way about anyone. Now he had an idea what the word *love* actually meant.

He also began to think about what would happen after they reached Morocco. Mia didn't have a job; she'd told him that. That meant it might be possible for her to move to Berlin. Could he ask her to do that? Or was she too attached to her home city? They'd definitely have to sort that out. Maybe it wasn't quite time yet, but they wouldn't be traveling forever, and he had no intention of giving her up.

Mia quickly pulled on a T-shirt and shorts, and then she grabbed a towel and made her way to the showers. She was exhausted and sticky, and slightly sore between her legs. At the same time, she'd never felt so good. She felt loved, and she was in love—it was pure joy.

But as the warm water ran over her body, darker thoughts started breaking through. Now that she knew what it was like to have a man to love, she wanted to hold on to him as long as possible. Levin wanted to go to Morocco with her, but what was next? He said he loved her and that they belonged together. Mia felt exactly the same way. But how could they go on? Sometime he would ask questions, and if she didn't tell him the truth, he might find out anyway. *And if he doesn't find out?*

Was she allowed to do that? To just not tell him? She loved him so much, though, and didn't want to lie to him or hide anything. But the truth would drive him away from her. That was clear to her.

She wanted him to remember her well—as a girl who'd loved him—and not as what she really was.

15

"Hey, look, I got us something to eat." Levin bent down to give Mia a soft kiss. "Yum, you smell good. I have to go take a shower, too," he said.

Mia set the table outside the camper. She was unusually hungry, and Levin usually ate three times as much as she did.

"Shall we go swimming?" he said. Mia nodded enthusiastically. It was early evening but still pleasantly warm.

The beach was almost deserted as Levin and Mia entered the water. They splashed around for a while, and then Levin pulled her against him and kissed her passionately. "I want to make love to you right here," he whispered in her ear.

"But anyone could see us," she protested, laughing.

"There's no one here," he said with a grin.

"Someone could come," she said. "Besides, we don't have any protection with us."

"I'll be careful." Levin took her face in his hands. "I know it's risky, but I won't come inside of you—I promise." His eyes enticed her, but her instincts made her protest.

"I don't know," she said, shaking her head. "No, Levin, I don't want to."

"OK, you're right," Levin said, resting his forehead on hers. "You're more sensible than I am, sweet thing."

"It only seems that way at the moment," she said with a giggle.

"Mia?"

"Hmm?"

Levin tenderly pushed a wet curl off her face. "When we're back home—back in Germany, I mean—I want to make love to you without condoms. Do you think you could get on the pill?"

Her sad feelings started breaking through again, but she tried not to let them show. "Of course."

"Mia, today I was thinking about our future. Maybe it's too early to make plans, but I don't want to give you up. I love you, and I mean that very seriously. Would you consider moving to Berlin?" He looked hopefully into her eyes.

Mia swallowed hard. "We'll figure it out," she said, evading the question.

Levin kissed her and said, "OK."

For the next three days, he avoided broaching the subject. He didn't want to give in, but maybe it really was too early to make long-term plans. And at the moment, it was simply a dream to be with Mia. They traveled a ways down the coast every day and looked for places to camp in the early afternoons.

Now they were almost to Barcelona. Levin was curious to see if Mia would like the city. He'd been there with his parents, but that had been a while ago.

They took two days for Barcelona. Mia was amazed when she discovered the city, just as she had been in Paris. She was completely captivated by the experience, and Levin's presence made everything more perfect, if that was even possible.

"It's just over five hundred miles to Tarifa," Levin explained as they drove out of Barcelona. "From there we can take the ferry to Tangier."

Mia's excitement grew. Morocco! Soon they'd actually be there.

"We could take a shortcut on the highway, or we can continue down the coast like we've been doing," Levin said. "What do you think?"

"I'm not in a hurry, are you?"

"I was hoping you'd say that." He reached for her hand and kissed it. "The Spanish coast is beautiful. Let's take our time, OK?"

"OK."

The days seemed to fly past. Everything was so perfect—no stress, living day to day, and all of it with this beautiful girl. Levin let the sand sift through his fingers and observed Mia, as he did so often.

She lay next to him, her skimpy bikini covering few of her charms. It was crazy how he was so constantly hot for her, and the nights were never long enough.

Levin tried to figure out how long they'd been traveling together. It must have been at least four weeks. With every day, every hour, every minute, he fell more deeply in love with her.

He bent down and gave her little kisses on her bare midriff. She raised her head.

"How are you? Do you still have cramps?" he asked.

"No, it's not so bad. It's only like that on the first day, then it gets better." She subconsciously put a hand over her womb. She'd gotten her period yesterday. Thank goodness she had some supplies with her. She'd completely lost track of time and forgotten about it.

"If you're feeling better, then we could try without a condom," Levin said, making little circles on her stomach. He looked at her with hopeful puppy eyes.

"What? That's so . . . I mean, what about the blood? Isn't that unpleasant for you?"

Levin sat up. "No, no problem. I'd just like to feel you properly for once," he said softly.

It was just as good as he'd imagined it would be. Mia had escaped from the bed directly afterward to clean herself. She had blushed the entire time. For a moment he felt bad for embarrassing her, but now all that was forgotten as she cuddled up against him.

"Tomorrow we'll take the ferry, sweet thing," he whispered into her curls. "Then your dream will come true."

"My dream?" Mia gazed at him lovingly. "You're my dream, Levin." She kissed his bare chest. "Morocco can't be any better than what we've already found. But of course I'm still happy about going there."

Levin sighed. The long line at the ferry ticket window was moving slowly. The sun burned on his skin. He and Mia had opened the camper windows, but there was no cooling breeze.

It was finally their turn. Levin held out their passports to the customs officer. The man glanced into the vehicle and took a closer look at Mia. She smiled nervously. Then he typed something into his computer and reached for the telephone.

"What now?" Levin said. He noticed that Mia had suddenly gone as pale as chalk.

Mia panicked. She knew exactly what was wrong. Up until now, she'd tried not to think about anything like this happening.

"Please pull over and wait." The man looked severe.

"What's going on?" Levin asked.

"Pull over and wait!" The customs officer ordered angrily.

"OK, OK," Levin said, raising his hands apologetically. Then he saw more officers being summoned.

"They probably just want to search us," he explained to Mia. "Don't worry, it's not that bad. Just kind of annoying."

"Get out of the vehicle—both of you," the officer commanded. Levin realized that all the men seemed tense. He had a bad feeling.

Mia climbed out of the camper with wobbly knees.

"Are you Mia Kessler?" the officer asked her.

"Yes," she squeaked.

"You're being searched for all over Europe. Please follow me."

"What?" Levin's heart stopped beating for a moment. "This must be some kind of mistake!"

"No, it's not," the officer said with conviction. He and his colleague each took Mia by an upper arm and led her away.

Mia looked back at Levin, and the sadness in her eyes tore through him.

"Listen, this has to be a mistake," Levin said, trying to follow them.

But yet another officer blocked his path. The man was determined. "You will be questioned separately," he said.

"I will not accept this! My father is a lawyer, and we'll take you to court for abuse of authority!" Meanwhile, Mia and the other uniformed men had already disappeared into a building. Levin swallowed.

"Yes, you're welcome to do that," the officer said. Waving Levin along impatiently, he added, "Now please follow me."

16

Mia looked around fearfully. They'd brought her to an office. Two border-police officers stood behind her. An older officer sat at a desk in front of her. "Miss Kessler, do you know why you've been detained?"

Mia nodded.

"We're going to have to keep you here until someone can accompany you back to Germany. Do you understand?"

She was incapable of answering.

"Who is the man you were traveling with? Did he help you escape?"

Her state of paralyzed fear suddenly lifted, and she looked up in shock. "No!" she said. "Levin doesn't know anything about me or my past. We met at a highway rest area. He has no idea," she explained in a steady voice. If there was one thing she could still do, it was protect Levin. She didn't even want to imagine him being questioned, too. What had she done?

A wave of desperation spread through her. It was her fault; everything was her fault. How could she have been so egotistical? She could only hope and pray that Levin wouldn't get into any trouble.

"We'll find out if that's true," the older officer said before turning to the others. "Take her to a cell." He looked at Mia again. "You'll stay there until someone from Psychological Services can fly back to Germany with you."

Mia was pulled up by the arms again. She just let it happen. Her thoughts were only for Levin.

"This is a joke, a bad joke!" Levin blustered as he was led into an office. An officer stayed to guard him.

He wondered what they were doing with Mia. He was almost dying with worry for her. This could only be a misunderstanding. There could be no other reason for it. As soon as he was allowed, he'd call his father and ask for his help.

They let him wait. Levin thought he'd go crazy. Mia was surely scared. She was such a sensitive person, and Levin was afraid that they'd pressure her and make her panic.

Mia had been taken to a sparely furnished cell with bars on the window. She sat on the hard bed. It was only now that she realized her whole body was shaking.

Finally the door opened. An older officer entered and sat down facing Levin. "Levin Webber, correct?" The man gave Levin his passport back.

"Yes, that's what it says!" Levin snapped. "Can you *finally* tell me what this is all about? And where is Mia?"

"Can't you figure it out?" The man looked at him, probing.

"No, I can't—I don't understand what's going on here at all!" Levin said.

"How do you know Miss Kessler?"

"Is this an interrogation? Before I answer any questions, I want to know what you're accusing us of."

The officer took a deep breath. "No one is accusing you of anything yet. I just asked you a question."

"And if I don't believe you?"

"Miss Kessler already gave us her statement. What's your problem?" The man narrowed his eyes. Levin decided it was better to talk. After all, he hadn't committed any crime.

"I met Mia at a highway rest area, in Germany. She was hitchhiking, and she wanted to go to Morocco. At first I didn't want to take her, but then I saw a trucker approach her with a dubious offer. Mia didn't seem to understand what he wanted. She would have gone with him, and she had no clue what his intentions were. That's when I offered to take her with me. Since then we've been traveling together," Levin explained. "So you see, it's all completely harmless."

"How long have you been traveling?"

"About four weeks."

"And you never noticed anything strange?"

"About Mia? She's a bit gullible and naive." Levin was starting to get impatient. "And now I really want to know what's going on."

"Miss Kessler didn't tell you anything? About herself or her past?"

"No, she's always avoided the subject." Levin ran his hand through his hair. He was getting nervous. Something was extremely wrong.

The officer nodded. "I believe you."

"Well, that's nice of you," Levin said, his voice dripping with sarcasm. "Can I go, then? And where is Mia? Can I pick her up?"

"That's not happening. Miss Kessler will be returned to Germany as soon as possible," the man said.

"What do you mean?" Levin looked at him, aghast. He swallowed hard. This just couldn't be true. Why was he treating Mia like a criminal? "What is happening?"

The man looked at him with sympathy. "I don't know if I'm allowed to give you that information. Perhaps you should turn to the authorities in Germany."

"To which authorities? What is Mia being accused of?" Levin asked desperately.

"What is your relationship to Miss Kessler?" The officer seemed friendlier now. Maybe there was a chance, after all, that he'd learn something.

"We fell in love with each other during our journey. Please tell me what she's being accused of. I'm sure it's a misunderstanding. Mia is a wonderful person, and she would never hurt anyone."

The man hesitated, but then he took a deep breath. "OK, fine, but please treat this information confidentially. Understood?"

Levin nodded. He waited expectantly.

"We don't know any details, of course. I don't know the case. It also doesn't concern us. We were simply told that we should detain a Mia Kessler if she tried to leave the country. She was released from a mental institution about six weeks ago, but only under the condition that she attended therapy sessions and made regular contact with a social worker. She did that only once, and then she disappeared."

"And there's so much fuss about that?" Levin's eyes were wide with surprise.

"One has to be sure that Miss Kessler will not endanger herself or others."

"Endanger others? Mia?" Levin might have laughed out loud, but the part about the mental institution had hit him like a fist. A terrible chill crept up his spine. It felt like a strange kind of premonition— nothing concrete, but very disquieting.

"Around eight years ago, she killed her parents," the officer said, looking at Levin sympathetically. "We really don't have any more information than that. I'm very sorry for you, but maybe you should be glad it happened this way. Who knows if this girl is really healed? After all, she didn't stick to the conditions set for her, and she escaped at the first opportunity." He shrugged and added, "But I'm not a doctor—I can't judge her."

Levin heard the words, but they didn't really penetrate. Mia? A murderer? Could that be true?

Slowly he began to put the pieces together. *Eight years ago? Mia was only a child then.*

"Would you like a cup of coffee?" the officer said.

"No, thanks. Can I see that?" he asked, pointing at the file with Mia's name on it. "Please, it's very important to me."

The officer sighed. "I'm afraid I'm not allowed to do that."

Levin was about to voice his frustration again, but then something else occurred to him. "Do you know where they're taking Mia? Is there an address in Hamburg?"

The man regarded him for a long moment and then looked through his papers and wrote down an address. "This is the contact information for the responsible police department. But I can't tell you any more than that." He handed Levin the paper. "And you should be aware that she'll also be questioned in Germany."

Mia sat on the bed with her knees pulled up to her chest and stared out through the high barred window. She saw a blue sky without a single cloud. It was a beautiful summer day, like all the days before.

But Mia felt sick. She had caused trouble for Levin, the only person in the world who loved her. Why had she done that? Deep inside, she'd known they would be searching for her. But with every mile that took her farther from Hamburg, a bit more of her past seemed to fall away. It had all seemed so easy, and her longing for freedom had made her forget everything.

*You're so stupid, Mia. What have you done to him? Grandma was right—
you're the most horrible person ever born!*

She ran her hands over her face and discovered it was all wet.
She hadn't even noticed that she'd been crying. The cell door scraped
open. The sound of it startled her after the last few hours she'd been
surrounded by silence.

"Come with me," an officer said gruffly. Mia stood up fearfully and
followed him on shaking legs. They went down a corridor and through
another door. The bare little room held only a table and two chairs.
And Levin. Levin was there.

He'd been standing by the window, looking out, and now he turned
around quickly. He wore an expression of complete bewilderment.

The door closed behind them, and the officer stood in front of it
with a grim look on his face.

Mia turned to Levin. "I–I'm so sorry," she said.

17

Levin just looked at her, at first. Her eyes were red from crying, and she was shaking as though she'd been standing in a meat locker.

"Mia!" he cried softly, quickly moving to her side. He wanted to take her in his arms, but the officer abruptly let him know that he had to forget that impulse.

Mia looked at Levin anxiously. He was surely angry with her. After all, she'd made a lot of trouble for him. She wondered if he knew what she had done.

Levin looked at the tragic creature that stood before him. He felt so incredibly sorry for her. She was scared and totally desperate.

"Mia, is it true that they've been looking for you—and what they say you did?" he asked, his voice breaking.

Mia lowered her eyes. She felt so ashamed. "Yes, I killed him," she whispered.

He sprang back from her in shock, unable to process the information. "And why did you just leave like that? Why didn't you stick to the conditions? Jeez, Mia!" He paced around the room, fingers tearing through his hair.

"I wanted to go to Morocco so much," she said, sobbing softly. "Levin, I'm so sorry that you're in trouble because of me."

"What? That doesn't matter at all! This is about you." He stood facing her again. Seeing her cry that way broke his heart.

He turned back to the officer. "Please, can't I just hold her once? You can see how sad she is."

"No. You have to leave now, anyway."

Levin wanted to hit him, but he knew that wouldn't be such a good idea.

"Mia, you know I'm studying law, and my father is a well-known lawyer in Berlin. I'll call him right away and ask him to take your case. Maybe something can be done to keep things from escalating." *Or to keep you from being locked up again*, he thought. He didn't want to scare her.

"No, Levin!" Mia said. "Please don't do that. I've already made enough of a mess for you, and I'm so sorry about it. I don't want to bother your family with my problems, too. Please don't do it, please!"

She reached out a hand to touch his shoulder, but the officer pulled her back immediately and gave her a threatening look. Mia cowered.

"She's not going to hurt me, don't make a fool of yourself," Levin hissed at him.

"Rules," the man said. "And the time is up."

"Levin, please, you have to forget me, and if you do think of me, then please try to remember the good times we had together. Please remember the Mia you got to know, and not the real one." Her voice broke off.

"Forget you?" Levin shook his head. "Mia, I love you. I won't forget you, ever. I'll do everything I can to make sure you live free and happily."

"No, Levin!" she cried. "Don't do that. Live your life as you would have before you met me. Become a great lawyer. Promise me that, OK?"

"I can't promise you that, because that's not how it's going to work," he answered.

"Enough now." The officer took Mia by the arm.

"Mia? Tell me just one thing: Do you love me?" Levin looked into her eyes.

"Yes, but—"

"No 'buts.' I don't need to know anything else." He tried to comfort her with a smile, but he had serious doubts that he'd succeeded.

Mia was brought back to her cell, but she didn't register her surroundings anymore. Her thoughts were with Levin. He mustn't concern himself with her case. Maybe he would realize for himself that it would be better for him not to.

Perhaps she shouldn't have told him she loved him, but Mia had never been a good liar, and she had never been able to be cool.

Forget me, Levin, please, she continued begging in her thoughts.

Levin was allowed to go. As he stepped outside, the fact that it was a bright, sunny day seemed wickedly ironic. Nothing was the way it had been a few hours ago. His world had gone dark.

"Move your vehicle—you can't park there any longer," a customs officer said, waving him on.

"All right already!" Levin said.

Otherwise, he would have stayed in front of the building until they took Mia away—just for another chance to see her. But the officer wouldn't allow him that small consolation.

As he sat in the driver's seat of the camper, he angrily slammed his hands on the steering wheel. He found a parking place in the harbor area and then reached for his cell phone. According to the route planner, it was 1,864 miles back to Berlin. Levin groaned. It would take the camper at least three days to travel that distance.

Levin got up to make coffee for himself. He had to try to think everything through rationally and keep his cool, otherwise he'd be no help to Mia at all.

When he saw her things, he came up short. He couldn't help it. Tears ran down his face. He reached for the stuffed camel they'd bought at the Paris flea market. Mia loved that thing. Her eyes lit up every time she saw it. He buried his face in its soft fur and sobbed.

He didn't know how long it had taken for his tears to stop. He just knew he was annoyed with himself for losing time.

Think! he ordered himself.

So Mia had killed her parents, and she must have been around fourteen years old when it happened. But no child does something like that out of pure wickedness, and no one is born a murderer, so there must have been something terrible behind it. But without more information about her family situation and social circumstances, it was all pure speculation.

Why would a teenager kill her parents? It couldn't have been just a typical conflict of puberty, and Mia was in no way hard or aggressive. Was she actually mentally ill? Did she have a disease that would explain that kind of violent episode? Or had it been self-defense? Had she been abused? It turned Levin's stomach to think of what she must have experienced in her youth.

The fact that they had released her indicated that she was thought to be stable and nonthreatening enough to go out into the world. But she was so terrifyingly naive. How could they have believed that she'd be all right on her own? Of course, she was supposed to have been under supervision.

Levin's head was spinning, but he couldn't do anything from where he was. He had to get back, and the longer he sat there brooding, the longer it would take.

Suddenly a memory struck him like lightning, something Mia had said: *"Yes, I killed him."*

Killed *him*? Why had she spoken only of her father? What about her mother? She'd been accused of killing both of them, but Mia had only mentioned *him*. He also remembered that when they were on the beach, she'd said she missed her mother, but nothing about her father. He felt like he was going crazy.

Levin reached for his phone and called his father's number from his list of contacts.

"Hey, Levin!" His father sounded happy to hear from him. "Where are you? And when are you coming back? It's been four weeks already."

"We agreed on eight weeks, remember?" Levin said. "But actually, I'm on my way back to Germany now. I'm in Tarifa, though, so it might take a while."

"Tarifa? That's on the Strait of Gibraltar!" his father said with amazement.

"Yeah, I'd planned to go to Morocco, but something happened. Dad, I need your help," Levin said quickly.

"What's wrong? Was there an accident?"

"No, nothing like that. I met a young lady, and she's got some problems. Could you please see what you can find out about Mia Kessler? She lives in Hamburg, and eight years ago, she was accused of murdering her parents."

"What? And you're mixed up with someone like that?" He sounded suspicious.

"Yes, I am, and I want to help her. Please, Dad, I'm asking you as a lawyer, not as a son. I'll even pay you if you want me to."

"As if you could afford me," his father said. "But OK, I'll check into it for you."

Levin was relieved. "Thank you," he said.

"Don't thank me just yet."

"I know you must be curious," Levin said with a slight grin.

"It's an occupational illness. So you're coming back?"

"Yes, but it could take three days or so. I'll try to hurry."

"Drive carefully, Son," his father said.

"I will. Let me know if you find something out, OK?"

"Come home. By then I *will* know something."

"Aren't you hungry?" The officer observed Mia with a piercing glance. She cowered at the sound of his voice. She hadn't heard him coming. She was still looking out the barred window. It looked like the sun would be setting soon, but she couldn't see very well because the window was so high.

She just shook her head.

"At least drink something. It's very hot," the man said. He came a step closer, and she slid fearfully to the farthest corner of the bed.

"Don't worry, I'm not going to touch you," he said. "I'm certainly not going to dirty my hands with the likes of you."

He left and closed the door. Then her thoughts wandered to Levin. What was he doing now? Was he thinking of her? She was afraid he might be. Did he really want to help her? He shouldn't do that. But of course, if their positions were reversed, she'd do everything she could for him.

But then that thought struck her as ridiculous. How could she ever be in a position to help anyone? She wasn't particularly educated, she wasn't right in the head, and she definitely wasn't courageous. Mia heard herself crying, but the sound seemed to be coming from far away.

Levin tried desperately to concentrate on the road, but it was almost impossible. Since Mia's arrest, his head had been spinning. He simply could not believe that she was a murderer. In his mind, it couldn't be true. Or did he just not want to believe it? Had he read her wrong? Had she fooled him?

He took a sip from his water bottle. No, it couldn't be. And he shouldn't even try to judge her before he knew all the facts. He intended to become a lawyer, so he would stick to those principles, no matter how biased he was toward her.

He drove through, late into the night, and the weight of exhaustion started pulling his eyes shut. Levin sighed and headed for a parking area. He needed to eat something and get some sleep, even if he didn't want to.

He bought a sandwich at the rest area and chewed on it halfheartedly. It was almost unbearable to be in the camper, because everything in it reminded him of Mia. He stood up and gathered all her things, and then lay in his bed. It still smelled of her.

The last weeks had been beautiful—maybe too beautiful. So much joy had to be punished. He remembered his aunt's saying again: "Nothing happens without a reason." But what was the reason for this?

Levin set the alarm on his cell phone. He planned to get four hours of sleep before continuing.

Mia listened in the darkness. Could she really hear the ocean? She was in a harbor building, after all.

Morocco is right on the other side of the water.

How she'd longed to go there, but it didn't matter anymore. Now she was missing something far more valuable—the most important person in her life since her mother had died. It hurt—physically hurt—to be separated from Levin, and it was all her own fault. But if she hadn't run away, she never would have met him.

What was that thing his aunt had always told him? "Nothing happens without a reason." At least she found some small comfort in those words.

She couldn't sleep. Whenever she closed her eyes, she was tortured by nightmares. It was the first time in weeks that they'd come so strongly. Because she didn't have her things, she couldn't get her sleeping pills, either. She decided she'd rather stay awake, even if it was pitch-black.

Levin awoke with the first ring of his cell phone alarm. He was under far too much tension to sleep deeply. He missed Mia so badly, and her case agitated him. He hated having to sit there without being able to do anything.

"How are you, sweet thing?" he quietly asked into the darkness. "Can you sleep?"

He remembered how destroyed and fearful she'd been, and how she'd begged him to forget her.

"You can forget it, Mia," he scolded. He made a thermos full of coffee and seated himself behind the steering wheel.

"Good morning, Miss Kessler." A different officer came into Mia's cell the next morning. "I've brought you some breakfast."

Mia nodded. She really wasn't hungry.

When he returned later, he looked at the tray in surprise. "You haven't eaten anything. Are you ill? Shall we send for a doctor? You'll be flying back to Germany tomorrow. There were no earlier flights because of the holidays."

Mia shrugged. She didn't care if she was locked up here or in Hamburg.

"So, were you able to learn anything?" Levin rolled up the window of the camper as he held his phone to his ear. He could barely hear over the highway noise at the parking area.

"Levin," his father complained, "do you seriously believe I had nothing better to do than look up the case of some girl you met?"

"It's important and very urgent!" Levin argued.

"They all say that. I'm drowning in work here. I have two important trials tomorrow."

Levin couldn't believe his ears. He was furious. "You haven't done anything? You agreed!"

"I know I did. I called my colleague Hans Merker, who has a large law firm in Hamburg. He's taking care of it," his father explained calmly.

Levin breathed a sigh of relief. "Thanks, Dad."

"How do you know this young lady?"

"I met her on the road at a rest area, and she traveled with me for a few weeks. Now she's been arrested because she didn't meet certain conditions set by the court." Levin thought it was smarter not to tell him that he and Mia were a couple, but he wanted to tell him as much as possible. After all, he might be able to help.

"Did they charge you with aiding and abetting?"

"They questioned me, but I was found credible, and they let me go. I still might be subpoenaed in Germany, though."

His father groaned. "Something like that could only happen to you."

"Mia is a good person. I want to help her. She deserves to be free."

"Ouch," his father said.

"I'm not speaking as a lawyer," Levin snapped back.

"I'll get in touch as soon as I hear from Hans."

"OK, please tell him it's urgent."

"Of course." His father's voice sounded a bit cynical, but Levin knew he'd do it.

"Good morning, Mia. My name is Marta Alvarez. I'll be accompanying you on your flight to Germany today."

Mia pulled herself up from the bed. She looked shyly at the woman who'd entered her cell.

"They tell me you haven't eaten anything since the day before yesterday. Are you OK?"

"No," Mia answered. She just wasn't hungry. She felt endlessly sad, and she missed Levin so much it was making her crazy.

"I'm a psychologist, Miss Kessler—I'm not with the police. I want to attract as little attention as possible. I assume we both feel the same way about that."

Mia nodded.

"Then I'd like to request that you make no trouble for us. A plainclothes policeman will accompany us, so trying to escape wouldn't be very clever." Marta smiled at Mia. At least she didn't seem as unfriendly and grumpy as the officers here.

"I won't try to escape," Mia promised. She wasn't brave enough, and she didn't have any of her things, and aside from that, she'd miss Levin no matter where she went.

"Good. I'll be back in half an hour, and we can go," she said as she left Mia's cell.

Mia got up, still feeling tired, and gave herself a necessary wash. She was sure she didn't smell very good, because she'd been wearing the same clothes for the last two days.

Mia was nervous as the plane's engines started. She had never flown before. But it turned out that she liked it. She thought the world looked beautiful from above. She was reminded of visiting the Eiffel Tower with Levin. Everything had been perfect then.

Now she gazed at the clouds. They looked like big white puffs of cotton, and she felt almost as though she could reach out and touch them.

The flight was over much too soon, and Mia's nervousness grew. What would happen next?

Basically, it didn't matter.

Her dream was over.

18

"Hello, Mia. I'd been hoping we'd see each other again under nicer circumstances." Lydia was waiting in the airport office where they'd brought Mia after her arrival.

Mia nodded to her.

"My goodness, Mia, what were you thinking?" Lydia reached for her hand and held it tightly. "Why, Mia? You've made it so difficult for yourself."

"I just wanted to go to Morocco," she whispered.

"Yes, I know. You would have gotten there, too," the therapist said, smiling. "I see you're wearing other colors, and you have a healthy tan. It looks good on you."

Mia smiled at Lydia. She knew that Lydia just wanted to make her feel better. "Am I going back?"

"Yes, you have to stay at the institution until the hearing. Then it will be decided what happens next, but we'll clear that up when we're there."

Later, Mia got out of the car with shaky knees. Lydia and another caregiver who'd come to the airport took her between them as they entered the institution.

Mia fought back tears. She was here again. It was her own fault, and she knew that, but the thought of being locked in again was unbearable.

"First, we'll go see Director Schneider," Lydia explained. Mia nodded again. Nothing mattered anymore.

"Mia!" Director Schneider said, getting up from his chair to come and meet her. "My goodness, Mia, are you all right?" He checked her over.

"Yes," she answered.

"Sit down. We have a lot to talk about." He gave her a serious look and waved her to the chair in front of his desk. Mia couldn't look at him. She only stared at the floor. She could imagine what was coming.

"I have to say that I'm disappointed in you. *We* are very disappointed." He glanced over at Lydia, who'd also sat down. "What was it that you promised me? You promised to play by the rules—do you remember?"

Mia nodded.

"Then why didn't you? You disappeared, the first chance you got. I find that hard to believe!" Director Schneider pounded his fist on the desk, and Mia shrank back in her chair.

"You aren't ready to ramble off into the world, and it certainly isn't *allowed*. You put yourself in danger, and as long as your therapy isn't officially complete, and until it's been attested that you pose no threat for yourself or society, you must obey the rules!"

Mia bit her lower lip. It all sounded so dramatic. She didn't see it that way. "I would never hurt anyone," she said seriously.

"That's what you say. But the evaluators have their doubts," he said. "Aside from that, I'm personally disappointed in you. I put a lot of effort into finding an apartment for you quickly, as well as a therapist and social worker. And how do you thank me?"

"I—I'm sorry. But I just wanted . . . I just wanted to go to Morocco, just this once." Now she looked at him anxiously. His eyes became gentler.

"Yes, Mia, and I can understand that—we all can. But you didn't have permission for that, not yet. If things go badly for you, you might have to stay here awhile longer."

"And there's another thing," Lydia added. "After your disappearance, your grandmother requested to have you permanently committed. Do you know what that means?"

Mia shook her head. Now she was confused and alarmed. She knew well enough what her grandmother thought of her, and if she was changing things now, it wasn't a good sign.

"If you are permanently committed, then you will have to stay here forever. I don't know if she really wants to do that, but the danger is there."

Mia's eyes opened wide with horror. If what Lydia said was true, then she was sure her grandmother would try.

"She was outraged that you left the institution," the therapist continued. "But you should know that all of us here are on your side."

"Thank God they can't declare you incompetent anymore," Director Schneider said. "I may be disappointed by your behavior, but that would be going too far. And we also have a voice in the matter, if it should come to a trial."

Mia was shocked. Tears formed in her eyes. That was the last thing she wanted. "B–but I'm really not s–so crazy," she said, sobbing.

"No, Mia, you aren't, and you never were." Lydia took her hand. "But you have to understand that we must tell the truth. Your behavior has consequences, and you should have known that."

Mia nodded.

"Good, then," said the director. "We've cleared that up. Until your hearing, you'll be staying with us. But now tell us what you've been doing." Director Schneider smiled and shuffled through some documents. "They picked you up trying to get on the ferry to Tangier. We suspected that you might be in Morocco, and we tried all the airlines, but obviously you took the land route. You were in the company of a young man named Levin Webber." He turned the page. "Mia, did he force you to do anything you didn't want, or harass you sexually? We have to know that."

Mia shook her head decisively. "No. I met him at a highway rest area. He saw that I wanted to go to Morocco, and he spoke to me." Mia briefly wondered if she should tell them about the incident with the truck driver. She decided it was better not to.

"What were you doing at a rest area?" Lydia looked at Mia, shock registering on her face.

"Hitchhiking," Mia said.

Lydia sighed. "Oh, Mia, that's so dangerous!"

"That's what Levin said," she admitted.

"You and Levin—were you together the entire time?" Director Schneider wanted to know.

"Yes." Mia smiled as she thought of her time with him.

"Mia, excuse me for asking so directly, but this is very important: Did you get to know each other intimately?" Lydia squeezed Mia's hand again. "Do you know what I mean?"

Mia lowered her eyes. She really didn't want to talk about it. It was her personal business. But she also understood that Lydia and the director didn't mean her any harm. And if what they'd said about her grandmother was really true, then it would probably be better to tell the truth. There was nothing morally wrong about it, was there?

"Yes."

"But he didn't coerce you or force you? Sorry, I have to ask again," Director Schneider said.

"No, not at all. Levin is a wonderful person. He was kind to me the entire time."

"That's good to know," Lydia said, smiling. "You aren't wearing white clothes anymore—is that because of him?"

"I wanted him to like the way I look." Mia sheepishly pushed a strand of hair behind her ear. "And he encouraged me to wear colors."

"I almost believe that Levin had more good influence on you in that short time than we did in all the years you've been with us," Lydia said. "It's nice to see you like this, Mia. Your journey seems to have been good for you."

"Nevertheless, it happened a little too soon," Director Schneider interrupted. "The court will want to hear what Levin has to say, too."

"Do they have to?" Mia looked frightened. "I don't want him to get dragged into this."

"That can't be avoided. He's already right in the middle of it. But nothing will happen to him. Unless, of course, he knew that you were released under stipulations."

Mia shook her head. "No, he definitely didn't know that."

"That's also noted in the file. Lydia will take you to your room." Director Schneider stood up. Offering Mia his hand, he said, "Goodness, child, I really wish things had worked out differently for you."

Mia was given a new room, as her old one was already occupied. This one was smaller, but that didn't bother her. None of it mattered. It had been much tighter in the camper, but she'd been happier there than anywhere else she'd ever been.

"Mia, do you still have a key to your apartment? You don't have any clothes here," Lydia said.

"Oh, no," she said, "all of my things are still in Levin's camper. The key, too."

"OK, then I'll sign an authorization for the landlord and get a few things for you," Lydia offered. Mia desperately wanted to change out of the clothes she'd been wearing for the last three days.

Lydia returned later with a small bag. Of course all the clothes in it were white, but Mia found it fitting to wear them again.

After a shower, Mia sat on the window seat and looked out into the park. Now that she'd gotten to know the world outside, being trapped here was even more unbearable.

And Levin, where was he now? Would he continue his vacation, or was he on his way home? Was he thinking about her? She missed him so much. She longed for him, and yet she knew it would be better for him if she never saw him again.

"Darling, there you are! You look tired." Sonja Webber spread out her arms and hugged Levin.

"Hi, Mom. Nice to see you," he said, smiling.

"Come in, your father is still in his office. You know how he is, working all the time." His mother took his arm and led him into the living room. "Would you like something to eat?"

"Yes, please," Levin said. To save time in the last three days, all he'd eaten were sandwiches and snack food. But after a while that diet had become tedious.

"We still have some of the roast—I'll warm it up for you," his mother said enthusiastically. She still loved to spoil him. At the moment, he didn't mind. He was incredibly glad he didn't have to drive endless miles on the highway anymore.

"Levin, it's great to see you!" His father came in with a stack of papers under his arm. Levin had to hold back his curiosity to greet his father properly.

"How was the trip?" his father asked.

"Long. But the camper made it. I'll clean it carefully tomorrow," he said.

"Don't worry about that! We'll have it cleaned and checked over by the garage. How are you feeling?"

Levin groaned. The most honest answer would have been *like hell*, but he didn't want to admit it. After all, he'd taken this trip so he could relax. Now he felt burned out *and* incredibly sad.

"Good. Just all the stuff about Mia, you know."

"I understand," his father said. Then he waved the papers he was holding. "What do you know about this case?"

"Only what I told you," Levin said, impatient. "Why didn't you call to tell me you'd already found something?"

"Because this isn't something you can talk about on the telephone. This is a complicated case."

"Please, I want to know what happened back then. What happened, and what exactly was Mia accused of?"

"Do you have to do this now? Levin just got back from his vacation, and you're already talking about some case." Sonja Webber seemed annoyed as she returned to the living room. "The boy hasn't even eaten."

"That's OK, Mom, I'll eat in here. I asked Dad if he would find out about this case for me."

"Oh, yeah? OK, well, I'd wanted to hear something about your trip, but this seems more important," she said curtly, disappearing into the kitchen again.

Levin was in no mood to worry about his mother's oversensitivity. Mia's situation was more important.

"So, here I have the court's decision and reasons for the judgment. And here are a few newspaper articles about the case. It got a lot of publicity at the time—I remember it, too. A young girl killing her parents is not an everyday occurrence."

"Mia said she only killed her father."

"My God, what are you talking about?" Sonja Webber interrupted. She set down a tray of delicious-smelling food.

"Mom, please don't be offended, but this is important to me. I'll tell you all about the trip later, OK?" Levin gave her a kind smile, and she seemed mollified.

"OK, my boy. Do you want to sleep here? You look tired." She stroked his head.

"Good idea." He didn't even feel like driving back to his apartment tonight.

"I'll get your bed ready. If you two have a lot to talk about, I'll go watch television."

"Do that, Sonja," James Webber agreed. He turned to Levin. "It says in the verdict that she has responsibility for the death of both of her parents, if you could call it that."

"What do you mean by that?"

"OK, first things first. The death of her parents was discovered because her mother's employer was worried. She hadn't shown up to work for two days, and hadn't called in. Mia's mother was seen as very reliable, and it was well-known that there were tensions between her and her husband at home."

"Tensions? Did he abuse her? And Mia?" Levin caught his breath, and his heart sped up.

"Nothing was known about the girl except that she was a good student who kept a low profile and didn't have much contact with other children. She was isolated, kind of an outsider. In any case, the apartment had been broken into. Mia was found in a huge, partly dried-out puddle of blood next to her parents' bodies."

Levin stared at him, his eyes wide.

"Mia's hands and clothes were covered with blood. She held a knife in her hand, which later was proven to be the murder weapon."

Levin just shook his head. This was all so unbelievable, so terrible. He couldn't possibly imagine Mia doing anything like that.

"Shall I continue? You look like you could use a cognac," his father said.

"Yes, I could, please." Levin put down his fork and gladly took the drink his father offered.

"Go on," Levin said after draining the glass in one swallow.

"The murder weapon had only Mia's fingerprints on it. It was proven that both her parents had died of knife wounds."

"Did Mia make any kind of statement?" Levin asked with a shaky voice.

"No, none. Mia couldn't speak at all for over a year after it happened. The evaluators certified her with serious mental illness, and the court committed her to a mental institution."

"But Mia can talk now. She says she only killed her father, and I believe her. There must be some kind of explanation. Maybe the father abused the mother, and Mia, too—maybe it was a panic reaction to his violence?"

"That's possible, but there were never traces of abuse found on Mia or her mother. The autopsy revealed that the mother had already had several broken ribs, but that's only a vague indication. There had never been a complaint against the father."

"That doesn't mean anything," Levin said. "She could have been too scared to say anything."

"It means enough that he was a respected citizen. Mia was the only suspect, Levin. That's how the court saw it. Maybe someone should speak with her therapists. There may have been statements from her later, but Hans hasn't found anything yet. Now there will be a hearing to decide what happens next with Mia. I assume she'll be put back in the institution for the time being. Did she commit any crimes during her trip? Do you know of anything?"

"No, of course not," Levin answered with annoyance. There were so many different thoughts swirling in his head. Something was terribly wrong with this story; he was absolutely certain. Mia was no killer.

"What did they say about the motive?" Levin asked.

"That was speculated about, too, of course. In the end they explained it with mental illness. That's also why she wasn't sentenced but was committed for an indeterminate amount of time. And the way it looked a month ago, they were of the opinion she was healthy enough to be released."

"I have to find out what really happened," Levin said. "I won't settle for this. Anyone can see that something doesn't fit here."

"Could be, but in my opinion, the court decided correctly. The evidence spoke very clearly, and it didn't turn out so badly for Mia. She wasn't pronounced guilty."

"As if a mental institution is like a spa," Levin said bitterly.

"She has two human lives to answer for."

"One! She only speaks of her father!"

"All right, then *only* one," James Webber said, smiling cynically. "Isn't that bad enough?"

"I'm going to Hamburg," Levin said.

"And then what? You aren't a lawyer. What do you plan to do?"

"I want to speak to the therapist. I want to know everything I can about Mia."

"She's very important to you. Or am I wrong?" His father looked at him sharply. Red lights started flashing in Levin's head. He could easily imagine what his father would think about his relationship with Mia.

"Yes, I like her very much," he answered carefully, "and I care what happens to her. She's a nice girl who also happens to be very naive and innocent. She's a wonderful person, Dad, so it's easy to like her. That's why it's extremely hard to imagine her doing something like that."

"Levin, I've defended child molesters who seemed like very nice men. You can't see inside their heads."

"I know, but I want to be a lawyer to help people. You're my example." Levin smiled at him, and his father returned it. He obviously felt flattered, which was Levin's goal.

"It's not going to work to talk you out of this, is it?" He poured Levin another cognac.

"No, it's not." Levin finished his dinner. It was cold now, but he didn't care. He ate everything.

"If you really want to go to Hamburg to help Mia, then go to Hans's firm. He's already spent time trying to understand the case. He'll help you and Mia, if she wants. Unfortunately I have no time. I have more than enough to do."

"I know. Thanks, Dad." Levin reached for his hand. "I really appreciate it."

"It's an interesting case, and I hope you can learn a lot from it."

Levin nodded. It was OK if his father wanted to believe that. As long as he didn't make trouble about Mia.

Levin said good night and went to bed. The last three days had been stressful, and it only took a moment for him to fall asleep.

The next morning he went to his apartment. The first thing he did was listen to his answering machine. The last message made him stop and pay attention.

"*Hello, my name is Lydia Noll. I'm Mia Kessler's therapist. I'd like to talk to you about her. Could you please call me back?*"

Levin's heart beat faster as he dialed the number. He could hardly believe that she'd called him—this was going to be much easier than he'd imagined. He paced around the room as he was connected through the main office of the psychiatric clinic.

"Hello, Mr. Webber, I'm so glad you called," a woman said. The voice sounded kind. Levin tried to relax.

"Hello, Ms. Noll. I wanted to get in touch with you anyway," he explained quickly.

"I'm happy to hear that. You certainly know why I called. A month ago, Mia ignored the orders of the court and ran away. Now she's back with us until it can be decided what will happen next. Mia said the two of you have a very close relationship. I'd like to find out more about that if possible. In view of the upcoming hearing, it's important."

"I understand," Levin said.

Mia had talked about him. He was glad to hear that. He'd been secretly afraid she would try to deny everything that had happened between them, if only to protect him.

"But it's inconvenient to do this by telephone. Would it be possible for you to come to Hamburg?"

"I planned to come, anyway. I would very much like to learn more about Mia and to see her. Would that be possible?"

"If Mia wants to see you, I don't see why not. So I guess I'll see you soon?"

"I can leave right away and be there this afternoon." There was nothing keeping him in Berlin.

"Excellent. See you soon!"

Levin packed his bag quickly, and he made sure to grab the backpack with Mia's things. Then he jogged out to his car, ready to go. He hoped Mia would want to see him.

19

Levin arrived at the psychiatric clinic in Hamburg around three in the afternoon. When he saw the huge building, he got an oppressive feeling. The Art Nouveau house looked elegant and was surrounded by a park, but many of the windows had bars on them. Levin hoped desperately that Mia wasn't being kept in a room like that. "Oh, Mia," he whispered. Then he got her backpack out of the car.

"Can I help you?" A burly security officer greeted him at the gate. Levin's stomach turned.

"I'd like to see Lydia Noll. She's expecting me."

"One moment, please." The man reached for the telephone for confirmation, and then waved Levin through. "Second floor, third door on the left."

Levin continued toward the house, where another officer received him. The man searched Levin and asked him to open the backpack. He was getting impatient; after all, he had an appointment.

It felt strange to walk through the halls. Some of the inmates were obviously mentally handicapped, and with others, it was hard to tell why they were there. He really didn't want to know. But in any case, they all examined him curiously. Several even called out to him, and he tried to greet them politely while moving along.

A friendly-looking woman in her forties met him in the stairway to the second floor. "Levin Webber?" she said, smiling.

"Yes, that's me." He breathed a sigh of relief.

"I'm Lydia Noll. Please, call me Lydia," she said.

"Sure," he said.

The therapist brought him to an office and asked him to sit down. "What's in the backpack?"

"These are Mia's things, they were in the camper. I mean, the camper we were traveling in," he explained to her. He was nervous and kept running his hands through his hair.

"Mia said she met you at a highway rest area," Lydia said, looking at Levin seriously. "She was hitchhiking?"

"Yes, actually." His mood darkened. "I wonder where she got such an idea and why she didn't know how dangerous it was."

"What do you know about Mia's case?"

"Only what can be discovered from the court files and newspaper clippings. My father is a lawyer, and I'm studying law. I want to help Mia."

"How do you feel about her?"

"I care for her deeply, as she does for me." He returned her probing look.

"Yes, I could tell. Mia spoke very well of you when we talked after her return. It's important for me to know whether you love her."

"Didn't I say that?"

"Caring for someone deeply isn't the same as loving them," Lydia said.

"Yes, I love Mia. And it's important to me that she's set free as soon as possible."

Lydia nodded. "I'm happy to hear that, because I think she feels exactly the same way. Unfortunately, she's closing up more and more.

She only told us what was absolutely necessary, and we're afraid that in the worst case, she'll stop talking again altogether. What's more, she's refusing to eat. We experienced that with her eight years ago, and it worries us very much."

"What? Oh, no!"

"When Mia came back to us, she looked good. She wore colored clothes and had a healthy tan. We'd never seen her that way."

"Why did she always wear white?" Levin asked.

"White is the color of innocence. It has a strong symbolic meaning for Mia. She wore it in protest."

"Is she innocent, then?"

"Of the death of her mother, yes, we're pretty sure of that. She killed her father with a knife," Lydia said in a soft voice.

"Please tell me what happened," Levin begged.

"You know the court records—Mia's version is different. But unfortunately, at the time of the trial she couldn't speak, she was apathetic and silent. Only her eyes spoke, but that didn't count. Mia has very expressive eyes." Lydia smiled to herself. "You can read so much in them."

"I know." Levin felt impatient again. "Please, Lydia, go on."

"We worked with her very carefully. She only progressed in small steps, and there were many setbacks. She only wanted to hear one song, constantly. Later it turned out that the song had been playing on the radio while she killed her father, but she only started to talk a year later. We had taken her to a horseback-riding therapist. A horse nudged her with its nose. That seems to have touched her, in the truest sense of the word."

Levin nodded. He thought about the camel and the glow in Mia's eyes when she looked at it. He opened the backpack and took out the stuffed animal.

"I can imagine," he said, showing it to Lydia.

She laughed. "A camel?"

"It's a symbol of Morocco. I bought it for her at a flea market in Paris." Levin's voice cracked. Then he pulled himself together. He wanted to hear Mia's story.

"It took another year before she told us the truth about what happened," Lydia said. "At least we here are convinced that it's the truth."

"And?" Levin prompted her.

"Mia told us that on the day it happened, she went to school as usual. Upon arrival, she discovered she'd forgotten her calculator. The math teacher was strict, so Mia ran home to get it. When she opened the door, she saw her father in the kitchen, washing a knife. He yelled at her for being there, and Mia explained about the calculator. He ordered her not to go to her room, but he was drunk, and Mia managed to slip past him. On the way, she had to go through the living room. She found her mother lying in a puddle of blood. Her father tried to calm her down, mumbling something about a burglar, but Mia said she knew immediately that he'd done it. He had hit her mother often, and Mia, too. Besides being a drinker, he also had serious problems with jealousy. Mia had recently heard him complaining about her mother's waitressing job, saying he didn't like customers flirting with her. Mia believed they'd fought about it again and he'd stabbed her."

Levin listened closely, barely daring to breathe.

"Mia told us that, in the moment, she felt nothing but hatred. The only thought she could act on was to run into the kitchen, grab the knife that was still lying by the sink, and run back to the living room. Her father was sitting in front of her beloved mother's body. She stabbed him, again and again. She wanted to be sure."

Lydia covered her face with her hands. "That's what she told us after a long silence. And we have no doubts that it's how it happened."

"But why didn't her father defend himself? Mia was only fourteen."

"He did. There were clear signs on his hands and lower arms, just like those on his wife—but he was too drunk to stop her. Aside from that, he would have been surprised by Mia's attack. Neither Mia nor her mother had ever defended themselves when he hit them. You can't underestimate what people are capable of in an extreme state of rage. Mia was in such a state. Afterward, she was paralyzed and stayed by the bodies. She was found that way, two days later. We assume she hadn't moved away at all—that she just sat there in her parents' blood the entire time."

Levin took a deep breath. It was difficult to understand what he was hearing. He had no abhorrence for Mia's actions, only endless pity for her. "Does the court know this version?"

"Yes, we presented it, but that doesn't change Mia's position. She wasn't sentenced to prison. She was sick and needed psychological care. She could only be released when she was shown to be stable—and that she posed no threat for herself or others."

"Mia is so naive. How could you have released her with so little preparation for life? She almost got into a truck with an extremely sleazy guy. He made her obvious offers, and she didn't understand at all."

"Mia was prepared, Levin. She has a high school equivalency. She can cook and knows how to budget. Of course that's all in theory, but naïveté and inexperience are not criteria to keep someone in an institution. It's only possible to gather life experience *in* real life. Of course Mia should be supervised—that's why she had a social worker and a therapist assigned to her. We couldn't predict that she would hitchhike. But that's part of the risk we have to take. And Mia could have left earlier, but she stayed voluntarily. We always supported her, but we also felt it was right to gently push her back into a life outside. Of course I underestimated her excitement about Morocco. I never dreamed she'd just run away."

"Was there no possibility of her staying with relatives?"

Lydia laughed bitterly. "Her mother's family is dead, or impossible to find," she said. "She only has one grandmother—her father's mother—and that woman firmly believes Mia killed her parents out of spite. She thought of her son as a saint. She actually filed a request to have Mia permanently committed."

"What?" Levin said, shocked.

Lydia nodded. "We were afraid that she could have Mia locked up here forever. But she won't be able to manage that, even though Mia's disappearance has helped her case."

"Does Mia have a lawyer? I know a good firm in Hamburg."

"She will have one assigned to her, but if you have connections, then we can ask Mia if she wants that," Lydia said.

"What do you think will happen?"

"Mia's disappearance creates more problems, but she didn't do anything wrong, other than defying the stipulations. We think she'll have to stay here awhile longer. In the worst case—a year."

"That long?" Levin said. He'd hoped to be able to take Mia back to Berlin.

"If she has a positive social prognosis, then it might be less." Lydia's eyes gleamed.

Levin looked at her hopefully. He had an idea what she was trying to say, but he didn't dare say it.

"In that case, her grandmother wouldn't have a big chance."

"I'll do anything to help Mia get out," Levin answered, nearly breathless. "I want to have her with me. I can take care of her. I'm sure she'd be able to integrate quickly."

"Levin, you're a young man at the beginning of your professional career. With Mia, you'd be taking on a big risk and responsibility. You should think about it carefully. If it goes wrong and you realize it's not working, it could create a terrible setback for her. Pity isn't enough here—something like this would only work with a lot of patience and love. Are you confident that you can handle it?"

"Yes. I love her, and she loves me. We were together for four weeks, day and night. I like to think I know her," Levin said enthusiastically.

"Think about it."

"No, I don't have to," Levin said, letting his emotions get the better of him.

Lydia nodded. "We'll take things slowly. Besides, we can't decide anything behind Mia's back. She has the right to her own opinion." The therapist stood up.

"Could I please see her?" Levin said.

"I'll go and tell her you're here." Lydia took the backpack. "Please wait."

Levin took a deep breath. He hoped she wanted to see him.

"Mia?" Lydia knocked and stuck her head inside Mia's door. Mia looked up, despondent. She was sitting on the window seat and had been looking out into the park, just as she'd done every day since her return.

"Mia, you have a visitor," Lydia said, coming in.

Mia's head jerked up. "Is it . . . my grandmother?" she asked in a low voice, her heart racing.

"No, don't worry. Look." Lydia brought out the backpack from behind her. "Can you guess who's here?"

Mia froze. This couldn't be true. It wasn't *allowed* to be true. "H–he should leave," she said.

"But—"

"He should leave!" Mia shouted.

"But why, Mia? He says he loves you, and you love him." The confusion showed on Lydia's face.

"I'm no good for him. He should be preparing for his career, and . . . his parents—if they find out who I am? Oh, God!" Mia covered her face with her hands. "No, no, this is not good, it can't be good." Her whole body began to shake. "He should go—tell him that!"

"Mia, calm down," Lydia said. "Levin gives the impression that he's very serious about wanting to be with you."

"He's kind, but it's pointless," Mia whispered. "All completely pointless."

"He said he's studying law and his father is a lawyer. Mia, he wants to help you. He can, and he loves you. That's so incredibly valuable—don't throw it away." Lydia came closer and stroked her arm. "You're allowed to accept help, you know. There's nothing wrong with that."

"Yes, there is." Mia could barely keep control of herself. "I'm not good for him. He has to realize that."

"He's an adult and can decide for himself."

"He has to forget me," Mia said, sobbing.

"How is that supposed to work? It's impossible to forget someone you love, just as impossible as it is to forget bad things that have happened. Love can't just be pushed away."

"It must be possible." Mia looked at Lydia desperately. "I don't want to see him."

Lydia could only shake her head. "OK, Mia, I'll tell him. Please think about it carefully, all right?"

Mia nodded, but she knew there was nothing to think about. It was just wrong. Levin would have to understand. She felt an unbelievably deep pain in her chest and an equally deep longing. Sometimes you had to be sensible, even when it hurt so terribly.

20

Levin jumped up when Lydia returned to the office. She wore an apologetic expression, and Levin knew something wasn't right.

"I'm so sorry, Levin. Mia doesn't want to see you," she said, confirming his fears.

Levin's heart stopped for a moment. "I was afraid of that. When we parted in Spain, she asked me to forget her. But I can't, and I won't," he said stubbornly.

Lydia smiled and said, "I'd hoped you'd say that." She invited him to sit down again. "Mia is afraid to cause difficulties for you. And that's not really such a far-fetched worry."

"It is for me, because her past doesn't matter to me. I'm planning for our future!"

"Yes, and that's good. But you can't just ignore it, either. What about your family? Would they accept Mia with open arms?"

Levin lowered his eyes. That was a good question. He knew how snobby his parents could be and how much value they placed on their reputations. "To be honest, I can't answer that question. But I would stand by Mia, no matter what."

"I'm impressed. But Mia is stubborn, and you'll have to be patient."

"I will be. I'll take a hotel room nearby, and I'll be here again tomorrow."

"I'm glad to hear that." Lydia offered her hand. "See you tomorrow, Levin."

First he had to come to terms with it. Mia didn't want to see him. He'd suspected it could happen, but it still hurt. If he could only convince her she had nothing to fear. She was good for him. Without her, he suffered.

He found a room in a bed-and-breakfast, not far from the clinic. He had some dinner and then called his father.

His father answered after the first ring. Levin suspected he'd been waiting for the call. He knew how fascinated his father was by cases like this.

"Hi, it's me. I just came from the clinic."

"And? Were you able to discover anything?"

"Yes. I spoke to Mia's therapist, and she has a different version of the story."

"What would that be?"

Levin told him what Lydia had said. James Webber listened carefully and asked a few questions.

"So what do you think?" Levin asked.

"If what Mia told the therapist is true, then I'm very sorry for her. I hope she can overcome this and lead an independent life. It must be hard to come to terms with something like that."

"I hope she can, too." Levin didn't want to reveal too much.

"And now? Do you still want help from Hans's firm?"

"I don't know. I haven't had a chance to talk to her yet."

"Why not? Is she not allowed to have visitors?"

"Something like that," Levin said, avoiding the difficult questions again. "I'm going to stay in Hamburg for a few days to try to help her."

"If she wants your help. Levin, don't forget about your education. That's more important than this girl, no matter how much her fate concerns you."

If you only knew! Nothing is more important than Mia. Nothing! "Sure, Dad. You'll hear from me."

"Don't forget what I said, Levin." His father's voice had become strict again.

"How's Mia?" Levin said, appearing punctually at Lydia's office the next afternoon.

"She's not doing well. She cried all night. We had to give her a sedative," she answered.

"I want to see her, please. I'm sure I can persuade her to let me help her," he insisted.

"I'm sure you could," Lydia said, nodding. "But unfortunately my colleagues are of another opinion. They want Mia's wishes to be respected and want to wait until she makes the decision on her own."

Levin groaned. "Listen, that's probably the right thing to do, but I can't stay here forever. I have to get back to school soon." He ran his fingers through his hair.

"I understand that, but at the moment I can't do anything except keep trying to talk to her."

Levin started feeling desperate. "What if she never changes her mind?"

"Then we'll have to accept that." Lydia shrugged.

"That's a bad joke." Levin laughed bitterly. "I know what's good for Mia, I know her. I'm not a complete idiot. I've seen her truly happy. Her eyes had a light in them when we were together. Now you tell me she isn't well and I'm not allowed to do anything? Do you want Mia to sink into this craziness? What kind of a therapist are you?" Incensed,

Levin jumped up from his chair and paced around the office like a caged animal.

"I understand your anger. I promise you I won't give up trying to talk her into it, but I can't do anything else at the moment. Please, trust me," Lydia begged.

"Yeah, sure," Levin said, glaring at her. "And you prepared her so well for life outside, too."

"You don't know what you're saying. You're angry." Lydia shook her head.

Levin decided he'd better shut up. She was his only ally. He didn't want to risk annoying her. "I'm sorry."

"Don't worry. I'll go to her now. I'll call you if anything changes." Lydia stood up and offered him her hand. "I'm on your side, you know."

"Mia, can you hear me?"

Mia opened her eyes. She was so incredibly tired. Why wouldn't they just let her sleep? At least then she didn't hurt.

"Mia." The voice was more insistent. She realized it was Lydia.

"Hmm?" she murmured.

"How are you, dear?" Lydia asked, smiling gently.

"Good," Mia lied, hoping she'd go away.

"You haven't eaten anything. This has been going on for days. We'll have to do something about it soon. You know that, I hope," she said.

"I don't care." Mia pulled herself up to a sitting position. She immediately felt dizzy. She hoped Lydia didn't notice.

"You should care. And you should care about your boyfriend, who's still here in Hamburg and wants to see you."

"Levin?" Mia felt the sharp pain in her chest again. "Why didn't he leave yet?"

"Because he loves you, Mia. And you love him, too. Otherwise you wouldn't be suffering so much. Pull yourself together—it's important for both of you."

"I can't." She shook her head. "I want to be alone."

Levin was truly at a loss. He'd been in Hamburg for four days, and he still wasn't allowed to go to Mia. His anger was slowly growing. He was almost out of time. He felt terrible, and the fact that Mia was suffering made it that much worse. But what could he do? His hands were tied. Everything depended solely on Mia coming around.

As he had done every day, he returned to Lydia's office and hoped for positive changes.

"Mia, you can't go on this way," Lydia scolded, as the doctor who'd hooked Mia to an intravenous feeding bag left the room. "I can't watch this happen anymore."

"What do you mean?" Mia asked fearfully. She didn't want any of this, either—the artificial feeding, or Lydia's endless questions. She just wanted to be left alone to grieve.

"Why haven't you unpacked your backpack?" Lydia gestured toward the corner of the room, where the bag still stood, untouched.

"It doesn't belong here. Not in this life," she said. "You can throw it away."

"Oh, no, I won't!" Lydia's voice became more forceful. "No, Mia, it's part of *your* life. Just like the young man who's been waiting for you for days. There is no 'here' and 'outside'—it's all part of the same life, and you have to learn how to put it together."

"I don't want Levin to have trouble because of me. And I don't want him to see me like this," Mia protested.

"He loves you. He would accept everything in order to be with you, Mia. Solving problems is part of life, and you're not alone. You have a partner, and you have us. Stand up and take some responsibility for yourself!"

"I want to, but not with Levin. I can't ask him to do that."

"And I can't sit here and watch you waste away." Lydia shook her head and left Mia's room.

"I'll have hell to pay, but I can't stand to see the two of you suffering anymore." These were the words Lydia greeted Levin with the next day. "My colleagues don't agree with me, and I want that to be clear. But I don't think I have any other choice."

"What are you trying to say?" Levin dared to hope.

"That we're going to see Mia now," Lydia said.

Levin hadn't been this nervous for a long time. As the door to Mia's room opened, he came up short. She lay there in her bed, completely dressed in white, her face turned toward the window. She seemed so fragile, and Levin barely dared to approach her bed. There was a bandage on her hand with a tube coming out of it. He'd heard that she was being fed intravenously, but it still came as a shock to see it.

"Mia." His voice came out as a scratch.

She turned her head toward him, and her eyes went wide. This couldn't be! She didn't want to see Levin. Why hadn't they listened to her?

Levin came over to her bed. Her beautiful, dark eyes stared at him, so terribly expressionless. Lying there before him was the empty, bleached-out shell of Mia.

21

"Mia." He fought to speak over the lump in his throat. Then he pulled himself together enough to sit on the edge of her bed. He took her hand. She seemed almost like a doll.

Mia could hardly believe Levin was actually there. It was all so surreal. "Why are you here?" she asked him, sitting up.

"Why? Because I love you—have you already forgotten? I want to help you to get out of here as quickly as possible."

"I'll leave you two alone." Lydia went to the door, and Levin nodded at her gratefully.

"But you're supposed to forget me, Levin. I'm not good for you—don't you understand?" she said weakly.

"No, I don't, and it isn't true, Mia." He stroked her pale cheek. What had happened to her color? Where was the shining creature he'd held in his arms not so very long ago?

"You *are* good for me," he insisted. "I've been feeling awful since we've been apart. I can only think about you, and I will fight for you, sweet thing. Do you hear me? I'm not giving you up. You can forget that. And I don't care what anyone else says." Levin took her face between his hands. "I love you. You're the most important person in the world to me. I don't want to live without you, no matter how difficult things might be. Don't you understand that yet?"

Mia listened to him reverently. It all sounded so beautiful. But could she believe him? Did they really have some kind of future together? It seemed too good to be true. Mia had never been lucky before. Why should that have changed?

"Mia, did you hear me?"

"Yes, but—"

Levin interrupted her with a kiss.

"No buts," he murmured against her lips. He kissed her more intensely, being careful not to pull on the IV in her arm, and Mia felt that warm feeling, that tingle. Suddenly she was completely aware of him. His smell, his taste. Levin. Levin was with her, and the big, heavy knot in her stomach slowly began to untangle. She snuggled close to him and felt his warm body against hers.

Levin breathed a sigh of relief. "I've missed you so much," he whispered. "This has been the most terrible time of my life."

"I've missed you, too." She managed a small smile. Levin saw some of the spark return to her eyes.

Levin buried his face in her shoulder, inhaling her scent. Then he looked at her again. "What are you wearing?" He ran the edge of her white T-shirt between his fingers.

"It fits in here," she said.

"Maybe, but it's not right for you anymore." Levin kissed the tip of her nose and then moved back to her lips. He put his arms around her gently. He could feel her ribs. "Why aren't you eating?" he said.

"I–I can't. It's like I have a heavy stone in my stomach," she said, trying to explain the feeling.

"But you have to eat, Mia. Otherwise they'll keep you here longer. Do you understand that?" He looked at her seriously. "Promise me you'll start eating."

"OK."

"Mia, I wish I could take you with me right now," he said. He kissed her pale face. Her brown eyes seemed much larger over her hollow cheekbones, and it worried him.

"Take me with you?" Mia said, furrowing her brow. "What do you mean?"

"I already mentioned it during our trip. Mia, I want you to come with me to Berlin. Please, let's try. My apartment is big enough for two. But if it's really important to you to stay in Hamburg, then I'll try to finish school here. I want to be with you."

She looked at him incredulously. He actually meant it. He was making plans for the future that included her. She could hardly believe it. She began to weep again, but this time she cried tears of relief.

"Mia, what's wrong?"

"I—I love you so much. So much," she said softly, holding Levin tightly. "But I'm scared that I'll make your life difficult."

"It only makes my life difficult if you can't be with me, my angel. We'll make it, do you hear me? Maybe it won't be easy, but we'll find a way."

"That would be wonderful," she whispered. "But, I mean, should I really move in with you?"

"Yes, let's try it. We already lived together for four weeks in a very tight space, and it worked fine. Please, Mia," he said, pressing his forehead against hers.

To live with Levin . . . was all this just a beautiful dream? She dug her fingernails into the palm of her hand. It hurt—she wasn't dreaming.

"That would be so perfect," she said.

Levin's eyes shone. "It will be." He kissed her tenderly. "One more thing." He gently pushed her back from him so he could look her in the eye. "I know a good law firm here. I'd like to use one of the lawyers for your hearing."

"I've already been assigned a lawyer."

"But I want you to have the best," Levin argued.

"Can I afford that?" She'd heard that good lawyers could be very expensive.

"I'll take care of it for you," he said.

"But I don't want you to spend—"

Levin put a finger over her lips. "Mia, I would do anything for you. Please let me do this, OK?"

Mia just looked at him for a moment. Her heart beat wildly. The idea that she actually had a chance to be with him flooded her with an almost unbearable feeling of happiness.

"Yes," she said through her tears.

"Don't cry, sweet thing." Levin stroked her back.

"I don't deserve you."

Levin laughed. "I can be mean, too."

"I can't imagine that." She looked up at him, and he grinned impudently. Now she had to laugh. "I love you, and I'd do anything for you. I just want to make you happy, but I'm afraid I won't be able to do that," she said, her voice fading.

"You can, and you do, Mia. It will all work out."

"That would be so great," she said, smiling fully for the first time in what felt like ages.

There was a soft knock at the door, and Lydia entered the room. "I'm sorry, but it's time to go now, Levin." She looked at Mia. "Mia, you're smiling again! That's so nice."

Levin stood up and gave Mia one last tender kiss. "I was able to convince Mia to let me help her. I'm going to contact a lawyer now who'll take over the case."

"Very good." Lydia went to Mia. "Levin was right—he knows you well. I'm so glad you changed your mind. Life is waiting for you, Mia. And it's worthwhile to fight for it."

Hans Merker, attorney, met Levin in his office. He was an impressive figure, just like Levin's father.

"Levin Webber, you look a lot like your dad." Hans Merker shook Levin's hand.

"Yes, everyone says that," Levin answered.

"So, we shouldn't waste any time. I understand you're concerned with the case of Mia Kessler," he said. "This is my colleague Joern Becker," he added, introducing Levin to a young lawyer who had just entered the room. "He knows all the details and will handle the case."

Levin would have preferred to have the head of the firm involved, and his misgivings showed on his face.

"You can trust him," Mr. Merker said, winking at Levin. "He's very good."

"Pleased to meet you," the young lawyer said, shaking Levin's hand. "When can we speak with Mia?"

"Tomorrow," Levin said. "The hearing must be soon. And there may be a problem with the grandmother. She wants to have Mia permanently committed."

"It's unlikely she'll succeed. Something like that is difficult to achieve, and if you can testify that Mia is definitely in a position to lead an independent life, she can forget it. Unless, of course, the therapist thinks she's not capable."

"The therapist is on Mia's side."

"Then it should be easy," Joern Becker said, dismissing the problem.

The next day, Levin introduced Mia to Joern. "Mia, this is your lawyer." Mia wanted to make a good impression. She hoped he didn't think she was crazy.

Levin sensed her anxiety, so he put an arm around her shoulders and kissed her on the temple. "Don't worry, he's nice," he whispered in her ear.

"Hello, Miss Kessler," Joern said. "How are you?"

"Well, thanks." Mia offered her hand.

"Let's all sit down," Lydia said, leading them to a table. Director Schneider was there, too. "The hearing is in three weeks. We all hope Mia won't have to stay here any longer than necessary."

"I can't imagine the judge will make it difficult if you all speak for Mia," Joern began. "Of course there will also be a neutral evaluator present in response to Mia's grandmother's petition to have her permanently committed. But even that shouldn't be a large hurdle. The worst they could do is impose stricter requirements for her release—for example, reporting daily to a social worker instead of once a week. It's not possible for anyone to have Mia locked up. She did ignore the stipulations, but she neither hurt anyone nor committed any crimes."

"There's one more thing that could help," Levin said, clearing his throat. The lawyer didn't know yet that he and Mia were together. "Mia and I are a couple, and I want to take her to Berlin. She could live with me. I'm still a student, so I'll be at home a lot. She wouldn't be alone— she'd just have to move to another city."

"Oh!" Joern said, raising his eyebrows. "That's really a positive turn of events." He smiled at Mia. "We've got this wrapped up, then—now I'm certain of it."

They had a lot to discuss. Mia tried to follow the conversation, but it wasn't easy. She was still very confused. On one side, she had Levin, who held and stroked her hand the entire time. He seemed so determined, and that gave Mia courage. But on the other side, she still had doubts as to whether all this was such a good idea. But she didn't want to stay here forever, and the prospect of living with Levin was simply wonderful.

"During the hearing, your grandmother's request will be considered," the lawyer explained. "That's when the external evaluator will come forward."

"Yes," Mia said anxiously, "and what should I say to him?"

"You don't have to think about that," Lydia said. "The evaluator will just want to get an impression of you. Don't worry."

"Is it possible for Mia to be released until the hearing?" Levin asked Joern hopefully.

"That's unlikely since she already took off for Morocco once before. But all this won't take long. We're not talking about a trial, here. She'll just have to be patient for a few weeks." The lawyer looked at Mia and said, "Don't worry too much."

Mia nodded. People kept telling her that, but her fear remained. What would happen if she messed everything up and they decided she had to stay? She didn't want to disappoint Levin—and she very much wanted to be with him.

22

After the lawyer left, Levin walked Mia to her quarters. He hated her room and everything in that place. Even though the people cared about Mia, she simply didn't belong there.

"Mia, I have to go back to Berlin. I need to do something about school so I'll have more time when you get out," he explained while they were sitting on her bed.

"Oh, yes, of course." Mia tried not to look disappointed. She took his hand. "Thank you so much for everything."

"It was nothing, my angel. I love you, and I know you'd do the same for me." Levin kissed her on the tip of her nose. Mia nodded and laughed doubtfully.

"What is it? Is something wrong?"

"As if I could ever help you with anything," she said. "Look at me and you, Levin." She stroked his fingers lightly. "Do you really want to do this to yourself? I mean, I'm not particularly educated and not really intelligent, either. You surely have friends at school who are making something out of their lives. And what about your family? Will you introduce me as your girlfriend?" She looked at him sadly. "For me it's like a beautiful dream, but I don't know if I can really expect you to do this."

"Mia!" Appalled, he shook her gently by the shoulders. "Stop that right now!"

"But it's the truth." She couldn't look into his eyes.

"You may not have had the privilege of enjoying the same education that I have, but that certainly doesn't mean you're stupid. You just need life experience. How were you supposed to get any in here? Mia, we'll both manage this. We're an excellent team, and you know it." He took her in his arms. "And as far as my friends and family are concerned, they will accept it. They'll have to. My parents are, well, kind of difficult. At first it might be better to just tell them we're friends. Everything needs time, and we have time."

"We don't have to tell them anything at all. I mean, I don't have to be there when they come to visit you. I can leave, then," Mia suggested. It didn't surprise her at all that he wanted to keep their relationship a secret at first. In fact, she felt it was the only reasonable decision.

"My parents don't matter right now. The most important things are this hearing and your appointment with the evaluator. Do you think I should talk to your grandmother?"

"What?" Mia looked scared. "No, that wouldn't be a good idea. She'll never change her mind about me."

Levin didn't want to settle for that. He thought it was worth a try.

There was a knock at the door, and Lydia looked in on the two of them. "I'm sorry, Levin," she said, "I have to send you away now."

"OK." He embraced Mia one more time. "I have to go back to Berlin tomorrow, but I'll be here next weekend. Are you allowed to take phone calls?" He looked over at Lydia.

"I think that should be possible," she said, winking at him.

"Here's my spare cell phone—I'll leave it here for you. You can reach me best in the evenings." It was very hard for him to leave her. "Promise me you'll eat so you can get your strength back, OK?"

"I will." Mia caressed his cheek. "I love you," she whispered.

"And I love you," he said, smiling. Then he took his leave with a heavy heart.

Outside the door, he spoke to Lydia. "Did you get into any trouble for letting me see Mia?"

Lydia looked embarrassed. "My colleagues weren't exactly thrilled, but now they see I was right."

Levin nodded. He was glad to hear that her job hadn't been jeopardized. "I'm wondering if I should talk to Mia's grandmother. Maybe I can convince her to retract her request."

Lydia sighed. "Director Schneider and I tried that, but she hates Mia so deeply that we got nowhere. But you should try. It could hardly make things any worse."

Levin stood in front of the apartment building. His nervousness had grown on the way there. Should he really go in? What could happen? Worst case, she would just throw him out. Levin's curiosity got the better of him. How could a grandmother be so heartless? Had something gone wrong between them before it happened?

Levin took a deep breath and walked determinedly to the main door. He found the name "Kessler" and pushed the bell.

"Yes? Who's there?" said a woman's voice through the loudspeaker.

"Mrs. Kessler? My name is Levin Webber. I'd like to talk to you about your granddaughter," he said politely.

"I've got nothing to say. Are you from the asylum? You know my opinion already," she grumbled.

Levin held back his anger. "No, I'm not from the clinic. I'm Mia's partner."

There was a pause. "Partner? From where?"

"We met during Mia's trip." Levin tried to stay polite, but it was getting difficult.

"Trip? You mean her escape?"

"Could we please speak face-to-face? It's kind of difficult through the intercom."

"There's not much to talk about, but come up if you really want to."

Levin hurried up the stairs. The building was nice and well taken care of. He wondered why she hadn't taken Mia in to live here and forced himself to swallow his anger.

Mrs. Kessler waited for him at the apartment door. She had short gray hair and a judgmental look in her eyes. She had brown eyes, too, but the coldness in them made Levin shiver.

"Now, what was your name?" she asked.

"Levin Webber," he said with a fake smile.

She nodded and invited him inside.

The apartment was spacious and expensively decorated. Levin started feeling furious again.

Mrs. Kessler led him into her living room and asked him to sit. "Why are you here?"

"I wanted to ask you why you're trying to have Mia permanently committed. Do you think that's justifiable?"

"Is that a joke? You know she escaped. Mia isn't right in the head. She never was, and it's better for her and society if she's locked away forever."

"Mia *is* right in the head. She's a completely normal young woman with needs and wishes for a free, empowered life," Levin said calmly.

"Mia is a cold-blooded little schemer. She maliciously murdered my son and daughter-in-law. She's a dirty slut with serious brain damage and is completely useless. She's a danger to any normal human being."

Levin breathed deeply to try to keep his composure. What the old hag was trying to pass off couldn't be real.

"How can you talk about her that way?" Levin said. "Mia is a sensitive person with a good heart. Didn't you hear the therapists' opinion about the official statement Mia gave after recovering from the trauma?"

"Mia is a pathological liar. My son was an honorable man who never did anything to hurt his wife or his piece-of-shit daughter. It's all one big lie so Mia can get out of her punishment."

"I think you're deluding yourself. Your son beat his wife and daughter. He was an alcoholic—"

"Liar!" she screamed.

"No, I am not. I understand you're grieving for your son, but even you have to see that Mia isn't even close to being capable of murder."

"Young man, I've known my granddaughter a lot longer than you have, and I knew my son and that woman he married. I was always against that relationship—she wasn't good for him. And now you see what came of it: a depraved brat who stabbed *both* of her parents to death from behind."

Levin shook his head. Lydia was right. This woman was so caught up in her own hatred that it was impossible to get through to her.

"What about Mia's inheritance? She gets something, doesn't she?" he continued questioning. "She wasn't disqualified by mental illness."

"My son and daughter-in-law weren't rich. My son had unfortunately lost his job, and Anna went to work as a waitress. They had debts, and I settled them. I sold the furniture from their apartment to at least get back part of it. I only support Mia financially because I don't want people talking. So don't get your hopes up—you won't be able to get your paws on any money."

"That certainly was not my intention, I don't need Mia's money." Levin shot her an angry look.

"Oh, no? How nice for you," she said.

"I'd like to ask you to retract the request for Mia to be permanently committed. It won't work anyway, her lawyer assured me."

"Mia is dangerous and crazy!"

"Mia is completely normal. I want to take her with me to Berlin and start a life with her. If you hate her so much, then I'd think you'd be happy for her to disappear. Your request makes it more difficult for that to happen."

Mia's grandmother raised her eyebrows. "You want to care for her? Aren't you afraid that one day you'll get a knife between your ribs?"

"No, of course not."

"Then you're stupider than I thought."

"Please withdraw the request," Levin asked again.

"No." She stood up. "Mia didn't allow my son to be happy. Why should I want *her* to be?"

Levin shook his head in frustration and suppressed a nasty comment. He didn't want her to let out her anger on Mia any more than she already had. Getting up to leave, he said, "I hope one day you'll be able to see things more clearly."

"I hope the same for you. And remember to keep looking over your shoulder."

23

Levin couldn't sleep. He'd just talked to Mia on the phone—she'd tried to cover up her nervousness, but he could hear it clearly. The next day, the evaluator would be coming to talk to her. His verdict carried a lot of weight in the final decision, and she knew that.

Levin had spent a lot of time studying recently, but it was difficult for him to concentrate.

At least now there was finally a date set for the hearing. It was in two weeks. Levin could only hope that Mia wouldn't be confined in the home again. Joern Becker thought he could get her out of psychiatric treatment altogether, but Levin didn't want to have false hopes.

He had visited Mia on the last three weekends. She looked a bit better—she hadn't lost any more weight, at least, and her eyes had some of their shine back. It broke his heart every time he had to leave her there. He asked himself again and again how she'd been able to stand it all those years. He would have definitely gone crazy in that place. He could tell that Lydia and the other therapists cared for her very much, but they often didn't have enough time to give her the kind of attention she needed.

And something else was bothering Levin: He still had to talk to his parents, in case things worked out for the best and she was actually released. His father asked about the case regularly, but neither of his parents knew that he and Mia were a couple. Levin had decided to tell them she would share his apartment while he helped her look for a job and a place of her own.

He hated not being able to publicly acknowledge their relationship, but he really wanted to avoid conflict with his parents until he knew how things worked out with Mia. He just didn't need another problem right now.

"Good luck, sweet thing," he whispered into the darkness. He looked at his cell phone. It was already three thirty—too late to call her again.

"Good day, Miss Kessler. I'm Professor Siegfried Dobler. The court asked me to speak with you." An older man with a receding hairline and wire-framed glasses entered Mia's room. Lydia had brought him in. She smiled at Mia and left.

Mia offered him her hand. She hoped he wouldn't notice how much she was shaking. So much depended on this interview, and she was afraid of not presenting herself well.

"Nice to meet you, Professor Dobler." She gave him a shy smile.

They sat at the small table. "Miss Kessler, I gather you know why I'm here?"

Mia nodded and wrung her hands.

"The court asked me to evaluate your progress. They wonder if it was really the correct decision to release you from the institution over a month ago."

"I know."

"Initially, you stayed longer than you actually needed to—voluntarily. Why?" The evaluator looked at her. Mia's nervousness grew.

"I–I wasn't sure if I wanted to leave yet, or even if I could. I mean, living independently is so different."

"But when you were released, you obviously felt ready. However, you disobeyed the stipulations and ran away. Do you know why a social worker was assigned to you, and why you were supposed to continue therapy?"

"Yes, I do. But I felt the need to be free, and I didn't think about the consequences." She swallowed.

"No, obviously you did not." He shook his head. "It says here that you hitchhiked, and according to a statement made by Levin Webber, you almost got into the vehicle of a truck driver who wanted sexual intercourse as compensation. Is that correct?"

"I didn't understand what he wanted," Mia said. She felt like she couldn't get enough air and took a gasping breath. *This isn't going well, is it?* she thought.

"But you know it now, don't you?" Professor Dobler asked.

"Yes," she answered hastily.

"What are your plans when you get out again?" He leaned back in his chair and observed her carefully.

"I'd like to move in with my boyfriend. He's studying in Berlin, and he says I can live with him."

"Your boyfriend is Levin Webber, correct?"

"Yes."

"And then? What else do you want to do?"

"I want to look for a job or start an apprenticeship—if someone will accept me."

"Why would anyone not want to accept you?"

"You know why." Mia's brow creased.

"But I'd like to know if *you* know," he said, smiling.

"Well, because of my past, and the time I've spent here," she explained. "I imagine that many would turn me down."

"Yes, that happens, it's true. And what will you do if someone turns you down?"

"I don't know. I couldn't really do anything about it," Mia said. She didn't know the answer.

"Does the thought make you angry?"

"No, it's just the way it is. I understand that."

The questioning continued for another half hour. Professor Dobler asked about Mia's interests and her feelings for Levin. She answered everything as honestly as she could. But she often had to shrug when asked about more detailed plans for the future.

"I think I've found out all I need to know," he finally said. He gave Mia his hand. "I'll see you at the hearing."

"Yes, all right, then. G–good-bye," she stammered.

Levin had stared at his phone the whole time. How could he concentrate when his sweet thing was being questioned by an evaluator?

He was sure it had gone well for her. Of course Mia was naive and inexperienced, but there was no way that could be negatively construed.

He finally heard the ring he'd been waiting for. "Yes? How was it?" he asked.

"I don't know," Mia answered. "He wanted to know so much— and above all, he wanted me to tell him my plans for the future."

"Of course he would. It's all about your future," Levin said, trying to comfort her. Mia seemed anxious. She told him about the conversation and also that the evaluator had often asked about feelings like anger and sadness.

Levin had an idea what he'd been aiming at, but he didn't say anything. Nothing she told him about the interview sounded bad. But *he* wasn't an evaluator, and he was definitely not unbiased.

"Mia, it sounds like it went fine," he said gently.

"I hope so." She fought the lump in her throat. "I don't want to stay here anymore."

"You won't have to," he said, lending her courage. Then he realized she was crying. "Mia, I'll be there on Saturday, OK? Maybe we can go into the city, if Lydia doesn't mind."

"Yes, that would be nice," she said, tired.

"I love you, my angel, and I can hardly wait to see you again," Levin said softly.

"So Tuesday is the hearing?" James Webber looked at Levin curiously.

"Yes, I'm leaving tomorrow afternoon," he said.

"Well, then I hope it goes well for your friend. They should give her a chance."

"I don't know, James. Once crazy, always crazy," Sonja broke in while handing Levin a sandwich. But his appetite had just evaporated.

"What kind of unqualified statement is that, Mom?" he said, looking at her in amazement.

"Well, think about what the girl has been through. Something like that can affect you for your entire life. You can't get rid of it," his mother asserted. "I wouldn't be comfortable around her, in any case. Even if it *was* out of panic, no normal person reacts that way."

"I didn't realize psychology was one of your hobbies, darling." James Webber gave his wife a warning look. "I share Levin's opinion that your answer was very unqualified. Every person can change, and Mia was in therapy for years. I think she must have more or less processed it by now—otherwise they wouldn't have let her out."

"And where did that lead? She didn't follow the stipulations," Sonja said.

Levin knew his mother hated it when his father scolded her, but he was also grateful to his father for taking his side. He had not been capable of giving an objective response.

"She didn't hurt anyone! After that she was traveling. When someone is locked up for such a long time, I think that's understandable."

His mother stuck to her opinion. "No, it isn't. If she was a normal person, she would have followed the rules."

This was too much for Levin. "I'm going to hit the road," he said. "Thanks for breakfast." He grudgingly gave his mother a kiss and shook his father's hand.

"Call me on Tuesday to let me know what happened. I hope after this is over you'll be able to devote more energy to your schoolwork," his father said as a parting shot.

Levin felt guilty. At the moment he didn't want to imagine how they would react when he introduced Mia as his new roommate.

"Sure," he said, smiling at his father before making a quick escape.

Levin wasn't allowed to be present for Mia's hearing, but he had been invited to give information about their time together and to describe how he imagined their life once she moved in with him.

He was nervous, but that was nothing compared to how Mia felt. Lydia had told him that Mia was so rattled she'd thrown up a few times during the night. And she'd refused to take a sedative.

She looked good that morning, though. She wore the summer dress she'd bought in Paris and a bit of makeup. They let him accompany her to the court, at least, and he held her hand until it was time for her to enter the courtroom. He kissed her for luck just before she went in.

Mia felt like a wreck. Her hands were shaking, so she knotted her fingers together in hopes that no one would notice. She was in a large room that looked more like an office than a courtroom.

An older gentleman approached her, saying, "Good morning, Miss Kessler. My name is Peter Konrad. I'm the judge." He had kind eyes. Mia relaxed.

"Good morning," she said, her voice breaking slightly. Then she was asked to sit down.

Joern Becker took the seat next to her. He winked and gave her hand a reassuring squeeze.

"We are here today to decide if you will be sent back to the institution, or if you'll again be offered the possibility for outpatient therapy supported by a social worker. Less relevant is your grandmother's request to have you permanently committed," the judge explained. "Is anything unclear to you?"

"No," Mia said.

Siegfried Dobler, the evaluator, was there, too. He observed Mia carefully the entire time, which scared her even more.

"Miss Kessler, you did not honor the requirements for your release, and were then picked up at the Spanish border. How did that happen? Was it not clear to you that you were disobeying a court order?"

"I–I didn't think about it," Mia said quietly. "But I do know that it was wrong."

"Then why did you just leave?"

"Because I'd seen pictures of Morocco, and . . . it was so beautiful that I just had to try to get there," she admitted.

"That's understandable from one point of view, but from that of the court, you were not permitted. Did it not occur to you to at least ask your therapist or social worker about the possibility?"

"No," she said.

"That was a serious mistake," the judge said sternly.

Mia shrank into her chair, feeling smaller by the second. She glanced at her lawyer, hoping for help. He just smiled at her.

"The police report says you were hitchhiking, and Levin Webber found you at a rest area and took you with him. He said in his statement to the police that a truck driver almost took you, and that he expected sexual favors as compensation. Mr. Webber had the impression this was not clear to you. Is that true?"

"Yes, that's true. I didn't understand what the man wanted."

"But now you know what could have happened?"

"He could have raped me," she answered quietly.

"That's right. That was careless. Do you always go through life so rashly and gullibly?"

"Just because she would have gone with the truck driver doesn't mean that she always acts that way. Many young women who never lived in a psychiatric clinic have fallen into the same trap," the lawyer interjected.

"But they weren't told beforehand what that person was expecting," the judge argued.

Mia looked in confusion from one to the other. What did all of this mean? Was it going badly? She was so scared that she felt like crying, but she definitely couldn't do that. That would only make her seem more helpless.

"This isn't about punishing Miss Kessler—this is about her safety," the judge continued.

"Her safety is assured, to a great extent," Joern Becker countered, "because she's going to live with Levin Webber. I feel that in a stable environment, she'll integrate back into society without a problem. And if she also has therapeutic help, it will be easy for her."

"That's your opinion." Then he asked Mia several more questions about her plans for the future. She answered them all, hoping she didn't seem too insecure.

It was almost unbearable for Levin to wait outside the door. He was tempted to try to listen, but he managed to keep himself under control.

"Mr. Webber?" An officer of the court invited him inside. Levin breathed a sigh of relief. He could finally give Mia his support. He looked for her immediately. He smiled at her briefly, and she returned it.

After the introductions, he was questioned. They primarily wanted to know about the encounter with the truck driver—and in great detail. He cursed himself for having mentioned it to the police in Spain. He hoped they didn't think this event was a sign that Mia was incapable of living outside the clinic.

"What was your impression of Mia Kessler in the weeks that followed?" the judge continued.

"My impression was, and still is, that Mia is a kind person who is very interested in life around her. Mia is inspired by almost everything, and she is capable of communicating her joy. She's a warm, friendly person with a big heart."

"You fell in love with each other. One tends to see things more romantically."

"No, I don't, certainly not." He shook his head decisively.

"What do you think—would Mia find her way in society?"

"Yes, she would. And besides, we want to live together, and that will help, too. I'm studying law in Berlin, and I'd like Mia to move in with me there."

"If Miss Kessler begins therapy in Berlin, would you support her?"

"Of course. That goes without saying."

"I have no more questions, thank you," the judge said, dismissing him.

"May I stay?" Levin asked him.

"That's fine with me," he said, nodding.

Siegfried Dobler was invited to present his evaluation. Mia held her breath as he opened his file.

"This is the important part," Joern Becker whispered to her. Mia was so nervous that all she could do was nod.

"Miss Kessler can definitely be described as naive and inexperienced," the evaluator said. "But I have the impression that she is very aware and in a position to reflect on and learn from her behavior. She strikes me as absolutely nonaggressive. I can only repudiate the request for Miss Kessler to be permanently committed. And considering the fact that she has a serious relationship, I would see it as counterproductive to continue treating her as an inpatient."

"Do you not believe she could get herself into another dangerous situation?" the judge asked.

"Of course that could happen. But then all innocent young girls would have to be locked up in an institution. That can't possibly be a solution. I see ambulant therapy as appropriate. And in view of the serious relationship, I find the help of a social worker unnecessary. Miss Kessler should not be hindered on her way to reintegration in society," the evaluator answered.

"Then the question about permanent commitment has been settled as well," the judge said.

"It's completely unwarranted, and I can't understand the motive of the applicant." Siegfried Dobler shook his head.

Mia squeezed the lawyer's hand excitedly. That was surely good news! Joern winked at her, and a smile formed across his lips. Mia looked over at Levin, who also seemed relieved.

"We'll adjourn for a short deliberation," the judge said, nodding to the assembly.

Levin immediately went to Mia and pulled her into his arms. She clung to him like she was drowning. "That went very well, Mia," he whispered. "You'll see—everything will be fine."

"Oh, I hope so!" She released him and looked seriously into his eyes. "But I'm scared that I'll be a burden to you."

"Mia, the only thing that burdens me is knowing you're locked up," he assured her.

It went more quickly than they expected. Levin took that as a good sign.

After the break was over and everyone had taken their places again, the judge turned to Mia. "Miss Kessler, we have deliberated and come to the conclusion that it is no longer sensible for you to have inpatient care. We find that moving in with your partner is the best solution. However, we will assign a social worker to visit you occasionally. A therapist in Berlin will be recommended, and you must continue therapy without delay. Use this chance, Miss Kessler."

"I will, absolutely." Mia's heart beat fast, for joy this time. She felt like hugging the judge, but of course she didn't do it. "Thank you."

"No thanks are necessary," the judge said, smiling. "Make something out of your life."

"I will try," Mia promised him.

Levin couldn't stay in his place anymore. He ran over and hugged her. "What did I say, my angel? We're going to make it," he said.

"I love you." Mia gazed into his eyes. "And I'll never forget what you've done for me."

"Congratulations," Joern said as he approached them. "Any other decision would have surprised me."

"Thank you so much!" Mia hugged him, and the young lawyer laughed.

"I didn't have to do much. But now you have some work ahead of you—you're moving to Berlin."

"I hardly own anything," Mia said, dismissing the problem.

"How soon can I take Mia with me?" Levin asked Director Schneider. It had gone against his instinct to bring her back here again, but now it was just a question of time.

"I'm going to contact a few therapists in Berlin. As soon as there's a place for Mia, she can go," he explained.

"How long will that take?" Levin asked.

"Don't worry, I'll try to be quick," the director said, smiling.

"How'd it go?" Levin's father asked over the phone the moment Levin answered it. James Webber didn't believe in small talk.

"Perfectly. Mia is free," he reported.

"Excellent, I'm happy to hear that. So you're coming home tomorrow?"

"Yes. And I have some more news. Mia will be moving in with me. I offered to let her live with me," Levin explained, trying to sound casual. He held his breath.

"What does that mean?" His father's voice sounded sharp. "Don't you have enough to do? Are you training to be a social worker, or something?"

"I like Mia, and my apartment is big enough. It'll work out."

"You have two rooms—what's big enough about that? Is there something you're not telling us? What's going on here?"

"Nothing, Dad. We're just going to be roommates. It's cool. Mom is always complaining that my place looks like a pigsty. Mia is much tidier than I am."

"My God, Levin," his father said, "I hope very much that your grades don't suffer because of this."

"I don't see why they would. Mia is looking for a job or an apprenticeship. It will be fine," Levin said. He hoped he could convince his father.

"Your mother will not be amused, and I think you're starting to get out of hand."

"Oh, I'm just a nice guy, Dad," Levin said with a laugh. Then he ended the conversation and took a few deep breaths to settle his nerves.

24

"Do you have everything?" Lydia looked around Mia's room again.

"Yes, I think so. I really don't own very much," Mia said. No, she hadn't forgotten anything. All her things fit into two suitcases.

"Then, this is it." Lydia took Mia's hands in hers. "Please promise me you'll get in touch if you have any problems. Don't just leave—do you understand? In Berlin, there will be a therapist and a social worker to take care of you. And Levin, too, of course. I'll always be here for you. Don't get into any trouble."

"I won't," Mia promised. "I won't run away again."

"That's good." Lydia gave her a hug. "Do something with your life." Mia had heard that before. But unlike the judge, Lydia added, "I know you can."

Levin knocked softly on the door to Mia's room. He was so excited. Today was the day he'd be able to take Mia to Berlin. And even though she had to fulfill a few requirements, their life together could begin.

He'd spent the last two days cleaning his apartment. After all, he wanted her to like it. But he still had doubts as to whether she would. It was a practical apartment—no frills. But she could change that if she wanted.

"Yes?"

His heart beat faster when he heard Mia's voice. Lydia was with her. The therapist gave him a friendly smile.

"Hello, Mia, and hello, Lydia," he greeted them.

"Levin!" Mia flew into his arms.

He held her tightly. "Finally," he whispered against her neck. "Everything OK?"

"Yes," she said, nodding happily.

Levin turned to Lydia. "Thank you so much for everything."

"It's nothing. We're all so pleased for her. I told her that if she has any problems, she should let us know. The same goes for you, Levin. Don't hesitate to call us if you need to, OK?"

"Of course." He shook her hand and then took Mia's bags. "Are you ready?"

"I am so ready," she said with a big smile.

Mia suddenly felt shy once she was sitting in Levin's car. It all seemed unreal. Saying good-bye to the institution's employees had even made her a little sad. Not that she minded leaving—definitely not—but the place had been her home for years, and now she was moving to another city. Everything felt different than it had the last time she left. This time she was starting a new part of her life, and she felt that change keenly.

"Are you all right?" Levin said.

"Yes, of course." She smiled weakly. "It's just so hard to believe that this is really happening."

"I can understand that. But don't worry. Tomorrow I'll go with you to see the social worker and the therapist. We'll figure it out. You have all the time in the world to get used to it." He put a hand on her shoulder.

"OK." She reached up and gently stroked his fingers. "But I still don't know how to thank you for all this."

"You're with me, that's thanks enough." He took her hand to his mouth and kissed her fingertips. "And you'll have to live with my messiness."

"Now that I can deal with," Mia said. Levin noticed that she'd relaxed a bit. That meant he could, too.

As they drove into Berlin, he pointed out a few of the sights and told her a little bit about them. "We'll have enough time to see everything later, but this way you'll get a quick overview."

"This is such a beautiful city," Mia said.

"I'm glad you like it. After all, it's your new home."

"Yes," Mia whispered. So it was. Levin was right.

"This is where I live," Levin said, stopping on a street with beautiful old buildings. This part of the city didn't seem as chic as some of the others, but Mia liked the atmosphere. There were younger people on the streets, and she noticed the smaller shops and pubs. She stopped for a moment on the sidewalk to take it all in.

Levin observed her. There she was again, the Mia he knew from Paris and Barcelona. The young woman who absorbed every detail around her and looked at everything with wonder. She was completely engrossed in her surroundings and took time to look at everything from different angles.

After a while, she focused on Levin again. "OK, we can go," she said.

"OK." Levin picked up her bags and went into the building. He lived on the top floor.

Mia didn't know what to expect. How would his apartment be decorated? Now she was curious about Levin's space.

"So, here we are." He unlocked the apartment door and led her inside. Mia looked around with interest. There were wooden floors, and she liked that. The walls were painted white. "That's the living room," Levin said, pointing to the double French doors. Mia walked in and looked around with surprise. There wasn't much furniture—just an elegant black-leather sofa and a big, high-tech flat-screen television—with a glass coffee table between them. There was also a bookshelf against one wall.

"I'm not much of a furniture fiend," he admitted as he pushed his hair back, embarrassed.

Mia had to laugh. "No, one couldn't say that you are."

"We could go to a furniture store and look around sometime. You're welcome to do whatever you want, as long as you don't turn it into Barbie's Dream House or Cinderella's castle," he joked.

"You don't have to worry about that." Then she nodded. "But I'd love to look around in a furniture store."

"I was afraid of that." Levin took her in his arms and gave her a tender kiss. "Welcome to our home, Mia," he whispered against her lips.

"That sounds good," she answered.

"It *is* good." Levin didn't want to settle for little kisses anymore. He grew more passionate but stopped himself from kissing her onto the floor and making love to her right there. But his powerful longing made it difficult to step back from her. She was surprised by the kinds of feelings his kiss had brought out in her, and she hadn't tried to stop him.

"I'm so glad you're here, my angel," he said. "But I don't just want to fall on top of you."

"That wouldn't be so bad," she said. Her words turned him on incredibly.

"Then come with me." He led her into the bedroom. "Do you think there's enough space for both of us?" he asked, winking. He fell onto the bed and pulled her on top of him.

"I think there was less space in the camper," she said, laughing.

"It's true—this bed is almost too big." Levin turned her over and looked down into her eyes. Feeling her body under his made the wave of heat hit him again.

He looked into her beautiful, dark eyes and was lost in them for a moment. Then he began kissing her again. She immediately threw her arms around his neck. But now he wanted more than kisses. His hand caressed her taut stomach.

"May I undress you? I need to feel you again. It's been so long."

"Yes," she said.

"Oh, my God! I'm dead," Levin said, moaning. Mia lay with her head on his stomach. She, too, was worn out. But it was no wonder after everything they'd done in the last three hours. And from Levin's point of view, all of it had been totally necessary.

"Dead? Now that would be a pity." She gave him one of her breathtaking smiles.

"Hey, sweet thing, when we've got it all figured out with the social worker and the therapist, do you think you could make a doctor's appointment and get on the pill?" He looked at her, pleading.

"I'd planned to do that," she said.

"Hello, Miss Kessler. I'm Simone Klein. We'll be working together for a while." The social worker shook Mia's hand and then greeted Levin. She was a small woman with short hair and a friendly smile. She seemed nice. Mia was glad.

"May I call you by your first name?"

"Of course."

"Thanks, I prefer to be informal. I read through your files from Hamburg. I'm supposed to go with you to see some officials and visit you once a month. Do you already have an appointment with the therapist?"

"Yes, I'm going there today," Mia said.

"Very good. Mia, I want to annoy you and Levin as little as possible. But you should know that I'm available whenever you have questions. We can deal with all the red tape tomorrow, OK?"

"OK." Mia was relieved—she had absolutely no idea which officials she had to see. Her grandmother had announced that she would stop all payments. Mia didn't really mind, because she'd rather not depend on her, anyway. But until she had a job or an apprenticeship, she'd have to find financial help from somewhere. She didn't want to be a burden to Levin.

"Don't worry, we'll get all your ducks in a row," Simone said, smiling at her. "We'll get you to career counseling, too, so you can get an idea of the options open to you."

"She seems very nice," Levin said as they left the office building.

"Yes, she does. Now I have to figure out what I want to do. That might not be so easy. I want to earn some money, too."

"Mia, don't worry so much about it. You just got out of that place. You don't have to do everything immediately."

"But I'd like to," Mia said.

"First you have to take care of me," he said, putting his arms around her. "I need lots of affection."

"OK, let's go." Levin took Mia's hand. Together they followed the arrows on the floor through the furniture displays. Mia frequently stopped to take everything in. She hadn't been inside a furniture store since she was very small. A lot had changed, and some things hadn't changed at all, which she noticed with a glance at a bookshelf. She immediately found several things she'd like to have, but in view of her budget, she put them on her wish list for later.

Levin couldn't figure Mia out at the moment. She looked at everything carefully but didn't say one word about the furniture—and now they'd seen almost everything. "Don't you like anything here?" he asked, somewhat at a loss.

"Yes, of course I do. But you already have everything you need. I thought we could look for some decorations."

"I don't mind if you give me your opinion. Of course we can't refurnish the entire apartment, but we can afford a few pieces."

Mia lowered her eyes. "Then come with me." She took his hand and pulled him along.

Well, finally! Levin thought, realizing that with any other girl he'd have flipped out at the thought of going back through the displays.

"This table is so beautiful, and there's enough space in your living room. The kitchen table is very small, and you wouldn't be able to invite guests to eat." She looked at him nervously, knotting her fingers and waiting for his reaction.

"Good idea. The place in the kitchen has always been enough for me, but now that you're here, we can do with a bigger table." He pulled her close and kissed her on the forehead. "We should buy it."

Mia's eyes glowed. "Do you really like it?"

He thought he'd like anything that made her look this happy. "Yes, really," he assured her.

Mia was amazed by how much they had been able to fit in the car. She'd chosen colorful throw pillows for the black sofa, a few hurricane lamps, houseplants, and a lot of other decorations. They also had the table and four chairs. She had been surprised by the cost when they checked out and insisted on paying half. She still had money in the account her grandmother had set up for her.

They used the table that evening. Mia gazed at her purchases with satisfaction. She had decorated everything well. It looked pretty, and Levin seemed to like it very much.

"You have good taste, Mia. My whole living room looks much more welcoming now."

"Thank you. I'm so happy you like it," she said.

"But you're still the most beautiful thing in the apartment," he said.

After dinner, Levin took Mia's hand. "My parents invited me to their place for lunch tomorrow, sweet thing. I'd rather cancel, but they're incredibly curious about what's going on here with us," he said cautiously.

"With us? What do you mean by that? Do they think we're a couple? I thought you wanted to—"

"Mia," Levin said gently, "I didn't express myself very well. No, they don't know we're a couple. I would like to tell them, but at the moment that would be difficult. They have to get used to you being around. Everything else will come of its own accord. I just meant they probably want to hear how it's going with you moving in and everything."

"Oh, God, Levin!" Mia said. She looked scared. "What if they come here sometime? I mean, I'm sleeping in your bed. That won't work. We'll have to make it look like we have separate rooms." She nervously pushed a blond curl behind her ear. "How do we explain that?"

"No worries. They won't come over here anytime soon," he said. "Worst case, we'll say you're sleeping on the sofa."

"But that's not a sofa bed," Mia said. "We could say I use a sleeping bag on the floor."

"Mia, calm down." Levin stood up and put his arms around her. "Don't worry so much, OK?"

Mia took a deep breath and said, "OK, Levin." Maybe she was worrying too much, but she wanted to prevent Levin from having any kind of problems because of her.

Levin was not into this meeting with his parents. What's more, it went completely against his instinct to crawl out of the warm bed. He and

Mia had slept late after a night of passion. He'd skipped breakfast so he could eat the lunch his mother was preparing.

"Levin, darling," Sonja Webber greeted him, as usual. "You look tired," she said.

No wonder. "I didn't sleep well," he grumbled before kissing her lightly on the cheek.

"Levin, good to see you," his father said.

They all sat down at the table. Levin was reminded of his new table back at the apartment. It wasn't nearly so fancily set, but it still looked nicer and cozier than this opulent thing with the expensive damask tablecloth.

"How are you? And what's your new roommate up to?" his father asked. He never wasted any time.

"I'm doing fine, and Mia is, too," he said, nodding politely. "She already has a lot of official visits behind her. Next comes career counseling, and she'll be applying for jobs."

"I can't imagine anyone hiring her, not with her past," his mother said.

Levin shot her a poisonous glance. "And why not? Why doesn't she deserve a chance?"

"It doesn't have anything to do with whether she deserves a chance or not—it's because she killed her parents." She shrugged. "Who wants to hire someone like that?"

"She killed her father, not both her parents, and that was only because he killed her mother." Levin put down his fork. He couldn't eat anymore.

"Your mother is right, Levin," his father broke in. "People won't care if she's healed or not. People will judge her by the crime and the fact that she was in an institution."

"She'll manage," Levin answered. But of course he also shared the fear that his parents had just voiced. And he couldn't tell if that was on Mia's mind. She'd never spoken about it, anyway. He suddenly had an idea and he shared it with his father. "She could do an apprenticeship with you as a paralegal." Why hadn't he thought of this before? It was the perfect solution! And when Levin was ready to set up a firm, she could work for him.

"Have you lost your mind?" his mother protested. "Your father runs a respectable firm. What would he want with someone like *that*? It would be terrible for his reputation."

"Why would giving a young woman a chance be bad for his reputation? It would be a sign of social competence and tolerance."

"Well, for one thing, I already have two apprentice paralegals— and for another, I prefer to choose them myself." James Webber looked at his son sharply. "Aside from that, I always require a clean record from anyone I hire—that's absolutely basic. Mia can't provide that. And it's also impossible to know whether she'd be able to work under pressure. I wouldn't hire her."

"I should have known," Levin said bitterly.

"What do you mean by that?" his father said even more sharply.

"Nothing," Levin said, raising his voice.

"Your dedication to this girl is completely exaggerated. If the idea wasn't so ridiculous, I'd think you were in love with her," his mother said.

"No, Mia and I aren't together," Levin said, working to remain calm and not scream the truth in their faces. "But unlike you, I'm not a snob."

"Snob?" his mother said, offended. "What do you mean by that? Just because your father doesn't want to hire some psychopath doesn't mean he's a snob. I don't think this Mia is a very good influence on you."

Levin threw his napkin onto the table. "That's enough! I can hardly believe you're talking such bull." He turned to his father. "Sure, you pretend to be charitable when it comes to defending your image, but in reality you have the same prejudices as most people."

"I just know how to use my intellect and not let myself be carried away by my emotions. I lead a law firm, and that can only be done with a certain sense of responsibility. Maybe your Mia is a wonderful person—and maybe not. I have absolutely no desire to find out, especially not with her as my employee. I think your mother is right. Mia is a bad influence on you. Perhaps we should think about changing your arrangement. After all, *we* are paying your rent."

Levin jumped up from his chair. He had to keep himself from smashing everything in the room to pieces. "Then do it. Throw me out. I'll find something else," he said as calmly as he could.

"And what do you plan to use for money?" His father looked at him with amusement.

"I'll get student aid—and I can find a job. I have friends who do it." He turned to leave.

"Levin, wait," his father called him back gruffly. "Are you serious about this?" He approached his son slowly.

"Levin, please, be reasonable," his mother broke in.

"I am reasonable. Very reasonable," Levin answered calmly.

"I'm sorry—I went too far," his father said, offering his hand. "It's your apartment. It's just that this *relationship* with Mia is hard for me to accept. I shouldn't have reacted that way. Come sit with us again, won't you?"

Levin hesitated. He had no desire to sit at the table again. But he realized he hadn't been particularly honest with his parents. It was partly his fault.

He took his father's hand. "OK," he said, taking a deep breath.

They avoided the subject of Mia for the rest of the time. For the moment, that was better. Levin didn't plan to hide his true relationship with Mia forever, but he wasn't sure when to tell them, either.

25

"Hey, how was it?" Mia said when he returned to the apartment, after what felt like ages.

"Boring, as usual," he said, enjoying her embrace. He hoped she couldn't tell how badly the encounter with his parents had affected him.

"Boring? Why?" She studied his face.

"My parents are—oh, they're just such snobs," he said, evading the question. He looked around the living room. Mia was using the new table as an ironing board and was taking care of his laundry.

"Did you talk about me?" she asked nervously.

"Not really," he lied. He couldn't possibly tell her the truth. This was a horrible situation.

"Oh, good," Mia said, relieved. "I'm really not that interesting."

"I disagree." Levin pulled her into his arms and kissed her passionately. He needed to be close to her, to taste her, and feel her. "I disagree completely."

"I don't think it's such a good idea," Mia said. She felt queasy just thinking about it.

"Why not? My friends are really nice." Levin took her hand. He figured she would be hesitant, but he didn't want to give up so easily.

"I believe you. But what if they don't like me? That could ruin your evening." She bit her lower lip. She liked the idea of going out with Levin's friends, but she was afraid they might reject him because of her.

"Why wouldn't they like you? They aren't snobs, and they don't have prejudices. And they don't know what you did, either."

"But they'll ask questions about me. I wasn't at a normal school, and I lived in an institution," she said.

"We can tell them you had some personal issues. That's not a lie. You don't have to give a reason. Please, Mia." Levin kissed her fingertips. "It would mean so much to me."

"What if they tell your parents that we're together?"

"They won't. They're my friends, and if I ask them not to, they won't." Levin smiled. He saw her reluctance fading.

"OK," she said. "What should I wear?"

"Just jeans and a T-shirt. We're going to a beer garden because the weather is so nice." Levin's eyes shone. "I'm so glad you're coming with me."

Mia just nodded. She still wasn't completely convinced.

She looked around at the large beer garden in wonder. A band was playing, and almost all the tables were full. Someone called Levin's name, and a few people waved at him.

"Ah, there they are." He led Mia over to the table where his friends were sitting. "Hi, all, this is Mia," he said. "My queen of hearts."

"Oh, a queen of hearts!" a nice-looking guy with friendly eyes said, laughing. "I'm Kai, and this is my girlfriend, Geli." They took Mia's hand in turn. One after the other, Levin introduced her to all his friends. They looked at her curiously but not unkindly.

"Where are you from?" Geli asked.

"Hamburg," Mia answered. She was so nervous her hands shook. Levin stroked her back gently. That calmed her.

"Oh, cool. Hamburg is great. I saw a musical there recently, and we looked around the city the next day. Do you know the Bega on Musikantenstrasse? That's such a great bar."

"No."

"What about the Cocktail Bar on Hafenstrasse?" Geli continued.

Mia now felt even more nervous. She didn't know any bars in Hamburg. "No, sorry—I don't know my way around so well," she answered quietly.

"Where do you usually go? Do you have any insider tips for us the next time we're there?" Kai broke in.

Mia took a deep breath and looked at Levin for help.

He had sensed her panic and kissed her lightly on the cheek. "Sorry, we should tell them something about you. Is that OK for you?"

Mia looked at him doubtfully. "Is that OK for *you*?"

"If it wasn't, would I be here with you?" he said, winking. Then he turned to Kai and Geli. "Listen, Mia had some personal issues, and she spent a lot of time in an institution. That's why she doesn't know her way around the city and didn't get out much. Aside from that, my parents don't know we're together, and it has to stay that way for a while, OK?"

Mia felt like sinking into the ground. What an embarrassing situation for Levin. Why had she come? She should have stayed at home to watch TV, but she'd been so curious.

"No worries," Kai said. "Are you doing better now, Mia?"

"Yes," she said, nodding quickly. "Everything's OK."

Geli gave her a long, considerate look and smiled. "Levin tells us he met you during his vacation."

"Yes, that's true." Mia swallowed. "He was nice enough to take me with him."

"It was purely egotistical on my part." Levin wrapped his arms around her waist. "I fell for her pretty quickly," he said, grinning mischievously.

"And with this guy, that means something," Nele, another one of his female friends, said. "Levin isn't easy to land. There have been more than a few who've tried and failed."

"I'm not that bad. Don't embarrass me," he said.

"Yeah, sure." She grinned. To Mia, she said, "My best friend tried it out with him. Don't ask how long, but she didn't succeed. You should be really proud of yourself."

Mia looked at her uncertainly, but she was happy about what she said, too. "I–I fell for him pretty quickly, too," she admitted. "You can't help but like him."

Levin got a warm feeling inside. Mia was so incredibly sincere. It was easy for anyone to tell this wasn't easy for her. But if she wanted to lead a normal life, she'd have to be able to manage situations like this. He decided to leave immediately if he got the impression it was too much for her.

His friends wanted to know all about the trip. Levin gladly told them. Mia was silent most of the time and only spoke when spoken to. But after a while she relaxed some. Levin's friends were very nice.

They stayed for about three hours before saying their good-byes to the little group. Mia was glad. It had been fun, but her head was buzzing. So many new faces and scenes, and she needed to process it all. She kept wondering whether she'd made a good impression, or if they all just found her strange. It was important to her that Levin's friends like her—not for herself but for him.

"And? How did you like the gang?" Levin pulled her close to him in the bed. He just loved to feel her naked body against his.

"They were very friendly."

"But?" He knew when something was bothering her.

"I don't know if it was such a good idea for me to go. After all, they're your friends. What if they don't like me and then avoid you because of me? I could never forgive myself." Mia had to tell him how she felt; she owed him that.

"Mia, if they don't like you or reject you, then they aren't my friends—it's that simple. You are the most important thing in my life, do you understand?" He put a finger under her chin so she had to look at him.

"Levin, that's wonderful of you to say, but there's so much more for you than me. I mean, my reputation isn't the best, but with you it's different," she said.

"I don't care about my reputation," he said. "And besides, Mia, I'm sure they like you, OK?"

Mia nodded, but mostly to satisfy Levin. She wasn't at all sure.

"She's very shy, isn't she?" Kai asked Levin the next day after one of their classes.

"She's been through a lot, and she hasn't had it easy," Levin answered honestly.

"That's what we thought. But you're really head over heels, aren't you?" Kai said with a grin. "You've fallen pretty hard."

"She's really something special. I've never known anyone like Mia, but I have to be so careful with her. Her self-esteem is almost zero, and she always thinks people will reject her."

"Well, we all like her, and you can tell her that," Kai said.

Levin punched his shoulder, relieved. "Thanks. Believe me, that means a lot."

Levin was working at his desk in the bedroom when Mia came in carrying a pile of letters. "So?" he said, looking up from his books.

"Rejection letters, as expected," she said. She was very disappointed. She'd filled out so many applications, mostly to veterinarians who'd offered apprenticeships for assistantships—not directly in Berlin, but in the outskirts.

Mia thought she'd like to do something with children, but the occupational counselor had advised her not to. Her long treatment in the clinic—plus the murder and arrest—brought her chances down to nothing.

"I'm so sorry, sweet thing." Levin got up and gave her a hug. "Just keep trying."

"I wrote to all the zoos, too, but no one wants me." Mia tried not to show her sadness, but the constant disappointments were tough to stomach. "I'll try something different. I found two restaurants nearby that need extra help," she said, trying to sound determined. "They don't require any applications."

"Mia, you should keep trying for an apprenticeship." Levin looked at her seriously.

"I have the feeling I can forget about that," she said.

"Keep trying," he insisted.

"Yeah, sure." She smiled and put her jacket back on. "I'll be right back."

This small success made her feel better. She could start the next day in the café around the corner. She returned to Levin's building, relieved. She knew he wanted her to find an apprenticeship, but maybe she just needed to accept the fact that she had no chance. She was crazy, and who wanted to hire a psychopath? Aside from that, she was already old for starting any kind of trainee program. Mia understood that, and she hoped Levin could, too.

She entered the apartment, feeling excited. Levin greeted her immediately. "Where were you?"

"At the café. I start work there tomorrow, and the pay isn't so bad," she explained with a smile.

"Mia, don't get me wrong, I'm happy that you found something, but it's not a long-term solution," he said.

"But what's wrong with it? Plenty of people work in restaurants or cafés. Besides, I don't have another choice right now."

"You have excellent grades. Promise me that you won't give up, OK?" He felt so bad for her about the rejections. In his mind, he cursed his father. Why couldn't she do an apprenticeship with him? It would have been so easy.

"I'll do that. Maybe it will be easier when they see I'm already doing some kind of work. Levin, is it OK for you?"

"Of course." He held her close. "Even if you didn't work at all, it would be OK. And someday we'll have lots of kids, and then you'll have to stay at home, anyway," he said with a wink.

She punched him in the chest, laughing. "Levin!"

"What? That's the way it is. Of course, I'll have to earn plenty of money first, but you should know what to expect," he said.

Tears prickled in her eyes at the thought of a family of her own that loved and respected her. "That would be so wonderful," she said.

26

Mia stood excitedly in front of the café. She wasn't sure if it was the right thing to start working there, but she wanted to lead a normal life, and a job was part of that. She tried to breathe calmly. Then she opened the door and entered the little restaurant.

An elderly lady was just setting up the breakfast buffet. Mia walked over to her on shaky legs.

"Good morning, my name is Mia Kessler. I'm supposed to start work here today." She was careful to speak as clearly as possible, but her nerves made her swallow a few words.

The woman turned around and smiled. "Oh, it's you. My husband hired you yesterday. He told me to expect you. I'm Rita Heller—nice to meet you." She shook Mia's hand.

Mia was relieved, as the woman seemed nice. "Pleased to meet you."

"So, it will be your job to help set up the breakfast buffet and see that it's refilled throughout the morning. And you'll have to take drinks to the tables. Oh, we have a fancy new thing for taking payments. Just a moment—I'll go get it."

Mrs. Heller disappeared behind the counter and came back with a small device. "You just have to type in the different amounts. I told my husband I don't like this thing." Mrs. Heller's nose wrinkled, but Mia was confident she could figure it out. It didn't look difficult.

"OK," Mia said.

"Your shift will be from six thirty in the morning until two in the afternoon, and then someone will relieve you. I'll show you where to find everything."

Mia followed her into a storage room and listened carefully to what Mrs. Heller told her. She wanted to do everything right. Then she was given an apron and a belt with a purse on it. She was feeling more anxious. Hopefully she wouldn't make too many mistakes.

Mia was amazed by how many customers came here for breakfast, including plenty of young people. Many carried books, and Mia assumed they were college students. The prices must be quite reasonable, then. She had no idea about such things. It would have never occurred to her to go out for breakfast.

It was difficult to keep an overview of everything, but in the next few hours she started getting a feel for it. At least it seemed that way to her. She hoped Mrs. Heller thought so, too. The older woman mostly stayed behind the counter preparing various coffee creations, while Mia was responsible for the service.

Her relief came punctually at two o'clock. Mia was slowly starting to feel tired. She wasn't accustomed to being on her feet so long, and the stress couldn't be underestimated, either.

"Hi, I'm Evi," the other waitress said.

"Mia. I started today," she said, smiling.

"I heard. Silke didn't come to work again, and Mr. Heller fired her. It's her own fault. How was your first day?"

"Good. At least, I hope so," she answered. She looked over at Mrs. Heller.

"You did a good job, Mia. I'd like you to come back tomorrow."

Mia's eyes shone. "Thank you. I'd be happy to." She wanted to hug her. Instead, Mia shook her hand.

"And here are your tips—don't forget them," Mrs. Heller said.

"For me?" Mia's eyes went wide.

"Well, if you don't want them, I'll take them," Evi teased.

Mia joyfully made her way home. Levin's classes had been canceled, so he would be waiting for her. She wanted to tell him everything.

Levin looked at his watch. Mia would be back any minute. He was curious to hear what she had to say about her new job. He had wanted to walk with her to the café that morning, but then he'd decided to stay in bed. It wasn't that far. He'd thought it might be a good idea to take her there and pick her up, and then he'd get a chance to meet her boss. But then he berated himself. He didn't want to act like a father figure.

He heard the key turn in the lock. Now he couldn't wait any longer and rushed to the door. Mia's eyes got a happy glow when she saw him. She put her arms around him.

"Hey, beautiful." He buried his face in her blond curls. "That's a nice greeting. I guess that means it went well?"

"Yes, it did." She stepped back. Her eyes were bright. "The boss is nice, and she said I should come again. I have the job. Isn't that great?"

"Yes, it is." Levin kissed her nose.

"And I even got tips—look." Mia opened her wallet.

"Fantastic!"

Mia shrank back from him. How did he mean that? "Is it too little? Are you making fun?"

"What? Mia, no." Levin hugged her close again. "I'm happy for you. And for me, too, of course."

"Of course," she said, relieved. "I'll go shopping for dinner."

"OK, get a bottle of bubbly, so we can celebrate."

"Bubbly?"

"Champagne," Levin said, kissing her again. "Come to think of it, one can do lots of other nice things with champagne besides drink it out of glasses," he said, his voice getting husky.

"Phew!" Mia kicked off her shoes and sank into the sofa. She'd survived her first week at the café. It was a demanding job: she was on her feet all the time. But it was fun, too. All the interaction with so many people had scared her at first, but now she was beginning to enjoy it. They weren't all nice, and that made her feel a bit insecure. But Mrs. Heller had explained that she shouldn't take it personally, so she made an effort not to take everything to heart.

"Hey, you're back." Levin came into the living room. He examined her with concern. She looked exhausted. "How are you, sweet thing?"

"Good. The café was just very busy today. You can tell it's Saturday—lots of people have breakfast dates," Mia said.

Levin sat down next to her and started massaging her feet. "Should we stay in this evening?"

"I'd like to, but you can go out with your friends if you want." Mia leaned over and kissed him lightly. "I'm kind of tired."

Levin shook his head. "No, I'll stay here, too. We can have a nice evening, just the two of us, and tomorrow we can finally sleep in."

"You can almost always sleep in," Mia teased.

"But it's much nicer to sleep in with you."

Levin ordered Mia to relax for the rest of the day. He took over the cooking, just asking her for tips every now and then. After dinner they got comfortable on the sofa. Levin loved it, just lying there with her and cuddling.

Mia had turned on a music show about oldies. Levin barely noticed it, but then suddenly he noticed Mia had stiffened and was frantically searching for the remote.

"What's wrong?"

"I don't want to hear that song," she said. "I've heard it enough already!"

Levin caught a bit of the chorus before she was able to switch away. It was the same song that had upset her in the bar in France.

"That was the song, wasn't it?" he asked. He sat up and looked at her seriously. "The song that was playing when it happened."

Mia swallowed. She didn't dare look at him. Until now, she had always been able to avoid talking about it. It made her feel uncomfortable, even though she knew he'd heard the story. "Yes," Mia said. "My father always listened to a classic rock station on the radio."

"Mia," Levin said, twisting a lock of her hair around his finger. "Don't you want to tell me about it?"

"You already know everything from Lydia."

"But I want to hear it from you. It's your past, so it interests me."

"It's terrible and certainly nothing I'm proud of," she said.

"So what?" Levin said. "I don't want to force you, but it might help to talk about it."

"I doubt it," Mia said. Then she looked into Levin's eyes. "But I'll tell you. After that, though, I never want to talk about it again."

"Deal," Levin said. "How was your relationship with your parents?"

"My mother was a truly kind person. I loved her very much, and she loved me, too. She always tried to protect me from him, and mostly she succeeded."

Levin swallowed. "But not always."

"No. My father—he had always been a drinker. That was why he lost his job. I was actually happy whenever I got stuck at school longer and came home late. I hated being home alone with him. I never knew what kind of mood he'd be in or what to expect."

"Did he ever hurt you badly?"

"No, he never did. He never hit me as hard as he did Mama." Mia wiped away a tear. "I got a few bruises at worst."

"Why didn't you tell a friend or a teacher?" Levin asked.

"I didn't have many friends. Actually, I didn't have any. I didn't want to invite anyone to my house, so I always avoided contact. And the teacher couldn't have cared less." Mia shrugged.

"What happened that day? Lydia told me you'd forgotten something and gone back home for it."

"Yes, my calculator. We had a math test that day, and the teacher was very strict. I was scared he wouldn't let me take the test without it, so I ran back home."

Mia's voice kept breaking. Levin felt sorry for her, but he didn't want to stop her.

"He was in the kitchen, washing off a knife at the sink. At first I didn't understand what he was doing. I told him why I'd come back, and he yelled at me not to go to my room. But I ran past him anyway. I think he wanted to keep me from going through the living room. That's when I saw her. She lay in her own blood, and her eyes were open. I thought she was still alive and tried to revive her, but my father pulled me back and said a burglar had killed her. I knew he was lying." Mia buried her face in her hands. She could see it all, just as though it was happening again right then.

She went on. "I just stopped thinking. I suddenly felt such a deep hatred, something I'd never felt, before or after. I mean, I'd been angry at him many times when he'd hit Mama, but at that moment I went completely berserk. I ran into the kitchen. The knife was still lying there, and I took it. My father was still in the living room next to my mother. He was trying to cover her up or something. In any case I jumped on top of him and stabbed him again and again. He had his arms in front of his face for protection, and he tried to hit me, but since he was crouching there he lost his balance and fell backward. I know I aimed for his heart, many times, and then all he could do was gurgle. I watched him die. I couldn't feel anything anymore."

Mia took her hands away from her eyes. She looked at Levin but couldn't read his face. "Now you know. The actions of an insane person."

"No, the actions of a desperate young girl." Levin held her close. "And in spite of everything, you've become such a wonderful person," he said against her neck.

"Wonderful?" Mia looked at him with wide eyes. His words touched something deep inside her, and she started to sob.

"Yes, wonderful." Levin held her and let her cry.

"What about your grandmother? Why is she so stubborn?" he asked after Mia had calmed again.

Mia laughed bitterly. "My grandmother? She hates me, just like she hated my mother. I can't understand that. Mama was such a kind and beautiful person. But my grandmother never thought she was good enough for her son."

"What I don't understand is, why didn't your mother leave your father? If only for you—to protect you?"

"My mother loved him. She always told me that basically he was a good person, and it was the alcohol's fault. She tried to talk him into therapy." There was such a deep sadness in Mia's eyes, and Levin was sorry he had asked. "She had hoped she would manage to convince him."

"Shit," Levin said, taking Mia in his arms. "I still can't understand your grandmother. She still has a terrific granddaughter, and after all, you're part of him, too."

Mia pressed herself against Levin. "How can you love me when you know what I've done?"

"Mia, you're no killer." He looked into her eyes. "Anyone would be able to understand that."

"I've often asked myself why I didn't just run away and try to get help. I talked about it to Lydia many times, too. It tortures me. I'm scared of the way I reacted back then—scared I could do something like that again. Who can guarantee I wouldn't? Maybe I'm not healed at all, maybe there's a monster inside of me that I can't control."

Levin looked at her, shocked. "Where did you get an idea like that, Mia? That's bull. You reacted out of desperation. That kind of situation could have affected anyone the same way. Didn't Lydia or one of the other therapists make that clear to you?"

"They tried. Really. But I still have doubts." She bit her lower lip. "Sometimes I see it the way you do. And sometimes I think I'm a monster, and that my grandmother is right." Mia gazed at him. "Am I—a monster, I mean?"

"No, certainly not." Levin kissed the tip of her nose. Then he grinned. He had to lighten things up. "Except in bed, then you can be a real monster."

Mia was perplexed. How could he change the subject so quickly? But he looked so impudent, like a little boy. She had to giggle. "Oh, yes? Why do you say that?" She crawled onto his lap and straddled him.

Levin slid his hands under her shirt, caressing her soft skin. "You know why, very well, my angel," he whispered before kissing her.

27

"How about this one?" Levin held up an ad for Mia. A company was seeking a business apprentice.

Mia shook her head. "I don't know. I just think I have no chance."

"You have to keep trying." Levin stroked her cheek. "You can't always work in the café. I know you can find something better."

Mia sighed. She'd sent sixty applications for very different traineeships in the last four weeks, and the only responses she'd gotten were negative. She didn't think her job in the café was so bad, anyway. No, she didn't earn very much, but it was enough for most of the household money. She didn't want to argue with Levin—he only meant well.

"OK, I'll apply," she said.

"Mia, every time I see you, you look better." Her therapist, Silke Meier, greeted her kindly as usual.

"Thank you," Mia replied happily. She liked the therapist. She was just as nice as Simone Klein, the social worker.

"Is there anything bothering you? How's it going with the apprenticeship search?"

"I haven't had any success yet. Apparently people are put off by my past," she explained.

"I wouldn't say they're necessarily put off, but when they have the choice among many applicants, they choose one who doesn't have a potential for problems. Unfortunately, a lot of people close up when they see the word *psychiatry*. Don't take it so personally, Mia," she said.

"No, I don't. I can also understand those people somehow. But I'm sorry for Levin."

"For Levin? Why for him?"

"I–I'm afraid it bothers him that I'm waitressing. I mean, maybe it's not so respectable for the girlfriend of someone who wants to be a lawyer—or something."

"I can't imagine that." She furrowed her brow and wrote something down. "How was your week at the café?"

Mia told her about all the fun things and also about the things that had annoyed her.

"You're really making excellent progress, Mia. I'm proud of you. Perhaps we can have our sessions on a voluntary basis sometime soon," the therapist said after the session.

Levin looked up in surprise. Who could that be? He had been immersed in his studying. Mia was at the café, and he wasn't expecting any visitors. "Yes?" he spoke into the intercom.

"Hello, this is Silke Meier, Mia's therapist. Do you have a moment?"

Levin hesitated, shocked. Was something wrong with Mia? Was there a problem? His heart sped up. "Of course, please come up."

He recognized Mia's therapist at once. For her first couple of appointments, he'd accompanied Mia to see Silke—before Mia knew her way around Berlin. The therapist was a kind woman with an open smile.

"Hi, Levin, I'm glad you have some time. I'm sorry to burst in on you," Silke said.

"No problem. Is something wrong with Mia?" he said. He invited her into the living room.

"No, don't worry. It's nothing bad. It's more about you," she said.

"About me?"

"Yes, and to be clear, it's about Mia's job and the bad luck she's having with the applications. Mia's worried you could have a problem with her job in the long term, and she thinks what she does might not seem good enough to you."

"What makes her say that? That's ridiculous," Levin protested. "I mean, of course I think Mia has the potential to do more than serve people coffee. She has excellent grades. And it bothers me, too, that no one is giving her a chance to prove herself. But, no, really, I would never think what she does isn't good enough. Why does she think so?"

"You know that Mia's mother was also a waitress? And how her father reacted to it? It created tension between them. Mia's fear has a basis. She saw the kind of trouble that came from it."

"But she isn't seriously comparing me with her father, is she?" Levin said, aghast.

"No, of course she's not. But it affects her that way, anyway. Something like that doesn't just melt away. And Mia worships you. She loves you and would do anything to make you like her. So, please, don't take away the space she needs. Let her do what she has to do. The waitressing job isn't at all bad for Mia. She has to learn to work with people and solve conflicts. It's good practice." Silke smiled at him and said, "I know you only want the best for her."

"I never looked at it that way," Levin said. "What should I do?"

"Nothing. Don't talk to her about the job applications anymore. Just leave her to it."

"Sure, of course. Man, I worship Mia at least as much as she does me," he said with an embarrassed laugh.

"I can see that. But Mia is a person with extremely low self-esteem. She's just managing to free herself from that and is collecting good work experience. She's earning her own money and getting recognition for a job well done. These are all huge steps for her. Just leave her some space for that, Levin."

"Of course."

Silke got up and shook his hand.

"Thank you so much for coming," Levin said.

"No, I have to thank you," Silke said. "Can we agree that this little conversation will remain in confidence?"

"Sure thing," Levin promised.

"Hey, beautiful." Levin winked at Mia.

"Levin, what are you doing here?" Mia was happy to see him. He had never come to the café while she was working before.

"I thought I'd get a cappuccino and have a look at the sexy waitress."

Mia felt herself blushing. "You're nuts," she said.

"What's that?" He played offended. "Are you always so fresh?"

"Yes, to chauvinists like you," she said. "I'm happy you're here. There's a great new cake."

"Bring it on," he said.

Mia was nervous as she served him. She hoped she wouldn't make a mistake or drop something.

"Do you mind if I give you your tip in a different form?" he asked when he was finished.

"That depends," she said, haughtily raising her eyebrows. "What could you offer me?"

"A massage?" He looked at her innocently.

"You've got yourself a deal," she said, giggling. Levin got up and kissed her on the cheek. "I'll be waiting for you," he whispered. Then he left the café in high spirits.

"That was my boyfriend," Mia proudly told her boss as she returned to the counter.

"That's what I thought. He's good-looking. You made quite a catch," Mrs. Heller said.

"Yes, I think so, too." Mia's eyes glowed as she thought of Levin.

Levin kept his promise to the therapist. He didn't talk about the applications anymore and let Mia do things her own way. She put in just as much effort as before, but he could see how disappointed she was by the daily rejections that arrived in the mailbox. He wouldn't blame her if she decided to give up.

But in other areas, things worked out better. They met his friends more often, and Mia started feeling much more relaxed with them. Unfortunately, though, her past didn't stay concealed long. Thanks to the Internet, they soon knew all about her. So Levin decided to stop trying to hide it and just explain everything to them.

After that conversation, Mia wasn't very happy for a while. It was all terribly uncomfortable for her, but thank God his friends reacted well and didn't let her see how shocked they were.

Actually, things were going pretty well in general. Levin was happy with Mia, and he let himself be convinced that she was happy, too. Her therapy sessions now occurred on a voluntary basis, so Mia could finally do what she wanted without any stipulations. Levin could see that she was relieved to finally be free.

If only they didn't have to worry about the last little secret from his parents, who still didn't know about his real relationship with Mia.

While visiting them, Levin tried to avoid the subject or only mention it briefly whenever his mother pushed for information.

"Does Mia still work in that café?" his mother asked at Sunday lunch, as usual.

"Yes, of course," he said, "just like last week and the week before." Perhaps the question annoyed him so much because his conscience bothered him. After all, he and Mia had been living together for five months.

"Why are you so touchy? There's no reason I shouldn't ask," she snapped back.

"Of course you can ask, Mom." Levin squeezed her hand and answered more kindly, "Yes, Mia still works in the café, and she likes it a lot. It's a steady job, and she can work six days a week. Including the tips, she has a decent income."

"Oh, that's good to hear. Then it didn't work out with an apprenticeship?" his mother said, passing him the potatoes. Levin took some, even though the subject gave him a stomachache.

"Unfortunately not."

"Well, that was to be expected," his father broke in. "We told you from the beginning it would be that way."

"Yes, because all those people seem to think like you." It was difficult for Levin to suppress his anger.

"That's just what you call common sense," his father countered.

"You don't even know Mia," Levin said. "The people who do know her, like her."

"Except for her grandmother, or how was that?" His father looked at him sharply.

"I already explained to you where her hatred and stubbornness came from!"

"Well, we'll surely have a chance to meet her soon, won't we?" his mother said.

"Why?" Red lights and alarm bells went off in Levin's head.

"Your birthday, darling. You surely want to celebrate it. Or won't Mia be around for that? We wanted to come over for coffee with your aunt."

Levin stifled a groan. Of course, he and Mia had spoken about that. But actually they had just wanted to celebrate with his friends, and Levin had secretly hoped it would be enough if he visited his parents by himself. He couldn't forbid them to come. *Shit*, he thought to himself. "Oh, yeah, sure." He forced a smile. "I think she'll be around, at least for a while. Unless of course you don't want her to be there," he added.

"No, no, we would really like to meet your roommate. She's been a subject of conversation often enough, and she's been living with you for a long time." His father dismissed the objection. "And speaking of roommates, if she's earning so much, then can't she get an apartment of her own?"

"Why should she? I don't mind at all, and she's contributing a lot to the grocery money. We get along well." He looked at his father suspiciously. Was he getting ready for another attack?

"That's fine, but you must bring other girls home sometime. And with another young lady in the house, that must be difficult," his mother said. "Did I tell you Günter Hansen's daughter is single?"

"No, you didn't. But it doesn't surprise me—she's an arrogant bitch," Levin said, smiling back. He knew his mother saw the girl as a potential daughter-in-law. Her parents were stinking rich and only moved in upper circles. Levin couldn't stand her, and in any case he wasn't interested in any of his mother's matchmaking attempts.

His father laughed quietly and said, "That's true, actually." He reached for his water glass.

"What? I thought you liked Helene Hansen?" Sonja Webber barked at her husband.

"What does 'like' mean? She's nice to look at, but I find her kind of fake. If a woman feels the need to have her lips enhanced and fat sucked away at twenty-two, then I don't want to know what she'll do when she's forty."

Levin felt a little better. He just grinned and decided not to comment further on the subject.

"But how *do* you deal with that, Levin?" His mother wasn't giving up.

Levin played dumb to give himself time to think. "How do we deal with what?"

"When one of you brings someone home. Mia must have needs— and so do you."

"Mom, the problem hasn't come up, and since we don't live in one room, I'm sure we'd find a solution," Levin lied. "It works in other student apartments, too."

"Oh, well, good." She seemed unconvinced, but to Levin's relief she stopped pursuing the subject.

"What? Oh, God! Th–then of course I won't be here." Mia looked panicked as Levin told her about his parents' planned visit for his birthday.

"Of course you'll be here. They may not know that you're my girlfriend, but they want to meet you." Levin tried to put his arms around her, but she squirmed away. She couldn't believe it—*his parents*! They would come here. Her heart raced. What should she do? And of course they knew all about her. After all, Levin's father had engaged the lawyer in Hamburg for her.

"Mia, please stop worrying," Levin said. He'd expected a strong reaction from her, but she seemed downright scared. "If you really don't want to, of course you don't have to stay. But it would be a little strange, wouldn't it? And look at it this way: we have the chance to show them what a wonderful person you are," he added.

"But I live in your apartment. I caused lots of problems for you. Why would they like me at all?"

"Mia." Levin was able to catch her after all, and he pulled her against him. "So far, we've been able to solve all of our problems. We'll be able to do this, too." He kissed her gently on the forehead.

Mia didn't say anything else, but she had a bad feeling about the whole thing. A very bad feeling.

Mia ran around the table like a wild animal in a cage. She'd gotten a few recipes from her boss for delicious cakes. She'd even tested the recipes twice to make sure they'd come out all right. The table was set nicely. She'd put together a lovely floral arrangement and gone shopping with Levin to buy the plates and cups they were missing to complete a full coffee service. But she still couldn't stop herself from being nervous—she was aware of how important this meeting was. She was supposed to be his roommate, not his girlfriend, and she had to keep reminding herself of that. She hoped she wouldn't give something away.

His parents and Aunt Irmi arrived punctually at three o'clock. Levin opened the door for them. He was nervous, too, and he hoped Mia wasn't picking up on it.

His mother hugged him, as usual. His father was satisfied with a handshake. Aunt Irmi, his mother's sister, was his favorite relative. His father's side of the family lived in England.

"Hello, Levin. Happy birthday, my dear!" Irmi hugged him, too, and gave him a kiss on the cheek.

"Come on in." Levin invited them into the living room. Mia waited in the kitchen, coffeepot in hand.

"Mia? My parents are here!" Levin called.

Mia entered the living room. The first thing she noticed was the similarity between Levin and his father. It was truly remarkable. "Nice to meet you." She smiled at all of them, put the coffeepot on the table, and shook their hands.

"Won't you sit down with us?" Irmi asked her. Mia looked quickly at Levin, and he nodded at her. "He told us you're his roommate." Irmi gave her a friendly smile. "But he didn't tell us you were so beautiful." Irmi turned to Levin and winked. "A shared apartment is much more fun that way, isn't it?"

"Uh, yeah, sure," he said, throwing his parents a skeptical glance. They had greeted Mia kindly, but he knew they could change their colors quickly.

His mother gave Mia the once-over. She was smiling, but her eyes were cold. "Mia, we know your story. Are you doing well, or are you still seeing a psychiatrist? Do you need any medication?"

Levin wanted to strangle her.

"Don't you think that's kind of a personal question?" Irmi broke in. "We don't know Mia yet, and she didn't ask me why I use a cane."

Levin wanted to hug her.

"We don't have to pretend we don't know anything about her," Levin's mother said, as though Mia wasn't in the room. "After all, James was the one who contacted Hans Merker, the lawyer who helped her in Hamburg," she said. "What do you think, James?" She looked at her husband expectantly.

Mia squirmed in her chair. She felt like jumping up and running away. How should she react to all this? It just wasn't in her to be cool. She was so scared that she began to shake.

"That kind of curiosity isn't attractive, darling," James Webber said. He gave his wife an admonishing glance and looked over at Mia.

"First of all," Mia began quietly, "I want to thank you for your help." Her voice shook. Levin was worried. This had not been a good idea. She looked completely destroyed. He cursed his mother in his mind. "Th–thank you for engaging the law f–firm," she stuttered. "And thank you for asking about my welfare. I'm still seeing a th–therapist, but on a voluntary basis. I don't have any requirements to fulfill anymore."

"It was my pleasure, Mia," James Webber said. "I'm happy to hear you're doing well."

"You work at a café?" Sonja said.

"Yes," Mia said. Then she remembered her manners. "Would you like some coffee and a piece of cake?"

"Yes, please." Irmi held out her plate to Mia. "Is it homemade?"

"Not by me, don't worry," Levin broke in. "Mia was kind enough to help."

"That was very nice of you," Irmi said, "and we're all grateful."

"Where do you sleep, then?" Sonja continued probing.

"I sleep here in the living room. I have a guest bed that I set up in the evening," Mia said. She hoped they believed her.

"And I sleep in the bedroom. Any other inappropriate questions?" Levin gave his mother a look that could kill.

"I don't see why I shouldn't know how you've arranged yourselves. Since we're paying the rent, it's fair enough to ask."

Mia knew she wouldn't be able to stand the tension much longer. She could see clearly that Levin's mother had something against her living here with him. She was very cold with Mia. Of course Mia could understand that. As a mother, she'd worry, too, if her son had a friend with a past like hers. Still, it was hard for her to take.

Mia ate only a tiny bite of her cake—that was all she could swallow.

"The cake is delicious," Irmi complimented her.

Mia smiled at her gratefully. "The recipe is from my boss."

"Excellent. I think I'll go to that café with my friends sometime."

Mia was glad Irmi was there. She really seemed nice. But she couldn't stand the tension coming from Levin's mother anymore. "Levin, I should get over to the café. I think I told you I had to help this afternoon." They hadn't planned that, but she hoped he'd understand.

"Yes, of course. Thanks for your help, Mia." Levin understood completely.

"Oh, what a pity," Aunt Irmi said, looking genuinely disappointed.

"Yes, such a pity," Sonja echoed. But even Mia could tell she didn't mean it.

"It was nice to finally meet you." Levin's father got up from his chair and shook Mia's hand.

"Same here," Mia said, saying good-bye.

"I'll take you to the door," Levin said, following her. He felt so bad for her. He planned to give his mother a piece of his mind after Mia left.

"I'm so sorry about my mother," Levin whispered as soon as they were out of earshot. Then he pulled her into his arms. He hoped the body contact would help calm her. "She behaved terribly."

"She's your mother. She's worried, and I can understand that." Mia leaned her head on his chest. Then she looked up at him and smiled, saying, "I'll see you this evening."

"I'll call you as soon as the coast is clear," he said. Then he kissed her tenderly.

"The bathroom was here, wasn't it?" His mother's voice tore him away from Mia. He swallowed in panic as he saw her standing right there in the hall. He hadn't heard her coming. *Goddammit!*

"Yes, it's right there," he said, looking back at Mia. In her eyes was pure panic.

28

Mia drew away from Levin hastily, but it was too late. Levin's mother had seen their embrace. Mia swallowed, unable to make a sound.

"Hey, calm down," Levin said, stroking her face. "So, she noticed— so what?"

He hoped to be able to comfort her, but the look in her eyes pretty much said it all.

"Levin, I'm so sorry. Oh, God! I'm sorry." Then Mia groped for the door handle. "I think I'd better leave. Tell them I surprised you with that kiss, and maybe they'll believe it."

"I'll do nothing of the kind. I'm going to take care of this right now. Maybe it's for the best that it's out in the open."

Levin wanted to pull her in again, but Mia shook her head. "No, it's not for the best. I'm sure it isn't." The first few tears were leaking down her face as she opened the door. "See you tonight."

"Yeah, see you tonight, Mia," Levin said.

He wasn't happy letting her leave in such a state, but at least his parents and Irmi were still there. And maybe Mia would manage to regain her composure better when he wasn't around. It was a horrible situation, and it was his fault. He'd been careless, not Mia. Levin took a deep breath and went back into the living room. His mother wasn't there yet. That meant there would be a delay before the shit hit the fan.

"She's a pretty girl," his aunt said. "She has such expressive eyes and beautiful hair. One would think she's an angel."

"An angel who killed a person, but supposedly angels of death exist, too," Levin's father countered.

Levin gave him a nasty look. "But you know what happened, right? Mia acted in self-defense."

"Yes, or at least that's what she says," his father said. Then he grimaced. "Excuse me, Levin," he said, and his sincerity was audible, "my remark was inappropriate."

"What remark was inappropriate?" Sonja Webber entered the living room and sat down in her place. She looked at Levin.

"Nothing, honey." His father stroked her hand.

"Well, Levin, I never really believed you when you told me about this arrangement, and all I can say is I find it brash and impertinent that you lied to our faces!" His mother fixed him with an angry stare. "Was this your idea, or was it her influence?" His mother threw her napkin onto the table. "Answer me!"

"Sonja, what's going on here?" Aunt Irmi looked between Levin and his mother, flabbergasted.

"I'd like to know, too. Whatever has gotten you raging like this?" James Webber asked his wife.

"Mom saw Mia and me kiss. Just now when I took her to the door. Mia and I are a couple. We love each other." Levin took a deep breath. So now it was out.

"I'm not surprised," his aunt said. "Anybody with eyes and a bit of brain could see the way you two look at each other."

Great, Levin thought. But that didn't matter anymore now.

"So? How long has this been going on?" His father's voice was harsh.

"A long time," Levin said.

"You've been lying to us all this time?"

"Yes, I have. And I'm sure you can understand my reasoning," Levin exclaimed. "You and your prejudice. I suspected from the beginning that you'd give us nothing but problems."

"So, instead you went and made yourself a love nest with your little playmate here? How nice that we got to pay the rent for that, too," his father said, scoffing.

"You don't have to. Mia and I can get through on our own," Levin said. "I acknowledge that it wasn't nice to fool you, but it's been hard with Mia lately. She's only just brushing off the dust and learning to lead a responsible life of her own. Because of that, I wanted to avoid conflict for a while," he said more calmly. "I would have told you the truth eventually, but I wanted to wait until Mia was a bit more stable. I apologize for lying to you. You have a right to be angry."

"Well, how nice," his father said cynically.

"My goodness, don't make such a drama out of this." Irmi rolled her eyes. "Mia's such a nice girl."

"By your leave, Irmi," James Webber said, smiling at his sister-in-law, "Sonja and I have a slightly different view on the topic. This nice girl had, and obviously still has, big problems. I have to grant that she's not an ice-cold murderer, and that's not what she was sentenced for, but Mia was—and who knows, maybe she still is—ill. Mentally ill, and everybody knows how unpredictable those people can be. I can't accept that Levin has fallen for someone like that and possibly neglects his schoolwork playing the Good Samaritan. I think a relationship with Mia is a big mistake, not to mention the fact that it could be dangerous should her dysfunction return."

"What codswallop," Irmi said. "My goodness, James, you're a lawyer, and you should be seeing things more rationally. Haven't you learned that people serve their sentences for a reason? And that they are to be treated as *normal* people as soon as they are released? Doesn't that count for the mentally ill, too?"

"Of course I know that, but this is about my son. I allow myself to not be objective in this case. This is about his future—both private and professional. Levin is going to take over my firm one day. How is that going to look if he's with a mentally ill woman who killed her father? That she did it in self-defense, or for whatever reason, is beside the point. She *did* kill him. It's not like that kind of person is very trustworthy."

"Well, Mia won't have anything to do with my clients!" Levin shouted.

"But you will!" his father shouted back even louder. "People will doubt your ability to judge—and your sanity."

"James, what nonsense," Irmi said.

"It isn't nonsense." His mother's voice sounded mild. She felt vindicated. "James is right. I do hope Levin realizes that, too. He's completely deluded. The girl is gorgeous, Levin, and you're a young man. I can see why you're fascinated by her, but you can't continue this relationship. It would harm you—and even your father's firm in the end."

"And you're surprised that he didn't tell you the truth." Irmi rolled her eyes. "I wouldn't have, either."

Levin gave his aunt a grateful look. It was nice to have her as an ally, but he knew it wouldn't be much help. "I accept your opinion on our relationship, but that doesn't change the fact that I love her, and she loves me. I'm never going to give her up, no matter what." Levin looked between his parents. "I'm sorry for you."

"For us? You should be sorry for *yourself*." His father got up and gestured that they were leaving. His mother followed suit. Levin's father threw an envelope at him. He knew what would be in it: his birthday money. "Here's your present. Budget carefully, because from now on we are not supporting you. If you want to keep renting this apartment, you'll have to figure out how to do it yourself. Levin, I can only advise you to come to your senses."

"I've never been clearer about how I feel, thank you very much," Levin said, glaring at him.

"Levin," his mother said, "all Mia is doing is taking advantage of you. You're like a jackpot for her, don't you see? My God, I hardly recognize you anymore."

"That's because Levin is an adult," Irmi said. "Sonja, James—take stock of yourselves, sleep on it. Maybe then you'll see that you're on the wrong track here."

"We most definitely are not," Sonja said. "It's too bad you care so little for your nephew's future."

"Mom, Dad," Levin said, almost pleading, "Mia is a wonderful girl, and she means the world to me. Why can't you just be happy for me? Mia deserves a family who takes her in and loves her. Why can't that be *us*?"

His father shook his head. "Because we're rational people, it's that simple. I'm sorry we need to go so hard on you, but it obviously won't work any other way. Be reasonable, and all possibilities will become available to you again. We certainly won't be resentful." His father nodded at him and approached the front door.

"Levin, you disappoint me." His mother followed his father.

"Oh, dear," Aunt Irmi said. "What now?"

"Nothing." Levin shrugged. "All I can hope for is that all this isn't too hard on Mia. She was completely terrified."

"Well, then call her and ask her to come home." His aunt got up. "Levin, if I can help the two of you, let me know. I'll talk to James and Sonja again, too. It can't go on like this."

"Thanks, but I think it's better if you keep out of it. I don't want you in the line of fire, but I'm glad that you see Mia differently." He hugged her.

"I do." She patted him on the back.

"I'll drive you home," Levin offered.

"Thanks, that's very nice of you." Irmi heaped another two pieces of cake onto her plate. "And I'm taking this with me."

Levin didn't know whether he should still be angry at his parents. It was exactly the reaction he had been expecting. He found it sad, though, that educated, intelligent people like the two of them thought in such a way. Irmi had done her best to calm Levin down on the way to her house. But his main concern now was for Mia. He drove to the café and hoped she'd be there. Her boss showed him to the kitchen, where she was helping with the dishes.

"Mia, your boyfriend's here," Mrs. Heller said.

Mia looked up. Levin walked over and wrapped her in his arms. Mia pushed him away. "What about your parents?"

"They reacted like I expected," he said. "But that doesn't matter, Mia, it doesn't matter at all. We have each other, and that's all that counts, you hear me?"

"Oh, no!" Tears came to Mia's eyes. Her fears had been realized. "That's terrible. I'm so sorry."

"No, they should be sorry. They're so pigheaded!" Levin looked deeply into her eyes. "We'll make it." At that moment, he realized it was actually not such a bad thing that she wasn't doing an apprenticeship. With Mia's money from the café, they could get by fairly well. If he could get a job now, too, everything would work just fine. He would have laughed if it wasn't so sad.

"Levin, I–I don't know what to say. This is all my fault. If I hadn't come along, then—"

"Then all I'd be is a poor, unhappy idiot without love in my life. Do you remember my aunt's saying? *Nothing happens without a reason.*"

Mia tried to smile, but she felt just terrible.

"Hey, are you going to help me prepare my birthday party? Or aren't you allowed to leave yet?" Levin kissed the tip of her nose, hoping to distract her.

"I think I can go. I'm not scheduled." Mia didn't understand how he could be in the mood to celebrate now.

"I won't let them ruin my birthday," Levin said, as though he'd just read her thoughts. "OK?"

"OK."

29

It was hard for Mia to push away thoughts of Levin's parents. She'd stopped talking about it to him, but she couldn't think of anything else. Mechanically, she prepared everything for Levin's party. She'd set out some finger foods and made a big pot of goulash. His friends were taking care of the rest.

Levin was grateful for Mia's help. She'd made such an effort to make everything look nice. *If only my parents could see this*, he kept thinking. But he had decided to not let the situation ruin his good mood. This was his birthday, the first one he was celebrating with the girl of his dreams, and dammit, he wanted to enjoy it. He realized Mia felt differently about it. She just wasn't good at acting. Her sadness was visible, and that caused him more pain than the fight with his parents.

"Hey, sweet thing, that looks great," Levin said, stepping up behind Mia. He wrapped his arms around her waist and lightly kissed her neck. "What would I do without you?"

Mia wanted to say that he wouldn't have all of these problems if she hadn't come into his life, but she stopped herself. She knew Levin wouldn't want to hear it. She turned around to face him. "I love you so much, Levin. No matter what else ever happens, please never forget that."

She sounded so serious. "Of course not, my angel. And I love you, too. Do you hear me? You're my life, Mia."

She smiled. It seemed a little sad, but then she suddenly remembered something with a pang. "Goodness, I haven't given you my present yet." She put her hand to her mouth. With all the nervousness about his parents' visit, she'd completely forgotten about it.

"You don't have to give me anything," Levin said, but Mia had already separated herself from him and slipped into the bedroom. She came back with a small package.

"Happy birthday, Levin." She snuggled up to him.

"Thanks, but I'm already holding the best present in my arms." Then his curiosity won out, and he carefully unrolled the package. Out came two beautiful photos of Mia. "Hey, who took these?" he asked.

"A photographer Geli recommended. I didn't really know what else to get you. Then I had the idea. Didn't you tell me recently that you wanted to put a picture of me on your desk? And so I thought—"

Levin pulled her toward him. "It's perfect, Mia. There's nothing more beautiful you could give me right now."

"Right now? What do you mean?" She looked at him, confused.

Levin let his fingers glide down her neck, tracing her collarbone. "We talked about it recently. About family and that we want to get married. Someday you can give me your 'I do,' Mia Kessler. That would top even this present!"

His words had really hit home, and hard, deep inside. "Who knows what the future will bring?"

The sound of the doorbell brought them back to reality. "I can tell you already that the future brings a lot of visitors," he joked. He dragged her to the door with him. He had already guessed that his friends Kai and Geli would be the first ones to show up. That was perfectly fine with him, because they were bringing the drinks.

"Hey, help me for a sec," Kai panted as he pushed a small keg into Levin's arms. "Happy birthday and all that." He gasped for air. "I hate people who live on the top floor," he joked.

"Welcome," Levin said, grinning. "And you used to be in better shape, too."

"Happy birthday." Geli hugged Levin affectionately and planted a kiss on his cheek. Then she turned and said, "Hi, Mia."

Mia was genuinely happy to see the two of them. They were so wonderfully normal and always made her feel like they had accepted her into their group. "Hi, Geli—hi, Kai," she said.

Geli pulled Mia aside. "So? How did the photos turn out?"

Mia hurried to show them to her. "Here they are."

"Wow, awesome!" Geli said. "I told you that photographer has a good reputation."

"Yeah, he had some really good ideas," Mia agreed.

The two men set up the keg and tapped it. The four of them toasted to each other. Soon more and more of Levin's friends arrived. The table with the buffet on it gradually filled up. Once everybody had arrived, Levin asked his guests to help themselves. Mia had been worried because they barely had any seating. But a few friends had brought folding tables, and the party was spreading through the entire apartment. The mood was carefree and cheerful, and even Mia was slowly managing to enjoy the evening. But she still had a stomachache from the tension with Levin's parents. She couldn't eat a single bite.

Later in the evening, Kai pulled Levin aside. "So, is everything all right?"

"Yeah, of course, why shouldn't it be?"

"I don't know, you look like something's on your mind, and your sweetheart doesn't exactly look psyched, either."

Levin sighed. There was no point in acting in front of his best friend. They had known each other too long for that. "My parents know about Mia and me. Mom saw us today when I kissed Mia, and then it was out," Levin said.

"Oh, shit! I guess they didn't react very well to the news, huh?"

"Understatement of the year," Levin said, laughing. "They'll stop the financial support if I don't 'find reason.'"

"Well, I suppose it wasn't shocking that they didn't jump for joy once they heard you'd already been together for so long. But *that* is definitely a bit over the top." Kai shook his head. "Let them sleep on it for a few nights. Your parents adore you—they'll get over it."

"Maybe, but if they don't, I don't care. I love Mia no matter what they say. We can make it just fine without their help."

"So does Mia earn that much?"

"It's not much, but we can get by. And I can get a job. Maybe I can be a waiter in a club or stock shelves somewhere. I'll find something."

"How does Mia feel about that?"

"You can imagine. She thinks it's her fault and is just really sad. That's what worries me most, that she might do something stupid to try to spare me," Levin said quietly.

"Do you think she'd go that far? Maybe even break up with you?" Kai looked at Levin incredulously.

"I have no trouble believing she'd do that. But that can't happen. We've already talked about marriage. Not yet, but someday I want to start a family with her. I know that may sound extreme, but I just can't imagine a life without her. You know what I mean?"

"Wow, you're really in deep, huh?" Kai said.

"Truly, madly, deeply. Man, this had better not go wrong—ever." Levin's hand clenched his beer glass. "If only my parents could understand what a great girl she is, but all they see in her is a psychopath."

"Hey, like I said, just wait a bit. If they realize how serious you are about her, maybe they'll give in."

"I really hope so," Levin said with a sigh.

"And to think what you were like only a year ago. Back then I'd have bet anything that you wouldn't fall for anyone this fast."

"Same here—and then she came along." Levin tilted his head toward Mia. She was collecting used paper plates. He thought back to his discussion with her. Mia had wanted to borrow dishes from the café to avoid using paper plates, but he had managed to convince her it wasn't a problem. She wanted everything to be perfect for him. He was sure she'd sacrifice anything—why couldn't his parents see that? Why didn't they give her at least the tiniest chance? Levin didn't know anyone who deserved it as much as she did, and it drove him crazy to think that she might never have the courage to stand her ground in front of his parents.

"Mia, leave those, they're not going to run away." Levin looked at her sternly. She had been tidying up the apartment for an hour. He hadn't been able to persuade her to just leave everything until they'd gotten some sleep. Meanwhile, it was the break of dawn, and Levin could barely keep his eyes open.

"I'll be done soon—you should go to bed." She smiled at him. She, too, seemed exhausted, but he wasn't sure it was just from the party. She hadn't touched a drop of alcohol, and he doubted she'd eaten anything.

"No, I'm not going to bed without you," Levin said, pulling her after him. "Come with me." When he finally had her in his arms, he kissed her forehead. "Mia, about my parents and that whole situation . . ."

Her head jerked up. She gazed at him with a mix of insecurity and fear. "Yes?"

"I'm going to look for a job. They're always looking for servers in clubs and bars, or I can stock shelves somewhere. I'll find something, and together with the money you earn, we'll make it just fine."

Mia was alarmed. "But you need to concentrate on school. Maybe you won't have enough time if you work on the side," she protested.

"Other students work. I can handle it, don't worry," he said, but Mia shook her head.

"No, I don't want that. I heard in the café today that they're still looking for kitchen help in the Italian restaurant in Grazstrasse. I'll go there first thing tomorrow. Maybe I can help out there after my shift at the café."

"Are you nuts? You can't possibly work that much. I won't let that happen, my angel!"

"But, Levin, you just talked to Kai tonight about all your important exams coming up. I want you to be able to concentrate fully on them." Mia sat next to him and caressed his bare chest. Levin was wary. She'd figured out long ago that he was easier to talk into something when she made physical contact with him. He had to watch out that she didn't outfox him that way.

"I can pass those tests hands down," he said.

"Levin, please. I feel really bad already. This situation with your parents is my fault. Let me do this—it would help me deal with everything." She seemed so terribly unhappy, and it broke Levin's heart.

"But, Mia, I don't want you to work yourself to death for me." He pushed a lock of her hair behind her ear.

"But it's not forever." She bent over him and kissed him tenderly on the mouth. "Please, Levin, I'm never going to make it far, but all doors are open for you, and I want you to have the best chances. Please don't block me out. I want to help you." Her hands kept stroking him, going lower and lower.

"I can't possibly accept that," he said, moaning.

"Yes, you can," she whispered against his lips.

The next day, Mia made her way over to the Italian restaurant. The owner was a longtime friend of her boss, and Mia had asked Mrs. Heller to put in a good word for her. Mrs. Heller had been surprised that Mia was looking for another job and worried that she was thinking about working there instead, but Mia explained that she was looking for something extra.

"Don't work yourself to death, Mia," Mrs. Heller had admonished her. "Even though you're young, that kind of thing can be really hard on you."

"Oh, no, it's just temporary," Mia had said. Her boss's concern had been touching. Mr. and Mrs. Heller were always so nice to her.

She took a deep breath and entered the restaurant in Grazstrasse. Luigi Riccone was expecting her, and he welcomed her with a big smile.

"You are interested in the job for kitchen help?" he asked in his lilting Italian accent.

"Yes. Is it still open?"

"It is. I would need you here five times a week. From six until midnight. Is that all right?"

"Yes, of course," Mia said happily. "I work until two at the café."

"*Perfetto*. Can you begin tomorrow evening?"

"Yes, no problem."

"OK, *signorina*. We will see each other tomorrow night, then," Mr. Riccone said.

Relieved, Mia went home. A lot of pressure had been taken off her. With her job in the restaurant, she and Levin would manage. She knew that Levin wouldn't be thrilled, but she was determined that she could do it.

He was still lying in bed when she came back to the apartment. Apparently last night's party had left its mark on him. Mia had been very tired, too, but her inner restlessness hadn't allowed her to sleep anymore. And she—unlike Levin—hadn't had any alcohol. She quietly opened the bedroom door. He was lying in bed, his hair messy. The TV was on, and he looked grumpy.

"Where were you?" he said. "I was getting worried." Levin's head was throbbing, and the fact that he had woken up without his angel in his arms that morning—or wait, that afternoon—made it even worse.

Mia smiled sweetly. "I have good news." She kicked off her shoes and crawled into bed with him.

"Let's hear it." Levin pulled her up onto his stomach.

Mia snuggled up to him. "I was at that Italian restaurant, and tomorrow I can start there as kitchen help from six to midnight. Isn't that perfect?" She raised her head and looked into his eyes.

Levin thought he hadn't heard right. "You're joking, right?" He looked at her, dumbfounded. Slowly, vague memories of a conversation in the early morning hours started returning. He thought he'd made it clear that he didn't want that. She was already working hard enough.

Mia became insecure and looked at him, confused. "No, I'm not joking. Why would I joke about this?"

"Mia, I don't want you to start doing even *more* for me." Levin sat up in bed and moved his fingers through his hair. "Sweetheart, you're already working enough. I can't tolerate this."

"But I want to." Mia cleared her throat. She didn't like to fight with him, but she'd set her mind on this and was determined not to let him talk her out of it.

"No way. Besides, how is that going to look? I don't do anything, and you work like crazy every day," he complained.

"Why are you saying you don't do anything? You're studying, and one day you're sure to be an amazing lawyer." Mia took his hands. "Levin, please, just concentrate on school—that'll help us most!"

"Oh, Mia, not that look!" Levin groaned. "Don't you understand that I'd feel completely stupid having my girlfriend pay all the bills?"

"And don't you understand that it means so much to me to do everything I can for you? The other way around it would be exactly the same!" Mia stroked his stubbly chin. She liked it when he was so disheveled—it looked sexy on him. "I mean, this is the best I can do, because I'll never make it as far as you will. I can do my part so you can invest time in your schoolwork, and maybe—well, maybe your parents will think better of me if they see that I'm supporting you as best I can."

"Oh, Mia." Levin kissed the delicate skin on her neck. "You shouldn't do this for my parents."

"But if you finish school, I get something out of it, too, don't I? We want to build a future together, and this won't be forever. I mean, this thing with two jobs. Please, Levin, let me do it, OK? It would mean the world to me." Her expressive brown eyes looked at him so pleadingly that Levin's resistance melted away.

"How do I deserve a woman as wonderful as you?" he whispered. Her worry and commitment almost moved him to tears.

"Don't say that." She smiled shyly. "So then—it's OK?"

"Mia, no, it's not OK, not at all, but it looks like you're so determined that I just have to give in." He kissed her nose. "Believe me, sweet thing, when I'm done with all this, I'll pay you back a thousand times. You'll be my wife, and I'll worship you. I love you so much, Mia, so much," he said, kissing her again.

"Levin, you don't need to pay anything back. We're a couple. We're not supposed to repay things, just give to each other without counting, right?"

"Right." Levin sighed. She'd somehow managed to get her way again.

"Wow, Mia's really on her toes," Kai said to Levin. Then he toasted him with his beer.

"Stop," Levin said. "I can't even stand to think about her standing in that kitchen scratching leftovers off plates while I hang out here with you."

"Come on, you've been studying all day." Kai patted him on the back. "If it's OK for Mia, it should be for you, too."

"Yeah, but it should be *me* who takes care of her. With all that she's been through!" No, Levin hadn't come to terms with the situation yet.

For a week now, Mia had been working two jobs. She never said a word about it. She never complained, but he could see how tired she was when he picked her up at the restaurant at midnight.

"She's not made of porcelain, Levin." Kai became more serious. "Maybe you should just trust her more. I know you're worried, but just respect her decision. That might help her more than you think. Always putting her in a bubble can't be the solution, either."

"Humph," Levin grunted. Maybe Kai was right. Levin had also talked to Irmi about Mia's double load, and she'd reacted similarly to Kai. She had also been impressed by Mia's commitment and had wanted to tell his parents right away.

Levin was just fine with that. His parents *should* know about all the things Mia did for him. Since their fight over a week ago, Levin and his parents had not been on speaking terms. He'd resolved not to take the first step toward them this time. They would have to let him know they accepted his relationship with Mia. Until that, no go.

Like every evening, Levin picked up Mia from her shift. Letting her walk around alone at this time of night was way too risky for his liking.

"Hey." She wrapped her arms around his neck and cuddled up to him. "How was your evening with Kai?"

"OK, but not half as great as seeing you," he said.

His words made her happy. It took considerable effort to suppress her yawn. She didn't want him to notice how much strain the two jobs put on her. At least she had a free night tomorrow. It would be Monday, and the restaurant was closed. That meant on Mondays she only had to work in the café.

Mia walked very slowly, and Levin noticed. "What's up?" he asked.

"Nothing, it's just that my feet hurt." She didn't want him to think about how much of a toll constantly being on her feet had taken.

"OK, I'll carry you piggyback." He crouched down in front of her, and Mia looked at him, confused.

"What?"

"Come on, get on. If you don't, I'll see that you lose that job again," he said.

"Weirdo," Mia said, giggling. But the prospect of not having to walk anymore was pretty inviting. "Are you going to carry me all the way to the top of the stairs?"

"Don't push your luck." Now Levin was laughing, too. Of course there was no way he was going to show any weakness, so in the end he did carry his sweet burden all the way to the top.

"Wow, you're so strong!" Mia said once they were back in the apartment. She was impressed.

"I certainly am. Were you doubting it?" He was completely exhausted and out of breath, but her happy face made it all worthwhile.

30

Mia wondered what the visit was about. Was it good, or was it just wishful thinking on her part? She ran around the apartment, anxiously making sure everything looked tidy and clean. She had baked another cake, because now she knew Levin's aunt liked that kind.

Levin had gone to pick up Irmi. He was also curious about why she wanted to visit them, and so far she hadn't given any hints. He hadn't heard from his parents in over a month.

"Hi, Mia. How nice to see you again," Irmi greeted her.

"Hi, Mrs. Will. Nice to see you, too." Mia shook her hand and ushered her into the living room. "Would you like a cup of coffee and some cake?"

"Can't say no to that!"

They talked about anything and everything. Irmi asked about Mia's job and listened attentively. Finally, she turned to Levin. "Levin, I'm not visiting you just because I like Mia's cake," she began, "although that's a good reason, too."

He tensed. "So what *is* your reason?"

"You know that your parents are celebrating their silver wedding anniversary in a week. I was going to ask you if you'd like to come."

"Would I be welcome?" he asked.

"I think it would be a good occasion to make up with them, don't you?" Irmi said.

"How is that supposed to work? They don't accept Mia. Or has that changed?"

Mia could barely breathe—she felt sick. She wanted so much for Levin to get along with his parents. She felt that big, heavy rock in her stomach again.

"It might be better if you went alone. If they see you're making an effort, maybe they'll take a step toward you." Aunt Irmi laid her hand on his. "Make an effort."

"No, not after what happened on my birthday. I can't just act like I've forgotten their words." He shook his head.

"Levin." Mia's voice was shaky. "Listen to your aunt. I mean, they're your parents." She looked at him, pleading.

"It's completely out of the question. Either they accept our relationship, or this is settled for me."

His aunt gave him an annoyed look. "If both sides are so stubborn, this situation will never change. And you can't go on like this."

"That's not my problem. I didn't do anything to my parents. I didn't offend or hurt them, apart from the fact that I wasn't completely honest about my relationship with Mia. What they accused me of and how they're trying to put pressure on me is completely out of proportion." Levin jumped up and started pacing around the living room. "I will not be blackmailed!"

"Levin, please." Mia went over to him. "They're your parents, and it's their silver anniversary. That's an important celebration. You *have* to go."

"No, Mia, I'm definitely not doing that." Levin took her face between his hands. "Either they come to terms with my bringing you along, or I don't go."

He looked at her so stubbornly that Mia knew any argument would be useless.

"It's not as if I can't understand you, honey," Irmi said. "I'm so sorry about all of this. I hope for you two that James and Sonja come to their senses soon." She sighed and took another bite of cake. "Maybe we can hope for a miracle."

But that hope led nowhere, and Levin hadn't expected anything else. Aunt Irmi's attempts at communication came to nothing. All Levin's parents let him know was that they expected him to be at the party and that the invitation did not include Mia. Levin could only just barely conceal his anger from Mia. Although she had stopped trying to convince him to go, he could still tell that she was unhappy with the situation. But it wouldn't do much good to go to the party. Levin's anger about his parents' behavior would be like a wall between them, anyway. They would just have to answer people's questions about his whereabouts. That wasn't his problem.

Levin had to know how the celebration had gone. So on the following Sunday, he called his aunt. He had purposely gotten up early. Mia was still asleep; she didn't really need to hear this conversation. She had spent all of the last evening trying to persuade him to go to the celebration. She only gave up when Levin started ignoring her completely.

"Hi, Irmi," he said. Levin knew she usually got up early.

"Hi, honey. Well, are you calling for news?" She sounded serious.

"Yes, I'm curious," he answered honestly.

"Your parents were annoyed by your absence. I told them they shouldn't have expected anything else, but they wouldn't have any of it. The official reason for your absence was gastroenteritis."

"Guess that happens," Levin mumbled.

"Yes, I guess so. But now things are even worse between you. To make up for it, you'll really have to eat crow."

"Give me one reason why I should do that," Levin said. "As you just said, they shouldn't have expected anything else."

"All right, I've done my part to try to help solve this the nice way. I'll keep out of it now." He heard her sigh.

"Thank you, Irmi." Levin's voice softened. "I appreciate that you tried."

"Send Mia my greetings. I feel sorriest for her in this ordeal. It's clearly very hard on her."

"Yes, it is. But we'll deal with it," Levin said.

He set the table for breakfast, and then he crawled back into bed with Mia. She was still fast asleep. The two jobs and the situation with his parents were wearing her out. He carefully wrapped her in his arms and buried his face in her blond curls. "I'm so sorry for you, sweet thing," he whispered. Then he, too, fell asleep again.

Mia sighed quietly. She had a lot to do. It was a beautiful March day, and she had set the tables outside in front of the café. Many patrons were enjoying the first rays of the spring sun. Working outside was bearable in the area protected from the wind. Mia envied the patrons; she would love to sit down outside with a coffee now, too. She'd slept badly, just like the night before. Levin not going to his parents' silver-anniversary party was harder on her than she wanted to admit.

"Mia, you can take a break if you want," Mrs. Heller kindly offered. "I set up a table back in the yard, and you can take your break there."

"Oh, thank you," Mia said, pleased. She got herself a cup of coffee and seized the opportunity. She had just sat down when Mrs. Heller came back.

"Mia, there's a lady here who'd like to speak to you."

"To me?" She had no idea who it could be. "Did I make a mistake? Does she want to make a complaint?" Her heart started thumping. She thought back feverishly about her customers in the last few hours.

"I don't know. I'll ask her to come talk to you out here, OK? The café is too full."

"That's all right." Mia nodded, then got up from her chair. She still didn't understand. Mrs. Heller came back a few moments later, and Sonja Webber entered the yard behind her. Mia's heart just about failed her.

Sonja Webber was looking around her judgmentally. Her scowling gaze wandered over the yard and up the face of the building.

"Mrs. Webber," Mia said, her voice reduced to a scratch. When Sonja Webber glared at her, a shiver ran down her spine. The look was so hostile that Mia wished she could hide away in a corner somewhere.

"Mia, I'll be in the café," Rita Heller said.

"Yes, um, all right," she said. Then she pulled herself together and looked into Levin's mother's eyes. "What can I do for you?" she asked.

"Haven't you guessed, Mia Kessler?" she said coldly.

Mia tucked one of her blond curls behind her ear with a shaky hand. "Would you like to have a seat?"

"Here? No, thank you." Sonja Webber laughed scornfully. "Listen to me, Miss Kessler. I'm certain you know that Levin didn't come to our celebration on Saturday—and that was because of you."

"Yes, and I'm very sorry about that," Mia said.

"Are you? He embarrassed us in front of our relatives and our guests!" Levin's mother's voice kept rising. "This is all your influence, is it not? Levin would have never acted like this before he met you. He would never have exposed us to such a situation. He knows full well how important this celebration was. Good clients and influential citizens were present. But, no, he didn't come, and all because of you!"

It was only due to the busy atmosphere in the café that Mrs. Heller hadn't noticed anything. Now what should Mia do? She wanted to crawl under a rock and disappear. Levin's mother was right, and Mia was so terribly sorry about it all. Maybe she should just tell her that again. "Mrs. Webber, I–I just wanted to tell you that I really regret all this, j–just the situation and how it all turned out and—"

"Would you stop that stuttering," Levin's mother hissed. "So you're sorry, are you? Do you know what you should be sorry for? That you even put Levin into a situation like this! You have obviously seduced him so much that he's completely lost his mind. You are ruining his future and his reputation with this . . . this laughable relationship. Do you actually understand that? *That* is what you should be sorry for, Miss Kessler. You probably don't mind what people say about you. I'm certain you're used to people giving you strange looks. But it's completely different with my son. Unlike you, he actually does have something to lose. Do you see that?"

Sonja Webber's voice had become shriller and shriller, and Mia had inadvertently drawn back. This woman in front of her was unbelievably angry. Every word hit home. Of course she knew that Levin's mother was right, and she had every reason to hurl her anger at Mia. "I–I'm aware of that, but Levin and I, well, we love each other," Mia said over the lump in her throat.

"Love?" Sonja Webber laughed. "That may be what you believe—or better yet: That's what you want Levin to believe. He is your big chance to get a foothold in upper social circles. From psychopath to lawyer's wife! That's what you might call a quick promotion. But for Levin, this will be his downfall. Before you came into his life, he went out with respectable women—*educated* women with impeccable reputations. You're blocking him, Miss Kessler, in every way imaginable. Socially, professionally, and privately. If it weren't for you, Levin would surely already be in another relationship, but my son is much too decent to drop you. Don't you get it? He would stay with you out of pity, even if he were to look around elsewhere. And he will, sooner or later. Do you think you could ever be enough for him in the long run? You're very pretty, and your story is interesting, but that isn't fulfilling enough for a relationship." By now Mrs. Webber was practically screaming in Mia's face.

Mia tried to retreat, but Levin's mother just came closer and closer. She could feel how this woman was trying to crush her soul.

"You say you love him. If that's really true, you should have the decency to leave him so he can go on with a normal life. So he can fall in love again and have a relationship within his social class." Levin's mother's voice softened. Now she was even smiling at Mia. "Prove that you truly are a mature young woman. Use your wit, and make an effort. When we love, we only want the best for our partners—isn't that right?"

Mia fought back tears. What Mrs. Webber said was all true, and Mia knew it—deep down, she had known it from the beginning. She had been lost in an illusion, a beautiful dream. But now it seemed that the time to wake up had finally come. Mia had already ruined far too much for Levin. A tear rolled down her cheek and continued down her neck. Mia felt its path burning on her skin. "I–if we end our relationship, will you take him back? I mean, will you end your fight, then?" Mia asked hopefully.

Mrs. Webber smiled even more kindly now. "Of course, Mia. I see that you are reasonable. Levin, though, will be reluctant to end the relationship. He is much too stubborn right now. That's why I suggest that you leave him. You should write him a few lines, of course, because if you just disappear, he'd probably start a full-scale search. Levin is a responsible person, so I wouldn't put it past him." Then she opened her purse and pulled out a large envelope. "Leaving him will not be to your disadvantage, Mia. Here are ten thousand euros. Take the money, and start over. Just not in this city, please. I don't want Levin to be able to find you. Give him the chance to get his life back on track. Let him go."

Mia gave her a surprised look. What was this all about? Why would she take the money? It didn't mean anything to her. *Levin's mother is just being nice*, she reassured herself.

Mrs. Heller came out into the yard. "Mia, I need you out front again. It's very full, and I can't do it alone."

"I'll be right there," Mia said, hastily wiping a tear from her face.

"I won't bother your employee anymore," Mrs. Webber said, nodding at Mia's boss. "We're finished here."

Mrs. Heller went back inside. Then Sonja Webber turned to Mia. "I'm glad you understand me and will let go of Levin. You will be doing him a big favor, even though he may not be able to accept that at first."

Mia couldn't speak. The time she'd always feared had come. It hurt so badly, but she had been expecting the pain—and somehow, this sadness had always been in her. She had sensed it. Even with all her good luck recently, she had always sensed it.

31

"Mia, what's wrong?" Mrs. Heller's compassionate voice only made Mia's tears come faster. "What did that woman want?"

"Nothing. It wasn't important," Mia said. "There was some trouble, but we took care of it." Mia didn't know how she managed it, but somehow she forced a smile. "I'll just go clean myself up, and then I'll come help you."

"If you'd prefer to go home, I can call Evi or my husband." Mrs. Heller didn't look convinced.

"No, really! As I said, we took care of it." Mia gave Mrs. Heller's hand a short squeeze. "I'll be right back."

Mia slipped into the restroom. She looked terrible. The worst part wasn't even her tearstained face. She could see the deep despair that was mirrored in her eyes. *Get yourself together*, she ordered. She had seen this coming. The fear of this moment had always hung over everything, and now it was time to do the right thing. Levin had sacrificed so much for her; he'd done so much—now she had to give him his life back. That was her duty. Mia thought about the money. She still didn't understand what it was for. But she wouldn't keep it. It wasn't hers, and it was wrong to take it. Levin would surely be able to make use of it. With it, he could get by for a while after—yes, after she was gone. The tears threatened to come again, but then her sense of duty won out and she went back into the café.

She tried to concentrate, and the work did numb her a bit. But the worst was yet to come: seeing Levin. He always knew when something was wrong. It would cost her quite an effort to lie to him. It would probably be best if she told him something about a headache or nausea or something like that. Except she wouldn't be able to keep it up for long—she knew that much already. She'd have to act fast before she lost her courage. *And where would she go?* She didn't have to search long for the answer. She would go far, far away.

"Hey, sweet thing!" Levin called happily as Mia came home.

"Hi." Mia forced a smile and gave him a kiss on the tip of the nose.

"What's up? You're so pale." He took her face between his hands. "Did you see a ghost?"

"No, of course not." Mia shook her head, and then she turned away. "I just have a headache. There was a lot to do in the café."

That wasn't even a lie. By now, her head really was throbbing. She couldn't just turn off her thoughts, just like she couldn't get rid of the deep sadness that seemed to sit on her chest and keep her from breathing.

"Then go lie down. Are you hungry? I'll cook something for us." Levin put his arm around her shoulder and led her to the couch. He was worried. She looked almost as pale as when they first met. She'd seemed sickly to him then, too.

"No, I don't feel hungry." Mia stroked his cheek for a moment, then lay down on the couch. She wasn't tired at all, but maybe Levin would leave her alone for a bit.

She went to bed early. Now Levin was really worried. "Shall I drive you to see the doctor tomorrow?"

"No, you need to go to class. I'm sure I'll feel better tomorrow." She smiled at him again and went into the bedroom. It felt almost unbearable to lie down in this bed. It was definitely the most difficult place to be in this entire apartment. How many hours had they made love, laughed together, and made plans for the future here? Mia felt so awful. All this would be very hard on Levin. She could only hope for his sake that he'd start a new relationship as soon as possible. She swallowed. She couldn't bear to think of him holding somebody else in his arms, whispering tender words into her ear, making love to her.

Mia fought back tears. How had it even gotten this far? But the answer was so easy: she loved Levin more than anything else in the world, and she had been foolishly hoping they could have a life together.

When he came to bed, she pretended to be sleeping. Levin cuddled up and cradled her in his arms. He kissed her neck, just like he did every evening. All that familiar tenderness felt like torture now.

The next day, Mia went to a travel agency instead of the café. She didn't have the slightest idea how to book a flight or how much it would cost, but she had to start somewhere. She was lucky and got a flight for the next day to Casablanca. The friendly travel agent wondered about her not wanting a return flight. Mia had to confirm her wishes multiple times. The flight would cost almost three hundred euros. Mia was surprised it was so much. That would rip a gigantic hole in her budget, but she didn't want to hitchhike again. All she wanted to do was get far away very quickly. *One more day*, she kept telling herself, and then she made her way over to the café and the Italian restaurant. Mrs. Heller and Mr. Riccone had a right to know that she wouldn't be returning. Mrs. Heller was horrified and looked unhappy. Mia told her she needed to leave to take care of a sick relative. Luigi Riccone was initially angry because he wouldn't be able to find a replacement so soon, but then he showed some sympathy and hugged Mia.

"You can come back anytime," he said. Mia thanked him and nearly ran out of the restaurant—she didn't want to cry in front of him.

Levin was still at school when she came home. Mia took a sheet of paper and sat down at the dining table. Now she had to put this thing that was still so unbelievable to her into words. What should she tell him? She hated herself for lying to him, for hurting him—but that was exactly what she had to do now.

Later, Mia couldn't remember how many tries it had taken to write the letter or how many tears she'd shed in the process, but somehow she put the words on paper. Tomorrow, when Levin was at school, she would leave the letter on his bed, pack her backpack, and disappear from his life forever.

"Hi, sweet thing, how are you?" Levin found Mia in the kitchen as she prepared some dinner, and the smell was tempting.

"Fine, thanks." Mia tried to act as normal as possible and nestled up against him.

"How was your day at the café?" he asked.

"The usual. Very busy. The nice weather is attracting a lot of people. How was your day?" She kissed him on the nose and turned back to her cooking, glad to have something to keep her mind occupied.

Levin groaned. "God-awful, horribly boring—but I need to go to the lectures. This whole week is going to be terrible."

"Poor you." Mia attempted a smile. "We can eat in a minute."

"Great, I'm starving." He wrapped his arms around her waist and kissed the back of her neck, and then he let her go to carry a bowl into the living room. He was astonished: she had set the table beautifully and even opened a bottle of wine. Levin racked his brain for an explanation. Had he forgotten some date? "Is there some special occasion?" he asked, joining her back in the kitchen.

"What? No, I just thought I'd make it extra nice for us today," she said. For a moment she feared he'd realize it was a going-away dinner, but that was laughable.

"Great idea, sweet thing." He winked at her, excited about the food. And about Mia. Maybe this evening would be especially nice.

Levin wasn't disappointed, and Mia was very affectionate. He wholly enjoyed her caresses, although something seemed off. He couldn't put his finger on it, but there was a certain sadness in her eyes that had not escaped him. Still, the evening was just too perfect to worry about it. He could ask her about it tomorrow if she still looked so melancholy.

That night, Mia held on to Levin like she was drowning. She wanted to soak up as much tenderness as possible. She resolved to remember every second so she could invoke the memory when she was gone. And she didn't sleep; she watched just him. Time was too precious to waste on sleeping. When he got up the next morning, she had already made breakfast for him. She tried desperately not to let her emotions show.

"Hey, what's up?" Levin saw that she was shaking. Concerned, he reached for her hands.

"I slept badly, that's all," she said, trying to keep him from worrying.

"After that night? Incredible." Levin stroked her cheek. "Are you sure you don't want to see a doctor? You're so pale again."

"No, Mrs. Heller needs me. It'll be fine, don't worry." She shook her head. "You have to go," she reminded him.

"Yeah, unfortunately." Levin sighed. He didn't want to leave; his gut told him something was wrong. Mia was acting so strange. She seemed sickly again, and he didn't like it. But he really needed to get to class. And he knew that Mia was adamant that he take school seriously. He wanted to finish as quickly and as well as possible, because that was the only way he could take the strain of two jobs off Mia. "See you this afternoon." Levin pulled her into his arms once more. Mia gave him a long, tender kiss.

"See you." She lowered her eyes so he couldn't see her tears. But when the apartment door closed, the dam broke. She screamed out her pain, threw herself onto the bed, and cried hot, bitter tears. This was all so impossible; it just hurt too much. Mia got up, packed her backpack, and laid the apartment key and the envelope with the money on the bed. She'd added a thousand euros of her own money. She wished she could leave more for Levin, but she needed some, too.

The sound of the apartment door closing behind her seemed unnaturally loud to Mia. She hailed a taxi to take her to the airport. With her face puffy from crying, she wanted to meet as few people as possible.

"So, here we are." Mia jumped at the taxi driver's voice.

"Oh, right, thanks," she said. She paid the fare.

As he grabbed her backpack out of the trunk, he smiled at her. "Wish ya good luck with whatever you're doin'."

"Thanks, I think I'll need it," Mia replied, and then she entered the airport quickly, before she could change her mind. She stood in the big hall helplessly. Where did she need to go? And what did she need to do? Mia took a deep breath and went over to the help desk—she would start there.

Levin had no idea what was going on with him today. He just couldn't concentrate. He thought of last night's beautiful exertions. Afterward, he had slept like a log. But somehow there was a restlessness inside him that he couldn't explain. His thoughts wandered to Mia. He hoped with all his might that she was feeling better by now. She really had not looked good that morning. Maybe he should have stopped her from going to work. Levin resolved to call her during his break.

Mia had made it. Now she was sitting at the departure gate, waiting to board her plane. She pulled her cell phone out of her pocket and saw that Levin had called. She started shaking. Although she really didn't want to, she listened to her voice mails. Just to hear his voice one last time.

Hey, sweet thing, I just wanted to know how you're feeling. You were so pale again this morning. I'm starting to get worried. Please promise me that you'll go to the doctor if you don't feel good, OK? Can't wait to see you, my angel. Last night with you was beautiful.

Mia swallowed heavily. Then she ran into one of the restrooms and threw her SIM card into the garbage. It was time to let Levin go.

32

Levin looked at his phone in frustration. Either Mia hadn't noticed his call or she hadn't had the time to talk. He knew she was often so occupied in the café that she didn't hear her phone or couldn't call back—still, he was feeling more anxious by the minute. He couldn't tell where that feeling was coming from, but it kept getting stronger.

"I think I'm skipping lunch with you today," he told Kai.

"Yeah? Why? Don't feel up to the cafeteria food? Is Mia home?"

"No, Mia's not around—she's working at the café. But she was acting strange this morning and seemed sick. Also, she's not picking up her phone. I'm going to stop by."

"All right, you mother hen," his friend laughed.

"I know, I know." Levin felt like he'd been called out.

"Say hi to her for me." Kai thumped him on the shoulder.

Finally, the passengers were allowed to board. Mia anxiously clutched her boarding pass and followed the stream of people. She had chosen a window seat, remembering the flight back from Spain all too well.

It had been wonderful to look out of the window. Once in the air, everything else seemed so meaningless and small. Maybe she would feel better on the plane, but somehow she didn't quite believe that.

Upon entering the café, Levin was surprised to find only Mia's boss and another waitress. Mia was nowhere to be seen. The indistinct feeling became stronger. Now he knew something was wrong. Had she gone to the doctor? Levin headed for the counter where Mrs. Heller was making a cappuccino.

"Hi, Mrs. Heller. I'm Levin Webber, Mia's boyfriend," he introduced himself.

Mrs. Heller looked up. "Right, I remember. You've been here before," she said with a smile. "What can I do for you?"

"I'm looking for Mia. Is she here?"

"Here?" All the color drained from the elderly lady's face. "Mia resigned yesterday. She said a relative of hers wasn't well, so she needed to leave immediately to take care of her. She said she didn't know when she'd be back. Don't you know about that?" Mrs. Heller seemed downright shocked.

But that was nothing compared to what Levin was feeling. He was suddenly so dizzy that he needed to hold on to the counter for support. "Resigned?" he barely managed to choke out. "I don't understand." The feelings of helplessness and confusion were spreading through him and turning into a big, heavy weight centered in the pit of his stomach.

"I'm so sorry. I don't understand it, either," Mia's boss—no, her *ex*-boss—answered.

"Thank you," he said, and then rushed out of the café.

Levin didn't consciously remember the drive home, but when he arrived at the apartment building, he jumped out of the car and sprinted up the stairs.

At first glance, everything seemed normal. The kitchen was tidy. Nothing pointed toward anything being wrong. Then he wandered into the bedroom. He cried out when he saw a letter and a big brown envelope lying on the bed.

"No!"

Mia tensed as the airplane started moving. She watched the airport and the lively activity around it, but despite the distraction, there was a huge lump in her throat. She thought of Levin. He was probably still at school. She didn't want to imagine his reaction when he came home and found her letter. Mia tried desperately to swallow her tears, but it was pointless. She was afraid for Levin and afraid of the future. What would become of her? She had plans, and there were some places she wanted to visit. But then what? Up until now she hadn't had to think about it, but soon the time would come for her to deal with her life.

The plane reached its takeoff position. Mia heard the howling of the engines, then the thrust began, and she was pushed back into her seat. As the plane left German soil, Mia's deep despair came back in full force, and she started quietly crying.

Levin approached the bed as though moved by invisible strings. He ignored the brown envelope. He reached for the letter, recognizing Mia's handwriting. It felt like his insides were being ripped out.

> My dearest Levin,
>
> I'm sure you're wondering—with good reason— what all this is about, and it's hard for me to give you an answer. I thought for a long time about how

I could put this into words. But the time has finally come to not think about myself anymore, but about what is the best for you. I clung to you much too hard without thinking about the consequences for you. A future with me isn't good for you, and that has become clearer and clearer to me. There's no way for me to avoid making your life more difficult, and if there's something that I want more than anything in this world, it's for you to be able to lead a happy and carefree life. With me, that wouldn't be possible, although I really wished and hoped for it. I love you and always will. That's why I'm setting you free. Promise me that you'll become a great, successful lawyer, and please don't try to find me. Please don't worry about me. I'll be all right—just like you, do you understand? Thanks for the most wonderful time of my life, Levin. You'll always be in my heart.

Mia

PS There's money in the envelope. Please take it.

"No! No! No! Oh, fuck, Mia, no," he screamed.

Levin ran around the bedroom like a caged animal; then he tore through the entire apartment.

"Come back! Fuck! Come back right now!"

He kicked the couch and smashed everything in his path, but the short-lived pain couldn't really distract him from the all-consuming one that was now creeping through him bit by bit. He was so terribly angry at Mia, then drowning in despair, then angry again. It couldn't be true, and he refused to believe it. He was sure it must be a joke or a misunderstanding. They loved each other beyond all measure, and they belonged together.

Levin threw himself down on his bed and stared at the ceiling. He barely registered the tears running down his face. Then he jumped up, paced through the apartment again, and checked the bedroom closet. A few of her things were missing, and her backpack was gone. Slowly it began to sink in that it really was possible: She had left him. Mia was gone. Levin sobbed loudly. He had never heard himself cry like that, and it sounded surreal, not like himself. But then his pain wasn't from this world, either. Something had been ripped out of him, and he wasn't the same person anymore—not at all.

"Fuck!" he screamed again and again, but at some point his common sense broke through the despair. "Think, think!" he shouted at himself.

Something must have triggered Mia's actions. He wouldn't allow himself to consider that maybe she just didn't love him anymore. He had to stick to the facts and think logically. How did she come to the decision to take this step? She had been strange in the last few days; he had noticed that. Had something happened?

Levin jumped up from his bed. He looked for Mia's therapist's number. Thank God the slip of paper with her address was still hanging on the bulletin board. He feverishly punched in her cell number, hoping to God she'd pick up.

"Yes?" the therapist answered. She sounded a little gruff. Maybe Levin was calling during her lunch break, but he really didn't care about that in the slightest.

"This is Levin Webber, I'm Mia Kessler's boyfriend."

"Oh, right, hi. What is it? Is something wrong with Mia?"

"You could say that. She's gone. She left me. She just left me a letter and a lot of money, and I can't come up with any explanation for this." He swallowed his tears. "Please, do you know anything?"

"What? Mia's gone?"

Levin could hear the surprise and dismay in her voice, and his hope of finding a logical explanation faded. "Yes! Something must have happened—did she say anything to you?"

"No, I'm so sorry, I don't know about anything. I haven't seen her for a while. It's my lunch break right now. Do you have time? We could sit and talk a bit."

Levin was grateful for the offer, and he just had to do something now, so he grabbed his car keys and Mia's letter and drove over to the therapist's office.

"Thank you for taking the time for me." Levin tried to smile.

"No problem. I'm surprised by this turn of events." Silke invited Levin into the office. Levin handed her the letter, and she read it. "This is Mia's handwriting?"

"Yes."

"Has anything unsettled Mia lately? However insignificant it might seem?"

Levin told her about the disaster with his parents. Then he told her about Mia's second job and what her boss had told him earlier. "If all of this became too much for her to handle, she could have at least told me," he said.

"I'm sure everything in this letter is true. Mia loves you, Levin, I don't doubt that, but she also believes she's not good for you. Although it's not written in here, I think it has something to do with your parents and their social position. Mia has very low self-esteem. I'd thought it had improved with her job, but she wants to protect you, the person she loves more than anything else. And I think she's afraid that she can't. That's why she left."

"Do you think she might have gone to her grandmother's?" He didn't believe the story Mia had told her boss, but he needed to consider everything.

"No, I don't think so. Why would Mia want to be with her? And Mia would have told you about something like that."

"Should I call her and ask her about Mia?"

"The grandmother tried to have her permanently committed. If she hears that Mia's left now, she may try again. No, I think we can count that out, but wait a minute." Silke reached for the files and picked out Mia's grandmother's number. "Let's try something." She winked at Levin.

"Hello, Mrs. Kessler? This is Sabine Winter from the Workers' Welfare Association," she purred into the receiver. "Your neighbor told us you were feeling ill and asked us to send a caregiver to you. I wanted to ask when you would like us to come." There was a short pause. "Well, your neighbor notified us that you were in need of assistance. Have you engaged someone else?" Levin had to admit that she was a good actress. "Oh, I'm sorry, there must have been a mistake then. But I'm glad to hear that you're well. Good-bye." And Silke hung up.

"The old lady is vigorous and doesn't sound at all ill. She says that she doesn't need a caregiver and is doing fine on her own. I believe her," she said, turning back to Levin. "But there's something else: Where did Mia get so much money? You said she looked for a second job so you could get by. With this much up her sleeve, that wouldn't have been necessary."

"I don't know, either," Levin said with a sigh. "I can't imagine where she got the money. She used to have an account that her grandmother set up for her. Maybe it's from there." Levin ran his hand through his hair. "I don't think she borrowed it. Mia isn't the type to owe anyone something."

"So the only thing that remains is a reserve fund." Silke lifted her eyebrows and looked at Levin. "Can that be the only explanation?"

Levin laughed bitterly. "I know what you're thinking now. I thought of that, too, but no. My parents would never go so far as to offer her money. They're against our relationship, but that? No, it's impossible." Levin shook his head vigorously.

"Well, whatever the case, I can't help you any more than I have."

"And if you send out a search for her?"

"Search for her? What do you mean? A full-scale manhunt? There's no reason for that. Besides, do you really think you'd be doing Mia a favor by letting her get caught again? Levin, I know it's hard for you, but I suggest you respect Mia's decision. You should also consider that some relationships just don't last." Silke shook her head. "This seems strange to me, too, but I see no reason for action. I'm sorry."

"Well, that's just great!" Levin said with a snort. Then he pulled himself together. "Still, thank you very much."

"You should call Lydia—maybe she knows something."

"I'll do that." Levin hung his head as he left the office. He sat in his car for a bit, beating his fists on the steering wheel. Then he texted Kai to tell him he wouldn't be coming back to school today. He really didn't feel like focusing on his boring courses. He drove home and punched in the number of the clinic in Hamburg, but he didn't get anywhere with that, either. Lydia was just as perplexed as Silke had been. Neither of them could help. He couldn't stay here, though; he was starting to get cabin fever. He had to talk to someone, and he needed ideas and opinions. Everything inside him was spinning.

"Levin, honey. How nice," Aunt Irmi said, beaming at him, but then she grew serious again. "What's wrong? You're so pale," she said, offering him her arm. She guided him onto her couch. "Is something wrong with Mia?" she asked.

Levin silently handed her the letter. Irmi groped for her glasses and read it. "Oh, my goodness—that's terrible," she said. "What happened?"

"I'd like to know that, too," he said desperately. "We love each other so much. It can't just be over now." Tears filled his eyes. He didn't want to cry, but there was no stopping it. "What am I supposed to do without her?"

33

"I don't know what this is about. Only one thing is clear to me, Levin: Mia must love you very much."

"Yeah, so much that she left me." He stubbornly wiped the tears from his face, and then he looked at Irmi. "Do you think Mom and Dad have something to do with this? The therapist thought that might be the case, because Mia left me so much money and I can't explain where she got it."

Irmi shrugged. "They're definitely the strongest force against you and Mia. But would they really go that far? I don't know, I don't want to think so."

"I don't, either," Levin said.

"Shall I talk to them? I can see how they react. Or do you want to drive over there yourself?"

"And tell them that Mia's gone so they can be glad? No thanks!" Levin said.

"Oh, honey, I'm so sorry." Irmi hugged him. "Just what was the girl thinking? And where could she be?"

Levin shook his head. "Mia won't be easy to find. It's possible that she went to Morocco."

"Morocco?"

"That's where she was off to when we met the first time. I can't bear to think about her traveling alone. I'm damned scared for her." He tried to swallow the big lump in his throat. "I hope she doesn't do anything stupid."

"What do you mean?" Irmi asked, alarmed. "Do you think she'd hurt herself?"

"No! Uh, no, probably not. I hope not." Levin kept running his fingers through his hair. "But she's still so naive at times. I'm just scared she'll meet the wrong person."

"What can be done? Should we hire a detective to find her? Maybe she's still in town. Maybe she went into hiding at a friend's place."

"I'll call around, but I don't think she's here anymore. She would never put our friends in such a difficult situation." Levin hastily wiped away his tears. "But a detective might be a good idea. I have enough money now," he said with a sad laugh.

"I'm paying for that," Irmi said. "Who knows, maybe he can figure something out."

"Thank you." Levin planted a kiss on her cheek.

Levin began calling all his friends. It was early afternoon. He didn't reach everybody, but he got through to Geli, the most important person in his eyes. She was just as surprised as everyone else who'd heard about Mia's disappearance. At least calling around distracted him from brooding and his enormous fear for Mia's safety.

Later, Levin picked up Irmi so they could drive over to the private-investigation firm she'd found. He wasn't so sure it was right to snoop after Mia like that. Maybe Silke was right and he should accept Mia's decision. But then he stilled his conscience by focusing on his worry for her. If he found her, he vowed to just talk to her in peace—and if, after that, she insisted on her decision to leave him behind, he would accept it. Or at least that was his intention.

The detective asked for several photos of Mia and listened to their story. He promised to begin that day.

"I'll try my best, Mr. Webber," he said. "It's just that if someone doesn't want to be found, that's a tricky situation. But some folks may remember such a pretty blonde." He nodded at Levin. "I'll get back to you."

That night, Kai and Geli came by. Levin was grateful. He would probably have lost it, alone in the apartment. Geli was disconcerted; she, too, had tears in her eyes. "I just can't believe this. Gosh, you were such a great couple, and when Mia looked at you she was so happy. Your love was almost tangible." She looked at Levin seriously. "Sorry to say it like this, but all this only started when the trouble with your parents began. You really don't think they influenced Mia? And then all that money—where could that have come from?"

"I don't know what to believe anymore, but Irmi's going to talk to them. Maybe she can learn something. All I want is for her to come back!"

Mia examined the small room cautiously. She hadn't been expecting much for the price, but these quarters shocked her. The bedding was dirty, just like the towels, and she was sure she'd seen a creepy-crawly thing disappearing into one of the cracks in the floor. She began scratching herself involuntarily. This room repulsed her, but she was too exhausted to go find something different. Tomorrow she would get a train ticket to Marrakesh; she really wanted to see that city. *Keep busy!* she kept telling herself. She hoped she wouldn't think of Levin so much then.

She really didn't want to see the bathroom, but she desperately needed to pee. The next abomination was waiting for her there. It was dirty and didn't smell very nice. Thanks to the guidebook, she was prepared for a lack of toilet paper, but that was the smallest problem. Somehow, Mia brought herself to step into the shower. Afterward, she felt her tiredness more distinctly. She turned the bedding inside out, covered the pillow with her towel, and lay down on the sheets. She had barely closed her eyes when she heard something scurrying around.

"Whoever's there—please stay away from the bed," she said into the darkness. She noticed that her voice sounded shaky and rough, but that wasn't surprising. She thought of Levin and could no longer stop the tears from flowing. She wondered what he was doing, how he'd taken it. She tried to put herself in his shoes. In his place, she would probably feel betrayed and very, very lonely.

"I'm sorry, so endlessly sorry," she whispered. Then she remembered that she still had her sleeping pills. She thought about taking one but decided against it. She felt she deserved the pain, and who knew how things would develop here? Maybe she'd need the pills another time and be glad the package was still almost full.

The next morning, Levin didn't drive to school. He had no energy left, and his classes were the last thing on his mind. His aunt had invited him over for breakfast. Levin was interested in hearing what she had to tell him. She'd been with his parents last night. He arrived at Irmi's house.

"Levin—you look terrible," she chided as she opened the door.

"I know, I feel terrible, too," he said, groaning. He and Kai had gotten pretty wasted the night before. His head pounded.

Irmi had already set the table, and it looked old-fashioned but chic.

"Coffee?"

"Yes, please—gallons," he said. He wondered if he could stomach a roll. He wasn't hungry, but he knew he needed to get something in his stomach. Yesterday he hadn't been able to eat at all.

"I talked openly about all of this with your parents yesterday," she said. "I thought that was best. I hope you don't mind."

"So, did they break out in victory dances when they heard that Mia was gone?" he said.

"Your father seemed honestly taken aback but didn't seem to mind. Sonja didn't say much. When I told them how much money Mia had left you, they were both very surprised, or at least it seemed that way to me." Irmi sighed. "I don't want to accuse them of anything. I'm pretty sure your father has nothing to do with Mia's disappearance."

"But Mom?" Levin could feel his anger bubbling to the surface.

"Sonja has always been very ambitious when she wants something, but I can't believe this of my sister. She loves you, and even though she doesn't think Mia is the right choice for you, I can't imagine she would do that to her son." Irmi shook her head. Now she looked directly into Levin's eyes. "But your father wants me to tell you that he's sorry for you about Mia's disappearance. You're invited to stop by anytime."

"How nice!" His words were dripping with sarcasm. "If I visit them, it will only be to question them about this," he said. "But first I'm going to wait and see what the detective finds."

"I think that's a good decision. Maybe this will be solved in a completely different way," Irmi said. "And maybe Mia will change her mind and come back. Who knows, maybe her desire for you will win in the end."

"I can only hope so. I would welcome her with open arms."

"I can imagine. I've always said it, nothing happens without a reason, but I'm slowly starting to doubt if that's really true," Irmi said sadly.

Mia was glad to have caught the train to Marrakesh. She hadn't gotten much sleep last night—her lovesickness and her unwanted creepy-crawly roommates had kept her worrying. Now Mia was completely exhausted. She sat down with a sigh, untied her head scarf, and leaned into the upholstery. Hopefully nobody on the train would harass her. She'd discovered quickly that as a blond woman traveling alone in Morocco, she was constantly being confronted with all kinds of invasive attitudes. Mia found it hard to defend herself, and she usually just hurried to get away. Finally, she'd found a clothing store and bought herself a head scarf. At least now her blond curls didn't attract attention right away.

"May we sit with you?"

Mia groaned inwardly. She opened her eyes and saw an elderly couple. They weren't natives; their skin was a shade lighter. "Yes, of course," she answered. They sat down across from her.

The lady smiled at Mia. "Are you from Germany?"

"Yes," Mia said. "Is my accent that strong?" she asked, feeling insecure.

"No, that it isn't, but we're French, and we hear the difference right away," the lady said with a twinkle in her eye.

"Ah, I see." Mia cleared her throat, embarrassed. Up until now she had been getting along well with her French, and being recognized by real French people was really no disgrace. At least the two of them seemed fairly nice. Mia relaxed a bit. She was sick of all those pushy men, and she wanted her peace and quiet. Apart from that, it was much nicer here in the train than it had been in her dirty room in Casablanca.

"The ride will take about three and a half hours," the man explained to his wife. To Mia, he said, "May I ask you something?"

"Yes, of course."

"Are you traveling alone?" He pointed at the empty seat next to her.

"Yes."

Then the woman addressed her. "You're pretty courageous. I wouldn't dare do that." She grimaced. "The gentlemen here can be quite intrusive."

Mia sighed. "Yes, it's true. That's why I bought this head scarf."

"Are you going to Marrakesh, or are you traveling on?"

"I'm going to Marrakesh. I have a book about Morocco, and it looked like one of the most fascinating cities."

"I can confirm that." The man smiled at her. "I've been there a few times before for business. Now that I'm retired, I told myself I'd show my wife all the places that I liked best. And Marrakesh is at the very top of the list." He tenderly touched his wife's cheek. Again, Mia was painfully reminded how very alone she was.

"Have you already planned what you'd like to see?" he said, turning his attention back to Mia.

"Yes." Mia dug through her backpack and got out her travel guide. She showed him all the places she wanted to visit.

"Good choices. But I do have a few recommendations. Would you like to hear them?"

"Of course, please," Mia said with interest.

The man talked, and Mia wrote down everything he told her in a small notepad.

"You're welcome to join us if you like," the woman said, smiling at her.

Mia looked at her, unsure. Did she really mean that? She was traveling with her husband, and wouldn't Mia just be a third wheel? "Really?" she said.

"Yes, if you want to travel with two old folks," the man agreed with his wife.

Mia smiled back at them shyly. Maybe that would be a good idea, and maybe she wouldn't have to worry about unwanted attention so much. "I would love to accept your offer, but if I'm disturbing you, please tell me right away, all right? I really don't want to ruin your vacation."

"Why would you? We have two adult children who don't care for travel. We would be happy for your company," the man said.

A smile flitted over Mia's face. "Thank you."

"Have you found anything yet?" Levin drummed the tabletop impatiently.

"What do you think? We only started with this case yesterday," the detective said. "One of my coworkers showed the photo around the train station, but nobody remembered seeing her. Then we tried the taxi drivers. We were successful there. One driver remembered taking her to the airport. So your speculation that she might have traveled to Morocco seems to be correct. A colleague is trying to get his hands on the passenger lists from all the flights to Morocco that day, but it's not that easy—it's illegal."

"I know," Levin said sheepishly, "but it's important."

"We're also going to talk to the people in the café and the restaurant again. She may have dropped a hint where she wanted to go."

"I can do that," Levin offered. He'd been planning to talk to Mrs. Heller again. Yesterday he'd been too surprised and horrified to think about what to ask.

"OK, then. As I said, we're on it. We're using all our tricks. At the moment I can't tell you more than that."

Levin thanked the detective. Then he dug for a picture of his mother. He got a sick feeling. Was he really about to accuse her? Maybe he was wrong, but he really needed to know what happened. And if he found out that his parents had nothing to do with Mia's disappearance, he could at least allow himself the option of making up with them. Not yet, for the wounds were still too fresh, but he couldn't completely rule it out—nor did he want to.

He entered the little café, his heart pounding. Even this place made him nostalgic. It was here that Mia had taken her first steps into working life. She had been so proud about getting her job here, and she was so intent on doing it well from the very beginning. Levin fought that wistful thought. Then he caught sight of Mrs. Heller working the coffee machine behind the counter. "Hi, Mrs. Heller." Levin gave her his friendliest smile.

"Oh, hello." She smiled, then became serious again. "Have you found out anything about Mia?"

"Not very much," Levin answered sadly. "But I do have a few questions for you. Maybe you can help me."

"I would love to, but I don't think I know anything useful. Ask anything you want, though." She nodded at him.

"Had you noticed anything about Mia lately? Was she especially nervous or anxious? Was there an incident that troubled her?" His voice was rough; Levin was unbelievably nervous.

"Hmm." Mrs. Heller twisted her mouth. "She didn't have any problems with patrons, or none that I knew of. But one incident was strange, and that would have been three days ago. A woman visited Mia. The two of them talked in the yard. After that, Mia was in tears. I asked her what happened. She only said that there had been trouble, but it had been taken care of. I was going to send her home, but she declined and just went to freshen up a bit. After that she continued to work and seemed to have gotten a grip on herself."

Levin looked at Mrs. Heller in shock. "Can you remember what that woman looked like? Was she an elderly lady with short gray hair, about this tall?" Levin motioned at his shoulder with his hand. Maybe it had been Mia's grandmother. He didn't want to think of the alternative haunting his thoughts.

"No, the lady had dark blond hair, a pageboy haircut. And she was dressed elegantly in a ladies' suit that looked like it was from an expensive designer."

Levin felt the color drain from his face. He closed his eyes in shock. Then he pulled his wallet out of his pocket and took out a photo of his mother. "Was it this woman?" he asked in a shaky voice.

The elderly lady put on her glasses. Then she nodded. "Why, yes, it was. So you know her?"

Levin laughed. "Oh, yes, I know her—or at least I thought I did."

"So then you know now where Mia is?" Mrs. Heller inquired hopefully.

"No, but now I know why she left." He swallowed hard against the tears—this time they were tears of anger. "Thank you for your time."

"I'm glad to help."

"And please understand that right now I can't tell you more about why Mia left." Levin knew that she'd be curious.

"If you find Mia, please send her my best regards. She's such a nice and hardworking girl. The patrons liked her a lot. My husband and I like her, too."

"I will," Levin answered, touched. "I know she'd be happy to hear it."

Levin walked slowly back to his car. The shock had nearly paralyzed him. So it was really true. It had been his mother. Everything made a cruel kind of sense. He felt nausea rising inside him. He reached for his cell phone and called his aunt. "It was her. My own mother drove her away," he choked out painfully.

"What?" Irmi's voice sounded unusually shrill. "Are you sure?"

"Absolutely sure." Levin relayed his conversation with Mia's boss.

"Levin, I'm as shocked as you are. I wouldn't have believed that of her. My God, how could she go that far? What are you going to do now, honey?"

"I'll drive over there. One last time—and then never again," Levin explained.

"I'll come with you. I have something to say to my sister about this, too," she said.

34

Levin was too shocked to be angry. He tried to clear his head and somehow understand what had happened, but it was nearly impossible. Still, he remembered the money. He took a detour to pick up the envelope. Then he drove to Irmi's. She was white as a sheet when she got into the car with Levin.

"I can't believe all this, I'm actually feeling sick," she said, appalled.

"Then you're feeling the same as I am," Levin said. He had to force himself to concentrate on traffic. The closer he got to his parents' house, the hotter his insides boiled. Once they arrived in front of the house, Levin grabbed the envelope. He already had his hand on the doorknob when Irmi put a calming hand on his shoulder.

"Levin, even though you have every right to be angry, try to remain calm. Prove to them you won't come down to their level."

"I can't promise, but I'll try," he said, and then they approached the house together. Levin rang the doorbell even though he had a key. His mother opened the door.

"Levin. Irmi. What a surprise." She seemed nonplussed, but not truly shocked. Her gaze wandered to the envelope in Levin's hand. Her expression slipped for a moment. For Levin, that was all the proof he needed.

"A surprise? Why, Mom? How long did you think it would take me to figure out what happened?" His pulse was racing, but he was still relatively calm.

"I don't know what you're talking about." Sonja Webber was in control of herself again and played clueless.

"Sonja, aren't you going to invite us inside?" Irmi broke in.

"Certainly." Levin's mother smiled at her. "Come in, your father's in his office."

"Could you please get him? He should hear what I have to say. Then I won't have to waste my time repeating myself," he instructed her.

His mother seemed distraught, but she still kept a grip on herself. "You're speaking in riddles, but of course I'll go get him."

Levin kept the envelope clutched in his hand while they waited for his father. Irmi kept stroking his arm, but it didn't help. Of course it didn't.

"Levin." His father approached him with a serious expression. "What brings you to us?"

"Probably something other than what you were expecting."

His father raised his eyebrows. "Well, then, do tell." He motioned toward the couch.

"I prefer to stand," Levin said coldly. Then he pointed at the envelope. "Something in here belongs to you, isn't that right?" He turned to his mother.

"I don't understand," she said, turning up her nose slightly.

Levin's carotid artery threatened to burst. "Still? Fine, then, Mom, I'll explain it to you." He took a step toward her. "In this envelope are the eleven thousand euros you paid Mia so she'd leave me!" He threw the envelope at her, and she caught it.

For a moment there was a deathly silence; then James Webber spoke up. "What's all this about? Why should your mother have done something like that? That's completely absurd."

"*Absurd* is the wrong adjective," Levin answered. "Try *despicable* or *inhuman*." He scrutinized his father, but he couldn't tell if he was really innocent. He was too much of a lawyer and had a good poker face. Levin knew that all too well.

"How dare you assume that of me," his mother said. Her voice wasn't as firm as it had been in the beginning.

"Mom—do you really want me to explain how I know?"

"I demand to know why you're assaulting your mother with such accusations." His father looked at him seriously.

"She showed up at Mia's café three days ago. She talked to Mia, and after that Mia was crying. Mia's boss recognized Mom. I showed her a photo." Levin turned to his mother and gave her an icy stare. "Two days later, Mia disappeared. She left me a letter and this envelope full of money. Mia could never have gotten her hands on this much cash. At first I didn't believe anyone could have been so cruel as to offer her money to leave me, but after speaking with Mia's boss, I know the truth. I would never, ever in my life have believed you capable of something like this." He lowered his gaze, unable to look at her any longer. Levin's composure slipped.

"That is an outrageous accusation to make," James Webber exclaimed, looking at his wife. "What do you say to that, Sonja? Were you at the café? Did you talk to Levin's girlfriend? Did you offer her money?"

Sonja Webber was struggling for words.

Irmi took a step toward her. "Sonja, finish this. Tell the truth. Tell him what's going on."

"Why are you butting in?" Sonja Webber hissed at her. "This is none of your business!"

"I demand to know now if there's something to this!" His father's voice rose.

"And if there is?" Sonja Webber looked into her husband's eyes. "I did it for Levin! That girl is a bad influence on him, and you know it! What is he supposed to do with someone like that? She's ill, and who knows if she's dangerous! Levin has splendid future prospects, and you know very well that a girl like that can only do him damage—or have you suddenly changed your mind?"

"No, I agree. But goodness, Sonja—so it's true?" James Webber ran his fingers through his hair. "Did you offer her money to leave Levin?"

"Yes, I did." Sonja Webber crossed her arms in front of her chest. "I gave her ten thousand euros."

"That's unbelievable," James Webber whispered. "Have you lost your mind?"

"Don't act as if you aren't happy about it, too!" Levin's mother yelled. "You were just as much against her."

"Not against her, but against the relationship. That is true. But I had hoped Levin would see sense by himself one day." James Webber sank down onto the couch and poured himself a glass of whiskey from the side table.

"Ha, and what if it hadn't happened so quickly?" his wife defended herself. "Just think how Levin snubbed us by not coming to our silver-anniversary party. Did you really want to wait for something like that to happen again? For him to possibly even marry her? I have Levin's best interests at heart. I had to act this way!" Her voice was sounding shrill now. Levin looked at her with a mixture of disbelief and horror.

"I know of only one person who truly had Levin's best interests at heart," Irmi spoke up. "And that was the girl who took up two jobs so Levin could continue school undisturbed. My God, have you never grasped how much those two love each other? Mia left *out of love for him*. She made the greatest sacrifice for Levin that could ever have been asked of her. How can anyone be so blind and cruel? I'm ashamed of you, Sonja, like I've never been of anybody ever before!"

Levin's mother only waved her off. "Sometimes one must take the hard road."

"You'd better be quiet now," James Webber barked at his wife. Then he turned to Levin. "Levin, I'm sorry—your mother obviously went too far. Although I can understand her reasons, it wasn't right."

"Yeah? You think it wasn't right? Do you know how little I care about what *you* think? I only care about Mia." Levin shook his head. He really wanted to have it out with his mother, but that seemed so unimportant to him now.

"Where did she go? Could you contact her? You said she disappeared?"

"What's all this sudden interest in her, Dad?" Levin asked him bitterly. "Yes, Mia's gone, and I don't know more than that. We hired a private detective to find out more."

"A private detective?" Sonja Webber responded. "Isn't that a bit over the top? I mean, if she was so sure of her love, she wouldn't have left you in the first place. I could have offered her anything, and she still wouldn't have done it."

Irmi turned to her. "Mia's a girl with low self-esteem, and you know that perfectly well. You experienced firsthand how insecure she is, and you exploited precisely that weakness. She already thought she wasn't good for Levin, and then you came along and rubbed salt into the wound."

"Well, she isn't good for him," Sonja Webber responded.

"Mia is my life," Levin said quietly. "She's my everything. She would do anything just to make me happy." His voice was threatening to break. "She is good for me," he added. Then he turned to leave.

"Wait, Levin." His father jumped up and blocked his path, the envelope in hand. "You said there were eleven thousand euros in here, but your mother mentioned ten thousand. Did Mia add an extra thousand herself?"

Levin nodded. It only just sank in. Now she had even less money. His fear for her welled up again.

"Take it." His father handed him the envelope.

"No thanks."

"Then at least take Mia's money." James Webber reached into the envelope and handed Levin a thousand euros.

"I'm only taking it so I can give it back to her someday," Levin replied.

His father followed him to the door. "Levin, I know you're disappointed and angry now. As I said, I don't approve of your mother's behavior. But maybe we can have a quiet talk when you're not so shaken anymore. All sadness considered, you need to think of your future, too," he said urgently. "I mean, you'll be a lawyer soon, and maybe we could still get together sometime."

"My future just disappeared. I'm dying with fear for her. I'm more than just sad. Don't you understand?"

"I do, but—"

"We should get together? I'll only do that if you separate from Mom. Otherwise, we go our separate ways here," Levin said with a furtive glance.

"Don't be ridiculous." His father looked at him indignantly.

"What's so ridiculous about that? You expected the same of me." He laughed bitterly. "Don't worry, I'm not as pathetic as you. Stay with your beloved, upstanding wife. Maybe you even deserve each other. All I care about is finding Mia. I don't care about anything else right now." Levin reached for the doorknob, then doubled back.

"Irmi, I'm leaving. Are you coming?" he called.

"No, honey. You go ahead, I still have something to resolve here," she answered.

Back in the car, Levin inhaled deeply. He was astonished by his own composure. He hadn't wanted to make a huge scene in front of his parents, but none of that mattered anymore. His worry for Mia outweighed everything else. At least now he knew exactly why she'd left, and he could even understand what she'd done, from her point of view. Mia had been through so much rejection in her life that something like this would naturally throw her off. His mother had gone about it in a clever way. She had put her finger right in the wound, and Mia hadn't been able to defend herself. Levin rested his head on the steering wheel. How would he go on? He was about to lose his mind with worry. And if she was really in Morocco, where should he start looking?

Despair was spreading through him, but he pushed the emotion back with all his might. Maybe the detective would find out something. Even the tiniest trace would be helpful. He just couldn't give up, not yet. But his hope that Mia would return to him was shrinking minute by minute. The house door opened, and Levin became aware that he was still sitting in the car. He quickly started the engine. He had no intention of having another conversation with his father or—even worse—his mother, but it was Irmi who came outside. She glanced in his direction, astonished.

Levin got out and opened the passenger-side door. "Would you like a ride?" he called to his aunt.

"Yes, please, honey. Your father ordered a cab for me, but I'd prefer to ride with you."

"He didn't offer to drive you?" Levin inquired, aghast.

"He did. But I didn't feel like it." Irmi shook her head. "I'm so shocked. I can only say again that I'm ashamed."

"You don't have to be. You didn't do anything."

"You know what's the most tragic part?" Irmi said.

"No. What?"

"Both Mia and your mother acted out of misunderstood love for you. And both of them plunged you into the deepest despair with it."

"My mother can't possibly love me," Levin said. "Otherwise she never would have done that."

"Oh, yes, Levin. She loves you. Except she made a huge, unforgivable mistake. She still won't see it, but I just gave her my opinion about her behavior. And your father will also get it across to her what a disaster she's created. She'll see in time."

"Well, I don't even care," Levin said. "I can't forgive her for this. Ever."

"I can understand you, and right now you shouldn't bother yourself with her. There are more important things at the moment. But I truly believe your father didn't know anything about this. Maybe you should really get together with him once you've calmed down."

"As you said, there are more important things." Levin shook his head. "And my parents can both go jump off a cliff."

Mia looked around her room. It was austerely furnished. A bed, a closet. She didn't have her own bathroom, and had to cross the hall to take a shower. But at least it was clean. Philippe and Juliette had found the room for her. The friendly French couple was staying at a luxury hotel that was way out of Mia's price range. Philippe had used his connections and gotten her a room in this little guesthouse. It was near the hotel, and tomorrow they would tour Marrakesh together. Mia should have been excited. She was finally in the city that had fascinated her from the moment she had seen pictures of it, leafing through the travel guide. But now that she was alone, her grief welled up in full force. Her overpowering longing for Levin threatened to block out all other feelings.

Mia went to take a shower, where she let her despair flow unchecked. Nobody knew her here, and nobody cared if she was crying or not.

"Hello, Mr. Webber, this is Stefan Klein from the investigation firm."

Levin braced himself, nearly choking on his coffee. "Yes? Have you found anything?"

"We have, indeed. It was very difficult. Of course, the airlines wouldn't allow us to see the passenger lists, data privacy and such."

"Yes, yes, I know all that," Levin said impatiently.

"Well, my colleague managed to get them in the end. He turned on the charm and ended up telling them something about a life-or-death situation. That's how he gets them," the detective said with a laugh. "Your girlfriend flew to Casablanca, as you'd guessed. That was two days ago. The question is, how shall we continue? Your girlfriend has a head start, and who knows if she's still in that city."

Levin closed his eyes. So it was really true. Mia was in Morocco. He didn't even want to begin imagining all the dangers she could be exposed to there. Although he did, of course.

"Mr. Webber? Shall we stick with it? We can't do much from here."

"I'll get back to you. That's all for now, thanks," Levin said, and then he called his aunt.

"So, it's as we feared," she said. "This all sounds hopeless."

"I have to go there," Levin said.

"And then what? Do you want to run through Casablanca with a picture in your hand? That city has a population of over three million! Levin, be sensible!"

"Why not?" he answered. "Maybe I'll get lucky and someone will remember her. A pretty blonde isn't that inconspicuous!"

"She arrived two days ago and may very well be somewhere else by now," his aunt said, trying to reason with him. "Think what Mia wrote in her letter—that you shouldn't look for her. Maybe you should respect that."

"I can't. She acted out of desperation. I'm going." Levin stuck to his decision. He was already feverishly calculating how much money he had left. In that moment he thought it had been incredibly stupid not to take the money from the envelope. His parents should pay for this trip—it would be the least they could do!

"Well, I can see it's pointless to talk you out of this," she said. "I can give you two thousand euros, but then I have to pass."

"Thanks, Irmi." Levin felt his hopes rising. "I'll book a flight right now."

35

Mia was relieved to see Philippe and Juliette standing in front of their hotel, just as they'd arranged.

"So, Mia, are you ready to explore Marrakesh?" the friendly elderly man asked. Last night over tea they'd switched to a first-name basis, and Mia was incredibly happy to have met such nice people.

"Yes," she said, giving him a smile.

"You look tired," Juliette noted. "Did you not sleep well?"

"Um, I generally don't sleep well," Mia answered. She had been awake all night again, only falling asleep from exhaustion in the early morning. She secretly wondered if that would ever change. Would she ever be able to fall asleep again without crying over Levin?

They set off and aimed for a market first. Mia paused, dumbstruck, in front of some booths. Everything was colorful and loud. All sorts of different scents filled the air. Spices were being sold out of multicolored containers, and colorful bolts of silk waved gently in the breeze. She felt she would never tire of looking at the scene and was mesmerized by all the images.

At some point, Juliette touched her arm gently. "Mia, can we go on? There's so much more to discover. The bazaar only begins here."

Mia had lost track of time. That happened sometimes when she saw something new and wanted to absorb it. "Of course, I'm sorry, I was distracted."

"No need to be sorry. I find people with such an open-eyed approach to life very pleasant," Philippe said, winking at her.

"Really?"

"Yes."

The two of them laughed.

Levin sank onto a park bench. His feet hurt, and he was feeling more resigned. He had been in Casablanca for three days and had asked for Mia everywhere: the airport, the train station, the taxi stands—and he'd approached all the bus drivers he could find. One airport employee thought she remembered Mia, but of course she hadn't talked to Mia and didn't know where she might have gone. Now he had checked all the guesthouses. He had left out the more expensive hotels, but no one could help him there, either. It was the classic search for the needle in a haystack. Trying to find someone in such a megacity was probably borderline insane, but why shouldn't he have some luck? Levin refused to believe that his mission was doomed. Once he'd gone through the last two guesthouses, he wanted to stop by the police station and the hospitals. He didn't want to think about what he'd do if he failed to find her.

Mia was completely fascinated by Marrakesh. The city was gorgeous, and exploring it with Philippe and Juliette made her happy. Miraculously, it distracted her from thoughts of Levin, but the hours when she was alone were all the worse by contrast. It was still too fresh—she couldn't forget him, and of course she didn't want to. She wondered when it would stop hurting so badly. Right now she couldn't imagine the pain would ever go away, and the loneliness was hard on her. She had nice companions, but they were no substitute for a partner like the one she'd had.

"Mia, would you like to join us for dinner tonight?" Juliette asked her as they said their good-byes in front of the hotel.

Mia didn't need to think long. She didn't want to stretch her budget that much. Philippe and Juliette wanted to continue on to Fez and Meknes. She wanted to accompany them. She would still have enough money for that. But then what? She didn't want to think about it just yet. "No, you're sweet to offer, but I'm going back to the guesthouse," Mia said.

"You're invited," the friendly French woman said.

Mia felt caught. Was it so visible how worried she was about her finances? "Thank you, but I really can't accept—please understand," Mia answered awkwardly.

"All right. Then we'll see you tomorrow? We can buy the train tickets then, too," Juliette offered.

"OK, see you tomorrow," Mia said.

She had made it a habit to always walk quickly and look into no one's eyes when she was traveling alone. She usually wore her head scarf then, too. But now she realized she hadn't been paying attention. Suddenly she was jostled into a large group of young men and children. They angrily pushed her and tugged at her things. Fear flared up in Mia. She managed to pull away and hurriedly left the street. Relieved, she shut the door behind herself as soon as she arrived in her small room.

She felt sticky and decided to take a shower. As she was taking off her things, she noticed something was missing. Her heart skipped a beat when she realized her wallet was gone. She felt dizzy. She went through everything again feverishly in case she'd just stuck it in a wrong pocket. But then there was no doubt: the wallet was gone. It didn't take much to imagine where she might have lost it. It could only have been the group from before. Tears welled up in her eyes. She sank down on her bed, dismayed. Mia had brought nearly all her cash. She stored only her passport and a small amount of money in her room, but even that wasn't safe from theft. She could forget the journeys to Fez and Meknes now. She would barely be able to pay for her room for a few more days with what she had.

So now the time had come. She had to face the fear about her future. What in the world could she do? She had come back down to earth with a crash, something that she would have been happy to delay awhile longer. She was at a complete loss and paced around her room. Then she left the guesthouse and went back to the hotel. Luckily, Philippe and Juliette were sitting in the hotel's restaurant. They looked up, delighted to see her.

"Mia, how nice—did you change your mind? Come, sit with us." Philippe got up and pulled out a chair, then examined her, worried. "What's wrong? You're so pale."

"I–I was robbed. My wallet and most of my money are gone," she said. She was ashamed that something so stupid had happened to her, but the couple were the only people here that she knew and trusted.

"Oh, my goodness, that's terrible." Juliette brought her hands to her mouth. "Are you OK?"

"Yes, nothing happened to me, but I can't afford those tickets anymore. That's why I . . . well, because you're continuing on tomorrow, I wanted to say good-bye." She smiled sadly at her new friends.

"Will you fly back to Germany now?" Philippe asked.

"No." Mia shook her head. If there was one thing she knew, it was that she wouldn't be returning to her home country so quickly. There were sad memories waiting there.

"But what will you do, then?" Juliette asked.

"I thought maybe I can find a job here in Marrakesh," Mia answered. So she had come this far, but her plan was still on unsound footing.

"Do you have a work permit? You would also need a residence permit," Philippe explained.

"Where can I get that kind of thing?" Mia was already losing hope. Of course, why shouldn't bureaucracy exist here, too?

"Wait a moment." The elderly gentleman got up and nodded at her. "I'll call someone. What do I have friends here for?"

When he left, Juliette laid her hand on Mia's. "Mia, you can accompany us. Money won't be a problem—we have more than enough. We can buy you a ticket back to Germany, too. You're such a sweet girl, and I want to help you."

Mia swallowed. Juliette's words touched her deeply, but she didn't want to exploit these people. She liked them so much. Maybe one day someone would accuse her of only having wanted to bleed them dry. No, Mia didn't want them to bear her burden, because she would feel cheap.

"That's so generous of you, but I just can't accept. It was already nice enough that I could come with you. It meant a lot to me. Without you and Philippe, I wouldn't have gotten to know a beautiful city like this," Mia said.

"But I don't want you all alone in Morocco," Juliette said, becoming more insistent. "Mia, think about it. You can even pay us back sometime. It's really not urgent."

"No, I really can't." The first tear ran down Mia's cheek. "I—I'll get through somehow." She tried to sound confident, but she wasn't very successful.

"Oh, Mia." Juliette hugged her. Now all Mia's barriers melted. She began sobbing uncontrollably. Initially, it was awkward to her, but it felt good to be comforted.

"Hey, what's wrong?" Philippe had returned and was looking at her with concern. "Listen, I have a good friend in the office. He'll take care of everything tomorrow. Normally this kind of thing takes weeks, but he'll give you something temporary. And he'll give you all the forms you need. To get the permit of residence you'll need a job and an address." Philippe touched Mia's cheek. "Those are not impossible obstacles. Mahdi said you should try at the coast first. The season's just beginning, and maybe the big hotels will be looking for more staff."

"OK, thanks," Mia said. "Where can I find this Mahdi?"

"We'll go to him tomorrow," Philippe said.

"But didn't you want to continue your journey tomorrow?" Mia asked.

"Do you think we'd leave you alone now?" Philippe asked. "We have time. One or two days won't make a difference to us. And we'll give you some money, Mia, and I don't want you to object. If you want, take it as a loan. As soon as you have a job, you can pay us back."

Mia looked at him, dumbfounded. She was about to respond when Juliette laughed. "I had the same idea." She gave her husband a tender kiss. "We'll put you on a train to the coast. After that, we can't do any more."

All this was uncomfortable for Mia, but she was so touched. "Thank you." She nodded at the two of them.

"Yeah, she spent the night here at some point," the man said. Levin's stomach turned. He hadn't been expecting success, and this guesthouse was pretty shabby.

"And?" He could barely stand the suspense. "Did she give any hints where she was going?"

"No, she was only here for one night." The man shrugged. "I can't tell you more."

"Did she mention if she would be staying in Casablanca awhile longer?" Levin persisted.

"No, like I said, she was only here one night." The man leafed through a tattered planner and pointed at a date. "And that was a few days ago, now."

Levin left the guesthouse with slumped shoulders. It was driving him crazy. Finally he had a clue—yet somehow, still nothing. *What if something happened to her?* That question kept whirling around in his head. He granted himself another day, and then he would go to the police and browse all the hospitals, where he was praying that nobody knew anything about Mia.

"I–I don't know how to thank you." Mia was so overcome by their generosity that she could barely speak.

"Stop that, dear, you've thanked us enough." Juliette took Mia's chin in her hand. "Please write to us, OK? We'll be back in France in two weeks."

"OK, I promise."

Her train was already in, and it was busy on the platform. Soon she'd have to board if she wanted to get to Agadir. Philippe and Juliette had given her money for the ticket and a small sum to help her get by for a little while. To Mia, the two were her personal angels. The conductor gave the boarding signal. With a heavy heart, Mia detached herself from Juliette.

"Adieu, Mia-with-the-sad-eyes. I had always hoped you'd share your secret with us," Philippe said. "I wish you good luck."

"Thank you so much, for everything." She flung her arms around the friendly Frenchman's neck, hugged Juliette just as tightly, and then quickly got on the train.

"No, there's nothing about a Mia Kessler in our databases." The officer seemed annoyed, but Levin didn't care.

"So not nationally, either?" he said, pressing the subject again.

"Nope," the officer said, shaking his head. "Seems as though your girlfriend didn't attract any attention." Now he smiled at Levin.

"Thanks." Levin felt a slight relief. That at least was good news.

"Listen, it may be none of my business, but why are you still looking for her? Your girlfriend is probably already lying on the beach and living the good life."

"True—it's none of your business," Levin said.

"I'd leave it. All this trouble isn't worth it for a woman," the officer persisted.

"Then I'm sorry for you. You obviously haven't found the right one yet." Levin shook his head and left the police station.

"No, I'm sorry, we're currently not in need of staff." The man behind the reception desk eyed Mia through his glasses.

"All right, thank you very much." She smiled at him and left the hotel. That had been the sixth hotel she'd visited today. Although Mia was used to getting rejections, the frustration was still present. But there were plenty of other hotels in Agadir. Mia resolved not to give up hope. She *must* be able to find a job somewhere. She straightened herself and walked into the next hotel. She purposefully headed for the reception desk.

"Yes, may I help you?" The woman behind the desk seemed friendly.

"Hello, my name is Mia Kessler. I'm looking for a job and wanted to ask if you have any openings. I have experience in the hospitality industry as a waitress and kitchen helper, but I would be happy to do just about any job." Mia's heart was thumping hard as usual. The young woman regarded her quickly, then reached for the telephone.

"Please wait, I'll ask our staff manager," she said.

This made Mia even more nervous. But at least it wasn't a direct refusal, and her hopes were raised.

"Please proceed to the third floor," the young woman told her. "When you get off the elevator, turn left and follow the hallway to the last door on the right. Mr. Amani is expecting you."

"Thank you very much." A smile flitted over Mia's face. Then she was on her way. She knocked on the door hesitantly. A male voice asked her in. "Hello, my name is Mia Kessler. I would like to apply for a position," she said.

"Please, come in." The man stood in front of his desk. He smiled and looked her up and down. "So, you're looking for a position. What can you offer?" He grinned. His gaze lingered on Mia's breasts, and she felt uncomfortable.

"I've worked in the hospitality industry before, a–and I speak three languages," she said, stuttering.

The man approached her. He reached for her hair and played with a blond curl. Mia drew back, shocked. "What's this all about?" she asked.

"Well, if I'm supposed to give you a job here, I'd like to get some compensation. Know what I mean?"

"Compensation?" Mia frowned. Suddenly she remembered the trucker Levin had warned her about. "What compensation?"

"Oh, come on, such a pretty little blond thing can't be that slow, can she?" he said. His hand wandered down her neckline toward her breasts.

Mia fiercely pushed him away. He cursed her loudly in Arabic, but she had already reached the door and torn it open.

"German slut!" he called after her in her native tongue. "You're not usually such prudes!"

Mia was horrified, and all she wanted was to get out. She ran past the elevator and took the stairs. *Just get away from here as fast as possible.* When she was finally back outside, her heart was still pounding. Mia gasped for air. She looked around fearfully, but he hadn't followed her. Shaken, she closed her eyes. Never in a million years would she have expected that. Why couldn't she be lucky? Was everything against her?

Her pulse was still racing, and her throat felt all dry. She found a small kiosk and bought a bottle of water, and after a while she found herself on the beach. It was a pleasantly mild day. There weren't many tourists out yet, but the high season would begin soon. She sat down in the sand. She still hadn't calmed down completely. She felt exhausted and empty.

Maybe she should have eaten something today, but lately she had only been eating the bare minimum—partly because she didn't feel like it, and partly to save money.

She found the rushing of the sea calming. She gazed at the glittering surface, completely mesmerized, and memories came back up—memories of the trip with Levin. The images pierced her heart like scalding knives, and her thoughts flew to him. She prayed that he was all right. She wondered if he thought of her as often as she thought of him. Or were his classes distracting him? Had he made up with his parents?

Mia wiped the tears from her face, but more kept coming. She couldn't stop them. Finally she just let them flow freely. What was she doing here? Why had she even been born? Couldn't she have been spared all this? Nobody wanted her, and she couldn't even be with the man she loved anymore. What sense did any of this make?

Mia got up mechanically. She looked at the impression her body had left in the sand. That, too, would be gone soon, and then nothing would remain as a reminder that she'd been here.

She went back to her small guesthouse, opened her backpack, and fished out the box of sleeping pills. She squeezed them all out of the package and laid them on the bed. No, nobody would miss her. Even Levin would stop thinking of her one day. Mia thought about her mother—she could see her again. It would be so easy: all she had to do was swallow these pills, and they would be reunited.

36

Levin fell into his hotel bed, exhausted. He had been on his feet all day again. He'd had flyers printed with Mia's photo and laid them out in hotels and restaurants. He couldn't stop thinking about her. He imagined her in front of him when he closed his eyes. He was afraid that one day her image would fade and he'd lose her for good. He loved everything about her beyond all measure. Her beautiful, expressive eyes; her sensual mouth; those blond curls; and her soft, seductive body. He heard her laughter, her voice that had such a pleasantly warm quality to it. A smile came over his face as he thought of the kind of wonder with which she approached anything new. He had to find her, had to see her again. He couldn't lose her.

"Dammit, Mia! Where are you, you stubborn girl?" he cursed. "Please let me find you!"

Mia jumped, then shook her head. What was she thinking of? She recalled her time in the clinic. How many times had she wished then to be free? And now she was, free and unbound. She could do whatever she pleased. *No one promised you it would be easy*, she thought. Maybe she wasn't a good person—maybe she'd forfeited her chance for happiness by killing her father, and maybe giving up Levin was her punishment for it. But she was still here, and a spark of her will to survive suddenly flared up. She may not be good for Levin, but that didn't mean she didn't have the right to find her place in the world. Mia blotted her eyes and put the pills away. She knew it wasn't time yet to give up.

The next morning, the elderly woman who ran the guesthouse woke Mia.

"Yes?" Mia regarded her with tired eyes. She had slept badly again because of her near suicide—and because she couldn't stop thinking about Levin.

"You asked me yesterday if I knew where they're looking for staff."

"Yes?" Mia looked up, interested.

"Today in the paper they wrote that a hotel chain is opening here this spring, and they're hiring. Here!" The woman laid the paper down in front of her. But unfortunately, Mia didn't understand the language.

"I can't read Arabic," she said sheepishly.

"Of course, I forgot." The woman clapped a hand to her forehead. "I'll write down the address for you—it's right by the beach." She went to get a pen and notepad. "You should stop by."

"Thank you so much," Mia said.

"My pleasure. I can look around some more for you if you like," the woman said.

Mia had ironed all her things. She noticed that her clothes were starting to get too big. She had lost some weight, but she didn't want to know how much.

The hotel wasn't quite finished. There was still construction going on everywhere, but the reception desk was already occupied. In front of her were a number of people, both younger and older. Mia's hopes of getting a job sank. When her turn came, a young man asked for her qualifications. Mia told him about her jobs in the café and the Italian restaurant.

"But I would clean rooms or do other work, too," Mia added eagerly. She was terribly nervous. Would she fail again or finally be lucky?

"You speak three languages? French, English, and German?" the man asked.

"Yes, exactly. And I'll learn Arabic, too."

The man looked up quickly and smiled. "There are many applicants here, as you can see. Would you be willing to work here without pay for a trial week? We can offer meals and a place to sleep. If we're happy with you, we'll offer a fixed-term employment contract."

Mia accepted on the spot. She would put everything into getting this job. Maybe this was her big chance.

"Hey, honey, still no news?" Aunt Irmi asked on the telephone.

"No." Levin rubbed his eyes. "I distributed the leaflets. I hope someone with information about her will get in touch with me."

"Levin, I understand your dedication to this, but what about school? You can't stay in Morocco forever," his aunt said in a gentle voice.

"I can't think about that right now," he answered.

"But how much longer will you look for her? She could be somewhere completely different by now. You can't search the entire country."

"Who says I can't?" Levin answered stubbornly.

"Please don't lose *yourself* in your search for Mia. You have to learn to let go. Mia knows where to find you, and she's made a decision."

"But I can't let her go. I just can't," he said.

"Don't obsess over this, darling. It's not good for you. You can't do more than you already have, and the money won't last forever, either."

"I know," he agreed. "Give me another week. If I haven't found out more by then and nobody gets in touch with me, I'll come home, OK?"

"I'm taking you at your word," she said.

Levin stared at the baggage belt. He really had to concentrate to spot his suitcase. Now he was back in Berlin, but his mind was still so far away. He had fruitlessly looked for Mia for almost four weeks. The entire mission had probably been destined to fail from the beginning. Levin had begged another week from his aunt, and she'd given him more money. He'd tried two neighboring cities on the coast without success. She might just as well have been in Agadir, Marrakesh, or Tangier—or maybe she wasn't even in Morocco anymore.

Levin was sad, disillusioned, and also angry with Mia. His mother's comment that she wouldn't have allowed herself to be manipulated if she really did love him enough was still stuck in his head. Was there some truth in that? Why hadn't Mia trusted him? Shouldn't she have known he loved her so much that he didn't care about anything else? He scolded himself for the thought. He knew about Mia's self-confidence issues. Maybe he would just have to come to terms with the fact that he wouldn't see her again. It was very painful. Never in his life had anything hurt so badly, but one day he *would* have to find closure. He could accept that, at least, for now. He found his suitcase, which wasn't difficult, as by now it was the only one left circling on the belt. Levin grabbed it and went toward the exit.

"Levin! Hello!" It was his aunt's voice.

He looked around. How was this possible? Irmi didn't have a car, and they had arranged to meet for dinner that night.

"Here!" she said with a chuckle. Now he saw her; she was standing with Kai.

"Hey." Levin was genuinely happy to see them. He hugged Irmi, then thumped his friend on the back. "What are you guys doing here?"

"What kind of question is that?" Kai said, rolling his eyes. "We've come to pick up the eternal searcher. I stayed in contact with your aunt while you were gone," he explained.

"Thanks, I'm glad to see you both," Levin said.

"Your father asked us to tell you to please get in touch with him sometime," Irmi said as they got into Kai's car.

"Oh, yeah? And what if I don't want to?"

"Levin, he's really sorry. I think he understands now how hard this has been on you and how close you and Mia were. It's my opinion, too, that you have to start looking ahead now. At least talk to him. I think he wants to support you again. And you can definitely use a cash injection," she said.

"I'll work. I don't want his cash."

"Come on, dude, be glad," Kai broke in. "Don't make this harder for yourself. It'll be difficult enough to get everything back on track. Take this opportunity."

"Nope," Levin muttered. He didn't feel like thinking about it.

They all went out to eat together. Afterward, Kai joined Levin in his apartment.

"Oof," Levin groaned as he saw all the work he had to catch up on. His friend had collected everything for him. Levin stared at the mountain of papers.

"Well, you have four weeks to catch up, so knuckle down," Kai said seriously.

"I'll have to figure out how to do that. I need to find a job, too."

"Do you really want to do this to yourself? Man, you know your father wants to help you again." Kai shook his head.

"I don't want his money. For all I care, my parents can choke on it," Levin said, snorting. "I don't even care if I need another semester. I'll be fine."

"Levin—"

"No. I don't want to be dependent on my parents again. My God, Mia worked herself to death for me. If she could hold down two jobs, then I can at least handle part-time work." Clearly, he was far from over it. Just because he was back in Berlin now didn't mean he'd forgotten Mia or given up on her.

"You're still missing her a lot, huh," Kai said seriously.

"Yeah, of course. And I don't care if anybody thinks it's silly. I love that girl, and I can't imagine that ever changing." He blinked away a few tears.

"Didn't you find anything?"

Levin shook his head. "All I know is that she was in Casablanca and spent a night in a pretty lousy flophouse. I don't think she's in Casablanca anymore, but I have no clue where she could have gone. If I had the bucks, I'd be plastering the entire country with flyers, but who knows if she's even in Morocco now?"

"Man, I'm so sorry for you. We really liked Mia a lot, too. Hopefully—" Kai interrupted himself in the middle of his sentence and looked at Levin.

"What?" Levin said.

"I'm just saying, hopefully nothing happened. Such a cute blonde . . . well . . . you know what I mean."

"Yes," Levin said sadly. "I know."

37

"Mia, the staff manager wants to see you." Faizah entered the hotel room Mia was cleaning and looked at her seriously.

Mia looked up. "But why? Did I make a mistake?" She ran her hands over the bed she had just put fresh sheets on. "I'm not done with this room yet."

Mia's heart was beating like mad. Hopefully it wasn't a bad sign. She needed this job so badly, and she'd put so much effort into it. The hotel had been open for three weeks now. Mia had taken a job as a maid, and she was really working hard. In the evenings she always fell into bed completely exhausted. She was living in a small room on the hotel premises—she shared it with Faizah. The young Moroccan woman and Mia had become friends quickly, and Mia had already been invited to visit Faizah's family twice. She had a wonderful family, and Mia enjoyed their hospitality and openness.

"I don't know. Charda just told me to call you. Hurry, Mia," Faizah urged her. "I'll finish this room for you." Mia set off.

Nervously, she knocked on the office door.

"Yes?" the staff manager said.

Mia entered and cleared her throat. "I–I was told to come see you?"

"Yes, Mia. Please come in." Her boss smiled and asked her to sit. He didn't look annoyed.

"We employed you as a maid," he said, leafing through some documents. "But now we'd like to change that."

"But why? Did I not work hard enough? Are you firing me?" Mia's throat grew tight.

"Whoa, wait a minute," Mr. Chalid said. "You've misunderstood. I'm not talking about firing you—I'd like to move you into a different job. Aisha from services told me you spontaneously helped out on two evenings in the restaurant when we had a staffing problem, and she was very happy with you. Because we have many English guests and more and more German-speaking tourists here, your language skills would be a big asset. I would like to offer you a position in the restaurant. You'll have to keep in mind, though, that you may be assigned to work from early morning until late at night. But you do get a raise and one free day every week. What do you think?"

Mia could hardly fathom what she'd just heard. "I—well—thank you! I gladly accept, of course." Her eyes glinted, and she was sure that even he sensed the huge weight lifting off her shoulders.

"Great. Finish today's work, and then please report to Aisha tomorrow at six at the breakfast buffet." Mr. Chalid winked at her. "That's what I call a fast promotion. Congratulations, Mia."

"Thank you again." She smiled at her boss one last time and darted out of his office before he had a chance to change his mind.

Faizah looked at Mia anxiously as she came running back. Mia told her about the transfer.

"Oh, Mia, how wonderful! It's too bad we won't be working together anymore, but I won't hold it against you." Faizah gave her a hug.

As Mia lay in bed that night, she sighed in relief. She was so glad about her new position. Of course she would do her best to meet all requirements there, too. Besides, she really liked working in this hotel, even though it was sometimes hard and the hours were long.

It helped keep her mind off her ever-present memories of Levin. She had confided in Faizah about Levin, but the young Moroccan knew nothing about her past that—and neither did the rest of the staff. Mia was glad she hadn't been asked for any references or a résumé. She'd wanted to leave all that behind, and now it seemed like she was well on her way to doing that.

She had also gotten used to eating more again. The physical work demanded it, so Mia had started forcing herself to stick to regular mealtimes. With more money coming in now, she would be able to pay back Philippe and Juliette soon. That was very important to her. She didn't want to owe them anything. Mia turned over in her bed and looked out the window into the clear, starry night.

"Levin, I got a promotion. Isn't that great?" she asked wistfully into the dark.

Levin groaned. The doorbell had rung, but he didn't feel like having visitors. He was hunched over his books and had been studying all day. In just two hours he'd need to leave for his job at the bar.

"Yes," he grumbled through the intercom.

"Levin, it's me. Can I talk to you?" His father's voice made him groan again.

"I don't have the time, and I don't feel like it," Levin said.

"I know. You've told me enough times, but I'd still like to talk to you," he said.

Annoyed, Levin pressed the buzzer. He resolved to only cover the bare necessities with him and then ask him to leave. In the last few weeks, his father had tried repeatedly to speak with him, but Levin had always sent him away. It was probably time now to listen to him. He quickly cleared away some clothes that were scattered around his apartment. He wasn't much of a housekeeper, and since Mia had left he just didn't feel like making the place look nice.

A moment later, James Webber entered Levin's apartment.

"I'm here," Levin said. He was sprawled on the couch.

"Hi, Levin," his father said.

"Hi, Dad. Please keep it short—I have stuff to do." Levin had to force himself to stay polite—his anger at both his parents was still immense.

"How are you?" his father asked. He lifted some things off an armchair and sat down.

"Marvelous. Can't you see?" Levin said.

"No, I can't. The place looks like a battlefield, and you've looked more alive, too." His father stayed calm, but Levin could imagine it wasn't easy for him.

"I work at a bar, every night, but surely you already know that from Irmi. And during the day I'm at school or studying, even though it's summer. That doesn't leave much time to take care of the household. Plus, you've victoriously chased my only support out of town."

"Levin, I can only emphasize again that it happened without my knowledge and that I don't support your mother's behavior. She definitely overshot, and—"

"*Overshot?* Jeez, what a nice way to put it," Levin said, scoffing.

"I know you're deeply hurt. If there's anything I can do to make up for this, let me know." His father looked into his eyes. Levin felt he was being genuine.

"Something like this can't be made up for. If you want to do me a favor, then just let me live my life in peace. You've mixed in enough, don't you think?"

"Your mother misses you."

"That's her problem, not mine." Levin shrugged, uncaring.

"I'd like to offer you financial support again. Please accept my help."

"No. No way!"

"Don't be so proud."

"I'm not proud, I'm deeply disappointed in you. Not everything can be solved with money. When will you finally learn?"

"OK, I see you're not giving in. Levin, my firm will always be open to you." His father got up and held out his hand.

Levin got over himself and got up to shake his father's hand. "Thanks, Dad, but I can't tell you yet what I'll be doing after I get my degree. Right now I'm only thinking day by day."

"I understand. Have you heard from her at all?"

"Do you really care?" he asked.

"Yes, I do care. Maybe there can be a new beginning. For all of us." James Webber smiled.

"No, she hasn't been in touch. Not for three months now. She always wants to do everything right. That seems to apply to the breakup, too." Levin's voice briefly faltered.

"You won't believe this, but I'm very sorry." His father went to the door, and Levin followed. "You know how to reach me."

"Yeah, but don't expect to hear from me soon," Levin said. He had himself under control again.

"Are you coming later?" Faizah asked. Mia saw her encouraging look, but she shook her head.

"No, I don't feel like it. I'd like to take a break," she said.

"But you never come. It's really nice on the beach. And you know everybody."

"No, honestly. I'm not in the mood and would only ruin your fun."

"But you're still young. Why do you seal yourself off like this? Since I've known you, you work like a madwoman, and after that you stay in your room. Why don't you enjoy life a little?" Faizah took a step toward her.

"I don't want to," Mia said. She knew Faizah was only trying to be nice. Her other coworkers kept asking her to come, too. They met at the beach regularly. The group was slightly different every time, depending on who had time off when, but they were all quite nice.

"Today is your day off. It's warm, and we're by the sea," Faizah insisted. "Please, for me."

Mia sighed. She just wanted to be alone, to look at the few photos of Levin she had on her phone and dream of him.

"It's because of him, isn't it? This Levin? If you miss him so much, why don't you just contact him?"

"I can't. We can't be together—it's just not possible."

"I don't understand it." Faizah sat down on the bed next to Mia. "What reason can there be that two people who love each other so much have to separate?" She brushed a blond curl off Mia's face. "I mean, you're not a Muslim—you have so many more liberties than I do, and everything should be so much more relaxed."

Mia looked at her sadly. "I don't feel like talking about it, please, Faizah," she pleaded.

"Are you coming?" her friend pressed.

"If I come once, will you leave me alone then?"

"For a while, maybe." Faizah beamed at her.

"All right," Mia said. "I'll just go change."

Mia and Faizah were greeted enthusiastically when they arrived at the beach. Mia's coworkers seemed truly happy she had come.

"Hey, how great to see you here." Jorge approached Mia first. He was from Spain and worked as a host at the hotel club. He was an absolute chick magnet. Mia had often observed the swooning looks that the female guests gave him, and he never turned down a chance to flirt. There was whispering that he'd broken many hearts, and Mia could understand. He had a nearly irresistible charm and a boyish, joyful nature. From young girls to elderly ladies, he effortlessly wrapped them all around his little finger.

Jorge gave Mia two kisses left and right, Moroccan style. The others greeted her the same way. Some of them had brought food, and the non-Muslims had even brought beer and wine. Mia sipped on a beer. She hadn't had any alcohol since leaving Berlin. It wasn't available everywhere in Morocco. After the affectionate greeting, Mia was immediately included in conversations. She tried hard to seem relaxed and happy, but inside was a different story. The job helped distract her, and she did her work well and was often praised. But when she was alone, she constantly felt the sadness. She kept asking herself what Levin might be doing at that moment, and she wondered if he maybe already had a new girlfriend. It was all so hard, so damn hard. Sometimes she still thought about giving up completely. She had paid back Juliette and Philippe, so she didn't owe anyone anything. But wasn't that ungrateful somehow? At least she had a job and got by. She could even save money, although she didn't know what it would be good for.

"Why do you always have such a sad look in your eyes?" Jorge sat down in the warm sand next to her. He smiled broadly. "I think I need to take you to the club sometime."

Mia saw the glittering in his eyes and chuckled. "Silly!"

"Excuse me? What did you just call me?" He planted himself in front of her. This made Mia anxious, but then she realized he was only joking. "As a punishment, you have to dance with me." He held out his hand.

"What? Here?"

"Sure, we have music." He pointed to the boom box someone had brought along. "Turn that up!" he called to Mohammed.

Mia was embarrassed at first, but finally some of her coworkers followed suit, and she let herself be pulled into Jorge's arms.

"What did you say you were doing tonight?"

The blonde that had been watching Levin all evening had come over to the bar to approach him for the umpteenth time.

"The same thing I must have told you five times already today," Levin said with a grin. "I'm going home and falling into bed."

"Alone?" She pursed her painted red lips. "How boring."

"Yeah, I'm a bore. Totally. But do look around, a few other guys are still here." He winked. Then he went back to putting away glasses. He was glad he'd be done in an hour. The job was OK, but he didn't get much sleep, and classes and studying took a lot of time, too. At least the bucks were there. He got lots of tips, especially from women. He put on all his charm and was very popular with the guests. He knew that from his boss, and there was no shortage of offers, but Levin didn't feel the need. Thoughts of Mia still wouldn't let go, not even after four months. At the moment all he did was survive.

38

Mia surveyed the buffet one more time before going over to check the champagne glasses stacked in a pyramid. In half an hour it would be time. The old year would end, and a new one would begin. Mia wondered what might be in store for her. In the last two years, her life had changed so drastically that she'd gladly welcome a less turbulent new year. Today, of course, she thought of Levin even more than usual. They had spent the last New Year's Eve and Christmas before it together, and it had been beautiful. Especially during these days, the pain of separation was powerful, although Faizah's family had been lovely to her.

They had invited her over for Christmas Day and even put up a tiny Christmas tree decorated in every color on their dinner table. Mia had been touched by that gesture. They didn't celebrate Christmas, and she knew they were only doing it to cheer her up.

Faizah's father was pushing her to finally get married, and he didn't spare Mia from his interference, either. He thought she needed a man in her life, so every time Mia visited, he presented her with a potential candidate. But Mia always declined politely. She certainly didn't want to get married, and she wasn't looking for a new relationship. Levin still occupied her heart. She couldn't imagine that ever changing.

Certainly, a few young men—like Jorge—had made advances, but Mia wasn't interested. Maybe she'd just be alone forever. Maybe it was meant to be that way. And if it ever became too much to bear, then she still had her sleeping pills. She didn't think of that so often now, but the last few days had been so full of painful memories that it seemed like an option again.

"Mia, you've really made everything beautiful today." Aisha showed up next to her, chasing away her gloomy thoughts.

"Thank you," Mia said, blushing. She was happy about the service boss's praise. Mia wasn't just in charge of serving anymore but also of ordering the groceries. Apart from that, she ensured that the waiters kept the buffet stocked. In the beginning, Mia had shied away from giving people orders, and some of them had also consistently ignored her, but she had learned to be persistent. She'd earned their respect. The bigger responsibility also came with higher wages. Mia wondered if she should move into her own apartment. She was still sharing a room with Faizah. They got along well, but Mia longed for a modest, private space of her own.

The guests became more restless as midnight approached. On the beach there would be a big fireworks display, and later there would be another buffet. Mia would get to bed late, but that was fine with her. The less time she had to think about how happy she had been last year, the better. She glanced at her watch. One minute. She went over to help a coworker pour champagne. The seconds were being counted. Mia thought about how tightly Levin had held her and the tender words he'd whispered into her ear. They had talked about their future. She could almost hear his voice. *We'll always be together, sweet thing. Always. Nothing can separate us.* Tears filled Mia's eyes as the first champagne corks popped and people fell into each other's arms.

"Happy New Year, Levin," she whispered.

It was a stressful night, but it was worth it for Levin—his boss hadn't promised too much. He could just as well have worked at the bar, but he had also gotten a taxi license, and he definitely wanted to take advantage of New Year's Eve. Few people wanted to drive after the parties. His current passengers were talking without an end in sight. Levin didn't bother to listen. He just smiled now and then. His gaze wandered down to the clock on the dashboard. It would be midnight in Morocco now. If Mia was still there, she'd be clinking glasses.

He thought of the past New Year's Eve. They had celebrated with their friends on the banks of the Spree. It had been hellishly cold. Mia had cuddled up to get some of his warmth. Back then he would never have believed they'd be separated a few months later. He smiled to himself sadly. It was brutal how fast things could change. *Who are you celebrating with, Mia?* he asked her in his mind. He couldn't bear to think that she might be kissing another man now, wishing him a happy New Year. That was just too cruel.

His friends wanted to celebrate with him, of course—Kai and Geli had invited him. But Levin declined. Just like on Christmas, he had decided to work. He did at least meet his father and aunt for breakfast on Christmas Day, and it had turned out to be a fairly normal get-together. His dad asked him to give his mother another chance, but Levin wouldn't hear it. He couldn't forgive her for what she'd done, not even half a year later. On Christmas Eve, when the pub where he worked closed for the night, he'd roamed the streets with Kai for a while, and they ended up in a club. Levin got wasted to forget the pain, and then the next morning, to his astonishment, he woke up in a strange bed. That hadn't happened to him in ages. The girl was pretty—with blond curls—and he realized immediately why he'd left with her. He apologized to her profusely and explained that he wasn't looking for a committed relationship. For that, she had cursed at him wildly, and Levin hurried away. Afterward, he felt awful. He hadn't really cheated on Mia, but it still felt that way.

Lately, he'd made it a habit to scour international newspapers for possible news of Mia. A coworker who'd grown up in Morocco helped him look. So far there hadn't been any sign of an accident involving a young blond woman fitting Mia's description, and Levin didn't even want to think about anything happening to her. She just had to be alive—but if only he could find some clue. Sometimes he was terribly angry with her because she hadn't contacted him. Then he just felt sorry for her again. It must have been harder for her than for him, and there was no doubt that she'd loved him.

Jeez, Mia, he thought, sighing.

"You can stop here." The passenger's voice shook him out of his reverie. Levin pulled over and asked for the fare.

39

"Levin. Levin, hey, honey, you need to get up."

A familiar voice reached his ear. He opened his eyes, drowsy. "Why? What time is it?" he grumbled.

"Almost seven. You have a lecture today." Sarah planted a tender kiss on his lips.

"Come here," Levin said. He grinned and pushed her onto her back. "I want to be woken up properly first."

"You're too late," she protested, laughing, but then he always *could* persuade her that it was much nicer to be in bed.

When Levin stepped out of the shower, Sarah had already set the breakfast table. "Yum, looks good." He thanked her with a kiss.

"I have to go soon so I can stop by Susanne's before the lecture," she explained. Levin listened to her detail her appointments. She was studying medicine and still had several semesters to go. He, on the other hand, would graduate soon. He was already wondering what he'd do then. There was still the question of whether to join his father's firm. At least they got along again—they even met at a bistro for breakfast once a month.

Levin still didn't have any contact with his mother, but she *had* tried to apologize to him several times. Making up with her wasn't an option for Levin, although he knew she'd like his new girlfriend. An aspiring doctor from a rich doctor's family—that was surely to her taste. His father had met Sarah and liked her, as had Irmi—but there was a certain distance where his aunt was concerned. Her opinion was important to Levin, and she had been happy for him when she met Sarah. For a long time, Levin had no thoughts of starting a new relationship, yet still it had just happened. Sarah had shown up at one of Kai and Geli's parties; an acquaintance had brought her along. Levin had liked her from the start. She was intelligent and good-looking, and something about her made him curious. He hadn't met a woman like that since Mia. Yet still—when Levin listened honestly to his inner voice, he realized it wasn't exactly the same kind of thing he'd had with Mia. Those incredibly deep feelings were missing with Sarah. But maybe they'd come in time? She was a completely different person, and who said that one had to have the same feelings for everyone?

They had good conversations, and she knew about Mia and had listened attentively when he told her what had happened. He hadn't withheld that Mia had been his one true love and that he wasn't sure he could ever feel the same about another woman. Sarah had smiled and suggested they give it a try. From Levin's point of view, that was fine. He didn't want to plan anymore, anyway. What good would that do? He'd learned firsthand that it could go wrong and everything could change from one day to the next. Mia had been gone for over two years now, so he'd given up hope of ever seeing her again. He had more or less gotten over her, and life went on without her.

"Bye, honey." Sarah leaned over for a kiss. "Hugs."

"Hugs back. See you tonight." He winked at her and poured himself another coffee.

"Mia? Mia, how are you feeling?" Faizah bent over the bed. Mia opened her eyes.

"Better, thanks," she said.

"Well, you don't look it," Faizah chided.

"No, I'm OK." Mia turned away and doubled up again, a new wave of cramps shaking her body. She got out of bed laboriously and trudged over to the bathroom. She had lost count of how many times she'd been in there now. She still had diarrhea. She was angry with herself for letting it happen. She'd gotten permission to accompany a group of tourists on an outing and had probably gotten a salad full of bacteria. A few other people from the group had similar symptoms, but they were already on their feet again. Mia was uncomfortable having to call in sick. This was the first time she'd been absent. Kindly, Faizah took care of her in her free time, and Mia was grateful.

Mia crawled back into bed. Faizah started talking about her future husband and the impending wedding. Mia was excited for the event. Her friend was jittery, and it was contagious. Faizah had stuck by her choice to marry a coworker—a cook. Her family had wanted another candidate, but in the end they gave their consent. With Mia, they had given up trying, because she'd made it clear that she wasn't interested.

"Oh, Mia, you're back." Aisha, the service boss, regarded Mia happily. "You gave us quite a scare. Are you feeling better?"

"Yes, thank you." Mia brushed a blond curl behind her ear. She was embarrassed that she had been absent for so long.

"If you don't feel up to working at any point, then make sure to take a break, OK?"

"I'm all right, thanks," Mia said.

"OK. You look a little thin—take care of yourself." Aisha patted Mia on the shoulder one more time, then gave her the grocery list. Mia got right to work. She checked the hotel's provisions and noted what was needed. She had been away for two weeks. The illness had been drastic. At one point, Mia had lost consciousness and had woken up in the hospital. She had been lucky that Faizah had happened to be there when she blacked out.

At first she had almost welcomed it. She had lost so much physical and emotional energy that she would have been content if it had just ended then. She was artificially nourished in the hospital because she had been unable to keep any solid food down. For Mia, lying around had been agony. Not only had the cramps plagued her, but so had memories of Levin. Everything she had so meticulously buried came back in full force, and if she had been capable of keeping down the sleeping pills, she probably would have taken them.

Faizah and her parents had visited her daily, and their kind words helped nurse Mia back to health. She still wasn't feeling particularly well, but there was a lot to do in the hotel, and her sense of duty won out.

"Congratulations, Levin. I'm very proud of you." His father stood in front of him, beaming. He toasted him with a glass of champagne.

"Thanks." He had finally reached his goal, and with better grades than he'd hoped for.

"So? What are your plans?" James Webber regarded his son curiously. Levin sighed. The question wasn't unexpected, of course. Now he would have to give his father a reasonable answer.

"If you still have a position for me, we can give it a try," Levin said. "If we see that it doesn't work, I can look for a different job."

"A wise decision," Levin's father said, looking relieved. "I promise to give you a free hand to practice. If you need any advice, I'll always be here for you."

"Well, that sounds good." Irmi joined them and hugged Levin tightly. "Congratulations, honey. You did very well."

"Thanks." He gave his aunt a peck on the cheek. "I'm glad that all the heavy work is over now."

"I'd say it's only beginning," his father said, winking.

"Oh, look, there's your mother." Irmi pointed toward the door. Levin tensed. Irmi had appealed to his conscience, and he'd agreed to invite her. Before that, he had celebrated with his close friends and hadn't wanted her present.

"Levin." Sonja Webber approached him tentatively. She had hardly changed, but she looked nervous. He wasn't feeling any better, either. Even though the issue with Mia was now two and a half years in the past and his anger wasn't so all-consuming anymore, he couldn't just forget about it.

"Congratulations." She held out her hand. He took it reluctantly.

"Thanks, Mom." He cleared his throat.

"I should thank you for having me here. I'm very proud of you." Tears sparkled in her eyes. Levin was touched. "Levin, I'd like to apologize for what I did back then. I'm so sorry. If I could turn back time, I wouldn't hesitate," she said.

"Mom, I can't forget it, but I accept your apology. So much time has passed. I think we should try to bury our differences."

"Thank you. That means a lot to me." She hugged him.

Levin let her for a moment, but then he moved away. "Let's leave it at that."

Levin looked around, searching for Sarah, and then he beckoned her over. "Mom, I'd like to introduce you to Sarah. We've been together for a few months now."

"Nice to meet you, Mrs. Webber," Sarah said with a smile.

"The pleasure is mine," Sonja Webber answered. "My sister and my husband have told me about you. You study medicine, and you're Dr. Felder's daughter."

Levin chuckled, then moved along to let them scope each other out in peace. He didn't see the slightest risk for Sarah. His mother wouldn't dare reject her. Sarah's family had an impeccable reputation and belonged to the upper class. She'd be a perfect daughter-in-law. Not that Levin was wasting any thoughts on marriage—at least not yet.

Levin had changed a lot. He was now self-sufficient and independent, and he didn't want to put that at risk. If he should notice his father restricting or patronizing him, he would leave so fast it would make his father's head spin; that much was clear. Levin wasn't afraid to do things the hard way anymore, but he wanted to try the family firm first. He owed his father that much. And maybe it would even work out.

40

Mia was happy to see the letter. She took it out of the mailbox and hastily went inside her apartment. It was from Juliette and Philippe— she'd kept up a steady correspondence with them. The elderly couple traveled a lot, and once they even visited Mia at the hotel. They had invited her to Paris again. So far, Mia had always declined, because she didn't want to be a burden to them. And apart from that, she had a lot to do.

Except for during her illness, she had never missed work and had let her vacation days pass by unused. She now had Aisha's job and managed service all by herself. Aisha's husband had started his own restaurant, so she'd left to manage it for him.

Mia was proud that she had been trusted with so much responsibility. At first she was afraid of it, but she adapted well. She also spoke very good Arabic already; she'd found patient teachers in her coworkers and always studied hard after hours. Mia read the letter attentively and then wrote back. She didn't broach the subject of the invitation but told them about her friends and her work at the hotel.

A week later, Mia's phone rang late one evening. She could tell from the number that it was an international call.

"Hi, Mia," Juliette said.

"Hi. How are you two?" Mia asked cheerfully. They didn't talk on the phone very often because Mia only had a cell phone, and calls were expensive. She was all the happier for the call now.

"Very well. Well, actually, no, not really," Juliette said.

"What's wrong?" Mia was startled. Had one of them fallen ill?

"Why don't you come visit us? We've invited you so many times now, Mia."

"But I can't just accept that," she said. She didn't want to offend them, but she felt like they had already given her so much that she couldn't accept more of their hospitality.

"Of course you can, or we wouldn't have asked. Mia, we would be so happy to see you again. How about Christmas this year? I'm sure you won't have so much to do then."

"I—I don't know. Quite a lot goes on here during the holidays."

"But you need to get out. Or have you already used up your vacation days?" Juliette pressed.

"No."

"Have you even been away in the three years you've worked there?"

"No," Mia confessed.

"You'll work yourself to death one of these days. Please, do us this favor, OK? Paris is beautiful during the holidays. Deal?"

"I'll need to talk to the staff manager," Mia said, dodging the question, but she sensed already that Juliette wouldn't give up this time. Mia's resolve was swayed. She really liked the two of them, and she didn't want to offend them. And Paris. She closed her eyes for a moment, and the memories came back in a flash. What a beautiful and carefree time she'd enjoyed there with Levin.

"Then talk to him. I'll expect a message from you tomorrow, Mia. And, of course, Philippe sends his best regards."

"But surely you're celebrating Christmas with your children and grandchildren. It's a family holiday, I mean—I'm not sure I belong there."

"You're like a daughter to us. It would mean so much."

"I'll try."

"Have fun!" Faizah hugged Mia again. She and her husband had driven Mia to the airport, and Harun, too, said his heartfelt good-byes.

"Thanks," Mia responded with a smile. She was already nervous. She had been in Morocco for three and a half years now, and it would be exciting to travel somewhere else. She enjoyed the flight, gazing out the window the entire time and observing the shapes of the clouds. On her last flight, Mia had been in deep despair, and now she took stock of her emotions. She wasn't much happier at the moment. She felt like a marionette going through the motions every day. Of course the whole situation was her own fault—she knew that full well. She *could* have gone out and tried to have more fun. Maybe that would have changed something.

But the deep sadness inside her prevented all that. There were days when she was better at dealing with the loneliness than others, but she always fell back into the hole. At least she got a lot of approval at her job. She was known as a hard worker and was popular among her colleagues. It hadn't been easy, but she'd done it. That was something she could be proud of.

Mia stepped out into the arrivals hall. She didn't need to search long. A big balloon with "*Bienvenue*" printed on it immediately floated into her line of vision, and on the other end of its string was a beaming Juliette. Mia ran over and flung her arms around her neck. Then Philippe pulled her into his arms.

"Welcome, Mia," he said. There were tears in his eyes, as well as in his wife's.

"How wonderful to finally have you here. Let me see you." Juliette inspected Mia. "You've become frighteningly thin. Don't they feed you there?" she asked.

"Yes, of course they do," Mia said, smiling.

"And you're so pale. Don't you go outside in the sun?" Philippe admonished her.

"I work a lot."

"Well, all right then—come, we'll spoil ourselves while you're here." Juliette winked and took Mia's elbow. "We'll get you back into shape."

Juliette and Philippe lived in an elegant Parisian apartment. Mia was surprised by its size. She was staying in their guest room, which was also generously decorated. After she had dropped off her luggage, they strolled through the streets a bit, and then Juliette prepared a gourmet dinner with several courses. Their children would be there, too. Mia was already excited. What would her friends' family be like? Her tension disappeared when she was introduced to the daughter and son with their partners and children. All of them were relaxed and cheerful. They welcomed Mia sincerely. She joyfully played with the three small children. It was so much fun to romp around with them that Mia could barely part from them at the end of the evening.

"Why didn't you take a job that has something to do with children?" Juliette asked Mia later over a glass of wine.

Mia felt trapped and nervously brushed a strand of hair behind her ear. "That didn't work out," she said, dodging the question.

"Too bad—it seems to come naturally to you. You immediately had the little ones' trust," Juliette observed.

"Yes, maybe," Mia said with a shrug. She hoped the two of them wouldn't press it. What reason should she give them anyway? Mia didn't want to talk about her past. She was almost afraid that Juliette and Philippe would reject her if she did. Thankfully, Philippe changed the subject, and Mia relaxed again. Plans were made for the next day, and Mia was already excited. Paris was beautiful in her memory, part of the reason, of course, having been Levin's company back then.

This time, Mia found Paris fairly cold. She was accustomed to the warmer temperatures in Morocco, and so first thing the next day she found herself in a department store, where she bought a winter coat. Now warmly wrapped up, she toured the city with Juliette and Philippe. As they strolled past the Eiffel Tower, Mia's stomach gave a painful tug. She looked up at the steel structure. When she'd been up there with Levin, everything had been so perfect. She would have given anything for another five minutes up there with him.

"Mia? What's wrong?"

Juliette's voice shook her out of her memories. "Nothing," Mia whispered.

"I don't believe it—you're crying," she said anxiously.

Mia was surprised. She hadn't noticed. But she quickly wiped the tears from her face.

"What is it, Mia? Don't you finally want to tell us why you're always so sad?" Juliette embraced her. Mia tried with all her might to keep herself together, but it didn't work. She cried more and more, the memories washing over her in powerful waves. She shook her head, but she sensed herself that her resistance was melting away.

"It–it's, well, I was up there once before w–with a wonderful person. He meant the world to me," she said through her sobs.

"And who was he, exactly?" Juliette asked.

Philippe strolled off.

"The man that I love more than anything."

"Where is he now?"

Juliette's gentle questioning made Mia cry even more. Finally, she answered, "I don't know. I think he's still living in Berlin. I had to leave him over three years ago."

"Had to? Why *had to*? I don't understand." Juliette stroked Mia's hair.

Mia swallowed heavily, and her heart started racing. "He's from a reputable family and wanted to become a lawyer. I would only have harmed him."

"How could you have done that?" Juliette frowned. "You're such a pretty, friendly girl. Why should someone like you harm him?"

Mia glanced at Juliette in shock. "I'm afraid you won't like me anymore if I tell you. And I wouldn't be able to bear that. I've done something terrible."

"Please, Mia, tell me. And trust my understanding of people, OK?" Juliette smiled tenderly.

Mia's breath caught, and then she looked up at the Eiffel Tower, hoping to find advice there. It didn't answer. "I–I was fourteen years old when it happened," she said. First, her words started and stopped, but then they finally came gushing out of Mia, as if they'd been waiting for her to finally speak them to someone. Juliette's expression changed from horrified in the beginning to angry, until finally she looked at Mia, disconcerted.

"My goodness, child," Juliette whispered. "Philippe and I assumed you were carrying around some heavy baggage with you, but this?" She shook her head.

"Do you not like me anymore now?" Mia asked in a small voice.

"Oh, Mia, why would we not like you?" Juliette hugged her again. Then she led her by the elbow over to Philippe, who'd been walking around them in larger and larger circles.

"You've made a mistake, a big mistake, Mia," Juliette said finally, gently touching Mia's cheek. "You should never have given that young man up, especially not like that, without talking to him first."

"But I couldn't have told him personally. I wouldn't have been able to leave him then." Tears ran down her cheeks again.

A worried-looking Philippe asked, "Is there anything I can do?"

"You can lead us over to a café where we'll all have a warm drink," Juliette said. Then she turned to Mia. "May I tell him your story, or would you rather do it yourself?"

After Juliette related Mia's horrible tale, Philippe said, "I'm so sorry—that's bad, child." He reached for Mia's hand. "But I agree with my wife, you shouldn't have just caught Levin by surprise like that. You should have stayed with him. A strong love can survive something like that."

"I didn't want to ruin his life." Mia sniffled into a tissue. She was slowly calming down again. They hadn't rejected her, and she was so glad.

"To think that they haven't seen each other in over three years now." Juliette shook her head. "That's tragic."

"Do you know if he's still in Berlin?" Philippe asked.

"I have no idea."

"Didn't you ever search for him on the Internet? Jacques showed me how, it's really easy," Juliette said.

"No, I don't have a computer, and I've never asked anybody to lend me theirs. I had to learn to get over Levin. That's why I avoided it."

"He may not be in Berlin anymore," Philippe said.

"Or he may have gotten married," Juliette considered. "He could have two children already." She looked at her husband, and they smiled at each other.

"Yes, yes, of course," Mia swallowed.

"Maybe he didn't even become a lawyer," Philippe said.

"I'm pretty sure he must be a lawyer, but I don't know, of course," Mia said.

"Well, all that can surely be found out." Philippe observed Mia carefully. "Let's just search for him on the Internet."

"Or you could ask him yourself," Juliette suggested.

Mia's eyes widened. "*No!* No, th–that w–won't w–w–work."

"Yes, it will," Juliette said. "Of course it will. You have to talk to him, Mia, and not just on the phone, but face-to-face. Maybe he'll slam the door on you, or his wife will do it for him. Maybe he hates you now or is inclined to believe that his mother was right. But maybe he still loves you and has been just as desperate as you have in the last three years."

"And even if it all turned out to be futile, even if he's fallen in love with someone else and there's no chance, then at least you'll have the closure your relationship deserves," Philippe added. "You have to do this, Mia. You owe it to your love."

"But so much time has gone by," Mia whispered. Her eyes brimmed with tears again. "And I've hurt him."

"You've been hurt, too." Juliette looked at Mia seriously. "Mia, you have to face up to it all. Please talk to Levin. He deserves that, don't you think?"

Mia lowered her gaze. She felt so helpless. Was it true what they were saying? "But what if Levin hates me now?" she asked fearfully.

"Then that's the way it is," Juliette said. "That's life. But you have to face the uncomfortable things as well. You've fought so hard before, and you can do this." Juliette took her hands again. "Besides, you won't be going to Berlin alone. We'll be there just in case and catch you if you walk away from it with a bloody nose."

"I can't ask that of you," Mia said.

"Yes, you can. We would do that for our children, and you're like a daughter to us," Philippe said.

Mia bit her lower lip. "I'm scared," she confessed.

"Yes, I believe you. But you'll be fine." Juliette patted her hand. "So, are we going to Berlin?"

41

Philippe and Juliette acted immediately. They drove Mia over to their son's house and asked him to search the Internet for Levin. It didn't take long to find him. Levin was working as a lawyer in his father's firm. Mia was glad, because that meant that they had made up. They also found Levin's address. He was still living in the same apartment. Should she really do it? She couldn't imagine how Levin would react to her. Maybe he'd be terribly angry, or maybe he didn't care about her anymore? What if he really was in a new relationship?

Then you should be happy for him, she reprimanded herself. *He deserves something better than a broken woman like you!*

"Well, Mia, that was easy," Jacques said. "I wish you good luck. When do you want to leave?"

"Right away would be best," Juliette said.

Her son regarded her in surprise. "Christmas is in three days. I thought we wanted to celebrate together, *Maman*."

"Yes, of course we will," she said. "I won't miss out on that. But we could try to get a flight on the twenty-sixth, right?" She looked at Mia.

"OK," Mia answered.

"Merry Christmas, honey." Sarah beamed at Levin and handed him his present. Levin could already see from the wrapping that it must have been expensive. Although she was still a student, her parents sponsored her very generously.

"But we weren't going to give each other expensive things anymore." He kissed the tip of her nose, then opened the bow. He hadn't been wrong. Out came a watch that had surely cost a small fortune.

"You need a reasonable watch." She wrapped her arms around his neck and began kissing him. Levin gladly responded. There was still some time until the meal at his parents'. He nudged her toward the bedroom.

A while later, Sarah said, "We really need to go now." She breathed tiny kisses onto his chest. "Otherwise, we'll be late."

"Who cares?" Levin said. He really didn't feel like sharing this Christmas dinner with his parents. But Sarah got along very well with them, and she would push him to go over there. He played with the necklace he'd given her—the only thing she was currently wearing. Meeting Sarah's taste was easy. All he had to do was go to the jeweler and choose something that sparkled. In return, he got something expensive back, which he really didn't care about. They would visit Sarah's parents tomorrow. Levin got along fairly well with them. They were real snobs, but because Levin was used to that from his own parents, he was able to deal with it.

"Levin!" Sarah became more insistent. She went over to the closet and tossed him a fresh shirt. "We have to go."

"Fine, I'm coming," he said, traipsing into the bathroom.

The villa door opened, and Sonja Webber greeted them with open arms. Levin hated this theatrical part of her.

"How wonderful that you're here!" she said as she greeted Sarah, Irmi, and Levin.

"Hi," Levin said tersely, and then wished his parents a merry Christmas. He and Sarah had picked up his aunt on the way. The relationship between Irmi and his mother was still a bit tense. Just like Levin, she still couldn't really forgive Sonja's behavior toward Mia. Even though Levin came to visit his parents more often now, it didn't mean everything was OK, and his mother knew that.

There was an abundant meal. Levin didn't like this gluttony on Christmas at all. He was already excited for Christmas Day. He wanted to meet his friends then, while Sarah was invited to be with her relatives. He should have gone there, too, but he had objected. It was already enough that he had to go to her parents' Christmas dinner tomorrow. He thought he should be able to do what he wanted on at least one day of his vacation. He wouldn't have that freedom taken from him.

"And you two, what are your plans for next year?" his mother asked as they were sitting together later over a glass of wine. Levin sighed. He could guess what she wanted to hear, but he wouldn't be able to give her that. He didn't have the least intention of proposing to Sarah. He liked her a lot, and it was nice with her, but he wasn't ready for more yet. He also knew she wanted him to move in with her, but he liked his little apartment and was in no hurry to leave it.

"Well, I'm hoping the firm will go on being so successful," Levin said, smiling. "And Sarah has a lot to do with school."

Irmi smiled. She'd also guessed what her sister had actually wanted to know. Irmi and Sarah got along well, and his aunt had never said a bad word about her, but there was a certain distance. It was different than it had been with . . . Levin shook his head. Why was he remembering Mia now? He hadn't thought about her in a long time and had given up looking for news. She was gone. All he could do was hope she was all right—but anything else, he didn't care about.

"There will be a big ball on New Year's Eve," Sonja Webber continued. "Are you two coming?"

Sarah looked up excitedly, poking Levin. "Do you feel like going?"

"Not at all," he said. That was all he needed. He wanted to celebrate New Year's with his friends, just like always. "You know that we're getting together with the gang."

"Well, that could be canceled for once." Sarah was annoyed.

"It *could* be, but it certainly won't be. You go."

"Maybe I'll think about it," Sarah said. Levin gave her a kiss, and she seemed mollified. "OK, we'll celebrate with friends," she finally gave in.

Mia fidgeted in her airplane seat. She wasn't at all sure this was such a good idea, but there was no going back now. The plane had just lifted off from Parisian soil. Juliette and Philippe had actually managed to get seats for the twenty-sixth. Mia had secretly been hoping that everything would be booked. They would land in Berlin in the afternoon and then check in to their hotel. Thank God it wasn't too expensive. So Mia could afford to pay for her own room, Juliette and Philippe hadn't booked a five-star hotel this time. She had insisted on that. What was next? Should she go to Levin's right away? Maybe it was better to get it over with. She almost passed out from the stress of just thinking about it.

In the last few days, she'd hardly eaten, though Juliette's cooking was fantastic. Juliette and Philippe were very worried about Mia in that respect, but she just couldn't manage to eat much. The Christmas holiday had been nice. The family had met, and it had been a loud, happy gathering. Mia had been especially excited to see the children again and had played with them a lot. She wanted children, too, and at twenty-six that wasn't such a distant possibility. But she couldn't imagine meeting another man she would love enough to want to start a family with him.

Juliette touched Mia's knee. "Don't be so nervous, sweetie. He won't tear your head off."

"Maybe he's not even home—maybe he's on holiday," Mia said, trying to fool herself.

"You're stalling," Juliette said. "It can't be avoided. Even if it doesn't happen while you're in Berlin, you can still leave a message to let him know how to reach you."

Mia nodded. She would probably do that. Now she could see that she never should have just left like that. But back then it seemed like the only way it could work for both of them. Would Levin understand? Would he even give her the chance to explain?

"Should we come with you?" Philippe asked.

"No, that's nice of you, but I probably have to do this alone." Mia swallowed heavily. They were standing at the end of the street, less than a hundred yards from Levin's building. Being there was completely surreal for Mia.

"We're going to drive downtown for a while. You have our number. Call us, OK?" Juliette touched her cheek.

"OK," Mia promised. Then she took a deep breath and walked down the street on shaky legs. She stopped in front of Levin's house and studied the names over the doorbells. Some looked familiar, and others seemed to have moved in recently.

Then she saw "L. Webber."

Mia was relieved not to see a new name next to his. But that didn't necessarily mean anything. She raised her hand to push the doorbell, but then she hesitated. Should she really do this to him? Just show up after all these years? Maybe she should approach him on the street—at least then he'd have the chance to leave right away and wouldn't feel quite so trapped or taken by surprise.

Mia crossed to the other side of the street and looked up at the front of the building. She saw a light on in Levin's living room. Her heart beat dangerously fast. She leaned against the wall. It was already dark, and he wouldn't see her right away when he left the house. And what if he wasn't planning on going out at all? Mia bit her lower lip, resolving to wait awhile—maybe an hour. She would ring the bell then if he didn't come out.

Levin grabbed his jacket and a bottle of vodka, his usual Christmas present for Kai and Geli, and then he set off. He was excited for tonight. Last night at Sarah's parent's had been quite formal. The two of them asked Levin and Sarah about their future plans, and Levin had given them the same answer he'd given his parents. He walked out the door. His car was parked directly in front of the building, and he laid the bottle of vodka on the passenger seat. As he opened the door, he heard something. Had someone just called his name? Levin looked around. The voice had been very quiet, but he was sure he hadn't misheard. As he looked across the street, he saw a ghost approaching him very slowly.

42

Mia's knees were shaking. She'd had to clear her throat a few times just to be able to call Levin's name. But he must have heard, because he turned toward her. His face showed complete bewilderment. She forced herself to walk, stepping into the streetlight's glare. As though she was being pulled by invisible strings, she placed one foot in front of the other. She approached him very slowly.

Levin couldn't believe his eyes. Mia! It was actually Mia—or was his mind playing tricks on him? But he'd had nothing to drink, nor was he extremely tired. Now she had almost reached him. She stopped at his car.

Mia could only stare at him. He was just as handsome as he had been three years ago; he hadn't changed at all. Her heart beat so loudly that she thought the entire street must be able to hear it. Still, she couldn't utter a sound.

"Mia, is that really you?" Levin registered that his voice sounded rough, but that wasn't surprising. She smiled shyly, and when she pushed a blond curl behind her ear, Levin saw that her hand was shaking.

"Yes," she managed to say. She could barely see through her tears.

"Where have you been all these years?" Levin had gotten over the first big shock, and now his anger welled up. "Did you get lost on your way to the store?"

Mia lowered her gaze, and a tear fell onto the pavement. "I'd like to talk to you. I—I'd like to explain," she said softly.

"You'd like to explain?" he asked, dumbfounded. He was working himself into a rage. "What if I don't want to hear it? What if I don't care anymore? It was a long time ago, remember?" Levin raked his hand through his hair. "And apart from that, I don't even have time. I have somewhere else I have to be right now." He got in the car.

Do something, everything in Mia screamed, and finally her paralysis lifted.

"Levin!" He gave her an angry look as she held on to the car door. "I know I have no right to just show up here like this, but I'll be in town for a few days, and maybe you can make some time for me. Please, Levin, think about it, OK?" Mia sobbed quietly. "I want to try to explain why I left you back then. It won't take long. And afterward— then I'll leave you alone again. It would mean so much to me." She dug a piece of paper out of her jacket pocket and handed it to him. "Here's my number. Maybe you'll call me?" she pleaded.

Levin took the piece of paper. She was crying so desperately. That didn't leave him cold; it never had. "We'll see," he said, then started the engine. Mia stepped aside, and he saw to it that he got away quickly. He glanced at her in the rearview mirror. She stood fixed in the same place and slowly got smaller and smaller.

Mia was in shock. Only when she'd lost sight of Levin's car could she step back onto the sidewalk. Now she noticed that she was freezing. She wondered if she should go to Mrs. Heller's café, if it still existed. But she decided against that. She was so rattled that she wouldn't be able to put together a coherent sentence. She was surprised by how well she still knew the streets. Finally, she found a small bistro and went in to warm up.

Levin still couldn't quite grasp it. He almost doubted his own sanity, but the small piece of yellow paper on the passenger seat confirmed that it hadn't been a dream. Mia was actually back. He had seen her, in the flesh, standing right in front of him, wanting to talk. What did she want to talk about? He already knew her reasons and where she'd originally gone. Was she kidding herself that everything could be the same now as it had been three years ago? Was she still that naive?

"Fuck, Mia, what the hell is this?" He cursed her. How could she just show up and throw his life into chaos again? He stopped at Kai's place and pushed the doorbell incessantly.

"Whoa, what's with the impatience?" Kai greeted him in surprise. "Was Christmas that bad?"

"Do you know what this is?" Levin angrily pushed the paper with Mia's number at him. Then he handed the bottle of vodka to Geli.

"Um, looks like a Post-it note with numbers on it," Kai said, chuckling. "Come in, and give me your jacket."

Levin followed him, looking somber. "That's Mia's phone number," he explained once he was inside.

Kai's expression changed immediately. "What?"

"Mia?" Geli joined them. She looked just as shocked. "Where did you get that number? How did you find it?"

"Oh, that was easy—she just gave it to me."

"Dude! You're kidding, right?" Kai was wide-eyed.

"What do you mean? Is Mia back in Berlin?" A smile flitted across Geli's face. "What does she look like, what did she say? Where was she, and what has she been doing all this time?"

"No idea. She said she wanted to explain everything to me. But I really don't want to be taken for a ride, understand? Who does she think she is? Does she really think she can just show up here and everything will be the same again?" Levin said.

"Is that what she wants? Did she say that? Does she want you back?" Geli asked, practically bouncing with excitement.

"I only spoke to her briefly and then left her there. What did you think? Should I drop everything just because she so mercifully came back to me?" Levin grabbed the bottle of vodka and took a gulp.

"But you're going to call her, right? I mean, once you've slept on it."

"I don't know. I have my life, she has hers. A lot of time has passed. So what is this crap?" Levin shrugged, trying to seem bored.

"Don't act like you don't give a damn." Geli poked him in the chest. "If you don't, then why is your blood boiling?"

"Because I'm upset by the audacity of it," Levin complained. "How can she just turn up here like this?"

"Mia seemed audacious?"

"No," Levin said, running his fingers through his hair. "She cried and seemed desperate."

"Man, Levin, you loved that girl to pieces. Don't you want to at least hear what she has to say?" Kai shoved the piece of paper at him.

"Now? Are you nuts? I won't let her ruin my evening."

"You won't be able to think about anything else, anyway. Go talk to her, and then come back over here again. And even if you don't come back here tonight, we can still catch up on this later without a problem, right?" Kai smiled and punched him on the shoulder. "I know this is a complete shock for you. I never would have thought Mia would turn up here again, but hey, what do you have to lose by finding out what she wants to say?"

Levin groaned. Damn that girl, why did she have to come back? Then he pulled out his phone, gave Geli and Kai an angry look, and punched in the number on the paper.

Mia jumped as her phone rang. She'd kept it on the table in front of her in the crazy hope that Levin might call. She expected it to be Juliette, but then she saw a different number. Her heart beat faster. "Yes?" She cleared her throat.

"Mia, this is Levin. You said you wanted to talk, so let's get it over with. Where are you now?" He sounded more resentful than he meant to, but at the moment he was just too rattled to have a grip on himself.

Mia almost fell off her chair with excitement. "I'm in the small bistro on Gezellinstrasse. Do you know that one?"

"I live in Berlin, remember? Stay there—I'm coming over now." He ended the call and looked over at his friends. Kai and Geli had moved off to the side to give him space, but Levin knew they'd heard everything. "I'm going to meet her. I'll probably be right back."

"Tell her hello for us," Geli said. "Maybe she'd like to get together with me sometime."

"Here's her number, call her yourself," Levin answered. Then he grabbed his jacket and hastened down the steps to his car. *What am I doing?* he asked himself as he drove toward the bistro. *Am I her loyal puppy or something?* He was still angry when he opened the bistro's door.

Mia was sitting in a corner, kneading her hands. She looked in his direction and stood up. *He's here. He really came.* Mia didn't know if she should panic or feel relieved.

"Hi, Levin, I'm glad you came," she said softly when he was standing in front of her.

Levin eyed her for a second. She was so incredibly thin. He remembered her as slim, but now she looked sickly. She was pale, terribly pale, and had dark circles under her eyes. His anger dissolved the moment he saw the tears shining in her eyes.

"Please sit down," she requested.

"OK, here I am. So, what did you want to tell me?" he asked, not letting her out of his sight for a second.

43

Mia didn't know what to do with her hands. She wrung them as she searched for the right words. She was close to tears. Seeing him again had flustered her.

"Mia? I'm listening," he said seriously.

Mia took a deep breath, trying to regain her composure. Then she looked into his eyes. "I–I want to apologize. I hurt you, and to just leave like that was a big mistake." Her voice sounded surprisingly firm, which astonished her. "I should have talked to you, but back then I thought I was doing the right thing."

Levin shook his head and laughed. "You're right, Mia—it was a mistake, a goddamn awful mistake. I almost died worrying about you. I looked for you in Casablanca and some nearby cities on the coast, but no one could give me any clues," Levin burst out. He'd wanted to stay as cool as possible and then leave again right away, but he was shaken, and everything was rushing back.

"What? You were in Morocco?" Mia was wide-eyed. "But why?"

"Why? Because you were there, or are you denying that?" he snapped. "Did you think I would just accept that you disappeared without searching for you? Irmi and I hired a private detective. He found out you'd gone to the airport and taken a plane to Casablanca. So that's where I looked for you. I was there for four weeks, Mia." He looked at her stunned face.

"But I told you not to look for me," she said, distraught. "Levin, I didn't want this, why did you do it?"

"I loved you, Mia." Levin searched her face, but that was a mistake. Her eyes, her beautiful eyes, where her soul lay bare—he could read everything in them.

"I left out of love for you, because I didn't want to stand in your way and be a b–burden," she said. What Levin had just told her was hard to stomach.

"Did you honestly feel like you were a burden to me?" He dropped his gaze to the table, unable to look into her eyes any longer. There was a huge emotional chaos inside him right now. Her appearance had unsettled him more than he liked to admit. "You were my life, Mia," he added quietly.

"And you were mine." Her voice threatened to break away completely. This was too much for her. She couldn't believe that he'd searched for her, and had been so close. "Levin," she added, "I hope you can forgive me. I never wanted to hurt you." She fought the tears again—and this time she lost.

"You weren't very successful, then," he said. She seemed totally destroyed, and his heart constricted painfully at the sight. He couldn't help it: he reached for her hands—which felt like ice—and stroked them gently.

"Man, Mia, why did you let my mother talk you into something so stupid?" He brushed a blond curl off her face. Her cheeks were wet from the tears.

"So you know that she came and talked to me?"

"Yeah, I went to talk to Mrs. Heller at the café. She remembered my mother, and you had left me so much money that it was clear it hadn't come from your piggy bank." He smiled. "Then I confronted my parents. My mother admitted that she'd offered you money to leave."

Mia nodded. She looked down at Levin's hands holding hers so tightly now. It was a beautiful, familiar feeling. Warmth flooded through her, permeating the cold in which she'd felt trapped for so long now. "I should have guessed you'd see through that right away." A wistful smile settled on her face. "I can only apologize again and again that I made you worry so much."

"OK," Levin said, pulling away. He needed more distance at the moment. This reunion was still very difficult for him. "So how have you been all this time? What do you do now? Where do you live?"

"I live and work in Agadir," she explained, hastily wiping some tears from her face. "After I left Berlin, I only stayed in Casablanca for a day. I wanted to see Marrakesh. On the train ride there I met a French couple, and we became good friends. In Marrakesh something happened. Well, my money was stolen, and I had to find a job right away. Philippe helped me get a work permit, and they lent me money so I could travel to Agadir. I was told it would be easier to find work on the coast." Mia looked at Levin uncertainly. She was afraid she was boring him, but he listened attentively.

"Your money was stolen? Did anything happen to you?" Levin had inwardly jumped at her story. He didn't want to imagine what else could have happened to her.

"No. In Agadir I found a job at a hotel and, well, I'm still there."

"Do you like it there?"

"Morocco is a beautiful country. I've gotten to know some nice people, and I have a good job," Mia said. "I even have a small apartment."

A smile flashed across Levin's face. "That sounds great."

"Yeah, it is." She smiled back at him. "I'm the service manager, so I supervise the waiters and am in charge of grocery orders—that kind of stuff."

Now Levin was truly amazed, and he nodded at her approvingly. "I always knew there was so much more in you. Congratulations, Mia."

"Thanks." Mia was happy about his praise. "I'm proud of myself."

"And you should be. You've made it in a foreign country, and I can imagine that wasn't easy as a woman in Morocco."

"No, it wasn't." She didn't want to admit more than that to him. She definitely didn't want to tell him about her despair and the pills that were still lying ready on her nightstand. "I hope I didn't bore you," she added quietly. "How have you been? I see you're working in your father's firm now, so . . . you're getting along with your parents again?"

"You don't bore me, Mia. I made up with my father, but it took me a long time, and at first I really couldn't forgive them at all. But my father apologized. He hadn't known that my mother had gone to see you and treated you so horribly. I work in his firm now, but I'm still not sure if I want to stay there. I'll see how it all develops."

"And what about your mother?" Mia asked tentatively.

"Let's just say that I accept her company now and then," he answered. Then he thought it better to tell the truth. He couldn't know what Mia's intentions were. It was a good time for honesty. "And I get along very well with Sarah. She's my girlfriend."

"Oh." Mia swallowed, then smiled at him. "That sounds great, Levin." She hoped with all her might he couldn't see how hard that news had hit her. Of course, she should have expected it. But imagining it was one thing—actually hearing it was quite another.

She wasn't a good actress, and Levin had observed her closely. She had lowered her gaze, but he still hadn't missed her look of sadness. Was she really hoping that they could get back together?

"Yeah, it is great," he continued. "At the moment everything's fine. And what about you? Do you have a boyfriend?"

Mia was lost in her thoughts about Levin having a girlfriend. He was handsome and probably made good money. And he was a very nice guy. It was only natural that women would line up to be with him.

"Mia?" he pressed gently. She seemed far away. "Mia?"

She startled. "Yes?"

"Do you have a boyfriend? A steady partner?"

"No," she said, "I don't—I mean, since we were together, I haven't been with, uh, anybody." She felt she must be blushing. Dammit, why couldn't she just stay cool for once and hide her feelings? On the other hand, why should she? She had nothing to lose, and she wanted to be honest with him. That was just the way her life was. She was alone, and that wasn't so terrible.

Levin really hadn't expected this, because she was a beautiful young woman, and other guys ought to have noticed that. But he did feel kind of touched by it, and he couldn't avoid feeling relieved. "Ah, OK, then."

Mia took a deep breath. She felt the need for fresh air and a chance to digest this meeting. She reached for her purse and took out her wallet. "I'd like to go. My treat, of course." She pointed to the beer.

"Really? Already?" Levin asked. Then he bit his tongue.

"Yes, I've stolen enough of your time. Please, just tell me if you're still angry at me." Mia studied his face.

Oh man, she's still going strong. Her eyes had that pleading look in them. He was incapable of saying anything else now, even if he wanted to. "No, Mia, I'm not. I mean, I knew about the circumstances. I just wish you had acted differently. But things have happened this way now." Levin reflexively reached for Mia's hand. "I'm glad you're all right and have your life under control."

Then he focused on her pallor and delicate stature and noticed that she didn't seem all that well after all. But that wasn't any of his business anymore now—it couldn't be.

Mia smiled. "Thanks, Levin."

"What for?"

"For your understanding and the beautiful time together." Mia's eyes brimmed with tears again. Quickly, she put the money on the table and reached for her jacket. "I hope I didn't keep you from something important," she said before hurrying out.

44

Levin stared after her, baffled. She'd already made it out the door. *Follow her!* he told himself. But for a brief moment his pride took over, and he hesitated. Wasn't it wrong to go after her? They weren't together anymore, and he was in another relationship. Maybe he should just let her go. They'd already talked things out. But on the other hand, she was still the same Mia he had loved, and he couldn't stand to see her unhappy. Her tears and her appearance touched him. He couldn't help himself. Levin grabbed his jacket and ran after her.

Mia inhaled the fresh December air. The cold felt good to her. She had done it. She'd talked to Levin and apologized for her behavior. They had cleared the air, and because of that, their life together had found a peaceful closure. She should have been glad now, but she wasn't. Seeing him again, being near him—that had shown her once more how much she still loved him. Mia let her tears flow freely. Then she slowly started walking down the street.

Levin looked around, searching frantically. She couldn't have gone that far. For a short moment he panicked that she had slipped away from him again. But then he saw her. She was walking slowly with her head down, and he could hear her footsteps on the pavement.

"Mia!"

She jumped and turned. Levin jogged toward her. She blotted her tears. For a moment, hope flared up inside her, but she pushed the thought away.

"Levin, what is it?"

Levin took a deep breath. What was he doing?

"I'll take you back to the hotel," he said hastily, grateful that he'd managed to think of something fairly plausible.

"Thanks, but you don't have to. I feel like walking."

"It's dark and too dangerous," Levin persisted.

"It's not. I'm used to walking alone at night."

Levin raised his eyebrows. "Just because you're used to it doesn't mean it isn't dangerous."

"I'll take the Metro and then walk the rest of the way," she answered.

"Where is your hotel?"

"In Koenigstrasse," Mia answered. She wondered why he wanted to know, but his interest was nice, too. It felt good to know that he still worried about her.

"But you'll still have to walk quite a ways," he said.

"Yes, that's what I wanted to do."

"I'll come with you," Levin said.

"What about your car? It's still parked here. And you said you had something else planned," Mia reminded him.

"Yes, I do. Seeing you to your hotel safely." He looked into her eyes. She wouldn't get rid of him so quickly.

"OK." Mia shrugged and walked on.

After walking in silence for a while, Levin finally spoke. "Mia?"

"Yes?" She glanced at him.

"I'm glad to see you again, even though I did react harshly at first. I think highly of you for coming here." He ran a hand through his hair.

"I had to resolve this, but I wouldn't have had the courage to come on my own. My friends from France encouraged me."

Levin was disappointed. He would have preferred it to be her own idea.

"I should have thought of doing it myself," she continued, and Levin wondered if she could read his mind. "But I was afraid of breaking back into your life. I didn't want to throw you off balance."

"Mia," Levin said, taking her by the shoulders. "You're here now, and we've talked it over. That's something, right?" He smiled. "There's nothing more to untangle."

"Yeah, OK." For the first time that evening, her smile was truly free. "I'm happy to see you, too."

"Come here." Levin pulled her in. He buried his face in her hair as he always used to. She still smelled just as good. "Mia," he whispered.

At first, Mia stiffened, but then she felt that tingling that only he could create in her. She returned his hug and enjoyed this precious moment with all her senses. Levin pushed her away gently. He felt himself blushing. Thank God it was dark enough that she probably wouldn't notice. "I just couldn't help myself," he said.

"I know," Mia answered. Now she couldn't hold back a chuckle. Levin seemed embarrassed, and Mia thought that was cute. Why should she always be the one to feel that way?

"What, are you laughing at me?" he asked. "Hey!"

"No, of course I'm not laughing at you." She worked up her courage and touched his cheek. Levin felt her touch like an electric shock, even as light as it was. His skin felt like it would burn away under her hand. But it felt nice. Beautiful, even.

He cleared his throat. "Come on, Mia, let's go, OK?"

"All right. I think we'll find the Metro station around the next corner," she said. It had been a strange moment, but now the atmosphere had dissolved again. Her phone rang, and Mia could already guess who was calling her.

"Hi, Philippe," she answered, smiling.

Philippe? Levin's ears pricked. Who was that? Then he remembered her saying something about a French couple. Was she in Berlin with them? Or was Philippe more than just a friend? Had she just lied to him?

"I'm on my way to the hotel," Mia explained.

"Did you meet him?" Philippe asked.

"Yes, I did. He's standing next to me right now. He's walking me back."

"Well," Philippe said, "I should hope so. That's the way it's supposed to be. Juliette and I are sitting at the hotel bar right now. Come if you feel like it, and bring your friend."

Mia smiled. She could imagine that Philippe and Juliette were curious about Levin. "I'll see," she said. "I don't know yet. See you later."

Mia turned to Levin. "That was Philippe, a good friend. I'm in Berlin with him and his wife."

Levin was somewhat relieved. "Ah, so you met here?"

"No. I was visiting them in Paris. Being here now wasn't part of the original plan," she answered.

"I see." He thought of her words from before. Then a memory came up. "Paris. I haven't been back there since then." Images popped up in his mind, those of a radiant girl who laughed a lot and had begun to discover the world, wide-eyed. He looked over at Mia, who also seemed to be lost in thought. Was she remembering? Apart from her insecurity, she had nothing in common with the Mia he'd known in Paris. She seemed unhappy, somehow ill, and was always holding back tears. Levin had never been able to bear seeing her that way, but what could he do? They had parted ways, and now both of them had established new lives for themselves.

"It was wonderful there," Mia said. *Everything was wonderful with you,* she added in her thoughts.

"Yeah," Levin agreed. "Definitely. The entire journey was great, except for the end." *And the time after that, too.* He remembered some very different things, too, things that had taken place in his bedroom. For a moment he felt very turned on. Then he pushed those thoughts away. He had Sarah now, and they had a happy relationship. Still, he was shocked at how quickly Mia had entranced him again. He couldn't allow himself to get too close, although he was enjoying her company more and more.

Despite herself, Mia had started to shiver. The walk from the station to the hotel was longer than she'd remembered. But she wouldn't have taken any shortcut in the world. Every minute with Levin was precious. After tonight she'd probably never see him again. She didn't even want to think about it. The thought of having to live without him now was just too cruel.

"Everything all right?" Levin asked. Mia was so quiet.

"Yes, I'm just a little cold," she answered.

"Ha, you softie, you're not used to German weather at all anymore," Levin said.

"That's true," Mia said, giggling. He stopped and pulled her toward him. Then he vigorously rubbed her back and upper arms. Mia tried to stay cool, but she started shaking even more. And that had nothing to do with the cold.

"Thanks, it's better now," she said, lowering her eyes.

"There's a bus stop up there. We could take the bus the rest of the way if you want," Levin suggested.

"No, I'm fine." She didn't want to lose a second of time with him.

When they finally reached the hotel, Mia's heart became heavy. "Thank you so much, Levin," she said.

"Not a problem. Are you still meeting your friends tonight?"

"Yes, they're waiting at the hotel bar." Then she worked up all her courage. "Would you like to come in for a drink? They'd love to meet you."

Levin hesitated. It wouldn't hurt to get a look at the people Mia was traveling with. "Sure," he said.

Mia was happy that Levin was coming inside with her. When they entered the bar, Juliette was already waving at them from far away. "There they are," Mia told Levin, reaching for his hand. But she quickly reconsidered that and let go right away. Then she went ahead to Juliette and Philippe's table. "I brought Levin," she said.

The French couple got up and greeted him jovially. "Nice to meet you, Levin. Please, have a drink with us."

"With pleasure." Levin sat down at the table with them. The small bench made it necessary to sit very close to Mia; he could distinctly feel her leg against his. He considered scooting away but stayed put.

"Were you born in Berlin?" Juliette asked Levin.

"Yes, I was born here, just like my mother."

"We haven't seen much of the city yet," Philippe said. "We arrived today. Mia's going to show us the sights over the next few days, and we're really looking forward to it. The wall was still up during our last visit—it's clear that a lot has changed since then."

"Yes, you could say so. Mia's going to be your tour guide?" Levin grinned at Mia shamelessly and added, "Do you still know your way around?"

"Of course I do! I used to live here, you know."

"But not for long," Levin said, looking into her eyes. They were sitting so close that he could feel her breath on his skin.

"Well, I'm sure a newcomer wouldn't be able to do it as well as a local. But if Mia doesn't know where to go, we do have our guidebook," Juliette said, waving the small book at Levin.

"You could give us some recommendations," Mia said. Levin was really close now. Not that it wasn't nice, but it did confuse her a lot.

"Sure, I could do that. What are your plans for tomorrow?" Levin asked. Juliette opened up their guidebook and showed him a few destinations. "Sounds good, and there's a nice place to eat right there, too," he said, pointing at a spot on the map.

"You probably have a lot to do tomorrow, right?" Juliette's eyes twinkled mischievously. Mia had seen it. She could guess what Juliette was trying to hint at.

"No, I'm on holiday," Levin answered truthfully. "The firm is closed between Christmas and New Year's."

"Would you mind taking the time to accompany us?" Juliette asked. "I'm sure Mia's a fine guide, but someone who was born here sees everything with different eyes and has much more inside knowledge."

"Juliette, you can't just ambush poor Levin like that," Philippe scolded gently, but Mia could see that he, too, was having fun with this game. For her, the whole thing was fairly awkward. What would Levin think now? Surely he wanted to spend his time off with his girlfriend. Mia hardly dared to breathe. Levin didn't have to think long. The two elderly people were so kind and sincere; why shouldn't he spend the day with them? *And with Mia*, he added in his thoughts.

"I'm not ambushing him—I'm just asking." Juliette smiled at Levin. "You can be completely honest. We will understand, of course, if you don't feel like sacrificing your time for us."

"No, it's not a sacrifice, I'd love to show you the city," he answered. "It's possible that Mia's forgotten a lot already," he teased.

"Excuse me?" she said. Levin thought the way she was looking at him so indignantly was incredibly cute. "I haven't forgotten anything, but I'm glad you're coming with us."

"OK, so it's a date," Juliette said. She was happy about the way things were developing. "When would be best for you?"

"After breakfast, I can adapt to you. Maybe around ten?"

"Perfect," Philippe said.

Mia took a deep breath. One more day with Levin—that sounded very, very good. But she could already imagine that saying good-bye would be even harder after that. Mia needed some distance.

"I just need to use the restroom for a minute," she said, excusing herself.

Levin watched as she walked away. She seemed just as surprised at the turn of events as he was. Maybe she wasn't even happy that he'd offered to show them around. But now it was too late, and should he notice her feeling uncomfortable tomorrow, he could still make up a reason to end their meeting.

Juliette spoke up. "We're glad Mia was able to see you."

"I have to admit that I was shocked," he said, "and also very angry at first. The circumstances under which we parted were less than pleasant."

"I know," Juliette said. "But I can assure you that it was hard for Mia. She's like a daughter to us, and we took her into our hearts immediately. Never before have we met such a sincere and selfless person. She's so special, and it breaks my heart to think what she went through."

"Yes, Mia's special. That makes what my mother did all the worse."

"Definitely. We're parents ourselves, and God knows our children have made some terrible choices before," Philippe said, "but who wouldn't like Mia?"

"Well, a lot of time has passed"—Levin fumbled with his coaster, lost in thought—"and things have changed."

"Have you found a new love? Excuse me if I'm being nosy, but that would be normal—it's just the passage of time," Juliette said.

"Yes, I have a girlfriend," Levin answered.

"That's how it should be for a young man. Good that you've found love again."

Levin only nodded, but his thoughts weren't with Sarah. "How has Mia been doing in Morocco? She hasn't told me much yet."

"Well, she hasn't told us much about it. She's really very secretive and doesn't talk about herself. But we've visited her in Morocco before. We can speak to Faizah there, a good friend of Mia's. Faizah told us that Mia cries a lot and is sad. And that she barely eats anything. Once she became ill with food poisoning, and Mia had to be taken to the hospital. Faizah said she'd been under the impression that Mia wanted to give up on herself completely there. It was shocking to hear, but Mia made it far in her job. She really fought her way up, and for that she deserves respect."

Levin looked at Juliette, stunned. But he'd also been expecting it somehow. It was clear that Mia wasn't doing well. But what was going on? He didn't want to imagine that she was still pining for him, but what if it was true? "Do you know—or, I mean, did Faizah tell you the reason for Mia's sadness?"

"Actually, I shouldn't have told anyone what Faizah confided in us, and I'd prefer not to say any more. But since you're such a good friend of hers, I guess it's not so bad," Juliette said. "I'm glad that the two of you could talk things out. Maybe Mia will feel better now."

Alone in the restroom, Mia let cold water flow over her wrists. She needed to calm down. The evening had taken an unexpected turn. On one hand, she was grateful that she could talk to Levin, but on the other, it was painful to see him, knowing that he was happy with someone else. But she loved him, and she should be happy for him because of that—that's what her mind told her, anyway. Only her stupid heart wanted to shatter from the sadness of it. She took a deep breath. She resolved to enjoy the time she had with him. She couldn't do any more than that.

When she returned to the table, Juliette and Philippe were immersed in conversation with Levin. They seemed to get along well, which made sense. All of them were open-minded people.

"Oh, there you are." Levin smiled at her. Mia's heart accelerated at the sight of him.

"Levin was just telling us a bit about the sights we'll be visiting tomorrow," Philippe said.

"Good," Mia said. She caught herself looking into Levin's blue eyes. He winked at her, and she blushed. Mia's tension was slowly decreasing. She drank a glass of red wine and let Juliette, Philippe, and Levin carry on the conversation. She began to enjoy the evening more and more. There was a lot of laughing, and when the elderly couple finally excused themselves, it was already after one o'clock.

"We need to get some sleep, or we won't be on time tomorrow," Philippe said. "We'll meet at ten tomorrow in the hotel lobby." Then he and Juliette said their good-byes to Levin and Mia.

"See you tomorrow." Mia hugged the two of them tightly, then glanced at Levin. "Maybe I should get to bed, too," she said.

"Sure, I'll be on my way then." Levin was pretty nervous. "See you tomorrow, Mia."

"Yes, see you tomorrow. I hope that's OK for you."

"Yes, completely OK." Levin bent down and gave her a peck on the cheek. He paused, inhaled her scent, and fought the desire to pull her into a kiss. *Are you completely nuts?* he reprimanded himself.

"Bye." Mia smiled at him one more time, then turned away from his gaze and tried to calm the butterflies in her stomach.

45

Levin wasn't quite sure what to do with himself. There was no way he could sleep right now. It was close to two, and he needed to talk to somebody. Irmi wasn't an option at this time of night, but he'd love to hear what she thought about Mia's appearance. He resolved to call her early the next morning. Then he called Kai.

"Hey, Levin, where are you?" Kai said. The loud music in the background signaled that the party was still going strong.

"I just came home," he said.

"Were you with Mia all this time?"

"Yeah, I just came back from her hotel."

"What? Dude! When Sarah finds out!"

"What do you mean?" Levin sputtered, but then he remembered that Kai probably wasn't sober at this point, and he backed off. "We just had a drink with her friends at the hotel bar. Before that we were in a bistro."

"So? What'd she say? What does she want?"

"She wanted to apologize for disappearing like that. She was honestly sorry, and we talked it out. It's OK now."

"Does she know about Sarah?"

"Yeah, she does. I'm giving her and her friends a tour of Berlin tomorrow. It feels good to see her, you know?" Levin closed his eyes and immediately pictured Mia in front of him. Way too pale, way too skinny—yet still beautiful.

"I understand. But do you think Sarah will?" Kai said, laughing.

"She has to. Mia has a steady job in Morocco, so she won't be in town for long. All I want is some more time with her."

"Well, OK, have fun then. Send her our greetings—maybe she'll feel like stopping by our place, too, while she's here," Kai offered.

"I'll tell her," Levin promised. As soon as he put down the phone, his mind wandered to Sarah. Did she need to know about this? It was only a sightseeing tour.

The first thing Levin did the next morning was call his aunt. He invited himself over for breakfast and was standing at her door with fresh, warm rolls a few minutes later.

"Levin, how nice that you called. And so early—don't you have a day off today?" Irmi ushered him inside.

"I do. But I have plans, and I didn't want to sleep in that long," he said, smiling.

"Are you and Sarah having a day out?"

Levin thought it would be better to wait until she had sat down and poured the coffee before answering. "No, I'm spending the day with Mia and her French friends. I'm showing them Berlin," he said as casually as possible.

At first Irmi didn't react, but then her head shot up. "Mia? *The* Mia?" she asked.

"Yes." Levin laughed. "*The* Mia. She suddenly showed up at my door yesterday wanting to talk."

"I can't believe this. But why now? What did she want?" Irmi took a sip of coffee. "I mean, what did she want to tell you?"

"She apologized for disappearing three years ago. She said she did it out of love for me, and she's sorry for hurting me," Levin explained.

343

"And how did you react?"

"At first I didn't want to talk to her. I told her so and went directly over to Kai's for a party. But he and Geli convinced me to contact Mia. Then she and I met at a bistro."

"What does she look like? What does she do now? Where does she live?"

"She's still beautiful, but she seems ill. She's so pale and frighteningly skinny." Worry for her rose up in Levin again. "Yesterday I also had the opportunity to get to know her French friends, a very nice couple from Paris. When Mia was in the restroom they told me she's apparently not very happy."

"She never got over it," his aunt said sadly. "She never got over the separation."

"Do you really think so? I mean, it's been so long now." Of course Levin feared that might be the reason for Mia's state, but that didn't make things any less complicated.

"As far as I can imagine, that has to be the case. Levin, with the way she used to look at you all the time, there's no doubt in my mind. My God, I feel so sorry for her." Irmi looked at Levin sadly. "That's really tragic."

"But there's good news, too. She has a great job in a hotel in Agadir, which is where she lives. She worked her way up—she has a career." He was actually very proud of her when he thought about it.

"I'm happy to hear that. Apparently people had no prejudice against her there, and it goes to show how much of a difference that can make. But how is this going to go on? You're meeting her today?"

"Yes, we agreed last night that I'd show her friends part of Berlin, and her, too, of course. It just worked out that way."

"And how do you feel about it?"

"I'm glad to see Mia. I mean, there's still so much that connects us. It's OK. Absolutely OK." Levin ran his hand through his hair. It was hard to answer that question.

"Yes, exactly. There's still so much that connects you. The two of you had an intense time together." She put her hand on Levin's arm. "Mia was your great love, and the woman who broke your heart. Can you really treat her as objectively as you're trying to make me believe?"

Levin just shrugged. "There are moments when everything comes back. She still feels familiar and close. But then I think of my current life—and hers. We've changed. She has a life in Morocco, and I have mine here with Sarah."

"Are you going to tell Sarah that Mia's here?"

"I don't know. I think it might be better not to. I mean, we're meeting totally casually today, and—I mean, it's nothing big, is it?"

"If it's nothing big, then you can tell Sarah," Irmi said with a kind smile.

"I'd prefer to wait and see how today turns out first."

"Levin, don't start playing any games."

"What games? What do you mean? We're going on a tour of Berlin, nothing more." He became impatient.

"I just don't want you to test out Mia's availability as a potential partner while keeping Sarah on the back burner."

"That's ridiculous. How can you think that? It won't go that far. As I've said, Mia lives in Morocco, and I live here—goodness, we only just met again yesterday. I'm not even thinking of anything like that!"

"I'm just reminding you to be fair—to both of them."

"Well, you think highly of me, don't you!"

"Yes, and I'm telling you this exactly *because* I do. Levin, I'm not blind, I can see that this is getting to you."

"Well, why wouldn't it? I mean, I used to really love Mia. Do you think it would be better if I called off the meeting?"

"Not at all. Enjoy your day with her, and do me a favor: Listen to your heart and not to your head. And remember that nothing happens without a reason." Irmi got up and tousled Levin's hair. "Some things just take their course."

Levin went out to his car. Then he reached for his phone and called Sarah. He didn't really think it was necessary to inform her, but maybe Irmi was right. Playing with an open hand was always better.

"Hi, Levin, how nice of you to call." She still sounded sleepy; she'd probably just gotten up.

"Hi, how are you?" he said.

"Fine, thanks. I'll jump in the shower quickly and then start studying," she said. "How was Kai's party?"

Levin bit his lip. "I didn't go. You won't believe this, but Mia visited me yesterday. She's in town with friends for a few days." He tensed up, waiting for her reaction.

"Mia? Your ex?" she said in a tone of disbelief.

"The very same. She lives in Morocco and wanted to check out Berlin with her friends." Levin had adopted a casual, conversational tone.

"Ah."

"Yeah, it was kind of strange seeing her again after all these years. We're meeting soon so I can show her friends a bit of the city," he continued.

"There are tour guides for that," she replied with annoyance. "Why do you have to do it?"

"Because I'm a nice guy? And because Mia's friends seem nice, too?"

"Or because Mia's here?" Sarah's voice slipped up a few notes.

"Sure, also because Mia's here. We haven't seen each other in such a long time. There's a lot to say," he explained.

"Well. I bet there is. Then have fun with her!"

"Hey, calm down. You know why she left back then. We still have a bit to talk about, and as I said, Mia lives in Morocco and will only be here for a few more days. Relax, OK?" He cursed himself for following Irmi's advice. He really didn't feel like having problems with Sarah, too.

"I am relaxed." Sarah softened a bit. "I'm sorry, Levin—I'm just a bit overworked."

"No problem. I'll get back to you later, OK?"

"Yes, please do. I love you," she said.

"Hugs back," he said out of habit, ending the conversation.

His talk with Irmi had made him think. He thought she was a bit off the mark. He wasn't considering a new relationship with Mia at all—that would be pointless, anyway. He wasn't too fond of long-distance relationships, and besides, there was still the question of whether Mia would want him back.

What are you doing? he scolded himself. Irmi had put this idea into his head, and now he wanted to ignore it with all his might.

He arrived at the hotel on time, and Juliette and Philippe were already seated in the lobby waiting for him. Mia was nowhere to be seen yet. Panic crept up—was it possible she wouldn't come? Maybe she'd had second thoughts.

"Hi, Juliette. Hello, Philippe," he greeted them.

"Hi, Levin. Mia will be right here. She just forgot her scarf," Juliette said with a smile.

"Oh, OK." He couldn't avoid taking a deep, relieved breath. A short while later, Mia arrived, and for the first few minutes he couldn't take his eyes off her.

Mia was terribly nervous. She was excited about the day with Levin, but she didn't know where it would lead. But, surprisingly, she had slept better last night than she had in a long time. The talk with him seemed to have calmed her, although she didn't feel consciously relaxed. Mia noticed Levin checking her out as she approached. She smiled.

"Hi, Mia, you're looking good," he said.

"Hi, Levin. You, too."

Levin hesitated, and then he remembered his aunt's advice. He should listen to his heart. He bent down and kissed Mia's cheek. "Nice to see you," he whispered. As he stepped back, he saw that her face was faintly flushed. Levin could barely free himself from her gaze. The eye contact didn't last long, but it was intense. That deep brown hadn't lost any of its magical effect on him. He had to force himself to remember Juliette and Philippe. "OK, let's get going, then," he told the group. He put a hand on Mia's back as they left the hotel. "This way," he said, pointing.

First, they went through the usual tourist program. Since Levin had come by car, he could drive them to the various destinations. Before heading to the hotel, he'd written down the addresses of a few Moroccan restaurants. He wanted to surprise Mia. It was fun to show the three of them his hometown. The French couple were very interested, and with Mia's help the communication worked without a problem. As far as Levin could tell, Mia's French was nearly perfect.

Mia was enjoying Levin's company more and more. The atmosphere was relaxed. Levin joked around, and Mia couldn't remember the last time she had laughed so much. When it started getting dark, Mia felt a chill. She scolded herself for not remembering to bring gloves. She kept rubbing her hands together.

"What's up? Are you cold?" Levin asked and looked at her with concern. He came over to her. Juliette and Philippe were admiring the architecture of a building that Levin had pointed out to them.

"Oh, um, yeah, I should have brought some gloves," she said sheepishly.

"Why didn't you say something? We could have gone into one of the shops," he said.

"I'm fine." Mia smiled at him, and Levin shook his head.

"You're impossible, Mia," he said.

"Maybe," she said with a chuckle. "But I'll survive."

"I don't want you getting sick," he said. Then he took her hands and put them in his own jacket pockets. They had done this before, too. He remembered it well, and he wondered if Mia did. Thank goodness this jacket had such large pockets that both their hands fit. He gently entwined his fingers in hers. "Your fingers are like icicles." He looked deeply into her eyes. She was very close to him now, but he wouldn't have let go of her for anything in the world. She couldn't tear her eyes off him, and the warmth radiating off his hands seemed to permeate her entire body.

"Do you still think of our time together?" Levin asked.

"Every day," Mia answered.

"When I found that letter, I nearly lost my mind. That was the worst day of my entire life." Levin swallowed hard. Everything was coming back. And he'd thought he had left all that behind him.

"It hurt so much to leave. Please believe me—I was sure I was doing the right thing," she said. The pain was still deeply rooted within her.

Levin pulled his hands out of his pockets and tenderly held her face. "It wasn't the right thing. I would have stood by you. I loved you so much, I would have gone anywhere with you. We wouldn't have needed to stay in Berlin. No one had ever been as important to me as you were then." His voice shook.

"I'm so sorry." Mia wept quietly.

Levin wrapped his arms around her, and Mia did the same to him. They just held each other up and cried. It was beautiful and sad at the same time. They were both crying for their love and comforting each other. Mia felt guilty—everything could have been so different. Maybe they'd still be a couple if she hadn't left then. But it was no use thinking about it. Levin had a girlfriend, and she wouldn't interfere. Mia carefully detached herself from him. She looked into his face, which was just as wet from tears as hers. "I would turn back time if I could," she said.

"Yeah, me, too." Levin forced himself to smile. He pulled a handkerchief from his pocket and wiped the tears from her face. He regarded her sadly. He had lost so much. Again, he'd been painfully reminded of that. Why did it have to happen? But what use was it to be at odds with fate? It had happened, and now they were leading completely different lives.

"We should go to Juliette and Philippe." Mia cleared her throat and tried to regain her composure.

"Yes, of course," Levin said, following her over.

They strolled awhile longer. Levin regretted that Mia had distanced herself from him again. Of course he knew that it was better that way, but he missed the body contact with her. *Levin, be careful,* he warned himself. He tried to think about Sarah and not to get any stupid ideas, but his aunt's words kept buzzing around in his head. He should listen to his heart, and it was magically pulling him toward Mia.

"Phew, Levin, thank you so much, but I'm exhausted, I can't walk another step," Juliette finally said to him. "We've already seen so much today."

"I have an idea where we could go for dinner." He gazed at Mia. "There are a few Moroccan restaurants in Berlin."

Mia's eyes began to shine. "Oh, really? That's great!" She looked over at the couple. "What do you think—would you like to?"

"Normally, yes, but we'll probably eat at the hotel tonight. I'm too tired, but don't let us hold you up." Juliette nodded at Mia.

"Would you like to join me?" Levin looked at Mia hopefully.

She didn't have to think. Of course she felt like Moroccan food and even more like being with Levin. "Yes, I'd love to." Mia was happy he didn't mind eating alone with her.

"All right, then, we'd best say good-bye here." Philippe extended his hand to Levin. "Thank you so much for your city tour. I hope we'll see each other again."

"No problem, it was fun. I'd be glad to help you out anytime."

"Oh, not that we'd be taking you up on that," Juliette said and grinned at him.

"I'll drive you to the hotel," Levin offered.

"No need, the Metro's right here. We'll find our way back just fine." Juliette said a heartfelt good-bye to Levin, and then she hugged Mia. "Enjoy your evening," she whispered into her ear, "and take all the time you need. You don't need to worry about us."

Mia blushed. "Thank you," Mia said.

"See you tomorrow at breakfast." Philippe waved one more time. Then the two of them walked toward the Metro station, arm in arm.

"They're really great," Levin said to Mia on the way to his car.

"Yes, I like them a lot. Without them . . ." She stopped and shook her head. She preferred not to think about how her life might look without their help. Maybe she wouldn't even be around anymore. Levin looked at her curiously, but Mia obviously didn't want to elaborate. He thought it better not to ask, or at least not yet.

"I hope the restaurant's good. I haven't been here before," he explained when they had arrived.

"We'll see," Mia said. The place was decorated in Moroccan style, and she took to it right away. It was crowded, which she took as a good sign. They were given a table in the corner. The waiter brought the menu. "It's pretty here." Mia looked around curiously.

"Yeah, very pretty." Levin looked into her eyes for a moment and realized he wasn't talking about the restaurant.

Mia could hear the waiter talking to his colleague in Arabic. They were speculating if *the pretty blonde over there was that guy's girlfriend*. Mia suppressed a grin. When the waiter brought their drinks, she smiled sweetly and said in his mother tongue, "The blonde isn't the guy's girlfriend. Do you always talk about guests that way?"

The man's eyes opened wide with surprise. "I—I'm sorry," he stuttered. "I had no idea. Where did you learn Arabic? You're very good." He tried to gloss over the situation with a smile.

"I work in a hotel in Agadir," Mia explained. "You should speak more respectfully about the people here. They're your guests, and you make money from them. Shall I speak to your boss about this?"

"Please, no!" He shook his head vigorously. "Please forgive me."

Levin followed the conversation, dumbstruck. Mia was rambling along in Arabic with the waiter, and all he could do was sit there looking amazed. "What were you talking about?" he asked after the man had left. Mia explained, laughing about what she had overheard. Levin gave the guy a nasty look. "Maybe you should have told him you're my girlfriend. I don't want him to hit on you or anything."

"I don't think he would dare do that now," Mia said, winking.

Levin was still in awe of her. She had really changed—the Mia he had known would never have reacted so confidently. He studied the menu and said, "What would you recommend?"

"I really like *tajine*. That's roasted ragout with meat or fish with vegetables. It's the national dish. Or *pastilla*, a potpie with filo dough." She explained the different dishes to him in detail, how they were combined, what they were made of, whether they were eaten in a row or together. Levin ordered what she recommended.

"How long will you be staying in Berlin?" he asked after they'd placed their orders.

"We're flying back to Paris on New Year's. And two days after that, it's back to Agadir for me."

Levin looked at her hopefully. "Then we could meet a few more times?"

His gaze confused Mia, and she quickly lowered her eyes to study the tablecloth. "Levin, I'd love to see you more, but what about your girlfriend? I mean, you probably want to do something together during your time off." It wasn't easy for her to talk about it, but the fact remained that Levin wasn't free. She had to accept that.

"Sarah's studying for her exams at the moment. And I'd like to make use of the time. We haven't seen each other in so long." Levin reached for her hand. "Please, Mia. You'll be gone again soon, and who knows if we'll ever see each other again after that?"

"I just don't want you to have any trouble."

"Don't worry about that—ever, ever again, OK? Please just let that be my concern, sweet thing." He raised her hand to his lips and kissed the tips of her fingers.

Mia froze. She knew she should pull her hand away, but she couldn't—it was like she was in a trance. He'd called her "sweet thing," just like he used to. She swallowed hard against the lump in her throat.

At that moment, Levin realized what he was doing. He dropped her hand as if it had burned him, and Mia pulled it back to her side. He mumbled something about old habits as the waiter came to his rescue with the first course.

"Tell me about Morocco," he said. He needed to calm down, as he was pretty stirred up. For a second he thought it might be better to never see her again, but that second didn't last, because then he looked into her eyes—they glowed as she told him about her adopted country, and she entranced him again.

46

Mia described her life in Morocco and the beauty of the country. She talked like a book. Then she suddenly realized what she was doing, and it made her terribly uncomfortable.

"Oh, dear! Now I've chattered too much. I'm sorry," she said.

"No, Mia, that was interesting, it really was." Levin reached for her hand again. "But I think you should be kinder to yourself. You've gotten so thin. You work too much, don't you?"

Mia shrugged. It was true. But it distracted her, something she couldn't really tell him—or could she? She thought about it for a moment. *Why not?* she thought. She wanted to be honest with him, not lead him on. "Work is really important for me. When I'm working, I don't think so much."

"And what are you thinking about?" he asked with a heavy feeling in the pit of his stomach. "Or rather, what do you not want to think about?"

Mia swallowed. She couldn't look into his eyes. "You know exactly what, Levin," she said quietly.

Levin looked at her sadly and recalled his aunt's words. *She hasn't gotten over it.* Was that true? Was Mia really still pining for him and their relationship after so long? If that was the case, then maybe he shouldn't be sitting there. He didn't want to get her hopes up. On the other hand, the time they had left together was so limited, and Levin enjoyed her company. He wanted to see her, to find out as much about her as possible. They had three years to catch up on. "Mia, I don't know what to say," he answered.

"I know, it's OK, but I didn't want to lie to you." She smiled at him. "So, you have a girlfriend now. How is she? What does she do? Or would you rather not talk about her?" Mia tried to sound cheerful, but she sensed that she hadn't been convincing.

"Sarah?" Levin frowned. No, he wouldn't like to talk about her. This evening belonged to him and Mia. "Sarah's studying medicine. She's ambitious, and I'm sure she'll be a good doctor someday."

"Oh wow, that's great." *A lawyer and a doctor*, the voice in her head was hammering. *Are you blind, Mia? The two of them fit together perfectly!* "Sounds amazing—you've got it made. Congratulations, Levin." She squeezed his hand. "I'm happy for you, I really am." And she meant it. It hurt like hell, but Levin deserved the best, and he seemed to have gotten it.

"Oh, Mia." Levin held her hand. Her words had touched him, and he even believed that she was telling the truth. "Let's not talk about Sarah, OK?"

"All right. So, then, tell me what you've been up to in the meantime," Mia suggested.

Levin told her about the fight with his parents, and that he had worked as a waiter and a taxi driver. Mia looked at him in astonishment. "But the money—I mean, what about the money your mother gave me?"

Levin touched her cheek gently. "Did you ever really think I'd have wanted that? How low would that have been? I only took the thousand euros you left for me. And I'll return them to you, of course."

"I don't want that. I didn't want you to have to work."

"I know, Mia. But it was probably for the best, anyway. I became independent during that time, and it did me a lot of good. I should thank you." He laughed. "Damn, Mia, I missed you so much." He toyed with her fingers.

"But you have a new girlfriend now. That's good." She didn't pull her hand away, even though it probably would have been the right thing to do.

Levin didn't answer. *Is it really good that I have a new girlfriend?* That thought was spinning around in his head. Somehow, he had no clue anymore. Until yesterday he'd have thought there was only one way to answer that. But now? Now this magical blond creature was sitting across the table, holding him in her dainty clutches again.

Levin's phone buzzed, and he jumped. When he saw that it was Sarah, he felt guilty. "Hi," he answered curtly.

"Where are you? You told me you were going to get back to me," she said. Levin suddenly remembered with a pang that he *had* promised her something like that.

"I'm at a restaurant with Mia," he answered. He checked his watch and saw that it was almost midnight. He had completely lost track of the time. "I'm sorry, the city tour took longer than expected." That white lie couldn't be too bad.

Mia sensed who he was talking to. She got up and walked toward the restrooms. She didn't like to eavesdrop.

"Ah. And what restaurant are you in?"

"A Moroccan one."

"Right. I'm going to assume I won't see you tonight, right?" Sarah asked scornfully.

"No, it's sort of too late now. I'll call you tomorrow, OK?"

"Fine—do that if you can remember to." Then Sarah hung up, and Levin didn't blame her. It really hadn't been right not to call her, but he had simply forgotten.

Mia took a deep breath. Maybe it was actually good that Sarah had called—it had brought her back down to earth. It was probably better, too, to end this meeting with Levin. When she got back to the table, she said, "Levin, I think I should go now."

"It's OK, I'll get the check."

"I'd like to pay for myself."

"No way, Mia. You were invited."

Mia sensed that resistance would be futile. As they left the restaurant, she told him, "I can get back with the Metro."

"Sure you can. But give me one reason why you should when my car's sitting right here," he said with a grin. He had recovered. At first, his phone call with Sarah had darkened his mood. But it wasn't guilt that bothered him, only the chaos inside him. His head was fighting his heart. That was probably exactly what Irmi had expected.

"But you'll have to take a detour," Mia objected.

"Those few miles? Don't yank my chain, Mia," he said, and then he just grabbed her arm and pulled her over to his car.

They arrived at the hotel. "Thank you so much, Levin. That was a really nice day. And thanks for being our tour guide, too."

"No problem, I enjoyed doing that a lot." He reached for her hand again. "Mia, I'd like to see you tomorrow. We haven't seen half of Berlin yet. Do you think that would work?" Levin was downright embarrassed. He felt like a teenager asking for the first date of his life.

"I'd like to see you again, too." She didn't feel like thinking about Sarah right now. That may not have been right, but he'd asked her not to worry about his problems anymore—well then, she wouldn't. And the meeting today had been harmless anyway. *Oh yeah? Really?* her conscience admonished her. *Don't kid yourself!* Mia pushed the thought away. She wouldn't do anything wrong—all she wanted was a little more time.

"OK, then, the same time tomorrow?" he said. "I mean, if Juliette and Philippe would prefer to do something with you alone, you can send me a text. Otherwise I'll just come."

"I don't think they'd object. They seem to like you, and it's not every day they'll find such a good tour guide." Mia smiled and reached for the door handle.

"I'm looking forward to tomorrow already." Levin gazed longingly at her face. Her features were so familiar to him. How he had loved kissing her. His stare rested on her lips. He could remember what she tasted like in every detail and how exciting her body was. He put his hand under her chin, and she looked into his eyes. "Mia," he said, his own voice sounding like a stranger's, and for a moment he forgot where he was. All he could perceive was her. Her presence made everything else seem unimportant. Levin slowly bent down toward Mia, powerless against the magnetic pull of her lips.

Mia was unable to move—there was such a strange feeling between them. She had sensed it on and off all evening. Just then, the air seemed to be crackling with static as she felt his lips touch hers. He started kissing her very gently. She shouldn't be letting this happen, but she had no strength to resist. She responded cautiously to his kisses. It was wonderful to feel him. She had longed for him and always hoped she would enjoy this type of moment again. And yet, it was wrong.

She drew back. "Don't," she said, her heart pounding.

Levin returned to reality, saying, "I'm sorry." Mia groped for the door handle. "See you tomorrow?" Levin asked. He hoped he hadn't scared her off.

"See you tomorrow." Mia smiled, then got out of the car.

Inside Levin, everything was spinning. He paced around his apartment. The parting with Mia was still fresh in his mind, and he was shocked by his own behavior. He would have kissed Mia, really kissed her—and if he was completely honest with himself, he would certainly have gone even further. Her reappearance had turned his life upside down. That made him stop and think, and he had to ask himself some uncomfortable questions. Was it only curiosity that attracted him to Mia? Or was it the old closeness? Did he just want to see if he could still have her, or was it something different altogether? He had been attracted to her immediately and wanted to see her again, no matter what.

But what about Sarah? He had completely forgotten her today. That had been thoughtless of him, and he was genuinely sorry. Levin resolved to drive over and talk to her tomorrow. Irmi was right: he shouldn't play games. He didn't know yet what he'd tell her, but she should know how he felt. She was his partner, and he still liked her a lot. Levin groaned. He was dreading that conversation already.

It was still dark when he unlocked Sarah's door the next morning. He had brought croissants and a small bouquet of flowers. *Looks pretty incriminating*, he thought. Levin went into the kitchen and turned on the coffee machine; then he set the table and snuck into the bedroom. As he'd expected, she was still in bed, an open textbook next to her. She must have studied late into the night. He lay down next to her, tenderly stroking her face. She wrinkled her nose, and Levin grinned. "Honey," he said, kissing her on the lips. Sarah made a grumpy noise and then opened her eyes.

"Levin," she said, looking at him in surprise, "what are you doing here?"

"I brought my busy little bee some breakfast."

A smiled flitted over Sarah's face. "You're sweet," she mumbled. But then she turned solemn as her memory returned. "Have you been feeling guilty?"

Caught me! The thought flashed through his mind. "Maybe, but not because I cheated on you or anything."

Sarah sat up in bed. She rubbed her eyes. "That sounds pretty serious, Levin."

"That's because it is. I need to talk to you."

"OK, give me a few minutes. I need a shower. I can't think straight yet."

"All right, I'll be in the kitchen." He took a deep breath—he'd made a start.

Levin stood in front of the fridge, looking at the many photos attached with magnets. Some of them featured Levin and Sarah smiling into the camera, and in one of them they were kissing. Levin listened to his inner voice. Did he want that? Levin and Sarah, as a couple? But he couldn't find an answer. That only confirmed that he needed to talk to her. She came to him a short while later. Her hair was still wet and pinned up with a hair clip, and she was wearing jeans and a T-shirt. Levin liked that look on her. She was one of those women who looked much prettier without makeup than with it. But that seemed to be the only quality she shared with Mia.

"OK." Sarah sank into a chair and reached for a croissant. "Something tells me your need to talk has something to do with Mia's appearance." She looked at him seriously.

"Yeah," Levin said. "Exactly. I'm meeting her again soon to spend the day with her and her friends."

Sarah swallowed heavily. "How nice."

"Nothing happened between Mia and me that I'd have to confess, Sarah. Mia knows about you, and she's happy for us. She wanted me to find someone who fits into my world better, and she sees you as that person."

"How generous," Sarah scoffed. "Well, then, everything's settled, right?"

"That's exactly the point. Nothing's settled, nothing at all—at least not for me." He ran his fingers through his hair. "I know it's harsh of me to say it like this, but I think it's better to be honest: I'm completely unsure about my feelings for you and Mia. I can't say I still love Mia—but I also can't say that's the case with you. I'm really confused right now. I don't know right from wrong. I'm kind of questioning everything at the moment." Levin observed Sarah closely, and she looked away. He felt so sorry for her. He went over to her and crouched down. "Sarah, I don't want to hurt you, but I know that's what I'm doing. I don't want to lie to you. I know I'm being an egotistical ass right now, but I just need to find out what I want. If you don't want to go through that, I'll have to deal with it. If you want to slap me now, that's fine, too."

"Yeah, the slapping idea sounds appealing." Sarah looked into his eyes, and he saw so much hurt that it tore his soul. "But I can't. You know, the thing with you and Mia was always somewhere in the back of my mind. I've been scared of this moment all along." Sarah's voice cracked. "I was always afraid that she'd come back, and now she's here and taking you away from me."

A tear ran down her cheek, and Levin wiped it away. "I'm sorry, I don't want to see you unhappy." He pulled her into his arms and stroked her back. "I won't ask you to wait for me to figure out what I want. That would be cruel. Maybe I'll find out that it can't go on at all—with either one of you. But I need to find out. Do you understand?"

Sarah pulled away, tears shining in her eyes. "I can understand, Levin, and I'm glad that you're being honest with me. You could also have been doing all this behind my back. But that doesn't make it hurt less."

"I know," he said, "I know." Then he turned around and walked toward the door.

"Levin?" she called after him.

"Yeah?"

"You won't be hearing from me. If you have something to tell me, then let me know." Her voice sounded sad, but he admired her for her composure.

Levin looked at his watch. He had another hour before he had to meet Mia. He went to the gas station and got himself a coffee, and then he called Kai. He preferred to tell him what was going on with him and Sarah before their group of friends started talking about it.

"Jeez, Levin, have you looked at the time? I'm on vacation!" his friend growled at him.

"Yeah, I have. I'm sorry, I didn't want to take away your precious beauty sleep, but I'll be meeting Mia again in a few minutes, and I wanted to tell you something before—"

"Mia? Her again?" Kai seemed wide awake now. "Yeah, so how was it with her yesterday?"

"It was very nice. We talked a lot."

"Well, I'll bet it was nice, or you wouldn't be meeting her again. But what about Sarah? Isn't she raging about it, or are you doing this behind her back?"

"That's what I'm calling you about. I was at Sarah's a minute ago, and I explained that I'm unsure about what I want."

"Oh, so still Mia." Kai took a deep breath. "Are you back together?"

"No, no." Levin played it down. "It's not like that. Like I said, I don't know what I want. But I thought it was only fair to be clear with Sarah."

"How did she react?"

"Well, she wasn't exactly thrilled. But we were able to talk reasonably."

"Sarah's a great woman."

"I know. That doesn't really make things any easier."

"And Mia's also a great woman. I wouldn't want to be in your shoes now. But I already know which one you'll choose."

"Oh, yeah? Who?" Levin pressed.

"You know the answer," Kai said. "It's just a matter of time before you admit it."

Levin bit his lip. Of course he knew the answer, but it wasn't all that easy. Mia wasn't living there anymore. And even if she still wanted him, could he ask her to return to Berlin? Now that she was finally getting the appreciation she deserved in her job?

"It's all so difficult," he said.

"Well, it'd be boring otherwise." Kai grew serious again. "Man, Levin, she shows up after so long and throws you completely off balance. That basically says it all, don't you think? I like Sarah—she's really an awesome girl. But you and Mia? That's something very special, and everyone can see it."

"You're sounding like Geli already."

"Yeah, I have to, or I'm in trouble," Kai said. "But seriously, when else are you going to meet somebody who knocks your socks off like this?"

"Probably never again, huh?"

47

Levin eagerly waited for Mia in the hotel lobby. He was early. He was excited, and despite having mulled everything over and talking with Sarah, he was happy to see her. She arrived with her French friends. The elderly couple beamed at him. "Levin, how nice to see you again today," Juliette greeted him.

"The pleasure is mine." He shook both of their hands, then turned to Mia. "Hey, you doing all right?" he asked.

"Yeah." She gave him a smile, and his heartbeat promptly faltered. "Everything's fine. I'm glad to see you."

Levin kissed her cheek. "Me, too," he said into her ear.

Mia felt goose bumps on her skin. She pushed all her concerns aside and kissed him back, then looked into his eyes. His expression sent a warm rush flooding through her.

"Kai and Geli would be happy to hear from you," Levin told her during their lunch break in a café.

"I'd be happy to see them, too." A smile came over Mia's face. "Do you think I can just call them like that?"

"Sure, definitely." He nodded and handed her his phone.

"Now?" Mia looked at him wide-eyed.

"Go on, Mia," Juliette encouraged her.

On the other end of the line, Mia heard Geli's cry of delight. "Mia! Levin told us already that you're back in town. Please, we have to meet. Come over for dinner tonight?"

Mia was glad that Geli reacted so positively. She asked Juliette and Philippe if it would be all right with them if she went to her friends' for dinner.

"You don't have to ask us. Do what you feel like," Philippe said with a friendly laugh.

"I'd love to come," Mia said into the phone.

"Great. Oh, yeah, and should you meet Levin by chance, he's invited, too," Geli said with a laugh.

Mia felt herself blushing, then looked over at Levin. "I'll let him know."

Levin went on with the sightseeing program. It was a really fun thing to do. He hadn't been to those places in a while; they hadn't been special to him anymore. He kept trying for physical closeness with Mia, but she was withdrawn—although he was sure that her eyes told a very different story. He thought about his conversation with Sarah this morning. He would have to talk to Mia, too, because otherwise this distance would remain. How she would react, he had no notion. Because she knew about Sarah, she would probably feel guilty; he still knew Mia well.

Early in the evening Levin took Juliette and Philippe back to their hotel. They thanked him warmly for the second city tour. Levin offered to show them around again tomorrow.

"You're so sweet, Levin," Juliette said. "How nice of you."

"Oh, it's not all selfless," he answered with a grin.

The glittering in Juliette's eyes revealed that she knew exactly what he was talking about.

Mia blushed, but she was happy about his words. And she didn't even want to think about leaving again soon.

"If I'd known I'd see Kai and Geli, I would have brought them something from Morocco," Mia fretted on the way to Levin's friends' place.

"You could still do that—when you come back." He gazed at her hopefully.

Mia swallowed. Would she? Could she come here again? Certainly not very soon, and she also didn't know if that would be so good for her emotional state. "Yeah, sure," she said.

Levin noticed the wistful note in her voice. He wondered if he should talk to her now, or if he should wait until after the visit with his friends. He decided to put it off. Depending on how she reacted, it would strongly influence the general mood, and because especially Geli was so excited to see Mia, he didn't want to risk ruining it for them.

Mia followed Levin through the hall to the apartment. They had moved, and Levin told her that the two of them were getting married in the summer. Mia was happy to hear the news. Kai and Geli had been together for so long now, and they were a good couple.

The door was thrown open, and Geli bounced out and flung her arms around Mia. "Mia, Mia! I'm so happy, it's crazy! You're back. This is so great!" She squeezed Mia tightly.

"I'm happy, too."

"Let's have a look at you." Geli pushed her back a bit. "You've lost weight. You were so thin already—what's all this about?"

"You know, all that work and stuff."

"And stuff?" Geli raised her eyebrows. "I want to know everything."

"Me, too, but preferably not out here in the hall," Kai put in his two cents. "We have a few rooms with seating options in there—hey, how about we just go inside and use them."

"Hi, Kai." Mia wasn't sure how he'd react to her. He was Levin's best friend, and he'd probably gone through everything firsthand with him.

"Hey, Mia." He hugged her lightly. "Nice to see you again. You gave us a scare back then, little one," he said.

"I know, and I'm very sorry."

Kai guided them inside. Mia looked around. Everything was decorated in a cozy way. Apparently Geli had finally enforced her style. While there had been a colorful mix of styles in the old apartment, everything here harmonized nicely. Something smelled appealing, and Mia realized she was hungry. It was the first time in a long while she'd felt that way.

"Ha, good thing I cooked something with lots of calories—we're going to fatten Mia up." Geli giggled while putting the casserole down on the table.

"True, you could do with a few extra pounds." Kai looked her up and down, a little too long for Levin's liking.

"How long will you be staying?" Geli inquired.

"Until New Year's Day."

"We'll be celebrating at the banks of the Spree. Are you coming?"

"I don't know." She really didn't feel like meeting Levin's girlfriend. New Year's was always a difficult time for her; she always became so gloomy then. Only one time, four years ago, had she actually been happy. "I'm here with friends. I'd like to wait and see what they want to do."

"Oh, by the way," Kai said, "tell us—and with all the details: Who are these friends? Where exactly do you live? What do you do? We want to know *everything*."

Mia smiled at him, and then she began filling him in. Levin held back and observed Mia as she spoke. She became more and more relaxed, seemed to lose her tension, and soon they were back to their old familiarity. It was clear that his friends liked her. Mia's eyes glittered when she told them about Morocco.

Doubts gnawed at him again. Was there a future for them? He could hardly work as a lawyer in Morocco. So Mia would have to come back here. And if his parents started to bug them in any way, he wouldn't hesitate to pack his things and disappear with Mia. There were other nice areas in Germany, and his degrees were good. He knew he could definitely get a job.

Why are you even thinking about all this? he admonished himself. It was so easy, and it had been obvious all along. He only needed to look at this stunningly beautiful woman and the way she told stories and gestured, how her eyes shone—and then there was the look in her eyes when she saw him.

"Levin! *Leeeeevvvviiiiiinnnn!*" Kai's voice interrupted his musings.

"Yeah?"

"We were just thinking that Morocco would be such a great place for vacations. Now Mia's made it so tempting for us. Could you try to answer now?"

"If you tell me the question again," Levin said.

"What would you think about a trip to Morocco? Marrakesh, Agadir, maybe the other royal cities?"

"Sounds good." Levin looked over at Mia. She seemed to be happy about this.

Mia had been astonished by Levin's embarrassment when Kai had spoken to him. He had seemed to be completely lost in thought. She wondered what had occupied him so, but then she scolded herself for her curiosity. Mia listened intently while they told her how the last few years had been. The subject of their wedding was brought up, of course, and Geli beamed at Mia.

"You'll come, won't you? Please, Mia," she begged.

"I don't know if I can get time off. Summer is the main season over there." She also didn't know if she really wanted to come. Levin would be there with Sarah.

"You have to, I insist," Geli said with a smile. The two girls began clearing off the table. When they were in the kitchen, Geli closed the door. "It's so great to see you again," she said. "How are you feeling?"

"Fine, I'm feeling fine."

"You know what I'm talking about. What about you and Levin?"

"I needed to explain to him what happened back then. And I'm so glad that we could talk about it."

"So?"

"So we're—well, we get along fine. I'm really happy about that."

"And?"

"It's so nice with him."

"And?" Geli was relentless.

Mia lowered her eyes. "Stop asking, you can imagine," she whispered.

"You still love him," Geli stated.

Mia could only nod.

"Mia, maybe this will sound far-fetched, but Levin isn't exactly indifferent to you, either. That's clear from looking at him." Geli reached for Mia's hand.

"He has a girlfriend," Mia said.

"He does, but it's not the same thing the two of you had."

"But she seems to fit him so well. I mean, she's going to be a doctor."

"Sarah's nice, she's good-looking, her parents have money, and she's on the ball. That's all true, but she's not the girl who holds Levin's heart—that's still you."

"It's over," Mia said. "I messed up."

"I don't know. Judging from the way he still looks at you, I'd say there's still a whole lot left." Geli hugged Mia and added, "I'd try to fight."

"No, I won't do that. I would never push my way into an existing relationship," Mia said.

"OK, so you're kind of right. It's Levin's business to change that." Geli winked at her. "But it's so strange—it seems as though you never left. Mia, we've really missed you."

Mia stayed until midnight. Then she said good-bye. She had to get back to the hotel, and she wanted to show up in time for breakfast.

"I'll drive you, of course." Levin got up, too.

"You don't have to—I can take the Metro."

"Are we starting this again?" Levin grinned at her. "We won't have to go through this every day, will we?"

"You're stubborn."

"Look who's talking," he said, then went to get her jacket.

"Please come see us again, OK?" Geli gave her a good-bye hug.

"I will," Mia said.

Levin opened the car door for Mia and waited until she was seated. Then he walked over to his side. When he had sat down behind the steering wheel, he took a deep breath.

"Mia, we need to talk," he began, his heart almost doing somersaults.

"Yes?" He sounded so serious.

"I had a talk with Sarah this morning."

Mia kneaded her hands. She could already guess what was coming. Surely, understandably, Sarah had a problem with the two of them seeing each other. But then he shouldn't have offered to show them more of the city tomorrow. "I understand," she said, swallowing hard. "Levin, it's honestly OK if . . . I mean, if we can't see each other again. You sacrificed a lot of time for my friends and me, and I shouldn't expect anything more."

Levin quickly placed a finger on her lips and smiled. "Please just listen, all right?" Mia nodded. "I told Sarah that I'm not sure about anything. Since you've been here, I've been shaken up, and I don't know what it is that I want."

Mia was stunned. What was he trying to say? But he wouldn't leave Sarah, not because of her—would he?

"I'm so confused," Levin went on. "I want to be with you, to touch you and kiss you. I want to feel you, Mia. And I don't want you ever to leave me again." His voice broke with emotion. Then he gazed at her. "I love you, Mia. I've always loved you, I only just realized. The thing with Sarah was a mistake. Maybe I wanted to distract myself or whatever—it doesn't matter anymore. I love you, and I want to ask you to stay with me." Levin reached for Mia's hand hesitantly.

She was wide-eyed and silent for a moment before saying, "But Sarah . . . you can't just hurt her. Surely you're a good match. I don't know what to think."

"I love you," Levin repeated. He saw that it hadn't quite hit her.

"But how can it work? Your parents, and your job?" Mia's heart was racing. She had trouble believing it. *This could only be a dream, right?*

"I love you, Mia." Levin smiled at her, bringing her hand to his lips. "Please don't let us be separated again. Of course, if you don't love me—"

Mia felt the touch of his lips on her skin. She watched as he planted tiny kisses onto her hand. Slowly, she began to grasp what was happening. Here and now, her future with Levin was beginning. "I love you, too," she whispered.

48

Levin let out a long sigh and beamed at her. "Come here, sweet thing," he said, pulling her toward him. He could tell that she still couldn't quite believe what was happening. For a moment, Levin just held her in his arms, but then he gently lifted her head so that she had to look into his eyes.

"May I kiss you?"

Mia was speechless. But that didn't matter. Levin kissed her gently. Mia's numbness began to melt like the ice from a long, cold winter under the first rays of spring sunshine. That familiar tingling sensation was back and getting stronger. She closed her eyes and let herself be carried away by this precious moment. She returned Levin's kisses carefully. An overpowering heat spread throughout her body. As though of their own accord, her arms wrapped themselves around his neck, and she returned his advances more and more intensely.

For a moment, Levin felt like he was floating. He held his Mia in his arms, and it was like she'd never been gone. She tasted so familiar, felt so irresistible—exactly as he had remembered her. He had her again, his love. "Come home with me," he said when they separated for a short moment.

"But I have to get to the hotel. I arranged to meet Juliette and Philippe for breakfast tomorrow," Mia said.

"I promise you we'll be there on time," Levin said with a smile. "I need you, Mia. And we still have a lot to talk about, don't we?"

Mia looked into his eyes. This was real—it was really happening. "Yes," she said as tears of joy filled her eyes.

She was eager to see his apartment. How much would have changed? Mia had no idea if Sarah had lived there with him, and she looked at Levin with uncertainty. "Did Sarah live there with you?"

"No, I didn't want that, I always felt that we weren't ready." He reached for her hand. "I also never gave a thought to marrying her. Maybe I should have asked myself why, at some point."

Mia understood that very well. It hadn't been any different for her, only she'd never been able to let anyone get close to her.

"I'm sure you have lots of admirers, don't you?" Levin inquired. Even though the subject was uncomfortable, he still wanted to know what had happened in the last few years.

"Well, define *lots*?" Mia only shrugged. "A few, maybe."

"Did they get pushy?"

"No, they didn't. I didn't care for any of them." She glanced over at him. "Are you jealous?"

Levin looked at her with indignation. "Of course I am!"

"Silly," she said, giggling. Levin lightly poked her side.

"Mia?"

"Yeah?"

"I'm really pretty damn happy right now."

Mia felt the tears again. "Me, too."

"All right, let's get inside, then." He held the door open for her and let her enter his apartment. The hall at least hadn't changed much. "Look around all you want, most of it should look familiar to you," Levin said, grinning. He was right. Apart from a few small things, the apartment was very close to the way Mia remembered it. In this respect, apparently Sarah's influence hadn't been that strong. There were a few pictures on the walls, and, of course, Sarah was in a few of them. Mia didn't want to be nosy, but she was curious what Sarah looked like. She'd expected her to be pretty, but the fact that she was so stunning swayed Mia a bit. She was beautiful; she was rich and well educated— so why did Levin want *Mia*?

"What are you brooding about?" He stepped behind her and put his arms around her.

"She's beautiful," Mia said.

"Yeah, she is." Levin pushed a few strands of hair aside and kissed Mia's neck. "But you are, too, and I love you."

Mia closed her eyes; it felt so good to be treated with so much tenderness.

"I'll talk to her again tomorrow and end it for good. But that won't come as a surprise to her," Levin said into Mia's ear. Her scent infatuated him, and holding her body so close wasn't without consequences. He wanted to take her to his bed immediately, but he wondered if that might be too much for her right now.

"I feel sorry for her," Mia said. "I know what it feels like to lose you. It's just cruel."

"Hey." Levin turned Mia to face him. "Look, Mia, we can't undo what's happened, and it was just as bad for me as it was for you—no, I bet it was even worse, because I had no idea whether you were even still alive. But what we have is really special, and no one is ever going to separate us again. OK?"

"OK." She smiled, and then she carefully put her arms around his neck. "It feels so surreal. Can you pinch me or something?"

"Pinch you? I know something that's much better." Levin pulled her even closer and began kissing her tenderly. But this time he couldn't hold back for long. He just had to feel more of her now, and he could only hope she wouldn't reject him.

This kiss threatened to drive Mia out of her mind. Her body pressed closer to him without her seeming to have any conscious control of it. She wanted much more of him, and he seemed to feel the same way. His passion was contagious.

"Mia," he murmured over and over again. "My God, sweet thing, I've missed you."

"I've missed you, too." She snuggled up to him. "I love you so much."

Levin's hands wandered over her body, and his fingers strayed under her shirt. "Can I feel you?" he asked, breathless.

"Please." Her chest was rising and falling rapidly, and she knew what was about to happen. The thought of it caused a sweet sense of tension in her lower belly. She had been deprived of that kind of touch for so long that for a moment she worried if she would still be able to satisfy him.

Levin slowly opened up her shirt button by button. When her lace bra appeared, he inhaled sharply. He pushed the fabric over her shoulders, exposing her upper body. His lips slid down her neck, gently touching her collarbone and finally finding the soft abundance of her breasts. "You're so beautiful." Levin whispered little kisses onto her delicate skin. He gently pushed the lace fabric aside. Very tenderly, he touched the hard pink buds with his tongue. Mia sighed softly, and her fingers clutched his hair. Levin couldn't stop himself any longer. He hastily opened the rest of the buttons and pulled her shirt all the way off. He kissed his way further down her body, and slid over her stomach down to the zipper of her jeans. He traced the seam with his tongue. He felt her shiver. Encouraged, he kept going.

Mia could barely stand the intensity of her pleasure. Every fiber of her being had been stimulated to the breaking point. She watched him push her jeans off and bury his face in her lap. Levin breathed in her seductive scent, then pushed her panties aside. He let his tongue glide over her smooth skin and found her little pearl, toying with it gently.

"Levin," Mia moaned. She could barely keep herself upright, as it felt like the ground was disappearing from underneath her. Levin could tell she was about to come, and he gently pushed a finger inside her, kissing her all the while. When she finally tensed, he pressed his face against her sweet cave and held her tightly.

Mia's vision went black for a moment, and her climax came with such force that she would probably have collapsed if Levin hadn't been holding her.

He straightened again, looking into her slightly dazed eyes. "Hey, sweet thing, looks like you're back," he said with a love-struck smile.

Mia blushed and leaned her forehead against his shoulder. "I don't know how I ever stood being without you for so long."

"Oh, Mia," Levin said, gently stroking her hair. "Don't think about it anymore, my angel."

Mia was reminded of his physique again. She gazed at him, seeing the still-unsatisfied longing in his eyes. She kissed him but more aggressively this time.

Levin responded immediately; he wouldn't be able to bear it much longer. "Please sleep with me, let me be inside you."

Mia smiled, and then she took his hand and led him into the bedroom. She looked around briefly—nothing had changed here, either, except that the bed was a new one. Levin pushed her ahead of him, then let himself fall onto the bed with her. He kissed her with such passion that her senses threatened to fail. Now he was no longer tender as his hands wandered over her body. Mia helped him undress. When she saw his erect penis, she felt her need return with all its power. She lay back on the bed and opened her legs for him. Now the last of Levin's barriers melted. He shoved into her with one joyful thrust, and Mia met him with her hips, showing him how ready she was. Levin searched for her hands. Their fingers entwined; their bodies met, familiar yet still new. He kissed her wildly and more impatiently. Mia felt him inside her, filling her up. He took what was his and gave her back everything he had. Levin pushed into her faster and faster, almost roughly. As Mia cried out, he felt her tightening and pulsing around him. Now he gave in completely to his lust, driving into her deeper. Passion rolled over him like an elemental force. He moaned as he came in hot, pulsing waves. He sank down on her in exhaustion, clutching her to him; she was breathing as heavily as he was. Her eyes were closed, and she was slick with perspiration. Levin traced her beautiful features with a finger. They didn't speak, but then Mia opened her eyes, and her look of love hit him hard.

Levin realized he was lying on her with all his weight. His conscience returned, and he quickly pushed himself up onto his arms to take some pressure off. Guiltily, he asked, "Did I hurt you?"

"No, it was beautiful like that." Mia pulled him down to her again. "I can still feel you deep inside me."

Levin sighed; her words had hit their target. "That's where I want to be, deep inside you." Suddenly another thought flashed through his mind. "I didn't use a condom."

"I'm on the pill," she reassured him, smiling. Levin carefully pulled back out of her. She immediately felt the emptiness inside of her, and he gathered her up in his arms.

"Why are you on the pill? I mean, well, you told me you don't have a boyfriend."

"It's more practical for me because I don't get my period so strongly then. That was always annoying while I was working, because I had to go change so often then." She looked at him, embarrassed.

"Oh, OK." Levin was relieved. The thought of another man in Mia's life was enough to drive him mad. Although that wasn't fair, of course. He'd started another relationship, not to mention the one-night stands that he'd distracted himself with in the beginning. Levin kissed her breasts tenderly. His longing for her wasn't fulfilled yet. It would probably be better to talk now, but they could still do that later.

"Is it even worth going to sleep now?" Levin finally asked her with a grin.

Mia lay with her head on his chest, completely drained. "I guess not," she said, smiling at him sweetly.

Levin stroked her blond curls. "Well, then, we can talk about what's next." Mia sat up cross-legged and regarded him seriously. She drew small circles with her finger on his chest. She could guess what Levin was going to say. "I can't work as a lawyer in Morocco. I'd probably have to start from the beginning again, and also learn the language on top of that. I know this is asking a lot from you, but can you imagine coming back to Germany?"

Mia didn't answer. It might have been cruel, but she wanted to hear what other alternatives he might offer.

Her silence made Levin nervous. "I mean Germany, not Berlin," he said. "I could work anywhere—I don't have to go back to my father's firm. And above all my mother still owes you an apology, and—"

"Levin," Mia interrupted, "I understand that you can't come to Morocco with me. It's OK if we stay here. I just want to be where you are. I do like my job, but I wasn't happy, not like I am now. And I don't expect an apology from your mother—she did what she did because she loves you and wanted to protect you."

"No, Mia. It's necessary, or I'll leave Berlin. If she can't understand, I don't want anything more to do with her."

"They're your parents, Levin. Be glad that you have any left," she said sadly.

"Mia . . ." Levin wrapped her in his arms. "It's hard to forget that they didn't care about my happiness—and my mother drove you away from me." He planted a kiss on her temple. "They didn't even try to see how wonderful you are."

"But I'm not," she objected.

"Oh, yes, you are!" Levin looked into her eyes for a long while. "Do you really want to leave Morocco?"

"I want to be with you, Levin. Maybe I'll be able to find a job here. I bet the hotel will give me a letter of recommendation," she said hopefully.

Levin kissed her body, from her head down to her stomach. "I'd have a job for you," he said quietly.

"Yeah?" Mia looked up.

"Be the mother of my children." Levin lay back down next to her.

"Isn't it a bit early for that?" she asked with a smile.

"OK, maybe not right away. I'm selfish and want to have you to myself for a while first. But, yes, Mia, I can imagine that clearly," he said.

Mia snuggled into his arms. "Who's the wonderful one here?" she whispered.

She eventually fell asleep, and when Levin woke up it was already light out. He looked at his alarm clock in shock—it was already after nine. He was still wrapped around Mia, and the memories of last night made him smile. It had really happened, the thing that he had dreamed of for so long: a future with Mia. He resolved to talk to Sarah that afternoon, and then he'd tell Irmi. His parents needed to know, too, but he didn't feel inclined to take care of that at the moment. "Mia? Hey, sweet thing," he said gently, stroking her face. "We need to get up. Juliette and Philippe will be waiting for us."

Mia grumbled something unintelligible, and Levin bit back a grin.

"Come on, time to get up," he repeated more urgently. His hand wandered under the covers. Her body was still warm from sleep. It felt soft and tempting. He could imagine many other more fun things to do with her besides getting up.

Mia opened her eyes and looked directly into Levin's. Immediately, everything came back, and a warm feeling flooded through her. "Good morning," she said with a smile.

"Good morning, sweet thing. We'll have to hurry to get to the hotel on time." He touched the tip of her nose.

Mia jumped up. "What time is it?"

"There's still time. We can pick up something for breakfast on the way," Levin said, and then he pulled her into his arms once more. "Anyway, I'm not letting you out of bed before I get another kiss."

Mia gladly did him the favor, but then she got up. "I'll just jump into the shower quickly." She blew him a kiss and slipped into the bathroom. Her conscience flared up when she saw Sarah's makeup on the counter. Mia had pushed her way into a relationship, and she felt guilty. She was sorry for Sarah, but at the same time she was so wildly happy that there was another chance for her and Levin. Right now everything was still a bit surreal, so she cautioned herself not to become too euphoric. Maybe something else would stand in their way. There was no guarantee for eternal happiness—she'd learned that the hard way. But she wouldn't make the mistake of leaving Levin again. She was grateful for this new beginning, and she wasn't about to mess it up.

They reached the hotel lobby punctually at ten o'clock. Philippe and Juliette were already there. Levin and Mia approached them hand in hand.

"Oh, you look tired," Juliette said. "But very happy."

"We are," Mia said.

"We're so happy for you." Juliette beamed at her. She hugged them both. "I assume you'd prefer to have some time to yourselves?"

"No, we'd like to continue our city tour," Mia said. "I'd just like to go put on some clean clothes."

"We'll wait, take your time," Philippe said. "Have you had any breakfast?"

"We ate something on the way here," Levin said. Mia excused herself to go up to her room, and Levin stayed behind.

"Mia has such a gleam in her eye. I've never seen anything like it with her before," Juliette said happily. "But what about your girlfriend, Levin? Have you taken care of that?"

"Basically. She knows that Mia's here and I'm confused because of her. I'm going to talk to her this afternoon."

"Yes, do that. You owe her that much," Juliette answered, but then she was smiling again. "Our Mia, finally she's happy."

Mia hurried to get changed so the others didn't have to wait too long. Levin greeted her with a warm kiss when she returned to the lobby. Then they went out into the city.

Levin stopped here and there to kiss Mia. At first she felt uncomfortable that he was kissing her in front of her friends, but the two of them seemed to be very happy for them, which relieved her. She enjoyed Levin's kisses all the more.

Her worries returned that afternoon when Levin said good-bye so he could go talk to Sarah. "I'll come to the hotel around six, OK?" he said.

"Yes, OK," Mia said.

"Hey." Levin could see the insecurity in her eyes. "I love you, sweet thing. Only you."

"I love you, too." She stood on her toes and gave him a kiss on the cheek.

49

Sarah was surprised when she opened the door and saw Levin. "Why did you ring the doorbell?"

"I didn't think it was very fitting to use the key," he said.

"I see." She lowered her eyes and invited him inside, walking ahead into the living room. "It's over, isn't it?"

Levin felt so bad for her, but what could he do? "Yes," he said, nodding. "I'd like to tell you how sorry I am, or something like that, but that won't make it any better, will it?"

"No, it won't." She shook her head, hiding her face in her hands. She sat down on the couch. "You know, I can't even really be mad at you—you were always so honest with me. And that pisses me off. If only I could just curse you and be done." She smiled at him.

"Go ahead, knock yourself out. It would be OK with me." Levin admired her attitude. She was just so classy, and he had always liked that about her.

"I also know that I've always loved you more than you loved me. But I'd somehow hoped it would be enough."

Levin came over and sat down next to her. "You're a beautiful girl. You probably don't want to hear it right now, but you'll find someone in no time who will love you the way you deserve." He gently stroked her back. Sarah leaned her head against his shoulder.

"But I want you," she said, starting to cry.

"I'm sorry," Levin said.

"OK," Sarah said, sitting up and squaring her shoulders, "let's do this in style." She wiped her tears away. "What should we do about our things?"

"Whatever you want, there's no rush. Just call me whenever you feel like coming over," he said. He could tell how hard this had hit Sarah, but he was grateful that she was handling it so well.

"OK, Levin, get out, I need to cry now."

"I wish you all the best, Sarah. We had a good time together." It pained him to see her like this.

"Yeah, we did. But it was too short," she said.

As Levin left her apartment, he first had to lean on the wall outside to take a deep breath. This hadn't left him completely unfazed. He felt so incredibly bad for hurting Sarah. Thank God she hadn't made a scene, although he would have understood if she had. Her tears didn't leave him indifferent, either. So now his time with Sarah was over. Levin sighed and went down the stairs. But he felt lighter and lighter with every step, as though a heavy burden had been lifted off his soul. It should probably shock him how easy it had been to separate from Sarah, but the more he thought about it, the clearer everything became. She simply hadn't touched his heart the way Mia had. A smile dawned on his lips. Mia. Now she was finally his Mia again, and they would build a future together. Levin decided to be happy about that and stop fretting about how much time they'd lost because of his mother. He looked at his watch. He'd told Mia that he'd be back at the hotel around six, but it was only four thirty. Levin decided to stop by Irmi's and tell her everything.

"Levin, how wonderful to have you here." She hugged him and ushered him inside. "Anything new with Mia?" she asked once he'd sat down on her couch.

Levin smiled. "You don't waste any time, do you?"

"Well, I'm old, see, so I have to make good use of my time—I can't waste it with unnecessary babble," she said with a laugh.

"I just came here from Sarah's," he said in a serious tone. "It's over."

"Oh. Well, that's sad to hear. I assume Mia is the reason?"

"Yeah." Now Levin couldn't suppress a grin any longer. "We're back together!"

"What? That's fantastic," Irmi said. "So it's true—miracles can still happen. Levin, I'm surprised but so glad. The two of you have the most special connection." Irmi got up and grabbed a bottle of cognac. "You, too?" She held out a glass.

"No thanks, I have to drive."

"So how are things going to work out? She's still living in Morocco."

"She's coming back here, then we'll see. If Mom and Dad show the slightest signs of resentment, I'll pack my things and take off with Mia. I won't risk losing her a second time."

"Yes, I understand. Should I talk to them first? That will prepare them, and I can tell you about their reaction."

"Maybe that would be best," Levin said. "I don't feel like seeing them right now, anyway. My time with Mia is too precious to be wasted on that."

"I understand."

Levin smiled widely. "It's wonderful, almost as though she never left. Irmi, I'm just so crazily in love with her, and I probably always have been."

"I believe that. I'm sorry for Sarah. She's a nice girl, but I've always felt it wasn't the same kind of thing you had with Mia. The gleam in your eye was missing with Sarah. Do you think you can come over with her sometime? I'd be so happy to see her again."

"How about you come to the hotel with me right now? I've arranged to meet her and her friends there at six. I'm sure Mia would love to see you."

Mia couldn't hide her anxiety. Although discovering Berlin with Juliette and Philippe was nice, her thoughts were with Levin and his talk with Sarah. What if he had a change of heart? He had been with Sarah longer, and maybe he'd realize that he couldn't bear to be separated from her. Mia bit her lip and calmed herself by remembering the previous night. Levin had been sincere, she knew, but still she had a nagging doubt.

"Mia, you'll see him again soon." Juliette took her hand and squeezed it. "Are you missing him that much?"

"He's at his girlfriend's place right now, and, well, what if he decides to stay with her?"

"Then he would be an incredible idiot. An idiot who denied his feelings. It's so obvious that he loves you, and he can't hide it. Don't worry," Juliette said with a reassuring smile. Mia returned the smile, but she still couldn't fully relax.

As planned, Mia was waiting for Levin with Juliette and Philippe in the hotel lobby. It was almost six, and the tension was palpable. When Levin entered, she saw that he'd brought his aunt.

Beaming, Levin hugged her tightly. "Hi, sweet thing—everything OK?"

"You tell me," she said.

"I took care of things." He kissed her lips lightly. "It's all going to work out."

Mia took a deep breath. "Thank God." Finally, she could smile in relief.

"As you can see, I brought Irmi. She wanted to see you again."

"Hi, I'm glad to see you," Mia said.

"Me, too, honey. My goodness, it's sad that so much time has passed. But it's nice that you're back again—and with Levin," Irmi said.

"Yes, I'm very happy, too," Mia answered.

"Irmi," Levin said, "I'd like to introduce Mia's friends. It's thanks to them that I got to see her again." Levin beckoned to Juliette and Philippe, who'd been watching the reunion from a few steps back. His aunt didn't speak French, so Levin and Mia had to translate. Mia's friends and Irmi immediately took to each other, and they decided to go out to dinner together.

"Unfortunately, Mia and I didn't get to know each other very well back then, but I hope we can catch up on that soon," Irmi said.

"Yes, we really should," Mia said eagerly. "That would be so nice."

"I'd like to apologize for my sister's unforgivable behavior. She brought so much sorrow to you and Levin. I still can't understand why she acted that way." Irmi looked sad.

"She loves Levin, and she only wanted the best for him."

"That's how she saw it, but I still wonder how one can be so insensitive and conceited." Irmi reached for Mia's hand and said, "Please promise me one thing, Mia: don't ever leave Levin again. He really suffered a lot."

"No, I won't. I just thought back then that leaving was the right thing to do."

"I know. I'm still impressed by your love for him. But now everything's going to be better—right, Levin?" Irmi poked his side.

"Absolutely," Levin said.

As they parted that evening in the lobby, Philippe said, "Mia, we plan to visit two museums tomorrow, and you don't have to accompany us. Have fun with Levin."

"Is that really all right?" Mia felt guilty—she wanted to take care of them.

"Of course it is," Juliette said. "Irmi invited us over for dinner tomorrow, so we'll see each other again there."

"OK, then!" Mia hugged her friends good-bye, and they went over to the elevators.

"So, what about us?" Levin pulled her in for a tender kiss. "The night's still young."

"Will you come upstairs with me?" she said.

"So you're taking me to your hotel room now?" He kissed her forehead. "Is your bed wide enough for the two of us?"

"No, you'll have to sleep on the floor," she said, her eyes twinkling.

"I can think of something much better. I could just lie on top of you or you on top of me. That's the way it usually works."

Mia looked around in embarrassment, but nobody had heard their exchange. She took his hand and led him to the stairwell.

"You're much too thin, my angel," Levin noted when they lay in bed a short while later, naked, tired, and happy.

"I can't eat much," Mia said.

"You have to make yourself." Levin gently traced the outline of her ribs.

"I'll try," she promised. Mia remembered that she hadn't taken her pill yet and opened the nightstand drawer to find it. She was just about to close the drawer when Levin reached for her hand.

"What's this?" he asked. He stared at a small plastic bag filled with loose pills. "Are you sick?"

"They're sleeping pills," Mia answered quietly. She cursed herself for storing the sleeping pills there. *How careless. Why didn't you leave them in the suitcase?*

Levin sat up. His pulse started racing, and he got a leaden feeling in the pit of his stomach. "Did you have to start taking them again?" he said. "Why aren't they in the package anymore?"

"Well, I don't know. It just happened at one point."

"Look at me," Levin said, taking Mia's face in his hands. "Why are the pills all out? Why? Why?"

"I went through a very unhappy phase. So . . . then I . . . it doesn't really matter, does it?" She lowered her gaze.

"It *does* matter. If it was just a phase, then why do you still have them?"

"I find it calming to know that there's still a way out."

"*That's* supposed to be a way out? Mia!" Levin tugged her toward him and held her tightly. "Don't you ever think that again!"

"I don't anymore." She kissed his shoulder. "Definitely not."

"Never leave me again, Mia. Ever." Then he got up and took the bag with the pills in it. "Come on, we'll flush them down the toilet together, OK?"

Mia nodded and followed him into the bathroom. Levin made sure she destroyed every last one of them. "Maybe you should talk to Silke Meier about this," he suggested.

"No, Levin, I don't want to," she said, turning to face him with determination. "I've talked to so many therapists in my life, and I'm sick of it. But I promise that you won't get rid of me that way, OK?"

"I believe you," Levin said.

50

Levin couldn't fall asleep. The episode with the pills was still bothering him. Mia lay half on top of him, breathing deeply. At least she was able to sleep well. Had she really once thought about killing herself? He swallowed hard. He never would have seen her again. Levin stroked her naked back. He could only hope that she was stable now—although he wished she'd consented to seeing her therapist. He resolved to talk about it again with Mia, but maybe not just yet. That wouldn't do any good anyway since she still had to go back to Morocco to take care of paperwork. For now he would give her all his love and pray that would be enough. But he was no psychiatrist: Would he even be able to tell if she started feeling worse again?

Levin sighed. He had his one true love back, along with the fear of losing her. Mia twitched in her sleep and murmured something unintelligible. Levin carefully bent over her to look at her face. She was smiling in her sleep. He felt warm inside. Yes, this time they would make it; he was sure.

The next morning, they went to his apartment. They had time to themselves until the evening, a luxury that Levin planned to take advantage of. He was already thinking about her return flight. It wasn't clear yet how long Mia would have to stay in Morocco, but she'd made it clear that she intended to finish her employment contract and not just disappear. Levin understood, of course. She wanted to get a good recommendation. But it was a mystery to him how he could stand to be without her. *You managed to survive without her for over three years,* he reminded himself. He shuddered at the memory of the early stages of their separation.

"What's up?" Mia said, cuddling into his arms. "You look like you're lost in the clouds."

"I can't bear to think about your going away."

"But we'll see each other again soon. What are a few weeks, after all we've been through?" she said with a smile.

"I'd like for us to look for a bigger apartment if we're going to stay in Berlin," he said.

"But this one is nice."

"It's not exactly huge, though," he told her with a wink. "And we can certainly afford a bit more space and luxury."

"I'm not high maintenance," she pointed out. "And I have no idea yet how quickly I'll find a job. I'd like to pay my share of the rent."

"You don't have to—I can take care of that."

"I know, but I don't want that."

"I lived off of your money, too," he said. "Mia, it's OK—I know that you're an independent woman who can take care of herself." He kissed her lips delicately.

"What about your parents?" Mia asked. She was still stewing over the matter.

"Irmi's going to inform them, and then I'll have a talk with them, but there's no hurry for me. If they make so much as one inappropriate remark, I'm out of that firm." Levin looked at her. "They won't put themselves between us again, understand?"

Mia lowered her eyes. She was afraid that Levin and his parents would fight again, and she didn't want that. But she didn't want to give Levin up again, either. The two of them had gone through hell, and that wasn't something she was willing to repeat. "OK," Mia said. "Maybe they'll accept me one day. And if not, then that's just the way it is."

"Exactly." Levin smiled. "I can't promise you everything's going to be fine in that respect, but I don't really care, Mia. I have you back, and I'm not giving you up. And like I said, there are so many other law firms in Berlin. And in Munich or Cologne."

Mia put a finger to his lips and kissed him tenderly. "We'll see," she said, sitting down on his lap. "Will you make love to me?" she asked with a sweet smile.

"You still haven't had enough?" he teased. Her request was enough to make his blood boil.

"We have to stock up for the next few weeks."

"And you're sure you don't want to celebrate New Year's with us tonight?" Geli said, regarding Levin and Mia in disappointment.

"Please understand, Geli," Levin said. "Mia's flying back tomorrow, and tonight is all we have left."

"Yeah, sure, I understand. But in case it's because of Sarah—she's not coming."

Levin's conscience nagged at him. "How's she doing?" he said.

"You know her, she's a tough cookie. But she's taking her time to get over it." Geli shook her head. "She'll be OK, though. She called this morning to tell me she'd decided at the last minute to go skiing in Switzerland with her brother. Maybe it's for the best."

"Yeah, maybe," Levin said. Although he still felt sorry for Sarah, he was glad it was over. That he and Mia only had one night left was much harder for him to take. Tomorrow evening she'd fly to France with her friends, and two days later she'd be back in Agadir.

Levin had prepared a surprise for Mia. They would be celebrating by the river, just the two of them, and he got excited just thinking about it.

Mia felt wistful. Today was New Year's Eve, and she'd be celebrating with Levin; she had wished for that for so long. And yet, tomorrow they would have to separate. That was a heavy weight in her stomach. Juliette and Philippe had offered to change her ticket so she could fly to Agadir directly from Berlin; then she would have had another two days with Levin. But Mia owed them so much, and she wanted to spend some time with them, too.

She paced her hotel room. Levin would be picking her up soon. He had been acting mysterious and wanted to get something done urgently. She had already wished Juliette and Philippe a nice evening. The two of them would be staying at the hotel, where there'd be a New Year's Eve buffet and a big fireworks display for the guests. There was a knock on the door. Mia ran over quickly.

"Hey, sweet thing, you ready?" Levin said as Mia threw herself into his arms.

"I sure am!"

"Do you have warm clothes? It's supposed to get cold."

"Yes, I do." She went to get her coat, hat, scarf, and gloves, smiling happily. First they wanted to cook dinner at Levin's, and then they'd go down to the Spree. Mia was feeling more and more excited.

She was amazed when she entered Levin's apartment and saw the dining table. He had decorated everything beautifully, and a bouquet of red roses stood in the middle. He hastily lit the candles. "Wow," she said.

"Do you like it?" He ran his fingers through his hair. "I'm not that good with decor."

Mia thanked him with a long kiss. "It's wonderful. Thank you, Levin," she whispered, touched.

Levin breathed a sigh of relief. She already liked this, so he took it as a good omen that the rest of the evening would go just as well. They took their time over dinner. Then, at around eleven, they got going.

"What is all this?" Mia asked him, peeking into a big basket.

Levin grinned at her. "You'll see, don't be so nosy," he said, pulling a tea towel over the basket. "You'd better dress warmly, I don't want you freezing to death."

Mia wrapped herself up like an Eskimo, then followed him out into the clear, starry night. Levin had a favorite spot by the river, and they were lucky that nobody else had claimed it. When it was five to twelve, Levin got out his boom box and told Mia to close her eyes. Mia eyed the device before complying. She felt Levin standing behind her. Then the music started playing. She recognized the first notes of Bruno Mars's "Marry You" and caught her breath. Levin encircled her with his arms, and then he turned her around and started dancing with her. Mia laughed happily, and in the background the first impatient people were already shooting fireworks into the sky. This moment was just too perfect.

"Will you marry me, Mia?" he asked her.

Mia stopped short and looked at him wide-eyed. "Wh–what?" She thought she must have misheard. But the song and his serious expression let her know it must be true.

With a dry throat, he repeated his question: "Will you marry me?"

Mia's eyes brimmed with tears, and she threw her arms around his neck. "Yes, yes, yes," she said.

The fireworks lit the sky in ever-changing colors, but neither Mia nor Levin had any attention to spare for them. They kissed again and again, holding each other tightly—and when they looked at each other, they were both weeping with joy.

"Hey, don't cry," Levin said.

"But I need to," Mia said, sobbing. "It's . . . it's like a miracle."

"I know." Levin buried his face in her neck. "I know," he kept saying. Then he collected himself. "I almost forgot!" He dug through his jacket pocket and produced a small box. "To make it perfect," he whispered.

Mia looked at it in astonishment, then opened the pretty velvet box with shaking hands. There lay a beautifully adorned silver ring with a semiprecious stone on it. She knew this kind of jewelry. It was Moroccan. Again, tears filled her eyes.

He'd had to search long that day for this piece of jewelry. He had never made such an effort for Sarah.

"Tuareg jewelry," Mia whispered, awestruck. "How did you know I love this kind so much?"

Levin breathed a sigh of relief. "I didn't know, I just thought it suited you well."

"The ring's beautiful, Levin. Thank you, thank you, thank you." Mia wrapped her arms around him again. "You can't imagine how much I love you," she said into his ear.

Levin gently slid the ring onto her finger. Luckily, it fit. "I can hardly wait to go look at wedding rings with you," he said in a voice thick with tears. "I love you more than anything in this world, my angel."

They held each other and cried for a long time. For Levin, this was the happiest moment in a long time, and he knew he'd never forget it. They stayed on the banks of the river for quite a while. Only when the night started to get quieter did they walk back to Levin's apartment with their arms around each other's shoulders. Neither one of them considered falling asleep. Time was too precious.

51

"Call me as soon as you arrive," Levin said when they were standing by the departure gates a few hours later.

"I will," Mia said. She didn't want to cry, but of course there were tears in her eyes. She still wasn't sure how long it would be until she could see Levin again, but it would definitely be several weeks, and she wondered how she'd survive.

Levin kissed her one more time, then collected himself and turned to Juliette and Philippe. "I don't know what to say. I owe you so much. You brought Mia back to me and I—"

"It's all right, you don't need to thank us." Juliette hugged him. "We did it gladly, and seeing the two of you like this is more than enough. And the ring is marvelous—much prettier than any diamond."

"Really? Good to know," Philippe added with a grin. He gave Levin a farewell clap on the shoulder. "We'll definitely be coming for the wedding," he told him with a wink.

"Of course, we insist that you do." Mia took her older friend's elbow.

"We should go now," Philippe told her gently.

"Yes," Mia said. "Let's go."

Levin had sat in his car for a while before finally getting himself to start the engine and leave the airport. He drove to Irmi's. She was waiting for him and gave him a hug.

"It won't be long now," she said, trying to reassure him, but that was barely possible. He was worried, and although it was silly, he was still insanely afraid that Mia might just disappear from his life again. He would probably only get over that fear once he held her in his arms again.

"How about we distract you by stopping by your parents' house?" Irmi asked with a grin.

"Oh," Levin said, groaning. His conversation with them was still pending. They already knew from Irmi that he'd broken up with Sarah and was back together with Mia, though. They had immediately asked to talk to him, but Levin ignored them. He didn't want to deal with them while Mia was still in Berlin.

"Why not?" he said, shrugging. He would have to get it over with at some point, and that might just as well be today. And maybe today would decide his future in his father's firm. Irmi went along for the visit, which was fine with him. She would be able to help him curb his temper should he become too emotional.

His mother opened the door. She was surprised, but she looked at Levin joyfully. "How nice—we already tried to reach you today," she told Levin. "Happy New Year, honey." She hugged him, and Levin tensed.

"You, too," he said, and then he and Irmi followed her inside. His father was sitting in the living room by the fire, reading a book. When Levin and Irmi entered, he put the book aside.

"How nice that you're here," he greeted them.

Levin sat down in an armchair and eyed his parents furtively, ready to leave should the conversation take a bad turn. "I know Irmi already told you that I broke up with Sarah." He decided to get right to the point. He really didn't feel like small talk.

"Yes, she did." His father nodded at Irmi. "You can imagine we were shocked and also surprised to hear that Mia had come back. Irmi said she was here with friends."

"Yes," Levin said. "And just to make this clear: I asked Mia to marry me last night, and she said yes. As soon as she comes back to Germany, that's the first thing we'll do."

His mother opened her eyes wide. "You're getting married?"

"Yes, we are. And just so we don't waste any time here: if you can't accept that, I'll quit my job at the firm immediately and look for something else. I want to spend the rest of my life with Mia, and no one must ever try to push themselves between us again," Levin said. He glared at her as he waited for a response.

"Levin, please listen to me." Sonja Webber had collected herself and was looking into his eyes. "I know I made a big mistake back then, and I'm so very, very sorry. I promise you that neither your father nor I will oppose your relationship with Mia. Of course we're surprised how quickly this has developed, but that shows us you and Mia have always had a special relationship. We both liked Sarah a lot, and we were expecting you'd marry her. But things turned out differently, and if you're happy, then so are we. Please, Levin, you have to believe me. I may be a snob and have a certain pride of place, but I have a heart, too." Sonja Webber cleared her throat. "We wish you all the best, and of course we'd love to welcome Mia into our family. Provided, of course, that she wants that and will accept my apology."

Levin looked at his mother doubtfully. But she seemed sincere, and there was a silent plea in her eyes. He believed she had meant what she had said. "If you knew Mia, you'd know that she will definitely accept your apology." He held her eyes with a steady gaze. "I certainly insist on your making it."

"Of course, Levin." His mother got up and came over to him. "You're our only son. Do you think we'd want to lose you?"

Levin got up, too, and carefully hugged his mother. "I'm happy. Happier than I've been in a long time," he said.

"That's good," his mother said.

"Where is Mia now?" his father asked. "Did she fly back already?"

"Yes, I just took her to the airport."

"That's a shame—we'd hoped to invite the two of you for dinner." His mother seemed honestly disappointed. "When will she be back?"

"As soon as she's taken care of everything in Morocco. She has to resign and end her lease. That won't happen so quickly."

"Is she doing all that alone?" his father asked.

"Yes, I have to work, and we have important deadlines." Levin frowned. What was he trying to say? He knew what Levin had to do at the firm.

His father grinned at him, then went over to the bureau in the living room, got out an envelope, and gave it to Levin.

Levin watched in astonishment. "What?"

"Open it," his father said with a nod.

Levin was confused, but he opened it and couldn't believe what he saw. It was a plane ticket.

"You'll fly out tomorrow. That means you'll get there before Mia, if I'm informed correctly," his father said, winking at Irmi. "Your return flight is in ten days—oh, and I'm sure you'll feel comfortable at the hotel. We reserved two nights for you. I'm certain that you can find another place to stay after that."

"But what about the deadlines?" Levin was much too surprised to react appropriately.

"Klaus and I can take care of those," his father answered. "That'll be fine. Take care of Mia, that's much more important now," he said with a smile.

Levin could only shake his head and laugh quietly. "Thank you."

"You're welcome. I hope you can handle things so Mia can come back soon." His father was still grinning widely.

"I hope so, too." Levin still couldn't quite grasp what his father had done for him. He hugged his dad tightly. "Thank you."

Irmi had followed everything with a smile on her face. Levin realized his parents must have gotten all the information from her. He stayed awhile longer, constantly checking his phone. He sighed in relief when Mia finally called to tell him she'd arrived in Paris safely.

On the way home, Levin looked at his aunt. "What would you have done if I hadn't gone to my parents' place today?"

"Then James would have brought me the tickets, and I would have given them to you tonight. You ask a lot of questions, you lawyer, you," she said, chuckling.

"Did you have to appeal to their consciences much for them to relent?"

"No, not really. Of course they were shocked to hear that you'd ended things with Sarah. But they also understood very quickly that Mia is your one true love, and they can't try to drive her away anymore. I think once they get to know her, they'll also understand she's a wonderful person. It's going to be fine, Levin. I can feel it," she said, patting his leg.

Mia observed the clouds. She hoped to distract herself by trying to recognize shapes in the white fluff, but it wasn't working very well. She was sad she had to leave Levin and her friends for a long time, although it was nothing compared to the pain that had ruled her life such a short while ago. It really was a miracle. She would never have guessed that her life would take another extreme turn like this. Levin had told her how his parents had reacted, and she was very happy about that. However, when she thought about having to meet them soon— and this time for real—she felt queasy. She had talked to Juliette and Philippe about everything thoroughly, even about the guilty feelings she had toward Sarah. She'd stolen her man, and knowing that was hard on Mia. She knew very well how it was to lose someone you love. But Juliette reassured her: "You can only have something taken away if it belonged to you in the first place. And Levin's heart was never hers, not really. Otherwise, he wouldn't have returned to you so quickly."

Mia had to keep reminding herself of those words. Maybe Juliette was right, or maybe not. But all her brooding didn't help. Maybe it was just fate—or fortune—or kismet, as Faizah would say.

Levin was more than excited. He'd wanted to wait by her apartment door, as she had done for him, but then he decided against it. He would just go eat in the hotel restaurant that evening, like every other guest, and he'd wait for her to discover him. The hotel had been a pleasant surprise. It was part of a well-known international chain and was in the upper price class. That gave Levin hope that with her good references, Mia would find a job in Germany quickly.

He tried to imagine how surprised she would be. He knew she'd be happy, and his heart raced just thinking about it. He glanced at his watch. Her shift began in the afternoon. Levin could hardly bear it. He was ready to go to the dining hall now, but he resolved to hold out until the evening.

Mia took a deep breath and knocked on the staff manager's door. Just that morning she'd asked to talk to him. She wanted to get it over with quickly so she could tell Levin.

"Good afternoon," she said to her boss with a smile.

"Hello, Mia, how nice that you're back. Did you enjoy seeing your home country again?"

"Yes, very much." She cleared her throat. "Well, a lot has changed in my life, and I wanted to talk to you about that."

Mr. Soufany raised his eyebrows. "Yes?"

"I need to resign since I'm planning to move back to Germany."

"Oh!" He was surprised. "Such news, I don't like it at all. You're an excellent employee I don't want to lose."

"I'm happy to hear that, but I'm going to get married, and my fiancé and I aren't interested in a long-distance relationship." Her heart was racing.

"Goodness, I'm starting to think it was a bad idea to allow you to take a vacation." He shook his head, but his eyes were twinkling. "It seems all I can do is to congratulate you. Mia, I'm so very happy for you, although I don't like to see you go."

Mia took a short breath. "Thank you—I always enjoyed working here," she said, handing him her written notice.

"If you're getting married, I assume you'll want to leave soon?"

"As soon as possible, yes."

"The notice period is three months," he said, "but the position will be filled quickly considering our hotel's good reputation." He leaned back in his chair. "I'll advertise the job immediately. As soon as a replacement is found, you may leave."

"Thank you so much." Mia was sure he sensed her relief.

"I wish you all the best, Mia." He got up and held out his hand.

Mia sent Levin a text as soon as she left the staff manager's office. His answer came promptly: *Great! We'll have to celebrate!*

Yes, but it will still be a while. I love you, she answered.

Levin put his phone away. "Oh well, what are a few hours?" he said to himself quietly. He grinned and kept walking through the streets of Agadir.

Mia immediately went to tell Faizah her news. She was very happy for Mia. She herself had a lot to report, too, because she was expecting.

"Then neither of us will be working at the hotel much longer."
Faizah giggled and hugged Mia tightly.

"Looks like it." Mia laughed. "Poor Mr. Soufany."

"Come over as soon as you get a free moment. Harun will be happy
for you, too," Faizah suggested.

"I will," Mia promised her, and then she glanced at the clock. "I
have to get back to the restaurant now—talk to you later."

Mia had checked everything carefully. The food was appetizingly
decorated and arranged on the buffet. Then she opened the dining
room doors for the guests, greeting everyone with a friendly smile
before returning to the buffet.

Levin had already seen her, and his heart was beating fast. Mia didn't
seem to have noticed him. She was walking around enthusiastically,
giving orders to the waiters. He took a deep breath. Now he worried
she wouldn't be happy about his visit. Maybe she'd think it was too
intrusive or feel controlled? He felt a short, nagging doubt, but he
immediately pushed it from his mind. Besides, it was too late now.
"What do you recommend?" he asked Mia. She was just setting out
some more vegetables.

Mia looked up—that voice sounded familiar. She thought she
must be dreaming. "Levin!" she managed to say. "What are you doing
here?" She stared at him in wonder. The fact that he was really here still
hadn't registered.

"I was just asking my gorgeous fiancée what she recommends."

She quickly came around the counter and threw her arms around
him. "You're here. *You're here!*"

"Yes, I think so," he said, laughing. And all his doubts disappeared.
"I hope I'm not bothering you."

"What? Well, I do have to work." She pushed a curl behind her ear.
"When did you arrive, and how long will you be staying?" Levin was
here. It was unbelievable.

"I arrived the day before yesterday. My parents surprised me with the flight. They thought maybe I would be able to help you with all the paperwork here. I'll leave in a week. I hope you can spare a little time for me." He buried his face in her blond curls. "I missed you, sweet thing."

"I missed you, too." Mia closed her eyes and fought a lump in her throat. "Are you staying here in the hotel?"

"Yes, I have a reservation until tomorrow. Maybe after that I can find another place to stay." He stepped back from her, noticing the curious looks from the staff.

"My shift ends at midnight. Maybe I can leave early—I'll go and ask right now," she said, excited. "And maybe I can arrange not to have to work so long, so I'll have more free time. It won't work in the evenings, but during the day there's not as much going on." She still couldn't quite grasp it. "But you wanted something to eat! I can recommend pretty much everything. The fish is very good."

Levin observed her, smiling. She was completely beside herself but beaming at him happily.

"I'm so glad you're here," she said with tears in her eyes.

52

Levin had to be patient until Mia's shift was over. He'd already packed everything in his room, and soon he'd go with her to her apartment. He was curious to see how she lived. There was a knock on his door shortly after midnight.

"Hi, sweet thing." He greeted Mia with a kiss. "I've already packed, so we can leave right away. Or are you tired? We could just stay here, too."

"No." Mia beamed at him. "It's not far to my apartment."

Levin followed her. He knew where she lived, but so far he'd only been there during the day. They walked through dark alleys that got smaller and smaller.

"Do you walk home alone every night?" he asked.

"Yes, it's not that far," she said.

"But it's dark and dangerous."

"Nothing has ever happened. The area is relatively safe."

"Anything can happen anywhere, anytime," he persisted. "In the future, you should take a taxi."

Mia snorted. "Levin, are you nuts? I can't afford that in the long run, and I don't want to."

"I'm only worried about your safety." He looked at her seriously.

"I'll be careful." She stopped and gave him a peck on the cheek. "And now stop looking at me like that. We're here."

"I know—I was here before."

"I might have guessed." Mia giggled, unlocking the door.

Levin looked around. Her apartment fascinated him. Everything was furnished in Moroccan style. In the living room stood a beautiful old wooden cupboard decorated with artistic painted motifs. There were wrought iron tables and mirrors, and a wide, inviting couch.

"Do you like it?" She wrapped her arms around him and gave him a kiss on the back.

"Yeah, very much. Where did you get the furniture?" Levin turned to face her.

"From flea markets. Maybe I can bring some things back, if it isn't too expensive to ship them to Germany."

"Of course we can do that. And don't worry about the money— your future husband earns enough," he told her with a wink.

Mia snuggled up to him. "OK." She yawned. She'd have to get used to being on her feet all day again. "I have good news, too—in the next few days, I shouldn't have to work at the hotel too much. So we'll have lots of time on our hands. I can show you Agadir without time constraints."

"Hey, that's very good news." Levin kissed her blond curls. "But first you should show me your bedroom so you can get to bed." She cuddled drowsily against his chest. They had been planning to go to sleep right away, but then they couldn't keep their hands off each other. Levin made love to her very gently.

Mia got goose bumps just thinking about it afterward. She gazed at him proudly, her future husband. He'd already closed his eyes and seemed to be asleep. *My husband.* A smile played around her lips. *How perfect that sounds.*

Levin was nervous. He and Mia were invited for dinner at Mia's friend Faizah's house, and he wasn't sure what to expect. Mia had already introduced him to Faizah and her husband, Harun—the two of them worked at the hotel, too. Harun was completely different than Levin had imagined. He was very open-minded—and in their relationship, Faizah was obviously the one in charge.

"Ah, there you are, child." Faizah's mother greeted Mia with a warm smile, and then she greeted Levin just as jovially. "And this is your future husband, yes?"

"Yes, this is Levin." Mia led him inside.

Levin was overwhelmed by the hospitality of these people—and by all the different foods they served. He couldn't decide what he liked best, and he only stopped eating when he was too full for another bite.

"That was delicious," he praised Faizah's mother, who was happy to hear it.

"It's good that Mia's finally getting married," Faizah's father spoke up. "Being alone isn't good for a young woman."

"But, Baba," Faizah scolded, "nowadays that's not a problem anymore."

"But it isn't good," her father insisted. Then he turned to Levin. "You know, we've introduced young men to Mia before—good men who would have treated her nicely, but Mia didn't want them."

"Really?" Levin looked at Mia in amazement. "You didn't tell me anything about that."

"Why should I?" she said with a smile. "I didn't consider them options."

Faizah chuckled, and Harun started laughing, too. "And now we know why," he said with a wide grin.

"Who were they?" Levin asked her later on the way home. He couldn't resist.

"What do you mean?" Mia said, frowning.

"Oh, come on. The guys that Faizah's father introduced you to."

"Oh, them," Mia said, giggling. "As I said, none of them were my type. But they *were* nice." She glanced at Levin out of the corner of her eye; he looked annoyed.

"Who does he think he is, to just fix you up with men?" he complained. "It isn't the middle ages."

"He meant well. Don't forget where we are. Things work differently here."

"Apparently."

"Faizah's father views me as a kind of daughter. And parents worry about their children. They only want the best in life for them, right?" Mia gave him a serious expression.

Levin understood immediately. "Come here." He pulled her closer cautiously. "You're right. I shouldn't judge him, considering what my mother did," he said sheepishly.

Mia kissed his lips tenderly. "I'd like to invite Faizah, Harun, and her parents to our wedding. That's very important to me. And two other colleagues, too. Do you think that would work?"

"Of course." Levin caressed her blond curls. "We'll find them a nice hotel. You can invite anyone you want, sweetheart."

Somehow the time had flown by. Levin had enjoyed every moment with Mia. Now he was standing at the airport, with Mia in his arms, sad because they had to separate for him to go through security.

"Mr. Soufany said he's already invited applicants. I'm sure it won't take long," Mia tried to reassure Levin, but it wasn't clear which of them needed more comforting.

"I really hope so." Levin rested his forehead against hers. "Promise me you'll take care of yourself," he said.

"Of course I will."

"And I'll find a moving company," he said. "I can hardly wait. As soon as you're back in Berlin, we'll plan our wedding."

"Yes, we will." Mia tried to hold back her tears, but they were already rolling down her cheeks. "Definitely."

Time was growing short. Levin gave her one last passionate kiss and approached the security checkpoint with heavy steps.

Time in Morocco had flown, but back home it seemed to be crawling along. Levin was so excited that he hadn't been able to close his eyes at all the previous night. He had tidied and cleaned the apartment. Then he'd Skyped with Mia, who seemed just as nervous as he was. She had spent the last few nights at Faizah and Harun's place because her apartment was already empty. Her furniture would arrive in Germany in a few days. Since there wasn't enough space for it in Levin's apartment, they decided to store it temporarily at his parents' villa. James and Sonja Webber had been anxious, too. Mia and Levin were invited to come for dinner the following day, and Levin wondered how that would play out. He didn't seriously doubt that they'd accept Mia warmly. But there was still a tiny bit of distrust in the back of his mind.

The sliding door opened. Levin's attention focused on the first people coming out. He didn't have to wait long. Mia was one of the first, and she saw him immediately. She left the cart with her luggage and flew into his arms. Levin squeezed her tightly. To feel her again, to be able to hold her like that—how he had missed her.

"You're here, you're here," he kept saying into her blond curls. "Finally, my angel, finally."

Mia clutched him—how she had longed for this moment. "I love you," she whispered.

"I love you, too. And now our future together can begin," Levin said.

"This evening is ours. I warned everybody who might want to disturb us," Levin said as they drove home in the car.

"Who asked?" Mia gazed at him fondly. She couldn't get enough of Levin; it was incredible to finally be with him again. She had been sad about leaving Morocco and her friends, but now all that was swept away. She was with Levin, and she felt like she'd finally arrived where she was supposed to be.

"Well, everybody," Levin said. "What did you think? Geli, Kai, and all the others from the old crowd. We also owe them an engagement party. And then of course Irmi wants to see you—and my parents," he added with a glance in Mia's direction.

"Your parents?" Mia wrung her hands. Levin had already told her they wouldn't be an obstacle anymore, but Mia wasn't convinced.

Levin reached for her hand. "Sweet thing, how about we go over there tomorrow? If you feel uncomfortable we can leave again right away. But please listen to them once, OK?"

"OK," Mia said. She knew that there probably wasn't any way around it.

"But first we're going to have a nice evening," he told her with a smile.

Levin pampered Mia in all the ways he could. Still, he cursed himself for mentioning the visit with his parents. He could feel her tension about it. She had never been a good actress. He tried to calm her down, but it didn't really work. Nevertheless, they spent a night full of tenderness, and when Mia finally fell asleep in his arms, he was the happiest person in the world.

Mia took a deep breath as they stood in front of the villa. They had been invited for lunch, and she wondered what to expect. Sonja Webber opened the door, smiling at both of them, but she seemed uneasy. Levin gave his mother a last warning look, although he was pretty sure by now it was unnecessary.

"There you are," his mother said. "Please, come in." Mia followed Levin with shaking knees. He had his arm around her, and that gave her a sense of security. Sonja Webber still looked as good as she had almost four years ago, and Mia secretly admired her sense of style. But if she wasn't mistaken, Sonja also seemed quite nervous. That she felt the same was kind of a relief for Mia.

Levin's father was already waiting for them, and he approached Mia with a smile. "Mia, good to see you again." He held out his hand, and Mia responded in kind. He had a firm handshake.

"I'm glad, too," Mia answered, knowing full well that her words didn't sound very convincing.

"Hello, my dear." Irmi was already there and hugged Mia tightly. "How nice that you're finally here."

Sonja Webber cleared her throat and swept a strand of hair off her face. "Mia, I would like to apologize to you. I made a big mistake. I am aware that it's hard to forgive, but I still hope that you can do that. Maybe not right away, but maybe someday. Back then I believed I was doing what was best for Levin. I have come to understand, though, how wrong I was. I drove you away from him, and at the same time I drove him away from us." She swallowed hard. "I'm very sorry about how I treated you. Please—I really mean what I say."

Mia had been holding her breath. Mrs. Webber actually seemed embarrassed, and Mia wanted to believe that she really meant it. "Mrs. Webber, I can understand your motivation. You only wanted the best for your son, and even I believed the same thing. But the last few years have been very hard for me, and for Levin, too. I made the mistake of listening to your words and leaving him. Both of us made Levin unhappy." Mia looked into her eyes steadily. "As far as I'm concerned, we can let bygones be bygones."

Sonja Webber sighed in relief. "Thank you, Mia, you really are a generous young woman."

"She certainly is," Irmi confirmed. "It took long enough, but it's good that you finally realize that, too."

Levin's father approached Mia. "Shall we celebrate a new beginning?"

"With pleasure," she said, smiling shyly.

Levin watched her lovingly. Mia was really doing well. She was nervous, but who wouldn't be in that situation? She possessed a certain presence she hadn't had a few years earlier. She wouldn't be swayed so easily anymore. That was probably clear to all of them.

"I'm glad to hear that. And when I look at Levin"—his father smiled at him—"I can see that he's found what's good for him."

"Good, so we can start eating now. You shouldn't let an old woman go hungry," Irmi said, taking a bit of the tension out of the situation.

James Webber asked Mia all about her life in Morocco. She answered eagerly. His interest seemed genuine, and she relaxed.

"You had a demanding position," he finally said to her with an appreciative nod. "Are you planning to work in the business here, too?"

"I'd like to try. I have a very good reference, so maybe I'll be lucky," Mia answered.

"If you need help, I can look around for you. I know a few influential people," he offered.

"I don't know." Mia looked at Levin. Could she accept that? She wasn't sure.

Levin laid his hand on Mia's. "Do that, Dad." He winked at Mia. "Looking around can't hurt."

"Have you thought about when you want to get married?" Sonja Webber spoke up.

Levin grinned—he'd wondered when his mother would ask. This was definitely one of her favorite subjects. "For me it could be right here and now." He gave Mia a light kiss on the cheek. She blushed lightly, and he thought she looked delicious.

"I don't know if we can reach a registrar at this time of day." James Webber laughed. "But as soon as possible, then."

"Of course. We would have been married for a long time now if Mom hadn't messed things up." Levin looked at his mother firmly.

Sonja Webber looked down at the tablecloth, but then she found her composure again. "Your father and I would be happy to plan the wedding for you. You only have to tell us what you want."

"We couldn't accept that," Mia said, shocked.

"Of course you can," Irmi said. "That's the least they can do."

"I don't know." Mia glanced at Levin for help.

"Let them, sweet thing, if they want to do it." He gave her a quick kiss.

"Money isn't an issue," his father clarified. "We're happy for you. Really."

That night, Mia and Levin settled down on their couch.

"But a wedding is so expensive." Mia was uncertain. "Levin, we can't do that."

"Of course we can." He pulled her up onto his stomach and stroked her naked back. "It's their way of apologizing. Let them do it, Mia. It will make them feel better. And besides, it's normal for the parents to pay for the wedding. And since you don't have much family left, it's nice that they want to do it. We'll probably do the same thing for our kids later."

Mia buried her face in Levin's chest. Maybe he was right; maybe that was the way it was done. She knew it, too, from Moroccan families. She felt wistful. Her mother would have been happy to have seen Mia getting married. "Yes, maybe that's just the way it's done."

Levin looked into her eyes. Something about her tone alarmed him. "What's wrong, sweetheart?"

"Nothing."

"Don't lie."

"I was just thinking about my mother," she confessed. "Sorry for getting so sentimental." She turned her face away quickly, but Levin had already noticed her tears.

"If you're not allowed to be sentimental now, then when?" he asked. He lay down behind her and wrapped his arms around her. "I can't give you your mother back, but we'll invite all the people you love and who mean something to you."

Mia turned to face him. "You're so lovely. Thanks."

"I love you—it's that simple," he said. "And since I have time off next week, we have all the time we need to plan everything."

"Sounds good." Mia beamed. "I'll be your wife! I still can't quite believe this."

"You should," Levin said, laughing. At first he kissed her tenderly, and then more passionately.

53

"You look stunning." Philippe examined Mia from head to toe, and she gave him a grateful smile.

"I hope Levin likes it, too," she said. Mia couldn't recall ever being so nervous in her entire life. She was so often jumpy and restless, but this topped everything.

"You don't have to be afraid," Philippe reassured her. "Levin's getting a gorgeous bride, and you've already been officially married for a few hours anyway, so nothing can go wrong."

Mia looked at herself in the mirror one more time. Her dress fit perfectly. For this day, Levin's mother had ordered a seamstress to be ready in case of any last-minute changes. The dress looked like something out of a fairy tale. It was silk with a richly embroidered bodice, and a row of tiny seed pearls around the neckline. It even had a small train. Mia felt like a princess. And it wasn't even white. Mia had been clear about that from the beginning: she didn't want a white dress. This one was ivory. A shade of white. Mia was OK with that.

"We should get going now. Otherwise poor Levin will die of nervousness," Juliette urged.

"Two seconds," Faizah said, applying powder to Mia's nose. Giving her a peck on the cheek, she said, "I've never seen a bride as beautiful as you."

"I have—you," Mia said with a giggle.

"You're glowing from the inside, everybody can see your happiness." There were tears in Faizah's eyes.

Mia hugged her, which wasn't so easy anymore with Faizah's baby bump in their way. Mia was so happy that Faizah had been able to come to the wedding with Harun. Harun was a worried father-to-be, and he'd had second thoughts about the flight, but as was usual in their relationship, Faizah was able to talk him into it.

Levin's parents had rented rooms for the wedding guests at an expensive hotel. Mia had given up trying to protest the amount of money they were spending. Levin had asked her to just let them do their thing. But Mia would probably never get used to dealing with money that way. She knew all too well how hard life could be, and the times in Morocco when she had gone hungry were still fresh in her mind.

Of course Mia also benefited from the Webbers' generosity. She was happy and grateful that all the people close to her heart could be here now. Lydia, Director Schneider, and Robert—one of the other therapists—had come from Hamburg to be with Mia on her big day. Mia already knew she'd cry a lot; she hadn't even gotten through the registry-office wedding without spilling a few tears.

"Mia, we really need to go now," Juliette said.

Mia let go of Faizah and followed Juliette and Philippe. She'd dressed at the Webbers' villa. Levin's parents had already gone ahead to the church. Mia didn't notice the drive at all. She turned the bridal bouquet around and around in her hands. Finally, Philippe reached for her hand and squeezed it lightly. "Everything will be all right, child," he told her with a wink.

Levin took a deep breath. He felt like a wedding cake that had been ordered and not picked up. The church bells were ringing, and he wondered if Mia had arrived.

Kai grinned at him. "Whew, dude. Now it's for real, huh?"

"Just you wait. I'll have a smart mouth at your wedding next week, too," Levin said.

"Don't worry, she'll come. I had all the flights to Casablanca checked," Kai said, chuckling.

Levin groaned and punched him on the shoulder. He had a fitting answer on the tip of his tongue, but then he remembered they were in a church and bit it back. He couldn't really be annoyed at his friend. If it were the other way around, he would be teasing him, and he'd get his chance for revenge next Saturday. Levin surveyed the church. The pews were full. His English relatives had flown in. There were also friends and former colleagues of Mia's from Morocco, including Faizah's parents. Juliette and Philippe from France would arrive in a moment—so all in all it was a very colorful congregation. His parents sat in the first row, and his mother regarded him with pride. Levin winked at her. Since Mia's return, her behavior had been exemplary. She really seemed to have learned from the whole situation. Her relationship with Mia was even quite good now, although Mia still was somewhat reserved toward her.

James Webber had supported Mia's job search, and thanks to his contacts she'd found something quickly. She now worked at an upscale restaurant as a manager and the boss's right hand. Her boss was very happy with her. Mia had a knack for dealing with the waiters, and her experience and language skills helped a lot in her dealings with the patrons who came from Asia. His eyes scanned the rows. Sarah had come, too, which made Levin happy. She didn't have a new partner yet. Geli had told him that she was totally focused on school at the moment. The separation had been hard for her, but she wasn't angry with Levin or Mia. He gave her a lot of credit for that.

Finally the organist started playing. Levin noticed Juliette and Faizah darting to their seats. That meant Mia must be there. He looked eagerly toward the door. Sunlight came flooding in as it opened. They were in luck—it was a beautiful, pleasantly warm day in May. Even the weather seemed to be on their side.

"It's OK, let's go," Philippe whispered into Mia's ear. She took one last deep breath as they walked through the church doors. Mia was glad to have her friend's arm to hold on to, because her legs were shaking. Although the guests were all smiling at her, she didn't quite register seeing them. But it was different with Lydia: Mia saw that she had tears in her eyes. And Robert gave Mia a thumbs-up, which made her chuckle a little. Then she looked ahead to the altar, where Levin was waiting for her with Kai. Her groom was so handsome in his suit; of course she'd already admired him at the registry office.

Levin couldn't take his eyes off his bride. Mia looked like an angel—so beautiful it was otherworldly. But at that moment, he couldn't have even described her dress. All he wanted was to look into her eyes—those wonderful, fascinating dark eyes. Finally, she reached him. A proud Philippe handed her over, and Levin felt his heart speed up as Mia smiled at him. The priest spoke a few introductory words that Levin barely heard. He kept looking over at the magical creature next to him. Some of her blond curls were clipped at the back with a mother-of-pearl barrette; the rest tumbled over her shoulders in soft waves. Levin reached for her hand and squeezed it gently. They smiled at each other for reassurance.

Mia tried to concentrate on the priest's words, but that wasn't so easy with the man of her dreams standing next to her. Mia's heart was practically bursting from all the happiness in it. When they finished exchanging vows, Levin bent down and kissed her.

"I love you," he whispered in a husky voice.

"I love you, too. So much." She gave him a radiant smile. The priest cleared his throat, then translated the vows into French.

The rest of the service breezed by for Mia and Levin. Luckily, they'd be able to watch the whole thing on DVD since his mother had remembered to have the day recorded.

As Mia and Levin walked out into the bright sunshine, their friends were already waiting for them. More and more guests trickled out of the church to offer their congratulations. Mia fought back tears. She looked into the faces of all these people who loved her. They meant so much to her. Everything was so perfect, and for Mia this was certainly the happiest day of her entire life.

Without warning, Levin pulled her toward him. It was nice to receive all these good wishes, but now he just needed to feel her close. She beamed at him, and he was again lost in her eyes. Their lips met, and he finally kissed his wife, his love, his Mia.

About the Author

Ki-Ela began publishing her work online and as e-books, with five novels released in Germany and more in the works. *Shades of White* is her English debut.

For more information, visit www.facebook.com/Ki.Ela.Stories.

About the Translator

Kate Northrop grew up in Connecticut and studied music and English literature in the United States and the United Kingdom, until she decided to try out life as a musician. Her travels took her to the German-speaking part of Switzerland, where she has lived since 1994 with her Swiss husband and their two bilingual children. She now works as both a professional translator and as a lyricist. She has written lyrics for more than two hundred songs, and her many credits include songs signed to major publishers and lyrics for a song on the sound track of an award-winning German film. She has translated several novels.